STREET SMART ON A DEAD END

A NOVEL OF CLASHING CULTURES

BY

M. J. Brett

Blue Harmony Press

Blue Harmony ♫ Press

528 Southern Cross Drive
Colorado Springs, CO 80906

First Printing, June 2008

Copyright by M.J. Brett
EBrettMBour@aol.com
Website at www.mjbrett.com

Printed in the United States of America

Without limiting the rights under copyright reserved above, no part of this novel may be reproduced, stored in or introduced into a retrieval system, or transmitted, in any form, or by any means, (electronic, technological, mechanical, photocopying, recording, or otherwise), without the prior written permission of the copyright owner.

Though based loosely on the lives of real and fictional persons in a real place, this is a work of fiction. Names, characters, and incidents, are either the product of the author's imagination or are used fictitiously, condensed, or expanded. Except for public figures of the era, any other resemblance is purely coincidental.

Dedication

I sometimes think an author documents an unsuccessful endeavor not just for conflict inherent in a good novel, but because ever since the Biblical stories of the Prodigal Son, and the Lost Sheep, writers, like most fishermen, are intrigued not with the "successful" catch, but with "the one that got away."

Teachers are successful with the vast majority of their students, and parents are successful with the vast majority of their children, yet what of the one child we could not, for all our love and effort, save? This will be the one who haunts our memory. The one for whom we forever ask, "What if...?"

All of us are only human, and children still do not come with an instruction manual, nor is their any test for parenthood. How can we be sure we are doing it "right?" And what is "right" anyway? Teaching and parenting are both tough work.

Teachers do not get a boy or girl at birth, but after they have already experienced at least four or five years of early learning. In most cases, this early learning will be similar to their own value system, and the child easily conforms to society's requirements.

But once in a while, there is a child who has been exposed prematurely to an ugly side of life, whose needs are more serious, and whose value system has been damaged by his early learning. Success then becomes hard to define. Can we help this child become emotionally compassionate, physically strong, financially successful, intellectually curious, and get him to conform to the rules of society so that he stays out of trouble *all at the same time*. Can we erase early patterns and substitute new ones when, according to psychologists, most behavioral patterns are already set in stone by about age six?

This novel is dedicated to all teachers and parents who try, and sometimes fail, to solve the challenging problems of the children in their care. It is a tale of one who got away.

Foreward

During the late 1960's, a more innocent world before dialing 911 brought emergency personnel, before cell phones, computers, message machines, juvenile rehabilitation centers, laws to protect kids from abusive or neglectful parents, and safe police detention for juveniles, school officials are basically left holding the bag as children become addicted to gangs and drugs at younger ages.

What can be done if a child confides a drug problem, yet is afraid of both their violent parents and equally violent gangs and drug dealers? As those who love all children, even the troubled ones, teachers can find no other option but to keep trying to rehabilitate, on their own.

In an era when there are no outside resources, and even the police refuse to help find "...only one more druggie," can these dedicated teachers keep trying long enough to make a difference for their first young drug addict, or is there any difference that can be made?

Chapter 1

Kate Johnson entered Sunnyside School's office complex to find herself face to face with a scowling young kid. *Is it a boy or a girl,* she wondered.

Rough-cut straight hair, faded jeans, a tie-died sweatshirt, scuffed tennis shoes much too big, and a long, heavy chain slung from the belt left Kate with no inkling of the child's gender.

The kid aimed an insolent stare at the teacher as though from across a chasm.

Something in the dark features and almond eyes stirred a memory of photos of her husband's American Indian ancestors, and Kate felt sure the child was also Indian. She held out her hand and said, "I'm Mrs. Johnson. I teach fifth grade. Are you a new student for my class?"

The child turned away toward the window. The hard sneer on its face said more clearly than words that the inside air had somehow turned fetid.

Aha. We have an attitude, do we?

The child was the size of her own fifth graders, yet Kate saw something in the eyes--cold, brooding, angry--that seemed much older. A cardboard cigarette box was outlined prominently in the hip pocket.

Kate looked up as Nancy, the school nurse, and the principal entered the office. The principal cleared his throat noisily. "Oh, Olivia, I see you've already met Mrs. Johnson."

So it's a girl, Kate thought. *I would never have known.*

"Yeah," came the mumbled reply.

"Please say, 'Yes sir,' Olivia," said the principal. His tone was syrupy sweet.

The child looked at the floor and said nothing.

"Olivia, my dear, you must be more...." The principal paused, reaching out to pat the child's shoulder. She jerked away. "I'm *not* your dear!" she snarled, gripping her dangling chain and stepping backward one pace, every belligerent muscle tensed, poised to spring.

"I'm sor-ry," the principal responded with undisguised sarcasm. "Olivia, you'll be in sixth grade. Your mother said you were almost thirteen and should go to junior high, but...." Mr. Marken paused. He glanced nervously from Kate to Nancy and fidgeted with the key ring he'd pulled from his pocket.

Kate stifled a laugh that both principal and child were unable to go forward in this confrontation without holding on to something—a chain, a key chain--what difference? *Best to intervene before this escalates.* "Mr. Marken must be referring to your test scores, Olivia. Did you take a math and reading test at the junior high school?"

"Yeah, but it didn't do no damn good. I hate shitty schools." The child arched her neck and turned away again.

"Perhaps you'll be here only a short time for help with math and reading to get ready for junior high school." Kate ignored the offensive words for the moment and smiled at the child, hoping she would respond, even a little. "It might be easier for you, then."

Olivia's eyes grew icy. "Do I hafta be in your class?"

Kate felt the chill.

The principal stuttered, "Well, no, not exactly. Your teacher will be Mrs. Warner, sixth grade, but she's out sick, and we can't send you to the substitute teacher because....because...the sub might not know how to handle...I mean the sub has her hands full with a large class, so we're asking Mrs. Johnson to keep you until your teacher comes back to school. Do you understand?"

"I ain't no damn nitwit!" Olivia's steely black eyes flashed.

Mr. Marken recoiled. Then he stiffened his rotund five-foot-six inch height and blustered, "Young lady, you'll keep a civil tongue in this school."

"And I ain't no damn young lady either!"
Kate and the nurse exchanged glances. Things got ugly when their principal got red in the face. He was the only adult on campus who often needed calming as much as did the children. Kate wondered about the logic that had sent this particular principal to this particular low achieving, high-pressure school made up of teachers who volunteered for the difficult job. He was one of its major challenges.

Kate turned to Olivia. "Let's go down to my classroom now, and we'll get the paperwork done later. She extended her hand to guide Olivia toward the door, but she nodded at Nancy, signaling that Nancy was to distract the principal.

Mr. Marken was a nice man, nearing retirement, but he expected all children to be immediately pliable, and he seemed ill equipped to handle changes looming in 1968.

With drugs, free love, race riots, gangs, and anti-war demonstrations in the hippie culture and colleges, lawlessness seemed to have spilled over into a few difficult neighborhoods, even down to school level. Kate was as disturbed as anyone by negative societal changes in these few, localized areas of Los Angeles County. But, she didn't believe it was effective to jump to conclusions from first contact with a child and perhaps lose what little chance a teacher might have to help the child progress.

She wanted to talk quietly with this young girl when, hopefully, a few of Olivia's distrustful barriers had lifted.

Could such intervention be successful? Children at Sunnyside Elementary School were from the most desperate of homes—mostly single-parent families headed by women. Not only was the school in a welfare neighborhood, rife with dysfunctional families, alcohol, and abuse, but the children were also frequently neglected and given the poor moral example of hot and cold running fathers/uncles/boyfriends who mysteriously changed almost weekly.

As she walked the open breezeway with this child new to their school, Kate wondered what it would take for Olivia to become a warm human being. Many children took the whole six years to make the grade, yet for Olivia, they would only have what was left of this one year to make any progress at all.

Half way down the hall Olivia suddenly jerked her arm away from the contemplative teacher and yelled, "Don't think I'm doin' any shitty old homework!"

Kate sighed heavily. *Olivia is going to be a tough customer, even for Sunnyside.*

Days went by, during which the sixth grade teacher to whom Olivia was permanently assigned, Mrs. Holly Warner, returned to school and moved Olivia to her own classroom. Holly was about the same age as Kate, but she had married much later and still had young children, while Kate married at eighteen, so her children were teenagers. Always fashionably dressed and beautifully coifed, Holly exuded a charm that had somehow escaped tomboy Kate. But the two were fast friends, and were equally dedicated to the children in their care.

Holly remarked to Kate that perhaps she had come back to school too early, before she felt "…truly healed."

Kate smiled at her friend and commented, "That severely recurring headache wouldn't be called 'Olivia,' would it?"

Holly winked. "How did you guess?"

"Just my usual clairvoyance. She does seem particularly troubled, doesn't she? Could you get any information out of her?"

Holly shook her head. "Her mom dumped her off that first day and didn't show up at the conference we scheduled. That seems the pattern for these hard-core kids, doesn't it? Olivia's last school was in Tucson. Father died eleven months before Olivia was born, according to her very limited record folder."

"Eleven months? But…."

Holly rolled her eyes knowingly. "Yeah, I know. Her records show her kicked out of every class she's ever been in. All promotions must have been 'social,' since she hasn't mastered skill levels for any grade that I can find. I guess when each teacher ran out of options, or patience, they promoted Olivia to get rid of her."

Holly uttered a dramatically overstated sigh. "I can't even

say I blame them. Every time you have to stop her from mayhem on the playground, if she can draw you into a response at all, it becomes *her* argument. She can scream louder, be more obscene, more angry, and pretty soon you have no choice but to march her down to the office to keep her away from other kids and calm her down without an audience."

"That must be frustrating. We all hate to take a kid to the office, if we can find *any* other alternative."

"And did you get a load of her language?"

"Right from her first day. I've never heard anyone speak in such vulgar terms."

"Well, yes, but nobody talks that way around *you*, even adults. You sort of move in your own little bubble Kate, never seeing bad in anyone. I've seen the others clean up their language when you enter the teachers' lounge. Don't know why. You certainly don't *look* any different from the rest of us." Holly laughed at her friend.

Kate blushed. "Even Phil has never cussed since we were ten-year-old best friends, so maybe I've been sheltered. But it bothers me to hear a young girl like Olivia use gutter language. The little boys sometimes try out new words to shock us, and we can straighten them out, but this seems different." She bit her lip in concentration.

"Olivia's salty vocabulary spills out with as much fluidity as though it's her normal speech pattern," continued Kate. "I don't think she even notices if others are shocked. She's pretty hard-boiled about everything. She even uses those terms for bodily functions, so maybe she's had no one to teach her. Perhaps tactfully giving her new words to substitute for old ones will help."

"Now, that'll be an interesting experiment. How do we *tactfully* tell her to use 'defecate' instead of 'shit?' I'm afraid nobody trained me to be *that* tactful," said Holly.

The two tried out hypothetical word substitutions. Soon both were in stitches. "Thank goodness we can laugh about this, or we'd be crying," said Holly.

Holly waved as she headed to the teachers' lounge for

lunch hour, while Kate moved to the playground. She noticed more restlessness, arguments and fights than when she'd had lunch duty the previous week. She watched to find its source. Each time something stirred up, Olivia was in the middle of the controversy, arguing angrily with anyone who got near. Her smutty words screeched across the playground. Kate vaguely remembered seeing similar behavior in a *National Geographic* movie where gorillas menaced each other to establish primacy with one group and then moved to the next group of fellow gorillas. Was it possible Olivia was trying to establish some sort of playground pecking order where there had been none before? Kate strolled over to observe more closely.

She watched as Olivia grasped her chain, stuck out her chin, and glared at each child in turn, daring him to advance toward her. *Just like those gorillas.* When other children seemed taken aback at Olivia's menacing tone or expression, she moved toward them and watched them retreat with a sardonic smile on her face. Though Olivia was older, she wasn't any bigger in stature, so it seemed she manipulated others totally through her demeanor.

It was like a game, yet the threatening, bullying tone was apparent, as one by one, the other students backed down and moved off to other activities. Olivia always won.

As soon as she had the game figured out, Kate asked Olivia to come talk to her. The girl responded with a sullen stare of pure hatred, but Kate stubbornly held eye contact and waited. Finally, Olivia turned and jabbed her finger at the child she'd been menacing in one final unspoken statement and walked slowly over to where Kate stood.

"Olivia, you seem to be feeling a bit aggressive today, and you're using words we don't allow here. Do you realize you may be making some of these kids afraid of you rather than making friends?"

"I ain't doin' nothin' to 'em. Who tattled?" The girl glared at those nearby.

"No one needed to tattle, Olivia. I've been watching how you approach people, and I think we need to work a little on

socialization skills for you to make friends."
　　Olivia looked up at Kate with a bewildered gape, shaking her head. "Most times, I don't know what you're words are talkin' 'bout. And I told you, I don't need no friends."
　　"We'll talk about that again, Olivia. For now, I'll remind you not to smoke on campus."
　　"I ain't smokin'," said the child. "Who told you I was smokin'? I'll get 'em!" Olivia stood with her stubby Marlboro cupped in her curled hand.
　　Kate laughed out loud. "Then what's that little cloud of smoke hovering over your head, Olivia? Cupping the cigarette doesn't make you invisible, you know. You're a dead give-away, like Indians sending up smoke signals before they attack the covered wagon train."
　　Olivia looked down at her hand, and Kate thought she saw a flicker of a smile cross the girl's lips before she sullenly threw down the cigarette butt and stomped it.
　　"You can pick that up and put it in the trash, and then we'll go to the bench."
　　The girl obeyed, but Kate could hear her reluctance in the sound of dragging tennis shoes on the surface blacktop following behind her, agonizingly slow.
　　Kate pointed to the seat and said in the same quiet voice, "You're benched."
　　"What'd I do?" Olivia's voice rose loudly, as though to attract attention to an argument she hoped would ensue. "I didn't do nothin'. All you teachers do is bitch."
　　"Try 'complain,' Olivia, as in, 'All you teachers do is *complain.*'"
　　The girl looked bewildered. She seemed accustomed to getting the best of any confrontation.
　　So, if Olivia loved an audience, Kate refused to give her one. Quietly, she pointed again and repeated. "You're benched. Sit there until I come back." Without waiting for the child to comply, Kate walked away to supervise a jump rope group, offering to take an end of the rope so the turner could jump.

From the corner of her eye, Kate could watch Olivia. The girl turned full circle as though to see who might have observed her abrupt dismissal. Finally, she sat down on the bench. Apparently, without a confrontation, Olivia could think of nothing else to do except comply. She sat with elbows on knees and head against her balled-up fists, scowling.

As the play period ended, Kate strolled back to Olivia and sat down beside her.

"You wouldn't even answer me." The young girl sulked.

"You weren't courteous enough to deserve a conversation, Olivia. When you speak nicely to others, they'll speak nicely to you."

"But I didn't do nothin'."

"Anything. You didn't do *anything*, Olivia. That's the correct word for it, but you know what you were doing that caused a problem, now don't you?"

"No." Olivia looked down at her feet and shuffled them slowly in the dust.

"When you think you can tell me what you were doing, perhaps we can get on with this conversation." Kate rose and started away.

"Okay, okay. I guess I was smokin', and so what if I was pushin' the kids a little. They got no damn right to think I'm not in charge."

"What makes you think they need anybody in charge?"

"Somebody has to run this place, and it's gonna be me, not some paleface."

"You know, Olivia, it's probably comical to other children that you think somebody must 'run them.' They've done quite well all this time with each person minding his own business and taking care of himself. Why do you think that might be?"

"I don't wanna talk to you. You talk funny."

A warning bell rang, ending the lunch hour. Olivia started to rise. Kate restrained her lightly with a hand on her arm. "Wait a moment, Olivia."

"I gotta go shit before the bell. You can't keep me here."

"I think you can wait a moment before going 'to the restroom,' Olivia. I'd rather *that* be the way you refer to your private business. Would that be too hard for you to remember next time?"

"I ain't no dummy."

"I know that, Olivia. That's why I don't want you to use words that might make someone who didn't know you think you were. These students are all new to you. Wouldn't you like to make some friends and help them feel comfortable with you?"

Her black eyes shot fire from under dark lashes. "I told you, I don't need no friends here. I got friends in my gang, and we take care of each other just fine!"

Kate realized the child was waiting for a reaction. She gave none. Instead, she continued softly. "Perhaps, but, while you're here with us, our students would feel better around you if you cleaned up your language and let them run their own business. We'll not allow *you* to 'run them.' Do you understand?"

Olivia fidgeted.

"All right, Olivia. You may go to the *restroom* now, and then go on to Mrs. Warner's classroom. Don't be late. I'll see you at lunch tomorrow."

"You gonna be out here *every* day?" The child looked pained.

"As long as you need me to be, Olivia." Kate smiled at the girl and walked down the arcade to stand outside her own classroom, collecting her students to her side with good-natured hugs until they all tumbled into class. She glanced down the breezeway one last time and saw Olivia staring after them with a confused look before she entered the girls' restroom.

Kate sighed, wondering if she had handled that episode appropriately for this young girl, but she wasn't sure. Perhaps she and Phil had been sheltered in their own safe, happy little world, and Olivia somehow shattered her illusions about the innocence of children. *Olivia's a tough one. God help us all to figure her out.*

Kate joined her class inside to start a science lesson.

Chapter 2

For the next three weeks, the daily scene was much the same. Often the office secretary would call Olivia's house to ask that her mother come get her at the request of the principal. The mother was either not home, or didn't answer the phone. She never responded to notes. The secretary asked plaintively, "I wonder if Olivia's mother is even a real person, or is she missing or dead?"

If Olivia acted up when Kate had playground duty, she only repeated the two words, "You're benched," and walked away. In every case, the young girl didn't seem to know what to do except obey and sit down, if she couldn't make it into a public argument. Kate always went back before the bell to try a quiet conversation, or pass on a "new word of the day." The girl appeared to ignore her, but sometimes, she used the new word. Kate just nodded and smiled in response, not making too much of it.

Holly reported that Olivia seemed distracted in class. Or she became belligerent, followed by catatonic isolation, as though she was unaware of others nearby. Her behavior was distressing and unpredictable.

Lacking any parental response, teachers struggled on their own to devise strategies to help Olivia learn to curb her aggressive tendencies. She was often the topic of teacher lounge conversation as colleagues suggested interventions for Holly to try. Olivia seemed to attract negative attention more than positive.

"If we had a hundred kids lined up, you'd pick her out as trouble," said Fred, the colleague next door to Kate's classroom. "I don't understand quite what it is about her. Something in her body language or stance just comes off as aggressive. We'll have to figure it out before we can help her change the image."

"Does she even *want* to change the image," said Matt, the other sixth grade teacher teamed with Fred and Holly. "She's a mean one, all right. She hangs onto that chain like a weapon. Makes me wonder if it's for show, or if she'd really use it. I was hoping she'd stop wearing it when she felt safer here at school, but we may have to take it away from her by force. I've had to pull her off other students three or four times this week for fighting, and I'm afraid she might use it on someone."

"She talks about her 'gang' all the time." Sallie, a fourth grade teacher, had enjoyed playground duty until Olivia came along. "To me a gang is simply a group of friends or colleagues. To Olivia, it seems to be something entirely different—something with fights and weapons. I think we have a real culture clash on our hands. She has some kind of value system, but it's certainly not the same as ours, or anything we're trying to teach the other kids."

Ruth, another fifth grade teacher, added, "We all volunteered to be at this school because we felt we could make a difference. *All* our kids came to kindergarten with problems, and most don't even know how to dress or clean themselves. We get them with no vocabulary skills because no one has ever talked or read to them—usually no breakfast or lunch." Ruth emphasized her point by waving her finger. "Yet, we're somehow supposed to get them up to grade level before they finish sixth grade and have to compete with the well-fed kids coming from other schools to the junior high. We all know it takes almost the whole six years to do the job, and with Olivia, we only have a few months left. We've got to start making that difference for her, too, and quickly."

"Olivia is certainly farther out of the loop than the rest of our kids." Jeff kicked in with the statement. "Troubled as they are, she makes them seem quite normal by comparison. None of the usual ways we use to get kids to be cooperative enough to learn seems to work for Olivia. We need some new strategies."

Holly said, "It's hard to figure her out. I sure don't see any sign of her becoming less angry. It's also strange to me that sometimes she comes to school in slouchy old clothes that smell of smoke or bleach, and sometimes whips in with a brand new fancy outfit. Most of the kids around here can't afford those outfits, so where does Olivia get them?"

There were many mysteries about Olivia, but asking her anything resulted only in sullen silence or violent outburst. The faculty tried one technique after another to no avail. Olivia hated them all--kids, faculty, school in general. She didn't want to belong at Sunnyside and went out of her way to perpetuate this isolation. *Where does all this violence come from?* thought Kate. Some of the teachers felt they might as well just give up and hope the school year ended before Olivia killed someone. This was, of course, said facetiously, but all knew the girl was poison on campus. She had developed a small following of kids with a tinge of latent aggression—a worrying development. Olivia truly brought out the worst in everybody.

At noon, during the fourth Friday of Olivia's presence, Kate walked toward the teachers' lounge with her lunch sack, absorbed in thinking out a math procedure she would use to intrigue her students for the afternoon. Her class was difficult to spice up to the intrigue level but, like all the other teachers at Sunnyside, she stood on her head to try to accomplish the impossible. She loved her school, *and* her kids.

She was startled from her reverie in time to see Olivia staggering down the arcade toward her, looking pale, sweaty, sleepy-eyed, and apparently ill.

"Help me—I'm on drugs," Olivia mumbled, and she fell.

Kate dropped her books and caught Olivia before she hit the sidewalk. She struggled to lift the child. Though Olivia was small for her age, Kate found it impossible to run with the awkward load. Fred ran forward and took the child out of her arms. Together they raced into the nurse's office.

"What happened?" The nurse left her sandwich and rushed over to the cot in her office as Fred lowered the child's body on it.

Kate tried to catch her breath. "She just stumbled into my arms and collapsed saying, 'Help me—I'm on drugs.' Thank goodness Fred was there to carry her."

The nurse checked for a pulse, saying what Kate had already feared. "I think she's overdosed. She's out cold. Somebody get Mr. Marken." Fred moved quickly to do so.

Hearing the commotion, Holly entered from the teachers'

lounge, and the three teachers, the secretary, and the principal stood watching the girl, while the nurse took her blood pressure and peered behind her eyelids. "She's on something, all right," Nancy said. No one knew what to do next. It was an incident totally outside their experience on the elementary school level.

"If we call the Operator to get an ambulance company," said Marcia, the school secretary, "they won't treat her unless her mother is here for consent, and we can never find her."

"What about the police?" suggested the principal.

"The police will put her in Juvenile Hall," said Holly. "I know she's rough, but I don't think she belongs *there*." She sighed heavily and slumped to a chair beside the cot.

"If she's really overdosed, we need to get her to a hospital," said Fred. "Nancy, is there any way to tell how much she's had or how long it's been in her system?'

"Her pulse and respiration are good. She's a tough kid. I don't feel she's in any immediate danger, but I'd like to at least get her to vomit." Nancy sighed. "God, I never thought this could happen here--hippies, college kids maybe, but elementary kids?"

"We'd better leave her here to sleep it off, so the other children won't see her," said the principal. "We don't want to scare them all by an ambulance coming."

His fuss budgeting around the room stretched Kate's patience far more than any of the so-called problem children within the school.

"No, we need to keep waking her," contradicted the nurse. "She'll be groggy, but she'll wake soon, if she hasn't taken a massive dose."

"But, do we know that?" asked Holly, twisting her handkerchief around her fingers.

"Call her mother to come," offered Fred. "She can decide."

Marcia, dialed, letting the phone ring for several silent moments. Everyone in the room waited, hoping Olivia's mother would be there. Marcia slammed down the receiver, fuming. "Doesn't that woman ever stay home? She never gave us any work phone number or any way to reach her. Her daughter needs her and, as usual, she's missing."

Nancy applied a cold compress to Olivia's forehead while Kate massaged her wrists. The others stood silently transfixed, as the tiny nurse's office seemed to shrink to a cocoon, encapsulating six adults into an anxious little world of their own. Time crawled by, emphasized by the loud click of each second on the master clock, marking off the tense minutes while the group wondered aloud how they should deal with something that had never happened before to any of them.

"We can't leave her here indefinitely, and we can't send her home unless her mother is there to take care of her," said Mr. Marken, stating the obvious.

Olivia moaned. The nurse lifted her eyelids again. Her pupils were still quite dilated. Kate shook her gently and spoke to her, hoping a voice would stimulate some response.

Finally, the girl's eyes opened to half-mast, and she searched the scared faces hovering over her. When she saw Kate, she spoke shakily.

"I loaded up today, figurin' I'd pass out in class, or I'd find you and you'd do somethin'."

"Olivia, what do you want us to do? How can we help?" Kate asked.

"Get me off, Mrs. Johnson." Olivia shook her head back and forth on the cot. "Get me off--I'm gonna die if I don't get off." Her voice came slowly, as from far away. "You can always make me do what I don't want to...so make me do it."

With that, Olivia shut her eyes tightly, and they could all see the hot tears come from their corners. Not one of the adults could believe this child even knew how to cry. Still, no one knew what to do with the young girl lying there who suddenly seemed more fragile than before.

She turned again to Kate. "Take me home with you."

Kate gasped, "Why, Olivia, you have a family, a mother. Your records mention six older sisters, a brother. Your mom must be worried sick about you." *At least she's talking. The voice is vibrating, but it must mean she's not in immediate danger.*

"Mom don't know." With sudden strength, Olivia grabbed the hands of both Holly and Kate. "You won't tell her, will you? She'd kill me for sure!" Her words slurred almost to the point of incoherence, but the desperation in her tone spoke clearly.

Kate and Holly locked eyes. *She's genuinely afraid,* thought Kate. *Is her mother abusive? What if we send her home and her mother hurts her?* Teachers knew police wouldn't investigate cases of suspected abuse, since courts consistently ruled that what went on at home was a family's private business. Teachers weren't supposed to interfere. *Maybe someday there'll be better laws, but we need to do something for Olivia, now!*

"Where did you get the drugs, Olivia? Can you tell the nurse what kind you took, or how much you took? We need to know that too, I think."

"Won't tell you where...against the code. But they're downers...yellow ones."

Her voice seemed stronger and more coherent, but relatively docile, Kate thought. *Did these "downers" make even Olivia more quiet?* "How many did you take?"

"Dunno ...took some...didn't knock me out worth shit...took more."

"Oh, my God," said Holly. "Call the Operator for an ambulance, now."

"No...no, damn you." Olivia jerked away from Holly. "They call police." She choked as the tears came. "I came to you 'cause I thought you'd help me." She held tightly to Kate's hand and pulled her down to eye level. "You're the only one I can ask. Please." Olivia put her free arm over her eyes, wiping the offending tears on her sleeve.

"Olivia," said Kate quietly, "we're trying to help you. It's just that none of us has any experience with this kind of problem, so we're not sure what to do." She knelt on the floor beside the cot. "The hospital, the police, your mother—you're fearful of them all, yet those are the only resources we have. I wish there were a rehabilitation hospital for young people, but there isn't. They'd put you in with adult heroin addicts."

The girl turned on her side facing Kate. "I jus' need a place to crash 'til the damn stuff stops makin' my head fall over, so my mom won't know." Olivia's eyes were foggy and her voice pleading. "She'll kill me if she finds out, I swear."

Mr. Marken huffed and puffed around the office, mumbling, "I've got to call the police. We have no choice. We have to call the police." Three or four times he got as far as picking up the phone receiver before Fred took it from his shaking hands and hung it back up. The principal didn't argue. He uttered an almost grateful sigh of resignation, as though he'd be out of the line of fire if someone else took responsibility for the decision.

When Kate looked again at Olivia's face to see if she had heard the exchange, the child had gone back to sleep. Some color had returned to her cheeks. Kate touched her face, feeling the warmth. She hoped the girl would wake again, but she didn't really know what effect drugs had. She turned questioning eyes to Nancy.

"She's just sleeping it off, Kate. She'll be okay. We'll keep waking her every few minutes to make sure. I'm positive this is more an ethical problem of what to do for her immediate safety and eventual rehabilitation, than it is a medical problem."

"Since she came to us for help," said Fred, "she must think we can do something—but what?"

"I suppose someone could keep her just for tonight," said Marcia. We can leave a note on her mom's door with a phone number. We'll say she's staying over, someplace."

Her voice died away as Holly looked at her. "Could you?"

"Oh, not *me*!" said Marcia, almost stuttering in her excited refusal. "I wouldn't know what to do if she got sick or anything, and besides, my boyfriend would have a fit."

Holly looked a little guilty, as though she hadn't wanted to state her feelings. "I have a four and a five year old. I can't have them mimicking Olivia with every vile word they hear. I can't have that." She shook her head emphatically.

"You guys know I'm already having enough trouble with my own two teenagers," said Fred. "They're followers. I can't take the chance of having Olivia in my house. I really can't trust my kids not to try out drugs *with* her."

The principal spread out his hands in a helpless gesture. But they all knew the home of this nervous little man with his oh-so-conscientious wife who worried someone might step on her Persian rug or bump her antique Chinese vases was not the right place for Olivia.

All eyes turned to Kate.

"I...I'm not sure...." Kate was grateful Olivia was asleep and, hopefully, hadn't heard those pondering her fate. *But how can I take this foul-mouthed, doped-up young girl home to my family? Yet I can't leave her behind when the others don't want her?*

Kate thought about her big bear of a loving husband, Phil, who had already accepted Alisa, Ned, and James, who had come to live with them permanently. Nor did he seem to mind the steady progression of kids who stopped by for homework help, or a meal, or a few nights, when they ran into sporadic problems in their own homes. It was a challenge financially, as well as physically, to install bunk beds in every nook and cranny of their modest two-bedroom, one bath, and a den, starter home. They had even turned the combination dining/TV room they'd added on into a bedroom for James and Ned. The two boys had moved in at ten and fourteen, respectively, when James's parents didn't want him around, and Ned's step dad got abusive when drunk.

Sometimes Phil joked that there must be markings on the curb like the hobos used during the Great Depression to show where there was a family that would give them a free meal. He would even go out and look at the curb, shaking his head and laughing whenever a new kid showed up.

Could mellow Phil accept one more troubled kid, or would this one, with heavier problems than all the others combined, be the last straw--the breaking point for their having any time, money or energy left for each other or their own girls, Cindi and Cori?

Glancing out at the breezeway of this open, bright elementary school in the worst part of Whittier, Kate always felt a lump in her throat. *We're making progress here that probably couldn't happen anywhere else. Every teacher at this school volunteered to bend the rules when necessary to accomplish whatever the children needed. Is that what I'd be doing by taking Olivia home? Only one more kid?*

Her thoughts were interrupted as the others offered suggestions and arguments.

"Kate, your kids are all really solid now. They won't be influenced to be illegal or immoral by someone like Olivia." Fred apparently felt his kids *could* be influenced.

"Being around your kids who don't cuss may influence even Olivia to clean up her vocabulary," added Holly. "Besides, it'll only be for one night."

Funny, thought Kate. *Every child who moved into our house only came for one night, yet somehow the time stretched into years. Now they ranged from Cori, her youngest at twelve, through James, the gangly eldest of the group, who was sixteen and driving. What could she do with another child, when they could scarcely feed the ones they had on two teachers' salaries? What on earth would they do when the kids got to college age?*

"Do you think we'd be breaking any laws by one of us taking her while she dries out? Yet, if she's that afraid of her mother...." Kate's voice trailed off. They all knew that some of their children lived under dangerous conditions at home, and there was no agency, no law to intervene on a child's behalf.

Fred pounded the counter. "They've promised legislation for years to allow teachers to report incidents like this. But the lawmakers get hung up on parents knowing best, so no one should interfere. I don't see any degree required for parenthood. What is it going to take to protect the kids instead of abusive parents? Does one of our kids have to die first?" He slumped from his soapbox.

"Marcia," Holly asked, "You met the mother on the first day she brought Olivia to school? What she was like? Do you think Olivia is right, that her mom would hurt her, if she knew the kid asked us for help?"

Marcia looked down at the counter on which she leaned and pushed her hands together. "I remember all right. She spoke with slurred speech. I thought she might be drunk. And she just shoved Olivia into the office, slapped the record folder on the counter and left. I called after her that there would be some papers she needed to sign, but she just walked out. She never came back. You saw Olivia that first day--really angry and sullen. I have no idea what the mother is like."

"And the rest of us haven't seen her," added Fred, shaking his head. "Olivia might have good reason to be afraid. I don't know what to think. Are there rules for not notifying authorities until we can find out if the kid is in danger at home or not?"

Mr. Marken bustled up with the latest codebook for the district, labeled 1968, but he couldn't find anything about children *afraid* to go home. Nor was there any guidance on drugs, since that problem had not yet filtered down to the elementary level.

Mr. Marken scratched his balding head as he searched the codebook. "I'm not sure a drug overdose fits into the procedure for getting hurt on the playground or getting sick."

Fred added with a sound that was half harrumph and half sarcasm, "Okay, so there are no outside resources for us to consult, no child abuse or child rehabilitation services, Olivia doesn't quite need hospitalization or jail, she's afraid of her mother, and there's nothing in the elementary codebook about illicit drug use because we've never had any yet." He laughed with an ironic expression. "That about sums it up, doesn't it? I guess we teachers have nothing available beyond our own ingenuity."

The group had been so engrossed in Olivia's situation that they were startled when the warning bell rang loudly from the master clock. Lunch hour was over. Those teachers not on playground duty that day hustled from the teachers' lounge through the front office, and a steady flow of children waltzed by the open door on their way to class, jostling and giggling, oblivious to the drama unfolding within the nurse's office.

Kate sighed. They were out of time. She heard herself say she'd take Olivia for the night if Nancy could keep watch on her until after school, and if Marcia could keep trying to call the mother. All agreed it was the only solution, at least until they could be sure if this mother was abusive or not. Certainly the young girl needed counseling, not "juvie," the Juvenile Hall that had an abysmal record of repeat offenders and gang connections. But where could they begin to find counseling for a twelve, almost thirteen year old?

During the afternoon, Kate checked on Olivia, once finding her distraught and moaning, and once sleeping peacefully. Nancy checked pulse and blood pressure frequently and felt sure Olivia was merely sleeping off the drugs. Kate tried to call her husband each time she went to the office phone, too, but he was either in class or out coaching his high school track team. After her students left, she set up her classroom for the next day and went back to the office to get Olivia and call her own home again, but neither Phil nor any of the kids were there yet.

Well, it looks like Olivia will be a surprise.

Nancy waited with the fuzzy-minded, quietly profane Olivia, while Kate brought her old 1960 station wagon to the door. Together, they helped the girl in.

During the drive home, Olivia dozed one moment and woke with a four-letter expletive the next. Kate began to be concerned that the whole clan would be home by the time she arrived, Phil probably peeling potatoes while the kids set the table, waiting for her to make the main dish. How on earth could she explain Olivia, especially if the child's language and behavior were really obscene when she woke up fully? She would just have to trust the family to follow her lead and not over-react.

Olivia moaned and shifted her position to lean against the car door.

The closer Kate drove to her home, the more apprehensive she became. Her thoughts focused on one thing--*what have I gotten myself into this time?*

Chapter 3

Kate pulled forward to park behind Phil's car, since James's van wasn't there yet. *Probably working late at the malt shop,* she thought, wondering if she'd need to keep his dinner warm. She ran around the car to help Olivia, who leaned heavily against her. The girl's slow steps set their pace as they approached the brightly lit house, where strains of music and laughter escaped.

A heavy bougainvillea vine dominated the front entrance of the modest house, its blood-red blossoms hanging from where it almost covered the roof to within three feet of the rock flower bed below, creating a natural screen for their walkway and shade for their front porch. The bougainvillea vine was the pride of the neighborhood, attracting comment from neighbors and visitors alike.

Kate steered Olivia behind the bougainvillea screen. Glancing through the living room window, they could see Alisa, Alli, Cori and Cindi all playing a caroms game in the middle of the room with her husband calling the shots.

"Didn't know you had kids." Olivia mumbled with a marble-mouthed sound Kate was beginning to recognize. "Thought teachers had big houses."

"Teachers don't get paid enough for big houses, Olivia, and my husband and I are both teachers, so what you see is what you get. Are you feeling any better now?"

"Wobbly, but I can maintain." Her voice seemed clearer.

"Has this happened to you before?"

"Yeah, but just with my gang. We sleep it off the next day."

"Can you handle being with people, or would you prefer to lie down awhile?"

"I'll see what you got in there." She motioned toward the lighted living room. She giggled drunkenly. "They ain't gonna like somebody like me. Will you get beat for bringing me in?"

"No one here would 'beat' anyone else, Olivia. We're family, and we care about each other. They'll treat you like any other kids who've come home with me, or with Phil."

"Is Phil your husband? Are you *really* married to him?"

The question caught Kate by surprise. "Of course. Why do you ask?"

"Everybody I know just lives with a guy until they get a baby and get beat up, and the guy leaves 'em."

"This is a family, Olivia. They aren't going to hurt each other, no one will hurt you, and no one is going to leave." Kate took a deep breath, wondering where on earth Olivia got such totally foreign ideas. *Sallie was right—there is a deep culture clash.* Kate patted Olivia's shoulder. "Are you ready to go in and meet them?"

"What'll I say?"

Kate felt the girl's shoulders shaking. "'Hello,' would be nice." She smiled at Olivia, opened the door, and escorted her into the sparsely furnished living room.

Phil rushed over to kiss Kate passionately, bending her backward in good-natured glee. The teens said almost in unison, "Yuck!" But one could tell from their smiles they were accustomed to the scene. Phil grinned with mischief and hugged Kate once more. Then he bent to meet Olivia's eyes, saying, "And who have we here?"

"This is Olivia. I invited her to stay with us tonight." Kate smiled a bit too brightly with raised eyebrows as a signal. *Will they get the message?* "These are our girls, Cindi, Alisa, Alli, and Cori." Kate pointed them out around the caroms board, each waiting her turn to knock rings into the corner pockets with a cue.

Phil had placed a large barrel from the back yard in the middle of the floor to hold the carom board. At least, Kate assumed it was Phil, since he was always dragging something into the living room. He never liked to work alone. Instead, he brought whatever he was working on inside, to be near her. The last time, it was the engine block of one of the old junker cars Phil struggled to keep running. Oh, he put newspapers down to prevent dribbling oil from eating up the asphalt floor tile, but it was still unusual by most people's standards. They couldn't afford the wall-to-wall carpeting all the neighbors seemed to prefer. Carpeting had a lower priority than kids. *Is it any wonder everyone in the neighborhood thinks Phil and I are a little crazy in love, or maybe just crazy, for taking in stray kids like some folks did stray puppies.* Out loud, Kate said, "A barrel for a pedestal? You guys were pretty creative to think of a use for that eyesore from the back yard."

"It's right at waist height for the carom board, Mom," said Cindi as she leaned against the console hi fi cabinet. Their high fidelity console was their adventurous splurge and the biggest piece of furniture in the room. It held a modern reel-to-reel tape recorder, AM/FM radio, twin speakers, and a record player that handled both 78 and 45-rpm phonograph records with a spindle in the middle. They hadn't gone so overboard on the budget since they bought their house in 1957. The music of "The Mamas and the Papas" sprang forth from its radio and, in between turns with the carom stick, the girls lip-synced the words of Mama Cass with an imaginary microphone, "Say 'nighty-night and kiss me. Just hold me tight and...." They all loved the contralto voice of Mama Cass, though only Kate could actually sound like her, much to the amusement of the family, who otherwise giggled at her efforts to hit any note higher than middle C. "I think Mama Cass and I were both born baritones," she told them. She and Phil had sung together in their high school Acapella choir and still loved to harmonize on favorites until the kids either joined in, or dissolved on the floor in laughter.

But this time, Kate didn't offer her imitation of Mama Cass. The girls and Phil aborted their game to gather around Olivia and ask her questions.

"Are you going to stay here too?" Alisa asked.

Fourteen-year-old Alisa still harbored occasional remnants of insecurity from three years before when her parents divorced and left the state. Her mom took the three youngest boys, and her dad took the two oldest girls. Neither parent seemed concerned about Alisa in the middle. Alisa knew the Johnsons from being in Kate's first class at Sunnyside, taking part in her Girl Scout troop, and being a friend of Cindi's. She had been a frequent guest in the house. She turned up on the Johnson's' front porch one Sunday morning with a paper bag holding two pair of panties and her tennis shoes, with her guitar slung over one shoulder. "Can I stay here with you?" she'd asked, and Phi! put up another bed. No parent had ever called or searched, and there appeared to be no legal ramifications. *After all, we could never have turned away a child in trouble.*

Olivia stared around the room, as though taking in all the clues she needed to decide on her answer to Alisa's question. Kate couldn't help watching her. What would this drugged young girl see in their small home that might define their lives? Kate wondered whether the living room might look a little shabby to an outsider. Though small, it was clean and comfortable for an active family, and its tile floors could support both dancing and water balloon fights. When Olivia looked toward the kitchen, Kate glanced through the open archway to the narrow I-shaped kitchen, as well. The corner of the sink slab and refrigerator were barely visible. The kids took turns helping with cooking and clean up, but Kate needed to finish cooking dinner. First, however, she wanted to be sure Olivia could integrate herself into the group for this one evening.

"What the fuck is that?" said Olivia loudly.

An audible, collective gasp filled the room. All movement stopped.

Well, there goes the idea of Olivia integrating into the group. Kate jerked her head at the others. They went back to the carom board silently, not used to hearing such language in their home.

Phil moved over to again bend down to Olivia's eye level and answered quietly, "That shelf holds trophies the kids have won in track, softball, and football. We all like sports in this house. But we don't use those kinds of words, Olivia, so you'll need to remember to try another way of saying things. You can just say, "What is that?" and any one of us will answer you. Is that okay with you?"

Olivia nodded silently, her head bowed. She snuck a glance over at Kate, apparently for confirmation that it was okay for Phil to tell her the rules. Kate nodded at her.

With the first dialect dispute out of the way, Olivia resumed her survey of the small living room. She looked down at the large, circular, imitation-marble coffee table that held a half-finished jigsaw puzzle, and passed to the turquoise, slightly bruised, three-piece curved sectional sofa arranged around the table. A turquoise abstract painting with no frame hung above. Next came a low bookcase. Olivia steadied herself against the bookcase and ran her fingers across the books. She announced, "Somebody sure must read a lot." Before they could answer, Olivia continued, "Readin's dumb. I hate it."

No one spoke. There seemed no answer to her emphatic statement. Next, Olivia moved toward a wide door leading to a closed-in porch they'd added on, housing a set of bunk beds for the boys at one end, a battered TV and a table at the other. She counted eight table settings out loud. "You have more kids?"

"Yes, " answered Phil, "Ned's playing with the dog in the back yard, James isn't home yet from work, and Alli doesn't live with us all the time, but she's staying with us tonight. She and Renee are often here at homework and game time. We'll set another place for you." Phil moved to the kitchen to attend to that little chore.

Alli added with a sardonic laugh, "Yeah, sometimes Renee and I stay here when our parents don't like us for a few days. Then we go back home."

"But you know you're always welcome," said Kate with a hug for Alli.

Cori changed the subject by inviting Olivia to join the caroms game. Cindi handed her the cue stick, and Kate headed for the kitchen to finish dinner, watching as she worked through the arched doorway. She listened to the girls chattering in the living room, asking innocent questions about Olivia's background—all of which Olivia managed to deflect in some subtle manner. But she didn't raise her voice and seemed almost shy. Kate smiled. Olivia had not tried her bullying manner--perhaps she felt outnumbered or insecure in a strange place. But perhaps, just perhaps, she was figuring out it was not in her best interest, at least here on Kate's home turf. She felt content to leave Olivia temporarily with four normal girls with normal girl problems like what skirts and leotards to wear for school and how to get their hair fashionably straight when Mother Nature had provided curls.

Ned came noisily through the back door, hugged Kate on his way through the kitchen and sauntered into the living room. The family's Bassett hound and her constant companion, a straggly yellow cat, closely followed him. Walking up to Olivia, he said, "Hi, I'm Ned. This dog is Princess Cleopatra and the cat is Goldie Buttercup."

"Dumb names," muttered Olivia.

"You'd have to blame that on us," said Cindi. She giggled. When James came to live with us, he mowed a neighbor's yard to buy Cleo as a gift for Mom and Dad. They were too embarrassed to tell him they didn't want a dog." Cindi paused to take her shot at the carom board. "The names sound funny now, but I was seven, and Cori was six, and we thought we were giving them really sophisticated names." She grinned at her sister.

Ned added, "Cleo's mother was hit by a car before Cleo's eyes were even open. A mother cat adopted her, nursing her along with the kittens, so she still thinks she's a cat. She's never in her life barked, and she hangs out with other cats and the kids of the neighborhood, sometimes dragging home strays of either species."

"She gives herself baths by licking her front paws and swiping them over her head like a cat," said Alisa. "She even tries terribly hard to purr."

The kids broke into laughter as they tried to imitate the comic result of noises that were a sort of "gurgle" way down in the belly, half way between a growl and a rumble.

Olivia didn't seem to know if she could join in the laughter or not. "So what about that retarded cat?" She almost sounded interested.

Kate grinned from the kitchen doorway, listening to the historic recital of their animals that were certainly as eccentric as the rest of their family.

"Goldie Buttercup?" said Cori. "He's a special case. About the same time we got Cleo, I found this ugly yellow kitten someone tried to drown in the creek in a paper bag. Cindi and I wagged him home for Mom to save. Of course, she was just thrilled!" The two girls giggled at the memory. "Mom washed, deloused, warmed, and adopted." She paused to scratch the silly yellow cat between the ears. Goldie stuck his tongue out between his teeth in glorious pleasure.

"Yeah, he looks dumb, all right," said Cindi. "It was obvious Goldie was a few mice short of a meal. But he loved us, even when we fed him with a bottle, dressed him in doll clothes, and wheeled him in the doll carriage. He didn't care as long as we loved him back. Finally, he got strong enough to stagger around on his own."

Alli chimed in. "He still staggers, but it doesn't bother Cleo. They eat, sleep and play together. Don't you have any pets?"

Olivia shook her head vigorously and tried to ignore the animals when Cleo sniffed at her leg. She said, "Your dumb dog's belly almost drags on the ground."

"We know," said Cindi with her usual quick-clipped voice. "Cleo's actually smart, but yes, Goldie's dumb. He's got a good soul, though. Go ahead and pick him up. He won't hurt you."

"And Cleo is pregnant--again," added Alisa. "Everyone in the neighborhood waits in line for one of her puppies because they all turn out as mellow and as good a 'kid dog' as she is." When Alisa reached down to the hound, Cleo obligingly rolled her fat body over on her back. "She loves having her tummy rubbed. Watch." Alisa rubbed Cleo's belly and the dog's left hind leg scratched the air in pleasure. "Here, you can rub her belly too."

Olivia held back, seeming as suspicious of animals as she was of people. But Cori picked up Goldie and plopped him into Olivia's arms. Goldie immediately laid his head on Olivia's shoulder and wrapped paws around her neck. "He's hugging," yelped Olivia. "Somebody help!" In her alarm, she came close to dropping the cat, but Goldie hung on.

Ned roared with laughter, flopping his fourteen-year-old, short, stocky body on part of the sectional couch. "Everyone around here hugs, Olivia, even the animals. It's part of life in the Johnson house. You'll get used to it. We all have."

With Goldie hanging loosely around her neck and one arm warily supporting the cat, Olivia, guided by Alisa, very tentatively reached down to pat Cleo's belly. As Cleo's hind foot got going rapidly, Olivia actually laughed, and all the kids laughed with her.

"Don't worry, Olivia. We sort of grow on you," said Alli with a grin and a toss of her short, blonde hair.

Just as Kate invited the whole crew to the table, James arrived home. He was tall for his sixteen years, with dark, wavy hair and startling blue eyes. He greeted everyone and seemed totally unphased to find another strange girl there. He quickly removed his ice cream stained apron, washed his hands, and slid into his seat at the table.

"James, this is Olivia. She's staying with us tonight," said Phil, before all joined hands for grace. Olivia hesitated, but Ned grabbed her hand on one side and Cori grabbed her on the other. She didn't seem to know what else to do except bow her head when the others did. Kate had a moment of insight. *Olivia can rise to the occasion and meet expectations sometimes, if people assume she can.* She put the thought away for future reference.

Amidst the busy conversation at the table, Olivia suddenly yelped, "You don't think I'm gonna eat these damn trees, do you?"

"Those aren't trees," said Alisa. "They're broccoli. And they aren't damned. Vegetables will be good for the stamina you'll need to run with us in the morning."

"I ain't running no where."

"Everyone else probably will," said Alisa, "and you won't want to be left behind."

After dinner, there was the usual discussion between the kids over whose turn it was to wash dishes and whose to dry. A flip of the coin landed on Alisa and James. Cori and Alli carried dishes into the kitchen for them, and then joined as the rest of the crew melted into the living room and gathered on floor pillows around the 3000-piece jigsaw puzzle underway on the coffee table. James nodded at Kate, so she stayed a moment longer in the kitchen.

"What is it, James?"

"That girl's on drugs," he whispered. "Did you know when you brought her home?"

Kate also lowered her voice. "Yes, she overdosed at school, and none of us knew the safest thing to do with her. I sort of won her by default. How did you know?"

"Her eyes. I see some of the college kids at the malt shop who are doing drugs. You can tell they're on something when they come in. She's so young. Do the others know?"

"I don't think they can tell, James. I'll explain to them later after I take her home when her mother calls. The secretary left our phone number on her door."

"She won't call. She probably doesn't care, or the kid wouldn't be so out of it."

"We don't know that yet, James, so we'll give her mom the benefit of the doubt." Kate sighed. "I'm sure the kids could tell she has problems but, so far, they've done a good job of carrying on as though nothing is unusual about Olivia."

"Whatever made her do drugs before, I bet it'll make her do them again. What'll happen the next time, if you're not around to bring her home?"

"I'm hoping there won't be any next time."

The young man shrugged. "Maybe not. But you always think the best of everyone, even those who don't deserve it. I figured I'd better tell you, in case you didn't know. If you know, that's fine. I've got to help Alisa with the dishes." He moved over to Alisa, shook out a clean towel, and started drying the dishes she had already placed to drain on the sink slab.

"Betcha can't catch up," Kate heard Alisa say as she walked into the living room.

"Betcha I can." The dishes rattled alarmingly as James raced to clear the slab before Alisa could get further ahead. Points came for the dryer clearing the slab, or the washer getting two dishes ahead.

"I already have two points. You can't do it," sang Alisa.

Kate smiled...*just like real brothers and sisters*. Her mind raced ahead. *What if James is right--that Olivia will go back to drugs, no matter what anyone does? Olivia, at almost thirteen, might already be addicted. Is it too late for her?*

"Okay, guys," said Phil, smiling as Kate slid in beside him on the floor around the coffee table and its puzzle, now rapidly turning into a picture with eager hands grabbing pieces that fit. "How was everyone's day? You first, Ned."

Chapter 4

Olivia chose to sleep on the sectional sofa. She was small enough to fit comfortably. After the others went to bed, Kate stopped short of checking Olivia's pockets, though the thought entered her mind. She sat beside the girl and approached the touchy subject. "Olivia, you're welcome to stay over, but you mustn't ever bring drugs into this house."

"I wouldn't bring my dope here! These kids don't know nothin'. They're way too straight."

"Thank you. I appreciate your being responsible around other young people. Some of these in our home have had serious problems, too. They don't need new ones. I'm hoping you'll realize you don't need drugs either. What do you think?"

Olivia dropped her head. "I dunno. I wanted to kick today. I thought I could. But now, I wonder what my gang is doin'. I dunno if I can get through the night with no drugs. I'm kinda sick, and my gang'll think I ran out on 'em or ratted 'em out or somethin'."

"Do you think your friends would be angry at you for trying to quit?"

"I dunno. Maybe. My gang expects me to be with 'em, 'cause I'm a good fighter if we get jumped. And anyways, I don't know if I can quit, or if I want to—not all the time, anyways."

"Do you think you've been taking drugs long enough that you're already addicted, Olivia, or have you just been playing around with them for a little while?"

"A pretty long time...I dunno. I don't wanna talk about it."

"Okay, Olivia. Get a good night's sleep, and we'll see how you feel in the morning." She placed an extra blanket at the foot of the sectional, "...in case you get cold."

"What if I just walk outta here?"

"I don't think you'd do that, Olivia. We don't want to force you into anything, but we do want you to feel safe here. And I don't want to have to worry about you."

Olivia bristled. "Nobody worries about me. I take care of

myself--always have."

"But not always successfully, Olivia. People come into our lives for a reason, even if we don't always know what it is. You came to me for *some* reason today, and you're in our house now, so that means we're responsible for you. I don't 'have to' worry about you. I 'choose to.' There's a difference, and choosing is important in life." Kate reached down and hugged the girl, who seemed startled by the gesture. "Good night, Olivia. See you in the morning."

"I sure don't get you. I dunno what lots of your words mean, and I don't sleep so good alone at night, either. Can I turn on that music in the big stereo there and listen?"

"Will you keep it quiet enough it won't wake anyone else?"

"Yeah. Check it out and see if I don't."

Olivia selected a record and put it on the turntable. Kate noted the title, "Honey." Olivia knelt on the floor in front of the console, her ear against the speaker. They listened to the soft words. "See the tree, how big it's grown, but friends it hasn't been too long, it wasn't big...." As they heard the words, "The angels came...Honey, I miss you, and I'm being good." Olivia sobbed and hunkered down in fetal position on the floor.

Kate knelt by her side. "What is it? Can you tell me what's wrong?"

"Can't stand that song."

"Then why did you choose it, of all the other records in the console?"

"Had to. I hafta listen. It's like my boyfriend."

Kate was confused. Olivia wasn't old enough for a boyfriend--certainly not one with a deep enough relationship that she could feel such pain. "Can you tell me about your friend?" she asked tentatively. "Why does the song make you so sad?"

"He died, and I miss him. We laughed at this song, the singer all mushy and corny. We thought it was stupid because we'd always be together listening to it. And then he took too many pills and just died. The song was right. 'The angels came....'"

"I'm so sorry, Olivia."

"Why'd you be sorry? You wasn't nothin' to him...or me!"

The words came out forcefully--angrily.

Kate recoiled as though slapped. "I'm sorry, Olivia. Of course, I didn't know this boy. I just meant that I'm sorry his loss hurt you so."

Olivia picked up the needle arm, scratching the record, abruptly turned off the stereo console and slammed the lid. "I ain't hurt! Nobody hurts me." She stomped to the couch, climbed between the sheets, and pulled the covers over her head.

Kate sighed heavily. "I'm going to bed, Olivia. If you need me, you can call me."

"Don't need nobody," came the muffled reply.

When Kate climbed in beside Phil, he pulled her to him. "All quiet for the night?"

"I hope so. I'm sorry I had to spring Olivia on you guys with no warning. I tried to call several times but could never connect. I know she's a bit different."

He chuckled. "Dear Heart, they are *all* a bit different. Olivia is just 'differenter' than the rest."

She couldn't help loving this man. He was a gem. Most men would have had a fit for her to bring one more troubled child into their already crowded household, but Phil had welcomed Olivia. Kate hoped seeing a busy family in action would at least let Olivia know that there was another kind of life besides the one she'd known, and perhaps she would reach for a more normal one. *But what of Olivia's tears over some dead boyfriend? Olivia hadn't understood my concern and had gone to bed angry—something taboo in a household that never lets the sun set on a quarrel.*

There in the warmth of Phil's arms, Kate told him all that had happened with Olivia during the day and their last encounter before bedtime. They could still hear soft sobbing coming from the living room. "Maybe she just needs to cry it out and sleep it off, and she'll be better in the morning, Hon." Phil hugged Kate tightly. "We'll let her feel safe here with us until you can get her back to her mom tomorrow morning--unless you think we should keep her." He said this with his usual mischievous tone of voice.

Kate loved the way Phil could always tell what she was

thinking. They'd had that ability since sixth grade, when they became best friends, all through junior high and high school too—able to carry on a conversation from across a room with only their eyes. Or maybe it was ESP. They had often wondered.

"Do you think Olivia is totally an addict, or can she still be helped? She's awfully young for all this adult trauma." Phil's quiet question interrupted Kate's reverie.

"I don't know. I almost wish we had a little more time with her to find out. She behaved better with our kids this evening than she ever has at school. But her background has been so different from what we've created for our kids."

"Yes, it's quite a values confrontation isn't it? Like she just landed from the moon amid busy earthlings, with *rules*, yet. She must be as confused by our family as we are confused by her ideas. We'll need to work on her language skills, won't we?"

Kate grinned, thinking of her efforts with Holly to change language patterns.

Phil hugged her again and said, "We'll take it one day at a time, Honey. But right now, I just want you...."

About four in the morning, Kate awoke. She had what the kids called a mysterious sixth sense for when something in the house wasn't right. She gently disengaged herself from Phil's arms so as not to wake him, rose, and tiptoed through the little house, listening for even breathing and quiet sleep. The boys always slept like the dead. Alisa and Cindi both talked in their sleep from beds near each other, often seeming to answer each other, one talking and then the other talking in turn, on totally unrelated topics. Kate didn't worry about them. They would outgrow it. Cori, however, had been a sleepwalker since she first learned to walk. She was often the restless spirit. They had installed additional locks at the top of the outside doors after she once walked out into the night when she was eighteen months old. Of course, Cori being Cori, both determined and strong, by age three she had learned to shinny up the door jam, pushing her hands and feet against the sides, and both parents became *very* light sleepers. Kate listened. No, Cori was all right.

Kate passed into the small living room, moving by long practice around the bookcase and the end of the sofa where Olivia now thrashed and moaned. *It must have been Olivia's bad dream that woke me?* The girl had knocked off covers and was sweating, her straight, black hair plastered against her face. Kate hesitated a moment, wondering whether to wake her, or just try to calm her. She dampened a cloth in the kitchen, wiped the girl's face, straightened the blankets, and sat on the edge of the coffee table, stroking Olivia's forehead until she seemed more calm, though she kept murmuring something unintelligible.

As Kate gazed at the girl's face in the moonlight, she wondered how someone so young could be so angry with the world, and so suspicious of those who might try to be kind to her. What had turned her into a child feared at school, proud of her drugs and her gang membership, and wary of all offers of help? Of what fearful thing was she dreaming?

Kate had no answers. Once Olivia was again quiet, Kate rose and went back to bed, tossing restlessly until morning.

Everyone rose with the sun, except Olivia. The other girls let her sleep a half hour, but then Kate watched as they descended upon Olivia in a group and shook her off the sofa. She cursed, sputtered, ready to fight, until she realized where she was and calmed down, sleepily rubbing her eyes.

"You'd better get cleaned up before the guys get back from their run, because they'll want to shower before we go to the game," announced Cindi, unceremoniously.

"I ain't goin' to no game. What kinda game?" Olivia stretched and scratched her head. "Don't you ever let anybody sleep?"

"Not around here," said Alisa, laughing at Olivia's slow response. "There's always something to do, so you just have to get with the program."

Cori said, "Olivia, you can come along and watch our game today? It's against the Maywood Pirates. They're good, except not very sportsmanlike. Alli and Renee are on our team too, and lots of others, plus Alisa and Cindi and me. You can watch us and see if you'd like to join the team." Cori smiled brightly, waiting for Olivia's answer.

Rudely, Olivia jerked her head away and stalked to the bathroom without answering. Kate and the girls could hear the shower and sink running full blast at the same time. They looked at each other and shrugged.

"She must have had a bad night," said Cindi, glancing at her sister's hurt face. "Don't worry about it, Cori. She just doesn't know you yet." Cori only nodded.

But when Olivia came out, the breakfast table was set, and the guys were waiting in line for their limited three-minute showers. Olivia was quiet, making no overt gestures, but not fussing either. *Small gains may have to be enough,* thought Kate.

At breakfast, Kate suggested, "Olivia, why don't you call home and see if your mother is there. See if she got our note so she knows where you are and won't worry?"

"She don't worry about me," Olivia announced firmly. "We go anywhere we want, cuz' she works nights and sleeps days."

"You mean you go out at night while your mom's at work?" fourteen-year-old Ned asked as he slid into his seat, the damp blonde curls he hated framing his face after his hot shower. "I'd get killed." He shot a knowing grin at Phil, who nodded with rolling eyes.

"She don't know--she don't care. We go outta the window when she locks us in at eleven. So long as we're in bed when she gets home in the morning, and the door's still locked, she don't know. Sometimes we sleep all day and she don't know that, either."

"Who's 'we'?" asked Alisa.

"Me and my sister, Lynette, and brother, George. Lynette's fifteen and George is eighteen. There's five others older, but they're all gone now."

"So you're the youngest? Have you been doing this long?" Cindi asked.

"Hell, I don't know."

"Heck," corrected Cori.

"Okay, heck," repeated Olivia.

"I mean," continued Cindi, "why would you go out so late?

There's nothing open, nowhere to go. What do you do all night?"

"I can't remember when we didn't go out, so I guess I done it forever. We just hang out with the gang over at Norwalk in the 'One-Ways.' There's lots of kids on the streets at night over there."

"But isn't there a curfew?" Cori persisted. "After ten, what can you guys do? Even The Corner Store closes at ten. That's where all the kids meet after school to have cokes and get the latest news. Once it's closed, there's nothing going on. It's too dark for baseball or…or *anything* fun in the middle of the night."

"We sure don't play baseball!" Olivia snarled the words. Then she seemed to think better of it and said, "Somebody always has music and drugs, and we just party until almost time for Mom to get home. Then we take the back streets home so we don't run into any pigs, and we carry our bars and chains to defend ourselves if some other gang tries to jump us."

There was a stunned silence. The kids looked at each other, mystified.

Kate wondered what Olivia could be thinking. Was she trying to shock everyone, or turn the other kids away from her, or at least let them know what they were getting into by talking to her. She debated whether or not to jump in to change the subject when Cindi broke the silence.

"It sounds like you've had a hard time, Olivia, if your friends are out in the cold all night. And *policemen* wouldn't hurt you." She emphasized the word. "I hope you'll come today and see how much fun it is to sleep at night and play during the day…. " Her voice trailed off in the face of Olivia's stare. "You know, in the California sunshine and all. At least no other gang will chase you. We compete with other teams, and it's fun, and…." Cindi obviously didn't know what to say next, but she couldn't seem to shut up, either.

Kate stepped into Cindi's embarrassment, saying, "Olivia, if it's okay with your mother when we call her, it might be something new for you to go see the game."

Olivia looked from one to the other of the earnest faces surrounding her at the table and finally said, "Mom's probably not home. I guess I could watch." But she added with a sneer, "I don't have nothin' better to do, anyway." Various expressions seemed to do battle in her face. Finally, she smiled and said, "Okay, I'll go see what you whitey kids do on Saturdays in the daytime."

The girls whooped, and Ned rose and said, "Great. I'll get the equipment bag into James's van so the rest of you can pile in the back of the station wagon." The family grabbed jackets and uniforms, picnic lunches, and loaded the station wagon and the VW mini-van. James drove the van since he'd have to go to work before the game was over. Phil drove the station wagon, which had been known to carry the whole Mavericks team to an away game, all loaded in the rear cargo area, and singing all the way. They spilled into the sunshine at Mayberry Park, greeted by girls waiting for their coaches.

James and Ned carried the load of bats and equipment in a huge bag and began sorting it in the dugout. Ned would help coach at first base.

Phil worked hard all week with the girls, but his most important job on game day was stowing away the red licorice sticks his team needed to survive the game. Well, to be honest, the red licorice was Phil's passion too, so it was no wonder when his girls needed a treat, he had whole handfuls of the stuff hidden in his big jacket pockets. The red licorice had become a trademark of the team within the league and almost a joke among opposing teams. This gaggle of girls from ages 11-15 were convinced Phil had a "magic pocket" like the magic pitcher in fairy tales because they could never catch him without enough sticks to go around. They called their team the Mayberry Mavericks, but the girls had chosen black jackets with a red licorice stick for the logo on the back.

While Phil had the girls stretch and take a jog around the diamond to warm up, Kate made out rosters and score sheets and greeted the few parents who came regularly to the Saturday games. Most of the girls had no family members who came to root for them, so Phil, Kate, and the boys did a lot of encouraging chatter during games or practice sessions.

As usual with such community endeavors, the Johnsons hadn't *planned* to coach a team with their already limited time. But when their own two girls, Cindi and Cori, wanted to play at six and five, it quickly became a family hobby. But one coach moved away, another had a heart attack, and the teams would disband if no one came forward. For most, this was the only outside activity, so it was the sad eyes of the team's little girls that moved Phil forward to volunteer, "...only until you can find someone else." Of course, no one else was ever found. As their girls grew up, and one by one, the additional children joined their family, they grew into a sports-oriented family in spite of themselves. With softball every spring and track every summer, fall and winter for the boys' Pop Warner Football, they were busy. Vacations? Who could afford them? The Johnsons had neither the time nor the money. There was always a game, or a practice session, or a tournament or a track meet. As the kids grew, and their teams started winning more games, they also were in the post-season playoffs and championships, so one season merged seamlessly into another.

Kate wondered just how Olivia would accept this regimen, even for a day. Sure enough, the call to the girl's mother proved fruitless, so there was nothing else to do except take her along. But it made Kate's day a little tense. Where normally, she would breathe in the varied aromas of a park full of flowers, ball mitts, and kids, enjoying the day, she found herself sneaking many glances at Olivia to see if she was content or getting restless. *Would she perhaps run off, the way she did when her mother was working or sleeping*? Kate was used to having children do whatever she asked of them. *Is this a good idea?* She asked herself the question at least a dozen times during the morning.

James asked Kate if she needed anything more, as he needed to go to work. When she shook her head, he called out to the girls, "Go Mavericks," and headed for his van.

During the warm-ups and Phil's pep talk to the girls about just having fun together and maintaining their sportsmanship no matter what the umpire or the opposing team did, Olivia was shifting around restlessly on the bench behind the backstop. Kate asked Ned to take over for her in the dugout, while she went to sit with Olivia, just in case. *Just in case what?*

Olivia was quiet as the umpire flipped the coin. The Mavericks took the field first, and Cori stalked out strapped into her catcher's padded chest protector, shin guards, and facemask, plopping the ball forcefully into her catcher's glove to warm it up.

"What's she wearing all that stuff for?"

"It's just protective gear for the catcher in case she gets hit by a pitch or a bat."

"You mean they hit her--sorta like a gang fight? How'd Cori get that job? Is she tough? She's the youngest, ain't she? I'm the smallest and toughest in my gang, too."

Kate strained not to laugh. "No, Olivia, no one would hit her on purpose, but the catcher's in the middle of the action with bats and balls flying around. It happens almost every game. Cori's usually bruised up after a game. She is youngest, and she isn't the best batter on the team, but she's the best catcher—the only one strong enough to throw down to second base from a squat position. And she doesn't mind getting down in the dirt. Some of the girls get a little more persnickety about that as they get older." Kate could see that Olivia didn't understand much of what she was saying.

"It's a pretty dumb game. What do they get if they win?"

"Well, they don't win anything tangible, but they feel they win in teamwork, and strength, and sometimes they win the game too." Kate marveled that Olivia, for all her bravado and street-smart ways, really knew little about everyday middle class life. *Where had she been hiding that she had missed learning about softball?*

"They don't get money or nothin' for winning."

"No, but they have fun together, and we have fun watching them. If you have any questions, I'll explain the game as they go along, and it's okay to cheer if you feel like it."

"I wouldn't do that. It's sh--I mean, dumb."

Kate said nothing. The team members warmed up in position, firing the ball around the bases from glove to glove.

As the game started, Olivia watched intently.

When Renee took the mound and pitched straight to Cori's mitt, the umpire called. "Stee-rike." The Maywood batter immediately gave him a dirty look and kicked the dirt. Cori moved back a little to modify her squatting stance.

Olivia looked to Kate for an explanation of what was happening. Kate explained one play after another, answering the "Why do they" questions in rapid succession.

"It takes three strikes for the batter to be out, and that girl is mad because she just got the first one. Renee's good at strikeouts. She's both our best pitcher and our best batter. Most pitchers are good only for their pitching arm and rarely get on base by hitting."

Olivia seemed interested. "It looks easy. What about Cindi? Is she good?"

"Cindi can't get a lot of power on her hits because she's built pretty lightweight, but she has what's called a 'good eye,' so she can nearly always get a walk onto first base with four balls and then, because she's really fast, she can steal the other team blind."

"Steal? A goody girl like Cindi?" Shock registered in Olivia's eyes.

Kate laughed. "That's what they call it when the runner can get to an extra base while the pitcher is looking the other way, or the catcher doesn't throw fast enough, or someone bobbles—drops—the ball. They call it 'stealing a base.' Cindi is really good at it, so she often gets all the way around and scores after only getting a walk to first base. Keep watching, and you'll get the hang of the game."

When Renee struck out two batters, and Cori threw off her facemask to catch a pop-up, it was three outs, and the Mavericks were up at bat. Olivia seemed to be catching on. Half way through the inning, after Cindi walked to first base, Olivia began shouting out with the crowd to "Go, go, go" as Cindi stole second base and headed for third. When the team was again out on the field for the next inning, she shouted, "Pitch her out, Renee," as the pitcher readied her throw. As more innings went on, Olivia called out, "Hey batter, batter" to the team, and squealed and cheered and jumped up and down when one of the home team made a score. Kate delighted in the girl's excitement and did *not* remind Olivia that she had thought cheering was dumb.

"Those Maywood girls are big, aren't they?" Olivia commented as one of the Pirates' base runners slid into second base with feet upturned, hoping to hit Barbara in the legs when she tried to tag her. "If I was Barbara, I'd kick her--hard."

"That would be poor sportsmanship if Barbara kicked the girl, even though it wasn't right for the girl to slide in with her cleats up, either. This Maywood Pirates are tough, but they're sometimes called the poorest sports in the league."

"How do ya know?"

"They're good players and have girls with big talent. But they argue with the umpire--something Phil strictly forbids, whether the girls think the call is right or wrong. I've seen times I thought the Pirate coach encouraged their pitcher to deliberately throw at a base runner's head rather than at the first baseman's glove."

"But when our gangs fight, a*nything* goes. Why do ya have all these silly rules?"

"You need some structure for a fair competition. A team member can be ejected from the game if she gets argumentative with the umpire or deliberately tries to hurt someone. I don't know about gangs, but if someone is hurt in a game, it should be an accident, not a deliberate act." *Is any of this making sense to Olivia?* "The Maywood Pirate coach says Phil is too easy with his girls, but Phil feels what the girls learn from teamwork and sportsmanship is more important than winning or losing." Kate paused, running her fingers through her hair, trying futilely to make it lie down as the breeze picked up. "You know, Olivia, it's funny, because I think our Mavericks win games just on fun and good teamwork, in spite of the antics of their opponents. The Pirates are a strong team, quite skillful, but it's possible to be strong and still use your strength in the wrong way."

Olivia looked at her with a puzzled expression. "I don't know 'bout this sportsman thing. I'd just hit 'em, if they did somethin' bad to me."

Kate decided it was best not to argue the point. *Maybe she'll see for herself.*

Perhaps Olivia's interest was inspired because she knew some of the players. But, she heard the Maywood coach scold any girl who messed up, while Phil, after a mistake, said, "That's okay,

Barbara," "No problem, Fran, You'll get the next one." Olivia picked up on Phil's tone and soon shouted encouragement instead of moaning or nagging about errors. Kate smiled and began enjoying the day after all.

In the seventh inning, the Mayberry Mavericks were ahead five to three. The Maywood Pirate girls' temperament got more ugly with each Maverick pitch. Phil motioned with down-turned palms to remind his girls to stay calm and just keep playing good ball without responding to the taunts and threats.

Olivia said to Kate, "That Maywood gang's spoilin' for a fight, ain't they? The ump guy won't let 'em hurt our girls, will he?"

Kate noticed the "our" girls, but she didn't mention it. "I think the ump's keeping a close eye on them. He's seen them in previous games. Their coach should be reining in their comments, though."

They could see the Maywood girls, one after another, saying something taunting to each Mayberry baseman as they ran by. While Mayberry girls bristled a little, they were able to shrug it off and refrain from answering the taunts. They kept focusing on the game, as Phil had taught them. "Just play ball, Ladies," he shouted.

But then, with two Maywood girls on base, and with Renee holding the third batter at bay with her pitching, the first base runner ran for second to steal.

From her squat position, Cori threw the ball hard to Barbara at second, and little redheaded Barbara tagged the base runner out. A powerfully built girl who dwarfed Barbara, she grumbled something that made Barbara's lips quiver, and the girl shook her fist at Cori as she walked back to her dugout. Their coach ran over and said something to the runner still waiting at third base, and then nodded to the batter.

"They're gonna do somethin' bad. I feel it," said Olivia. Before Kate could stop her, she shouted, "Cori, watch out!"

Cori didn't turn around, as she was watching for Renee's next pitch. But they could see her body tense in the squat position.

As the batter leaned into her stance and hit a high ball to left field, the third base runner ran for home. Out in left field, Fran caught the fly ball, firing it straight back to Cori as the third base runner slid toward home plate. The runner hit Cori hard under her catching arm in an attempt to make her drop the ball. Cori managed to hang on to the ball and make the tag, anyway.

"Yer out!" screamed the umpire.

Blood gushed from under Cori's upper arm, quickly soaking her white uniform top.

"Time out," the umpire yelled.

Kate was already on her feet and heading for the field, followed by Olivia, when the umpire wiped away the blood with his handkerchief so he could see its source. "Pirate runner 14," he called out. "Get back to home plate, now!"

The runner was already mad from being called out on the play. She threw her bat down and started screaming at the umpire, when he told her she was out of the game.

The Pirate coach ran to home plate, yelling, "You can't kick her out of the game. She only was called out on the play at home plate."

The umpire lifted Cori's arm, wiped it again and pointed to teeth marks. "I've never seen a runner bite a catcher to try to make her drop the ball. This is way out of line."

"It had to be an accident," yelled the Pirate coach, toe to toe with the ump.

The runner screamed, "You told me to…."

"Shut up, you little tramp," interrupted the coach. Those in the stands were on their feet. The umpire threatened to oust the coach and call the game in the Mavericks' favor.

Cori's arm continued to gush blood. Her face was stoic as her dad applied pressure with a pad from the first aid kit, and the umpire decided whether to call the game or not. But Cori settled the dilemma when she slid off her facemask and catcher's glove and handed it to her sister, Cindi. "Barbara can take first base in Cindi's place," she said. "I'm not sure I can catch the ball without dropping it. Let's switch around for an inning until this stops bleeding, and then we'll change back."

The umpire said with disbelief, "You want to go on with the

game? If I call it right now, your team will be the winners. This was a blatant foul."

Cori said, "The rest of the team can keep playing until I stop bleeding. It's no big deal. I don't want Maywood girls saying we won by default. We'll win fair and square."

Olivia turned to the umpire, "You don't think these Mayberry girls give up a fight *that* easy, do you?" And she walked off to the dugout with Cori.

The umpire looked at Phil, who shrugged and said, "The girls want to play."

"Okay, then," the ump nodded. "Play ball."

Kate looked after Cori and Olivia for a few moments in amazement and then hurried to catch up with her bleeding daughter. But Olivia was already seated beside Cori in the dugout applying pressure to the wound as she had seen Phil do. Cori's white face was gradually returning to normal, so Kate left them alone.

With the changes in the lineup, Cindi never having been a catcher before, Renee not used to pitching to her, and Barbara a little slow at first base, the girls fought hard to maintain their lead in the game, but they did it. Cori, with the padding on her arm wrapped tightly with bandages from the first aid kit, came back into the game the last inning, and the final score was seven to six with the Mayberry Mavericks winning by one point.

Olivia cheered loudest of all. After the game, she whispered to Phil, "We gotta get Cori to the hospital now. She didn't wanna tell you, but in the dugout, she was sorta dizzy."

Phil looked in wonder at Olivia and then put his arm around her shoulder. "You're probably right, Olivia. Thank you. The girls practice Tuesday night at 5 p.m. You can come learn to play if you like. You need some red licorice now, don't you?"

And just like that, Olivia became a Mayberry Maverick; the red licorice gang of girls she admitted was not at all like her own gang. She announced firmly, "When Cori gave away her job to keep the game goin', I decided she was okay, and so was softball."

Phil quietly admonished the girls to keep smiling, keep behaving like ladies, and shake hands with the Maywood girls, no matter what they said. "We'll simply rise above this, ladies," he said. And they did.

 Though Alisa said they should probably give Cori tetanus shots since the girl who bit her was no doubt a vampire and had rabies, a few stitches fixed the arm. After the emergency room visit, Phil stopped at the malt shop where James worked to treat the team to ice cream cones. Then they drove Olivia home. She was right. Her mother wasn't there, but her oldest sister was. Betsy had a five-year-old daughter of her own and lived nearby. Betsy and Olivia's brother, George, assured Kate they would stay with Olivia until their mother came home. Olivia insisted she would be all right with her big sister. There was no mention of the drug incident—or the game.

 At dinner, the whole crew discussed Olivia's problems and decided she had made some great strides in just one day. Even James said he thought if Olivia could learn to show compassion for Cori and appreciate the spirit of teamwork, then maybe there was hope for her. They felt much more optimistic as they went through the rest of the weekend.

 But, Monday morning, Olivia did not come to school.

Chapter 5

"What happened over the weekend?"

Holly was waiting for Kate at the first recess break of the morning. "Was Olivia still out of it when her mother called?"

"No, she was fine after a good night's sleep, and her mother didn't call. We took her to the girls' softball game Saturday and then to her home afterward."

"How was she when you left her? Did she seem mad, or restless, or…. Gosh, I sound like I'm giving you the third degree, but I don't know why she wouldn't be here today after we thought she was rescued Friday."

"Holly, I can't even imagine what happened. She was in a good mood when we dropped her off, and we assumed she was fine. She seemed to make progress in her attitude, and she actually enjoyed the game."

"Did you see her mother?"

"No, she wasn't there, but I didn't know what else to do. We left her with her oldest sister and her brother who insisted they'd stay with her. Apparently they didn't."

"How can we help these kids when the family is the problem?" Holly unconsciously ran her fingers through her hair-do.

"The courts keep telling us to mind our own business. I guess we're on our own." Kate considered various courses of action. "Do you think we should call her mother and see if Olivia is sick?"

"We don't usually do that until a child is out three days."

"Olivia isn't the usual child. Three days might be disastrous."

"What excuse could we use?" Holly sighed, staring at her grade book and biting her lip. "We aren't supposed to butt in."

Kate shook her head, unable to think of anything. Then she brightened. "She showed some interest in coming to ball practice at Mayberry Park tomorrow night. We could ask if she'll be well enough by then to come, or if she has permission to attend."

"Great!" Holly said. Then she sobered. "Why are we so

worried about one kid not coming to school for one day?"

Kate said, "Call it the lost sheep syndrome. We take for granted the successes, and we worry more about the ones we lose."

Looking down, Holly muttered. "I think I feel guilty that I didn't take her home myself. She's my student, and I put her in your hands."

"Holly, you couldn't take her. My kids had enough trouble dealing with Olivia's language. Your little ones would be sporting a whole new vocabulary by now—one you wouldn't like." Kate pondered the statement. "Maybe putting her in my hands wasn't the right thing, either. If we'd done it right, wouldn't she be in school today? Would she go right back to the drugs? We're all so hopelessly unprepared for this. We need some training."

The two teachers worried their way to the office and tried calling the home number. A sleepy man's voice answered.

"Hello," said Holly. She covered the receiver with her hand and whispered, "It's some man and it sounds like I woke him up. What should I say?"

"Just ask for Olivia's mother."

Holly uncovered the receiver and said, "This is Mrs. Warner at Sunnyside School. May I speak with Olivia's mother? Olivia isn't here today, and we wondered if she was sick." She rushed to add, "Also, she wanted to come to softball practice tomorrow."

Even Kate could hear the angry words as the man shouted, and Holly's eyes got wide. Teachers in the office stopped to listen.

"How the hell do I know where that damned kid is? She took off with her sisters and brother Saturday night, and they haven't been home since."

"Do you know where she might have gone, or when she might be back?" Holly quickly fabricated, "I have some homework for her that I'd like to bring by."

"Don't! We don't want no damned school people snooping around, or no fuckin' county people, either. Do I know where she's at? Hell no, and I don't care!"

"Thank you, anyway," sing-songed Holly's *now, what do I do* voice. She hung up, blowing a relieved burst of air from her lips.

"That was strange. Who was that guy? Why is he answering for the mother? I thought she was a widow since before Olivia was born."

"I haven't a clue, and I'm sure they'd tell us it wasn't our business. I'm more worried about where Olivia might be. She's been gone since Saturday night and no responsible party knows or cares where she is."

"Where might she go that folks would know nothing about her?"

Kate thought over everything said Friday night and Saturday at her home. Then she knew. "The One-Ways over in Norwalk. She said that's where she meets her gang, although I can't imagine gangs over there. Of course, I haven't been there for years, not since I was a kid. It was a nice area back then, built as low-cost housing for military folks returning from World War II. I remember it with white picket fences and parks."

"I've heard it's a hotbed of illegal aliens, drug houses, and gang fights now, Kate. Nobody goes in there who doesn't have to."

"We might drive through. I think I can still find my way in those narrow streets."

"I can't go today. Bobby has a piano lesson. And you shouldn't go alone."

"It might be worth a try. Maybe I could wait until Phil gets home, but by then it would be almost dark." She grew silent, having already made up her mind.

As soon as school was out, Kate tooled her old station wagon the few miles south from Whittier and turned off Norwalk Boulevard into the One-Ways. If the attendance area of Sunnyside Elementary was deprived, the One-Ways was now considered out of control. Many children who lived there didn't attend school at all after elementary, and parents could not be persuaded to send them.

The One-Ways were a series of narrow one-way streets, a high-density area perhaps a mile square. Kate began to recognize the streets, but not the landscape. Former white cottages with roses and picket fences had given way to scaling paint and unkempt houses. She noticed a motor hanging from a tree as a makeshift A-frame lift. Where, as a child, she and her friends had ridden their bikes down to the store for Popsicles, she noticed the run-down business now had only Spanish language signs. Those were unreadable with graffiti on every square inch. It covered walls and houses. Even a broken light pole was covered with painted symbols and nasty words.

Seeing this street, Kate realized that she had come a long way in life. She'd grown up, gotten married, and was busy with teaching and children of her own. It had been several years since she had been in this section of Norwalk. The neighborhood had changed drastically after the military families moved on.

The small homes bulged with what looked like several levels of mixed families existing in the same house. With her car window down, she watched the crowded streets, hearing mostly broken English and Spanish from the crowds of kids hanging out. Their silent stares reeked hostility, following her as she drove slowly by. She could hear them resuming their conversation after she had passed. She drove carefully, trying to avoid hitting any of the children and young adults slouching in groups in the narrow street. No one moved over to let her pass more easily.

"Hey, Whitey," one youth called out. "Whatcha doin' here? This ain't your turf. Even the pigs don't come in here no more." He laughed. "You a pig?"

"Shit," said another, "we got rocks and bottles to rain on them pigs and city people. They know better than to come in here. 'Member them folks fixin' the sewer last week? Guess we fixed them!" The whole group dissolved into raucous laughter.

Kate glanced from her car window and suddenly realized they were yelling at her. The first young man was tall, swarthy, and looked about eighteen. The second speaker looked like a chubby twelve year old, either Mexican or Indian. *Why were they so hostile?* She shuddered. *Perhaps I shouldn't have come, but it's too late now. Olivia might be overdosed again, lying in a gutter this time.* Kate's mind raced to the worst-case scenario.

She drove away from the group, warily watching as the young men gave ugly hand gestures she could see in her rear view mirror. She peered down each alley, hoping for a glimpse of the small dark figure of Olivia, or perhaps George or Betsy.

Some young people leaned on sagging porch railings, laughing and shoving each other. Most gazed insolently at her through the windshield or side window. It was slow going. Her stomach tightened as she drove further into mysteriously hostile territory. Kate couldn't imagine why these young people seemed so unwelcoming since she would never hurt anyone deliberately. Why did they stare at her so intently? Did she look *that* strange?

She passed the small park where she had played as a child with friends. The merry-go-rounds, jungle gyms, and teeter-totters, now broken hulks, sagged toward the ground. Bars rose menacingly where supports for the swings had been vandalized. No longer was the park filled with young mothers watching their toddlers play. She sighed. *Why destroy a playground for children?* But it was not a time for reminiscence. She had to find Olivia and get her out of this place. Kate decided to ask a group of youngsters about Olivia's age. She got close enough to speak to them through the open car window.

"Excuse me," she said. "I'm looking for a young girl named Olivia. Do any of you girls know her?"

"Whatcha want with her, Gringo? You ain't part of this barrio. Whatcha doin' here?" Kate estimated the speaker's age at about fourteen. The girl banged insolently on the hood of the car.

The other girls laughed derisively. "You a pig?" asked one.

"No, I'm not from the police," said Kate. "I'm just a teacher from Olivia's school."

An explosion of laughter stopped abruptly when the older girl lifted her hand.

"We don't need any ole fuckin' teachers in here. Get out, while you still can." Another bout of malicious laughter followed.

Kate didn't find it particularly funny.

She forced herself to smile and ask again. "Look, I don't mean Olivia, or any of you, any harm. I'd just like to find her to see if she needs a lift home. That's all."

"Well, get on outta here. We don't know her, and we wouldn't tell you if we did."

"Thank you, anyway," said Kate. She drove slowly, looking for someone who might be more hospitable. She by-passed several older kids—mixed groups of boys and girls. Always as her car approached, the group would fall silent and stare at her as she drove by. After she passed, words rose to threatening shouts.

One group blocked her way then stepped to one side as a muscular young man pounded on the side of her car. "You better get outta here, if you know what's good for ya," he growled. His broad nostrils flared, giving Kate the feeling he was about to explode.

"That's the third time someone has said that to me. I'll go as soon as I find a young friend I was told might be here. She's kind of short for her age, about so high." Kate held her hand out the window at about Olivia's height. "Can you help me find her? Her name's Olivia." Kate wondered if she sounded as scared as she felt.

"What you want her for?"

"Just to see if she needs a ride home or if there's something I can do to help her."

The young man shouted out to the others of his group, "This nice old lady just wants to help Olivia." His simpering voice brought hoots of derision from his groupies. He turned his attention back to Kate. "Look, bitch, I don't know any Olivia, but if I did, I'd tell her to stay the hell away from somebody like you!"

"I'm sorry you feel that way, but I really need to move on. I need to find her. Thank you for your time." She drove away, trying hard not to look alarmed or rushed.

Kate noticed lines of young people trailing behind her car and off to the sides, led by the outspoken young man. She reminded herself that these were, after all, simply kids, apparently with nothing better to do. Perhaps she had unwittingly become their entertainment for a boring afternoon. They were not much different, she hoped, than some of the more difficult students she taught at Sunnyside and those whom she had welcomed into her home. She decided to get out and meet them on a more personal level. *What do I have to lose? They already have me surrounded.*

When she stopped the car and got out to approach a group of girls, all action on the street halted, as though there was a collective holding of breath to see what she would do next. *Please God, let me do this right.*

The boys following her slowly closed around her car. She ignored them and spoke cheerfully to the group of young girls. "Hi there. I'm Kate Thompson. I'm a teacher, and I wonder if you girls could help me."

"Depends," said the smallest of the group. There was no hint of friendliness.

Kate heard a slight noise to her rear, and turned to see one of the larger boys who'd been following raising a crow bar toward the back of her car. She smiled at him with a syrupy grin born more of fear than of confidence. "I'd really rather you not do that, son. This old Chevy has lasted me eight years, and I need it to last a few years longer." She again smiled at him, noting that his expression held more bewilderment than anger. Perhaps she had shocked him by not screaming. She deliberately turned away from the boy and spoke again to the group of girls. She braced herself for the sound of metal hitting metal, but the sound didn't come.

"I'm looking for a girl from the school where I teach—Sunnyside Elementary—a little north of here. I thought she might want a ride home, so I drove over to see if I could find her. Her name's Olivia, and she's short, about so high…" Kate knew she was babbling out of nervousness, but the girls looked back and forth at each other as though they were not sure how they should respond to this crazy stranger in their midst.

"Who says she's here?" challenged one of the older girls.

"Maybe she don't wanna be found," said another.

"She told me she came here often to meet with friends. When she didn't come to school today, I thought of looking for her here."

"She say who she'd party with?"

"Not really, but I think she came with her brother and a sister or two. She said she knew a lot of people over here. Do you think you might know her?"

"We don't tell outsiders nothin', lady. I don't really care who you are."

Kate sighed, defeated. "I'm sorry you feel that way. I'm only trying to help her."

As she returned to her car, one girl looked at the others,

shrugged, and followed her. "Wait. Are you the teacher? The one who's tryin' to get Livie off drugs?"

"I guess so. She asked me for help."

"Did you really take her home to your family Friday night?"

"Well, yes. She wasn't feeling well, and I didn't know where else to take her until she felt better. We couldn't find her mother."

"That's good. Her mom's a bitch. You don't wanna find her."

Kate thought it better not to comment.

The girl turned and motioned to the others of her group. "Hey, it's the teacher." They gathered around Kate while the trailing pack of young men walked to the sidewalk and clustered together, talking low.

"We thought Livie was lyin', like usual, sayin' she spent the night at a teacher's house. Do you really have a bunch of extra kids that all play games and stuff?" The older girl, apparently the leader, cocked her head as though eager to know.

"Yes, I guess you could say our family is pretty large, and the kids do like to play games." Kate couldn't imagine quite what was taking place, but the atmosphere had somehow changed. She didn't feel as much of an intruder as she did a curiosity.

"Hey, teacher," said the younger girl, "if you can get Livie off drugs, she might have a chance to get outta here. She was wasted Saturday and Sunday nights, and we couldn't find her brother or sister. She's gonna get herself killed one of these times, and it'll bring in the pigs lookin' around. They'll put her in juvie, and there's more drugs in there than here on the streets. If you can get her out of here, it'd be good." The girls all nodded and looked quite serious.

Was there honor among thieves...or druggies?

"Do you know where she is now?"

One of the kids pointed down the street. "Fourth house down there. She was there last night, so she might still be there. She was pretty bad though. Want us to come along?"

"If she's not there, I'll be back for more help. But if she's there, I think I can get her out." Kate stretched out her hand to the main speaker. "Thank you. What's your name?"

"Bettina." The other girls snickered. "My street name's Rory, but Bettina's my real name." She patted her ratted and spray-plastered, big-hair do, as though it might fall over.

"I didn't know that, Rory," said another girl. "Bettina, huh?" She laughed, but Bettina's harsh look shut her down immediately.

"It's a beautiful name," said Kate. "What about the rest of you?"

Shyly, the girls gave their real names and their street names, almost as though they were ashamed they had two.

"Mine's Alice, but they call me Punk." She looked about twelve, dressed in a tight sweater and mini skirt that did little to hide her baby fat.

"Did anyone ever sing you the song named for you--Alice Blue Gown?"

"You shittin' me? Nobody'd name a song after me."

"Well *somebody* wrote one. It's pretty famous." Kate hummed a few bars.

The girl turned away with a smile. "I got a song," she said.

A third girl, probably about fourteen like her own Cindi, said, "I'm Belle, but my street name's Sissy. Do I have a song too?"

Kate looked down at the youngster so expectantly waiting and smiled. "I'm not sure about a song, but there's a famous lady from the days of cowboys, Indians, and pioneer history named Belle Starr."

"I'm Sioux Indian," said Belle. The dark girl with teeth woefully in need of braces turned to her friends. "Do you guys think the gang would let me change Sissy to Starr?"

"Naw," said Alice. "The gang gives us names. You ain't gonna change it."

For each of the girls, Kate had some comment, or a little history of a great person by the same name. The girls seemed more at ease and smiled.

Bettina put her hand on Kate's arm as she turned to go. "Livie may not make it, but if she has a chance…." She paused and didn't seem ready to go on.

Kate said softly, "What about you, Bettina? Could you make it out of the One-Ways, too?"

The girl looked down at her feet and almost whispered, "It's too late for me. I already got an old man on speed, and I got a baby. Livie may still have a chance, if she's got you helpin' her. I don't think anybody can do it alone."

"Do you want help?"

"Hell, no," the girl said loudly, perhaps for the sake of returning to bravado in front of her gang. "I don't need no help."

Kate reached into the front seat of her car, tore off a scrap of paper from her grade book, and scribbled her phone number. She folded it into Bettina's hand, and said, "In case you ever feel ready, call me. I'll find someone to help you, too." She raised her voice for the benefit of the others. "And thank you…all of you." She waved as she jumped back in her car and headed for the fourth house. The sullen boys watched her go.

Even through a ragged screen door, the house reeked of stale urine, sweat, and marijuana smoke, plus a myriad of smells Kate feared to define. Peering into the gloom, she could see on a low coffee table what seemed at least 25 different kinds of pills, all shapes and colors. A rickety table in what must have passed for a dining room was crowded with empty packages of chips, cookies, snacks, with dirty cups and beer bottles nestled in between. A filthy and torn divan sagged in the living room. A youth of indeterminate age lay asleep in a ragged t-shirt and Levis, half on the couch and half on the floor.

Kate knocked, but only a growl from some back room echoed through the otherwise empty house. She felt fairly sure it was human and not canine, but she fought the urge to run. Looking back at the cluster of girls she had just left, she found they were watching her. Bettina motioned her to go inside. Still she hesitated. *I can't just barge in. What can I say?*

She opened the torn screen door, being careful not to get the jagged edges against her nylons. She called out, "Olivia, are you in here?" As she stepped gingerly across the stained, creaking floor, she heard a muffled groan as the young man on the couch readjusted his sleeping position. Kate jumped. The subtle noise might as well have been a cannon going off. *What am I doing in here?*

She stepped quietly into the dining room and kitchen, not finding anyone else. But she moved into a darkened hall, calling out, "Hello...hello...anybody here?"

Olivia lay limply on the floor, her head jammed against the smeared-up wall, with her knees crumpled against the other. Her mouth hung open, and a foul-smelling liquid seeped from under her head. Was she unconscious or merely sleeping, though it seemed that someone would have tripped over her in the dark hall—an unlikely place to take a nap. No, Kate was pretty sure Olivia had fallen where she lay. *And no one even cared.*

Quickly, she bent to feel for a pulse, first in Olivia's wrists and then at her neck. The girl moaned and shifted her head slightly.

"Olivia," Kate whispered. "Olivia, please wake up." She struggled to straighten the girl out on the floor and debated how she might get her on her feet to the car. Olivia had little muscle tone, and she was not responding. Kate looked around for a phone, but realized there was none usable. Only wires hung limply from the wall of the kitchen. Calling the operator to get an ambulance would mean leaving Olivia and driving to the nearest gas station where there would be a public pay phone. Kate decided against leaving Olivia unconscious in the house. She knew she could not stand the stench of the place much longer either. She bent again and pulled Olivia's arm up around her shoulders, rose to one knee, and pushed herself up, dragging the limp body along with her.

"Whatcha doin'?" Olivia mumbled as Kate fought to get the girl's bare feet on the ground where she could bear some of her own weight. She dragged the girl to the table and leaned her against it, as she readjusted her grip. How could she get her to the car?

Kate jumped when a gruff voice behind her snarled, "Whatta ya doin' with Livie?"

She turned to see a large-boned man, barefoot, and bare from the waist up, sweat dripping down his chest and onto his dirty, unzipped shorts. He had huge, matted Afro hair and a sparse black beard. His equally black eyes seemed unfocused. His belt buckle hung from one hand, with the belt menacingly wrapped around his fist as some kind of weapon.

Kate stuttered, "Olivia isn't well. I came to take her home. I hope you don't mind."

"Hell, why should I care...she's nothin' to me...just another piece a' tail. Didja bring us any more hash?" He looked around Kate at the table, as though something should have been deposited there.

"I don't know anything about hash. I just came for Olivia. I'm taking her with me now." Kate again put Olivia's arm around her shoulders and dragged her toward the door. She prayed she could get out into the street where there were at least other people before the young man decided to do anything with that belt.

Halfway across the living room, within mere feet of her goal, the man weaved toward her and said, "Whaddaya expect me to tell her brother? Ya can't just take her like this...her brother'll be mad that I let her go. Her sister's in the bedroom. We better go back there and see...."

"Please tell her sister and brother that Olivia's teacher took her home, and she'll probably be home by the time they get there."

The man shrugged, grabbed a handful of pills from the coffee table and muttered, "Oh, what the hell!" He lurched back down the dark hallway.

With Olivia half stumbling on her own feet and half allowing herself to be dragged forward, Kate manhandled her through the jagged door, this time snagging both her last pair of nylons and her leg on the torn and jutting wire. The girl then leaned forward off the porch and fell to the ground, pulling Kate along with her. Kate sat on the bare dirt, panting, trying to think what to do. She wouldn't be able to get this limp kid into the car alone.

She didn't have to. When she looked up, Bettina and her girls surrounded Olivia, already grabbing Olivia's arms and legs to carry her to the car. One of the girls helped Kate up, and she quickly ran to open the back door so the girls could lay Olivia on the seat.

Gratefully, Kate thanked the girls. Bettina said stoically, "Livie's pretty wasted again. If you take her straight home, that old lady of hers will kill her, sure as we're standin' here."

"What would you suggest?" Kate could hear the quaver in her own voice.

"Could ya take her home with you again until she wakes up? Once ya can get her awake and on her own feet, she can maintain really good. Most people can't tell."

"Maintain?" Kate was puzzled. "Olivia said that once before. What does it mean?"

"You know—maintain--pretend she's not using, walk straight and all that. Long as no one asks her big questions, she can maintain with the best of 'em."

"Thank you, Bettina, Alice Blue Gown, Belle Starr, all of you."

Belle's wide grin transformed her face.

"You've been a great help, girls. I appreciate your wanting to get Olivia out of here. We'll see if it works. But, if it does, it will be because you all cared enough to help her. Thank you again."

As she pulled the car away from the curb and waved, Bettina said, "Vaya con Dios. Good luck 'cause you're gonna need it. Livie's not gonna be happy when she wakes up."

Chapter 6

"Whadja do that for?" Olivia muttered angrily when she woke in the late evening. Kate, Cori, and Cindi sat beside her on Cori's bed. Phil leaned against the door. Olivia turned her face to the wall. "My friends are never gonna speak to me again. They'll think I ratted them out."

Kate dipped the cold washcloth in a bowl of water, wrung it out, and placed it again on Olivia's forehead.

The girl threw it to the floor. "I don't want nothin' from you." She turned her face to the wall.

"I'm sorry you feel that way, Olivia." I couldn't just leave you in that filth in your condition. You couldn't take care of yourself, and you *did* ask for help, remember?" She wondered if she should say anything more. "Besides, your friends in the One-Ways helped me find you, so I don't think they're mad at you or think you ratted them out."

Olivia rolled toward her. "They helped you? Who? What did they tell you?"

Kate could hear the suspicion in her voice and struggled for words. "Not much. Just that they felt you were in danger and needed help to get off drugs."

Olivia snorted in contempt. "That's funny. They don't even help themselves. They sure couldn't do nothin' for me—and anyway, I don't need no help."

Cindi frowned at her. "Olivia, does that mean you don't want out of the drug scene—that you don't like being here with us?" Though Cindi was a year older than Olivia, Kate noted that she seemed to feel some kinship with this child of the streets.

Olivia's voice softened for Cindi, as she said, "Sure, I like being with you guys, but Saturday night when Lynette and George said they was goin' to the One Ways, I didn't want 'em to go without me, ya know?"

"I sort of understand not wanting to be left out, but you

could do lots of things besides going with them when you know...when you know you'll be ...like this...afterward." Cindi finished lamely and shook her sandy blonde hair out of her eyes. "Shouldn't your brother and sister be looking out for you better?"

"They take care of me just fine!" Olivia bristled. "It's better to take me along instead of leaving me home alone. All the older kids, they always took me along--me and Lynette. Mom always told Betsy and Rita and George to look out for me and Lynette, so they took us along since I was three and Lynette was five, in Tucson. Now they go to the One Ways. Betsy lives in an apartment with her little girl, Rita's off somewhere in San Francisco, and we don't know where the others are. I don't 'member them much. George and me and Lynette still live with Mom."

It was a long speech for Olivia—more information than she usually volunteered. Cori took the wet cloth from Kate's hands and again placed it on Olivia's forehead. "This might feel good to you, now, Livie." Olivia didn't move away.

As the girl now seemed more lucid and quiet, Kate asked, "Do you want to tell us what happened to you over there? I found you unconscious in the hall of a house."

"You shouldn't a come in there alone. They could kill ya." Olivia quickly changed the subject from any show of emotion. "Was anyone with me?"

"No, you were all crumpled up on the floor, alone."

"That's just like the bastard to leave me there."

"Who, Livie?" Cindi took the girl's hand. "No one should leave you alone when you're...sick...."

"You mean wasted, don'tcha?" For the first time since Kate had driven home and needed Phil's help in getting Olivia into the house, the young girl laughed. It was a rather rueful laugh, but a laugh nonetheless, and the other girls responded in kind.

"Aren't you guys mad at me?"

"Not mad, Olivia. Just puzzled as to why you'd go," said Kate. "We really thought you were enjoying yourself at the game Saturday, and that you liked doing something a little...different." She struggled to remain neutral enough not to say, "something better."

Suddenly Olivia raised up and turned to Cori. "Is your arm all right? Let me see."

Cori lifted her sleeve to show the padded bandage. "It's better. The stitches pinch a little, but the doctor said they'd drive me even crazier itching when they start healing."

"That Maywood bitch was an asshole."

Cindi corrected, "That Maywood player was a poor sport."

"That too," said Olivia. Laughter broke the tension.

Kate felt the vocabulary lesson was under control, so she said, "Livie, I'm going to fix us all some sandwiches now, since it's pretty late for dinner, and you and the girls can talk, okay? Call me if you need me, but come on into the dining room in about..." She looked at her watch. "...twenty minutes."

Phil intervened, as Kate walked by him in the doorway. "Let's alter that order, Love. You may want to shower now, and let me fix the sandwiches. What'd you get into, Honey?" He grinned as Kate regarded her torn stockings, bloody legs and sniffed her clothing for the first time since she had arrived home.

"Whew! I guess I do need a shower. I'll be quick. And I don't think you want to know what I got into."

They both laughed. Phil patted her on the derriere as she moved by him.

Cindi suggested that Olivia might like a shower after her mom got finished, to get the gunk out of her hair. Cori pulled a clean pair of shorts and a t-shirt out of her drawer and offered them to Olivia. Olivia looked down at her rumpled, stained clothing, and, turned up her nose. "I do stink bad, don't I? Someone must've barfed on me...yuck!"

When Kate ran from the bathroom to her bedroom a few minutes later in her pink robe with dark, wet hair flying, Cindi helped Olivia up. She "maintained" under her own steam to the bathroom, taking the proffered clothing from Cori. "Thanks, guys," she muttered, and disappeared.

A different Olivia emerged ten minutes later, slid into a seat at the dining table, quietly held out her hands to the others, and bowed her head.

After grace, Olivia looked around and asked, "Where's everybody else?"

Phil answered, "James drove Alisa to drama rehearsal and Ned tagged along so they could hit a few balls at the batting cages on campus until she gets done. They'll be back about ten." Then he added, "Are you feeling better now, Livie?"

"Yeah, I guess so. I didn't mean to go to the One-Ways, but I was lonely, so I went. I thought I could go with 'em and not take any drugs, but everyone else was usin' candy, and they said I was trying to be better'n them if I didn't, and shit like that."

"Stuff like that," said Cori.

"Okay, stuff like that. Anyways, I didn't want 'em thinkin' that, so I took some pills too. And after everyone else is smokin' and dopin,' there's nobody left to talk to, you get really lonely and might as well get wasted. I felt dumb being the only one not usin'. I didn't know what else to do." Olivia slumped in her chair. "And maybe I think I really wanted the drugs, too."

"You may be experiencing withdrawal," said Phil, "but you don't owe any of them anything, Livie. You can be your own person. You're under no obligation to join them when they're doing drugs. Do you understand? They don't own you, and you don't have to go over there."

"Yeah, I sorta get it, but they're my gang, and I guess I...well...I don't want to be no snitch, or no hold out when I'm there. And if we're hitchin' home or walkin', they need me in case some other gang tries to jump 'em, don't they? How can I say no?"

"Olivia," said Kate. "I know what you're saying. You want to go along with whatever group you're with so as not to feel lonely. But in order to have some control over your own life, you need to make your own choices. We can't always control those around us, but we have the power to control our own choice of how we respond to them and their problems. Do you understand? You might be better off to try to stay with a group that doesn't do drugs." *What can I say that will get through to her?*

"Gee, Livie," said Cindi, "there are other things to do to

keep from being lonely. Besides the teams, we have Girl Scouts and drama group, and we belong to a band. I play clarinet and bassoon, Cori plays baritone sax and drums, Alisa plays guitar, Alli plays trumpet and Renee plays all the strings. You could probably play the tambourine or something. We have a good library here and lots of the kids come over to do their homework and play games, and Dad has a giant-sized kite it takes the whole neighborhood to help fly when there's enough wind, and...."

"Okay, okay, I get it." Olivia shook her head, and they saw tears in her eyes. "You want me to live a life like you do and forget about my gang, don'tcha?"

"That's one solution to drugs, Livie," said Cori, softly. "If you think you *have* to do what everybody in your group does, maybe you need a new group."

Kate and Phil had listened quietly. Phil met his wife's eyes and nodded. She knew he meant that the suggestions might come better from the kids.

"But what do I do when Lynette and George want me to go out? I can just see me tellin' 'em I'm gonna go be some old Girl Sprout. They'd laugh at me forever."

Cindi waved a hand dismissively. "Then don't tell them until you feel you're safely out of the drug kind of life. Just tell them to drop you off at our house whenever they're going over to the One-Ways or using drugs. You can do whatever we happen to be doing and see which kind of life you like best."

"You mean, it's okay with you all if I come over here when I get lonely, and they're leaving me to go out?"

Cori and Cindi looked from their mother to their father. Both nodded.

"Looks okay to me," said Cori with a grin.

"I guess I can try." Olivia stared at her hands in her lap. "But how do I know I won't mess up again? It's hard to just quit cold turkey. I tried before. Everythin' hurts and I get all jumpy."

"Then I guess we'll just keep starting over again," said Phil, "until you're free. We're as much in the dark about how to do this successfully as you are, but we're willing to give it a try, if you are. We can't do it for you. Are you ready to try again?"

"I think I want to. I don't know if I can. What if I doped up too much already?"

Kate took Olivia's hand. "If you're already addicted, it'll be hard. But we'll take it a day at a time and try to keep you too busy to miss drugs or your former activities." Olivia laid her head in Kate's lap and started to cry. Cori put her hands over her mouth to stifle a gasp. No one knew what to say. They waited quietly.

A few moments went by before Olivia sat up, mopped her eyes with her napkin and said, "That was dumb. I'm already acting like a baby, and I haven't even quit yet."

"That's okay, Livie," said Cindi. "We all feel like that sometimes. You're trying something that may be pretty hard. I guess you'll have to be brave to think out your whole life so differently."

Kate wanted to get them back to laughing. "Okay, girls, time to clean up. Who's washing dishes, and who's drying?"

Olivia looked up. "Can I dry?"

"Sure, Livie," said Cori. It's my turn to wash anyway. Come on. We'll race."

"I'll hang around and kibitz," said Cindi.

Phil and Kate left the kitchen to the three girls. Once in the living room, Phil pulled Kate into his lap. "We may have started something difficult, my love, but the kids want to help, too, so tell me what you're thinking. What kind of impact do you think we can have on Olivia? And, what kind of impact will she have on us?" Then he cupped her chin in his hand, kissed her on the nose and added, "And, Katie-Love, I don't want you going to the One-Ways alone again."

"You're right. I'll try not to. But I hope Olivia can stick with a plan and not backslide. I'm afraid she'll give up when it gets tough, or if she sees herself failing."

Phil caressed her cheek. "This will be a giant change for Livie, changing lifestyle, family, friends, gang, drugs, everything. I'm not sure how people change, but they must *want* to change and see something wrong with the way things are now. I'm not sure

she sees. She may fail a few times before she succeeds. And, it'll be a giant change for us, too, and for the kids. Can we handle it?.
"Can we all withstand the disappointment if she fails--if we fail? Are we strong enough to hope, yet maybe fail, anyway?"
"I read something good last night, and I'm sharing. This quotation said, 'A woman is like a tea bag. She never knows how strong she is until she gets into hot water.'"
Kate laughed. "You always find the right thing, don't you? Who said that?"
"You'd never guess. Eleanor Roosevelt. Does that not hit it on the head?"
"It does. I guess we'll all just have to try our best and hope we *and* Olivia are good tea bags." She nuzzled Phil's neck and whispered, "As soon as the girls finish giggling in the kitchen, I'll have to get Olivia to call so her mother knows where she is."
Phil nodded. "I sure wish we knew what that relationship entails. Olivia seems so reluctant to be with her mother."
"Her mom and siblings may be the worst influences, even more than the One-Ways' kids, but I hate to think that when I don't know the woman. Maybe she needs help too. Of course, how can we get to know her when she's never there?"
"Well, my dear, Olivia has come into our lives for some reason. We'll just have to see what it is she needs from us."
A half hour passed before the girls emerged from the kitchen, still giggling. Kate insisted Olivia call her mom.
Olivia appeared reluctant as Kate showed her to their phone attached to the wall in the kitchen and watched as she dialed. The clicking of the heavy phone's dial returning after each number was the only sound. One could count the numbers. Then suddenly, Olivia hung up and said, "What'll I say to her?"
"Just tell her where you are and ask if you can stay overnight and we'll bring you home after tomorrow night's softball practice." When Olivia hesitated, Kate coaxed, "Go ahead, Olivia. Your mom needs to know where you are. Try again."
Whoever answered the phone screamed so loud they could all hear his words. "Where the hell are you? Me and Lynette are

already home and mom's getting ready for work and you're not here. We told her you had to stop on the way. You'd better get your fuckin' butt back home right this minute if you know what's good for you!" Olivia's eyes widened, and she held the receiver in two shaking hands.

Kate grabbed her jacket and nodded at Olivia. She whispered, "I'll take you now."

Olivia muttered something into the phone and hung up. "That was George. I have to go now or he'll beat my butt."

Automatically, Kate said, "Derrière."

Livie looked puzzled, but repeated the word. She added frantically, "What'll I do if they're goin' out again tonight after Mom leaves for work?"

Practical Cindi could always be relied on for an answer to every problem. "Just say you're too tired and go straight to bed. Don't argue about it. Call us and we'll talk to you if you get scared being there by yourself. In the morning, get dressed and get to school early, before they all come home. My mom will be there early, won't you Mom?" Kate didn't have time to even nod.

"And don't forget we have softball practice after school," added Cori. "I'll bring along an extra glove for you. School's a good place to hide out from George and Lynette. You can talk to the girls from the team so you won't have to be lonely, okay?"

Olivia was silent, kneeling down to hug Goldie and Cleo stretched out on the floor. Cleo's happy tail thumped on the tile.

"Okay, Olivia? You can try for one night, can't you?" said Cindi. "Say it out loud."

"Okay. I'll try. They're gonna think it's funny that I want to stay by myself, and maybe they won't let me, but I'll try."

Phil bent to look into her eyes. "That's all any of us can do, Livie. Try. Just for one night and one day at a time."

"We'll see you tomorrow, Livie, don't forget," said Cindi, as Kate escorted Olivia to the car for the uncertain ride home.

Chapter 7

Kate watched Olivia saunter into her classroom half an hour early and plop her math book on a vacant desk. She pulled up a chair by the worn teacher's desk where Kate sat checking lesson plans. Kate refrained from mentioning the girl's white pallor and sweaty brow. Instead, she smiled a greeting and continued with her work, waiting for Olivia to tell her what happened in her own way.

Olivia watched in silence for a moment. "That was hard, ya know. They didn't wanna leave me home alone."

"But you talked them into it?"

"Yeah, but they was really mad. Said I'd let 'em down and sh...stuff like that when they got home this mornin'."

Olivia looked away, staring out the windows. "I couldn't sleep without the pills, though--had the shakes and hurts and sweats all night. Is that a bad sign? It sorta made me wish I'd gone with 'em, but it was too late anyways."

"You might have some nights like that, Olivia--withdrawal, depending on how addicted you really are. I'm proud of you for toughing it out, though, and all by yourself, too. You're a strong girl, and you're going to beat this."

"Had to change the sheets 'cause I sweated so much. I hurried to get out of there before Mom got home from work."

"But you got here, Olivia. That's the important thing. One day at a time is all we can worry about—and you made a great start. How do you feel this morning?"

"Hungry. I've got the munchies."

"What does that mean, exactly?"

"You're just hungry all the time after smokin' pot or hash."

"But you didn't smoke last night."

"No, but the munchies last a *long* time." She grinned mischievously. "Or maybe I'm just hungry all the time anyway."

Kate wondered if Olivia's hunger was from neglect. *Where*

can I find out if hunger comes after marijuana? She reached into her desk drawer for peanut butter and crackers she kept for those children she knew had no breakfast. She spread out a few for the girl. Olivia's hands shook as she reached for them.

"Wasn't there anything to eat at home?"

"Nothin' I could get without Mom knowin'. She doesn't like it if I take food."

"Does she fix meals for you, then?"

"Sometimes. But mostly she's workin' or sleepin', so we go out, and Lynette buys something at 7/11. I like hotdogs and Mars bars and Marlboros."

"That's not very well balanced, and cigarettes aren't food, Olivia—but while we're on the subject...."

"Oh, no you don't," screeched Olivia, shoving back the crackers. You ain't makin' me quit smokin' at the same time I quit drugs. I can't do it. I know I can't!" She clenched her fists and her voice quavered.

"Okay, Olivia, okay," Kate said soothingly. "One thing at a time. Drugs first. But I want you to agree not to smoke at school or with the softball team. Can you at least promise me that much? Phil and James both smoke, so it's not outlawed, but even they go outside to smoke. I'm hoping you can quit or cut back, at least when you're over this drug thing. Just don't be sneaky about it."

"It's hard, though."

Kate smiled. "A lot of this is going to be hard, Olivia. It's a big decision for you. But it'll get better soon, I promise."

"Okay, but you better stick these in your drawer until after practice, so I don't forget." Olivia held out her pack of Marlboros.

"Until after softball practice." Kate shut the drawer, smiling at Olivia.

"Yeah, yeah, I know." She sat back down, one hand braced with the other to stop the shaking. Sweat glistened on her brow, and she frequently wiped it back into her straight, short black hair.

Judging by her puffy eyes, Olivia probably hadn't slept much. Kate leaned back, hesitating to ask questions, yet she needed to know. "Olivia, it might help us help you, if you tell me when you first tried drugs? Was it recently, or a long time ago?" Olivia paused so long Kate was afraid she wouldn't answer.

"I don't always 'member things. Probably I was three or four. My big sisters, Betsy and Rita, took George and Lynette and me to a party. Betsy told me to sit on the floor and be quiet and watch TV while she and a guy were goin' at it on the couch."

"Going at it?" Kate hoped she had misunderstood.

"You know, fu..., I mean doin' stuff to each other nekked. The table where I was at on the floor had all kinds of candy on it, so I took some purple ones. I threw up on the rug and Betsy whupped me for gettin' sick. Her boyfriend hit me, too. But she didn't say I couldn't have no more candy. She just said I had to learn to maintain and not puke."

"And that was your first time?"

Olivia nodded, nonchalantly taking a bite of cracker as though this were the most normal childhood in the world.

"Were there other times?"

"Whenever we went out after that. Lynette and George and I learned to maintain and not puke, and that's all that bothered Betsy and Rita, so they didn't hit us anymore. Rita was selling then, and she taught me to protect myself."

"From what?" Kate held her breath, afraid of the answer.

"From guys too wasted to know they was hurtin' me."

"You mean they had sex with you? You were just a little girl!" Kate gulped back the bile forming in her throat. A visceral pain hit her, imagining children being so used. But, she knew if she over-reacted, Olivia would clam up.

"Yeah, and Lynette. After everyone's loaded up, nobody cares much who or where. Fu..., I mean goin' at it's just fun and nobody cares. Lynette's good. She makes enough money to buy her own drugs and food, and sometimes she buys mine, too."

Forcing herself to stay calm, Kate said, "Olivia, no one has the right to have sex with you just because they're on drugs. Didn't your sisters or someone *tell* you that?"

"No, but it didn't matter. I was wasted, anyway. Sometimes it hurt, but I didn't care--except this once."

"Why was it different?" Kate could scarcely modulate her voice to keep from screaming. Her stomach wrenched painfully. "Last year, the boy I told you about that O.D'd. I liked him. We went at it just 'cause we liked each other, loaded or not." Olivia snatched a tissue from the box on Kate's desk and mopped her eyes. Her hands still shook. "Yeah, I *really* liked him." There was a long quiet spell while Olivia stared at the blackboard, her eyes far away. She bit her lip and her brow wrinkled up.

Kate was aware that Olivia had deep and private thoughts, but so did she. *What can I say or do that will help this child? She's seen and done more in her nearly thirteen years than I've even known about in a whole lifetime!*

Then Olivia abruptly broke the silence by standing up, wadding the tissue into a ball and throwing it into the trash basket.

"Gotta go. You don't want me late to Mrs. Warner's class, do ya?"

Olivia flashed a smile that startled Kate with the sudden change of mood. But Kate fought to switch to the lighter tone, following Olivia's lead.

"No, you mustn't be late. Come here after school so you can ride over to Mayberry Park for ball practice with the other girls from Sunnyside. We'll meet the ones from Carmela Junior High and Loma Vista Elementary at the park."

"I'll be here." Olivia looked at her shaking hands and said, as an afterthought, "if I don't fall apart or melt or somethin'."

Olivia swaggered out of her classroom. Kate stared after her with thoughts racing. How could she explain to Olivia that nice girls didn't have sex at her age, when she'd been "goin' at it" since she was a small child and didn't see it as anything unusual? Rita was selling drugs, Lynette was prostituting herself to support her drug habit, and Olivia wasn't even eating regularly. Kate's bubble of happy sanity had been punctured by an absurd lifestyle—one she hadn't known existed. "Obviously, drugs and cigarettes are the tip of the iceberg," she muttered to herself before pasting on a shaky smile for the first of her students to enter the room.

"Hi, Mrs. Johnson," said Sammy, one of her normal, rosy-faced ten-year-olds who was excited about normal ten-year-old activities--a relief. "Are you going to be at the PTA carnival next week?" The comparison was impossible to miss.

Softball practice went surprisingly well. Olivia turned out to be agile, so it wasn't hard to teach her to run or catch a fly ball. Catching a fast, hard throw from Cori and batting would take some work. Phil let the girls explain the rules, and only intervened when Olivia let out a "Hell, Barbara, nobody's goin' to run by you—you always tag 'em?"

He then explained a few rules, himself. "Olivia, what about the language?"

But Olivia took it good-naturedly and changed to "Heck— that just slipped out."

Kate noticed Olivia caught herself a little more often and sometimes substituted an approved word for an unapproved one right in mid-sentence.

"Thanks for small increments of improvement," Holly had said only that afternoon, reporting that Olivia had shouted out in class only once. Kate smiled, remembering the conversation as she watched Olivia connect with the softball for the first time, and the whole team screamed for her to run to first. She stood watching the ball sail out to left field before realizing she was supposed to move. Then she took off. For such a short kid, Olivia was surprisingly fast. *Small increments of success--yes.*

But then, Cindi shouted, "Hey Dad, I'm going to teach Livie to steal bases."

Livie shouted back, "I already *know* how to steal."

Kate put a hand to her forehead to hold it steady and scrunched her teeth together.

"I think Cindi can teach you a better way, Livie," Phil said, smiling.

And the whole group of girls laughed. Somehow, it had become a team effort. Olivia seemed a "mascot," and the girls bought into the idea of helping her fit in. Kate wondered if Cindi or Cori had secretly enlisted their aid because they seemed to be trying hard to ignore Olivia's worst remarks, or correct her, while applauding when she did something right, or at least, if she did it wrong in a friendly way.

Kate also began to notice an element of compassion in the girl. Livie quickly became the "go to" person when one of the girls got a scrape or bump, and she was the first to run get the First Aid kit for Phil, sometimes before he even realized an accident had occurred. Olivia observed all with a wary eye. Where that morning she had slurred words and was exhausted and shaky, by afternoon, she was hyper-alert to what was happening around her--a huge contrast from when she was "wasted." On the ball diamond at least, Livie had quick reflexes, and her instincts seemed better developed than Kate had thought. *Perhaps her alert side might be an advantage to getting her wasted side under control. My God, what kind of twisted thought is that?* But the girls on the team appreciated Olivia's quickness and congratulated her often.

Kate drove home some tired girls. Cindi, Cori, and Alisa were all draped in the back seat of the Chevy while Livie slumped against the door in the front, holding Cori's mitt tightly to her chest. Olivia was still sweaty, but Kate couldn't tell if it was from drug withdrawal, or just from playing hard. *I know so pathetically little about this.* Aloud, she said, "It was a great practice, girls. You'll do well against the Huntington Park team."

Olivia roused to a straighter position. "Do ya think I'll get to play by Saturday?"

"Dad makes sure everyone gets to play," said Cori. "But you might have to wait on the bench awhile for your turn since you're still learning."

"I wanna try that stealin' bases again. That's fun."

Alisa laughed. "You'll have to get on base first, but you'll get the hang of batting soon. You need a 'good eye.' You still need to remember the rules, too."

Olivia sighed heavily. "Rules! Everybody's got rules."

Cori said, "Yeah, Livie, but remember that Maywood girl who didn't follow the rules. She bit me, got kicked out of the game, and they *still* didn't win."

"Yeah. I guess some rules are okay. I'll learn 'em for ya."

As they pulled up to Olivia's home, she drew in her breath suddenly. "Uh oh, Mom's home. The door's open."

"Would you introduce us, Livie?"

"I dunno. She's sorta funny. She doesn't like outsiders."

"Well, at least she would know who we are when we come pick you up or call you for practice." Kate hoped she could at last meet the woman Olivia seemed to fear.

"I guess. Come on, and I'll see if it's okay." Olivia's obvious discomfort made Kate wonder if they should leave this step for another time. But Olivia ran to the door as Kate and the three girls walked behind.

"I'm home, Ma'am," Olivia called out, as she went through the screen door. "I brought friends to meet you. Is it okay, Ma'am?"

Cindi whispered to Cori, "What's all that Ma'am stuff? Can't she just call her mom, 'Mom,' like we do?"

Olivia appeared again at the door, holding it open while the Johnson girls trooped into the house. The strong smell of bleach coupled with cigarette smoke assaulted the nostrils. "Ma'am" was almost invisible in a worn, dark-colored robe, hunched into an equally worn and dark-colored recliner. She didn't get up. It was Olivia who asked them to sit down on the flowered, slip-covered couch. The room contained only the two pieces of furniture plus a wooden table placed against the wall, but the house was clean.

As Kate's eyes adjusted to the darkness of the room, the mother became more visible. A broad nose dwarfed the woman's eyes. Her thick eyebrows connected at the middle made Kate think of John L. Lewis. Her skin was much lighter than Olivia's native Indian brown, but her hair was equally black, though hers was frizzy like a new perm. Smoke from her cigarette curled above a beanbag ashtray perched on the chair's armrest. It was full to the brim of spent cigarette butts. The woman kept muttering to herself. Her reptilian, black eyes flashed each time she glanced in the direction of her unwanted guests. Kate shivered. But she kept smiling, hoping the woman might become more hospitable to her daughter's new friends.

A tall, Indian girl with black hair that looked ratted to the ceiling and makeup an inch thick stood in one corner with a broom. "I'm all done, Ma'am," she said.

Kate tried not to stare and wished the girls could turn their gaze from that hair. They couldn't. Cindi's jaw was half-slack, and Alisa's eyes popped.

The mother waved the older girl away as she would a bad odor and turned to stare at Olivia's guests.

"That's Lynette," Livie said, as the girl walked from the room. "She's my sister."

Kate said to the woman, "I'm Kate Johnson. I teach at Olivia's school. These are my girls, Cindi, Alisa, and Cori. Forgive us that we're all sweaty, but we've just come from softball practice. Olivia did well for her first day. You'd be proud of her."

"Why would I be proud of her for playing some stupid game? She has work to do *here*." Her hazy slur told Kate she'd been drinking. The woman turned to Olivia and said, "Who'd you say these people were?"

Olivia scrambled up. "Ma'am, these are friends from the softball team. I told you 'bout 'em last week. I joined the team, Ma'am. Is it all right?"

Cori spoke up excitedly. "Livie's getting good at softball, isn't she, Mom?" She turned to her mother for confirmation when Livie's mother did not respond. Kate nodded, wondering why the woman looked at them with such suspicion.

"I'm teaching Livie to steal bases," said Cindi. "She's really fast, isn't she, Mom?"

Again Kate nodded. "All the girls have taken a liking to Olivia, and I think she'll make a good team player. She tries hard, and she's learning fast."

Olivia seemed pleased at the words, but twitched constantly and kept glancing back at her mother's face as though expecting hot lead to fly. Kate couldn't quite fathom the electric tension between the two.

Lynette drifted back into the room and bent to pick up

something from the floor near her mother. A Marlboro pack was clearly outlined in the back pocket of her Levi's.

Suddenly the mother said loudly, "Lynette, are those cigarettes in your pocket?"

"No, Ma'am," said Lynette, quickly standing up and moving toward the wall.

"See," said the mother suddenly. "*My* girls are courteous. I notice your girls don't say 'Ma'am' to you. They aren't brought up right. I don't want my girl around yours."

Kate tensed. *At least my children don't broad-faced lie to me!*

Olivia wilted. "Excuse me, Ma'am. They're nice to me."

Alisa turned to the woman. "Excuse me, *Ma'am*."

Alisa's stressed sarcasm was apparent to Kate, but she glanced quickly at Olivia's mother and saw it had been lost on her. She sighed, thankfully.

"I think the word 'Ma'am' is used more in the south," continued Alisa. "I don't hear many people using it here."

"And I've never found the word necessary as long as children speak to adults in a courteous manner," said Kate. *And as long as they're honest*, she couldn't help thinking.

"From what I see, kids in …." The woman turned to Olivia. "Where are we?"

"California, Ma'am."

"Kids in California are rude. I prefer my kids to speak *respectively* to their elders." She seemed unaware she had used the incorrect word. Her words slurred and she frowned, looking bewildered as she searched all around for something, patting the seat and armrests of her chair.

Olivia squirmed in discomfort. Kate struggled to bring the agonizing visit to a close. "Will you allow Olivia to play on the softball team? We'll pick her up and bring her back on practice and game days."

"Please, Ma'am." Olivia practically kowtowed waiting for her mother's answer.

"Lynette," the mother asked her older daughter as though

she hadn't heard the younger. "Lynette, do you think Livie can play this silly ball game?"

"Yes, Ma'am. It can't hurt her any that I can see."

"All right, Livie, I suppose you can play, but only so long as you keep my kitchen spotless and don't break anything again. I won't have you breaking my things." As she spoke, her vacant eyes roamed the ceiling rather than her daughter's face.

"Thank you, Ma'am. I won't break stuff again, I promise."

Kate couldn't stand this conversation any longer. Olivia quivered all over when she lifted her hand in a tiny little secret finger wave, and all three girls returned it.

"I'll see you at school tomorrow, Olivia. You may come in early to help again, if you like. And we'll pick you up Saturday morning for the game," said Kate. "Be rested."

Cori added, "Livie, we can pick you up *anytime*, if you want to come *practice* sooner. Just call us and we'll come get you, do you *understand*?"

Kate hoped Olivia's mother was too far gone to notice Cori's emphasis.

Olivia nodded quickly, as Kate and the girls made their getaway. Olivia kept her eyes on her mother's face the whole time.

Is her glance wary, apprehensive, what?

As the girls stepped out the door and scooted to the car, Kate resisted the impulse to run with them to get out of earshot.

But they couldn't get away fast enough not to hear the mother screaming.

"What do you mean bringing people here? And you didn't get that kitchen counter washed good enough to suit me, either. And Lynette, Miss Hoity-Toity, finding lint on the floor of *my* house when you're supposed to clean it right. You'll both do every bit of it over again, right now! You girls are nothing but lazy, no-good...."

"Yes, Ma'am. I'm sorry, Ma'am."

Kate and the girls didn't wait to hear more. Silence engulfed the car as the scenery flashed by on the way back to their normal life.

Chapter 8

Olivia wasn't at school a few days later, and once again Kate decided she'd have to drive to the One-Ways after she finished with her class. Holly was ready to go with her, but then Bobby split his lip on the playground during recess. Holly sighed and rolled her eyes at Kate as she picked up her son and ran to her car. "I'm sorry," she called out.

Kate went alone.

This time, however, there seemed a different demeanor among the young people loitering on the street. While it was not friendly, the kids more or less ignored her except to move over a little as she passed. No one waved, but no taunts or screams or threats followed her, either. The word must have been out that she was harmless.

As she drove slowly, glancing left or right for a clue, she suddenly saw movement, and one of the girls, Belle, from Bettina's group, ran out to her car.

"She's down here. Follow me."

Kate followed behind as Belle jogged down the block, calling out to those on the side, "It's okay; it's the teacher." Young people near the houses watched, but made no attempt to harass or stop her this time. The girl ran into a yard and disappeared into a different house from before. Kate slammed on the brakes and got out, not sure what she should do. Within moments, Olivia came staggering out, buttressed by Bettina and Alice on either side. Kate ran to help them. Olivia had a huge welt and two angry, bloody gashes that had not quite closed just under her left eye. The eye was black and swollen shut. Kate sucked in her breath and asked, "What happened?"

"We dunno. She got here like this last night," said Bettina. "Lynette brung her."

"She was bleeding bad, and we didn't know what to do," said Alice. "She smoked dope and got wasted on pills. Said she hurt too bad not to. We couldn't stop her."

Kate gently touched the deep gashes on Olivia's cheek, and blood ran out where the wound hadn't congealed. She fished in her purse for a tissue to staunch the flow. She couldn't see the bone, but the swelling was enormous. "What caused this?"

Belle said, "I bet it's that mother of hers. She gets real bad drunk. Olivia and Lynette get hit 'cause they're the youngest." Belle brushed Olivia's hair from the wound.

Bettina added, "You gotta get her outta that house, or she'll be back here every night."

Kate didn't know what to say. Olivia had agreed to call if she needed help, and somehow it hadn't worked. Maybe she couldn't get to a phone or was too badly injured.

"We told all the gang to watch for ya," said chubby little Alice. "Was that okay?"

"Of course it was, Alice. Thank you, girls, and please give them all my thanks, too. I appreciate the help."

"Can you take her home with you again? She can't stay here, and she can't go to her house." Bettina fidgeted nervously with her cheap, pot-metal locket. "You gotta get her out of here before my boyfriend catches me helping you."

"Yes, if we can get her into the back seat."

Olivia was limp and almost slippery with sweat, and the girls had trouble holding her upright. The larger boy who had threatened Kate's car with a crowbar on her previous venture into the One-Ways stepped forward, scooped up the faltering Olivia, and moved toward Kate's Chevy. Alice opened the back door for him, and he plopped his burden unceremoniously on the seat. Livie was short enough her feet didn't even hang over the edge. He closed the door and walked away without a word.

"Thank you," Kate called after him. He didn't acknowledge her words.

Kate turned to the girls and said once more, "You've been good friends to Olivia. I don't know what we can do to keep her from coming here, but we're trying."

"You won't give up, will you, teacher?" Bettina asked.

"No, of course not. But we've got to teach her not to give

up on herself, and we don't know how to do that yet. We don't have any training." Kate stopped. These girls would have no concept of proper counseling or drug abuse care. *To whom can I go? Where can I learn? We must find out, now.*

Bettina said, "You go. I gotta go feed my baby, and my old man is mad at me for leaving." She motioned to the other girls to follow her.

"Don't get yourself in trouble, Bettina. You've done well, and I hope to see you soon--under different circumstances." Kate smiled ruefully as she climbed into the Chevy to drive home, her hands clenched in a tight, white grip on the steering wheel.

James pulled into the driveway behind Kate as he arrived home. He carried Livie, who suddenly became a fighter, so that he had difficulty holding on to her as she writhed and turned.

"How could she go there again?" Alisa was angry as she tried to help James with the wildly thrashing Olivia. "We can't trust her out of our sight for a minute."

"What're ya doin'? Olivia screamed.

"Kate caught up with the struggling pair and said soothingly, "It's okay, Olivia. You're here with us. Let's get you inside where Phil can see your wound." The girl quieted and allowed James to carry her in to a dining room chair by the table.

Phil got the first aid kit and examined Olivia's eye. It was still swollen shut. Livie winced whenever he touched the area.

"I'm just trying to make sure the eye itself wasn't damaged, Livie. I know it hurts, but please bear with me and let me look."

"It's not *in* the eye," came her weak reply. "Below...."

"What hit you?" James asked. "Was it some kind of weapon? Who would do this to you?"

Olivia didn't answer.

She winced again as Phil washed the wound with peroxide, mopping up the spilling pink bubbles with a paper towel. "It's all right, Livie. Just a moment more."

"I'm sorry," wailed the girl. "I wasn't goin' back there, but Lynette got me out of the house, and I hurt so bad I took the pills she gave me. I messed up again." She pushed away Phil's hands and put her head on her arms. "It's all no good. I'm no good."

"Shh, Olivia." Kate wrapped her arms around the sobbing girl's shoulders, being careful not to get near her eye. "Don't talk that way. Let's just worry about the cuts by your eye now, and we'll talk about the other later."

"Livie, can you tell me what she hit you with?" Phil asked. "I want to be sure it wasn't something that would cause an infection. It sure wasn't her hand!"

Olivia straightened up, a frightened look on her face. "Nobody hit me! Who told you she hit me?"

"I'm sorry, Livie, I just assumed from what the girls told me about her being angry when they left you yesterday."

"She didn't hit me! Don't you say she hit me!"

"Then what are these two gashes that have made your eye swell shut, Livie?" Kate hugged the trembling girl tighter. "Please tell us, so we can treat the wound properly."

"Those...things...sticking out on the toaster plug," she whimpered. "The cord swung like a whip. I didn't see it comin' to duck in time. Most times, I'm faster to duck."

Phil gasped. "You mean the prongs on the plug—an electric cord?"

Livie nodded, then winced at the movement.

"Did it bleed right away?" Cori said, "Usually if something bleeds, it won't get infected, will it?" She looked to her father for an answer. "Livie, I'm so sorry. Did she hit you because you took us in the house with you?"

"I dunno. She hates us bringing any outsiders, and...and...." Livie gulped and then the words came out in a rush. "She was drinkin', and I didn't get the kitchen counters clean enough, and she thought you was comin' to inspect from her welfare check office and she thought she'd lose her welfare check, and when I dropped the fork, she *had* to hit me. But, I didn't *mean* to drop the fork. I really do try and be quiet when she's been drinking. Lynette says noise sets her off worse." She paused and touched the wound gingerly. "I don't think she *meant* to do it. I just make her mad all the time. She says I never do anythin' right."

Livie struggled to quiet her sobs, still hiccoughing and gasping for air with the effort.

They all exchanged glances over Livie's bowed head. Cori's eyes were round and startled. Kate didn't know what to say or do, either. "Livie...."

"How bad does it look? It sure hurts."

"Maybe it'd be better to look later," said Cindi.

"I wanna see it now."

Cindi went to get a hand mirror while Ned let Cleo and Goldie in to comfort Olivia. Goldie immediately hopped into Olivia's lap, and Cleo laid her head on the girl's knee. Livie patted them both and said, "At least, *they* don't think I look that bad. You all should see *your* faces." A crooked grin was all she could manage with her lopsided face and eye swollen shut. She took one glance at the mirror and shrieked, took a second look and wailed, "Shit! I *do* look that bad. This'll have a scar, won't it, Coach?"

Phil looked closely again and said, "It might, Livie. It didn't get cleaned right away. Let's get the swelling down so we can find out."

"I'm sorry, I meant 'shoot'."

"We know, Livie. One thing at a time," said Phil, as he gently dabbed at the eye.

Alisa filled the rubber hot water bottle with ice and brought it back with a cloth wrapped around it. "Here, Livie, keep this on the eye. The swelling will go down faster."

"Thanks. You guys should hate me. I didn't mean to go. Honest. Lynette said for me to...."

"It's all right, Livie," said Kate. "Lynette was right to get you out of the house under the circumstances. If this ever happens again, ask Lynette to bring you here."

"Lynette don't know you, and I was too hurt to ask anything. She didn't know no place else safe. And anyway, if my mom looked for me, she don't ever go to the One-Ways."

"Where was Lynette when I got there to pick you up?"

"Probably with one of the guys. She makes about a hundred dollars a night, ya know." Olivia was proud of her older sister.

"That's good for her bein' only fifteen, don'tcha think?"

There were wide eyes around the table as the kids waited for Phil or Kate to say something. Kate was too stunned for the so-called "teachable moment." Phil was speechless, as well. Kate shrugged helplessly, sick at the events of the evening. *What can we actually do to help clean the cobwebs out of that head of hers?*

Cleo broke the tension by rolling over on her back. Olivia winced when she tried to reach down, holding the ice bag with one hand. She quickly laid her head back on the chair, so Ned took over the semi-compulsory job of scratching Cleo's belly for her.

"Homework time, crew, then bedtime," announced Kate. "Take turns with the shower." There were perfunctory groans, but the kids settled around the dining table with their books.

"Livie, you need some rest," said Phil. "You can lie down. We'll find out if we need to take you home or keep you overnight."

"I hurt too much to care, Phil. Lyin' down is good."

They left her in the bedroom with her ice bag. Cleo kept her feet warm, and Goldie curled under her arm. Kate looked at Phil and smiled, shaking her head, as she turned out the light. "The animals always seem to know who needs them most, don't they?"

"We can't send her back in this condition, and we can't keep her unless her mom's gone," said Phil, as they sat together in the living room. "She's worried about a scar on her face, but I'm appalled at all the scars she carries on the inside already."

"So many weird things go on in that house--Olivia's early drug use, her sexual activity, Lynette's 'profession,' the beatings. And Olivia thinks all that is *normal*! How do we change her whole value system--her whole life?" Kate felt hopelessly ill prepared.

Phil wrapped his arms around her and said, "First, Love, I mean it about not going back to the One-Ways alone. Wait for me next time."

"But...."

"No buts. Wait for me! For *now*, let's call Livie's house to see if anyone's there." They padded into the kitchen to dial.

A young female voice answered, "Gonzaga residence."

"Is that you, Lynette?"

"Yes, Ma'am, this is Lynette speaking." Then her voice changed to an urgent tone. "Is this the teacher? Is Livie with you? The kids said the teacher came and got her."

"Yes, Lynette. She's safe here. Her eye is swollen shut, and that welt will probably leave a scar, but she'll be okay. We were unsure whether to bring her home or keep her overnight."

"You'd better keep her there. Mom's gone to work 'cause she had a date first. She didn't miss Livie. I told her she was staying with friends in Norwalk for a few days."

"That didn't bother her?" Kate thought about how she'd feel if one of her brood just disappeared for "a few days" with no explanation, or if they lied to her about it.

"She don't care, and she's still mad at Livie, anyhow." Lynette paused. "I don't know what you're doing to Livie, but she didn't want to go to the One-Ways last night. It was the only safe place I could think of. I had to drag her out. Who are you, really?"

Kate wondered how much she could tell Lynette. "I teach at Livie's school. She told me she was on drugs and wanted help to get off. Our family is trying to help her. We aren't even sure how to do it, since we know nothing about drugs. We try to keep her busy with heavily physical things, like softball, hoping she won't be tempted to go to the One-Ways and get wasted." Kate sighed, wondering if she'd made a mistake in trusting this fifteen year old. She couldn't get her mind around Lynette's prostitution, but she hoped there'd be a shred of decency in the girl, and she'd want to help her sister.

There was a long silence, yet Kate could still hear Lynette breathing on the other end of the line. "If you have any ideas...."

"I don't know why Livie told you all these lies. What *else* did she tell you about us? She shouldn't have told you anything! It's our private business. Livie's got to learn not to talk to a narc."

"Lynette, I'm not sure what a 'narc' is, but I don't think I am one. I can understand you don't want strangers interfering in your business, but we mean no harm to any of you. We only want to help Olivia, because she *asked* for help. She must feel *something* isn't right before she'd ask, don't you think?"

"And what's it to you?" Lynette paused. "There's nothing wrong with Livie that isn't wrong with everybody. This whole family's screwed up, and everybody's hooked on something or other." Suddenly Lynette gasped. "You aren't turning us in to the county, are you? Mom would kill us if she lost her welfare check."

"No, of course not, Lynette. We're only trying to help Olivia get her life straightened out, and we may need your help from time to time, that's all."

"Why do you care? What's in it for you?" *So much suspicion in her voice.*

"We want nothing, Lynette. Just to help Livie, *if* we can. And I guess that's a big 'if.' But, Lynette, you did a good job of getting Livie out of the house last night. It shows you care about her. We care too, so perhaps we can work together to help her."

"Nothing you can do will help Livie any. She's too far gone--hooked harder than any of the rest of us. You're wasting your time. I shouldn't talk to you at all. Just bring Livie home. Now. I'll fix her face up. I can take care of her."

"Lynette, please wait! Don't hang up. Tell me *why* you think Olivia is hooked harder than anyone else?"

"Look, maybe you mean well, teacher, but Livie's been on drugs since she was little. She's mixed about every kind of dope, pills, pot, heroin, speed, sniffing, and LSD, sometimes all together. She's overdosed a gazillion times. There's something in her that makes her not even care *what* she uses. I think her brain is already scrambled. She forgets stuff, she's moody, and she does terrible in school. All she wants to do is get high, and fuck, and fight."

Kate ignored the word. She hadn't been *asked* to help Lynette. "Look, Lynette, some of the other girls said Olivia would die if she didn't get out of the One-Ways and off drugs."

"Yeah, probably."

Lynette's matter-of-fact tone chilled Kate. *Maybe I said too much.* "Can't we try? You care about Livie or you wouldn't buy her food or get her away from your mom when she's hurt."

"Suppose I do? She's still bad news. She'll get us all in deep shit one of these days. No one else can control her, so I *sure* don't think *you* can! What can *you* do?"

"Honestly, Lynette, I don't know yet. I know nothing about drug culture or addicts. Maybe we've been sheltered, but we've never seen it before. We're playing it by ear, learning as we go along. But, we're willing to try. Will you help us?"

"Maybe, but I don't see how you uppity folks with all your rules can help her. You're not going to turn narc, or report us to welfare or tell my mom…or anyone?"

"No, Lynette. That's not our purpose or our business. We just try to keep Olivia occupied as much as we can to see if family activities will get her over addiction and past withdrawal. We don't know if it'll work. You're a smart girl, Lynette. You know what Olivia's life will be if she doesn't get out of this lifestyle soon."

"Yeah, it's like that for all of us. I'm saving money to get out of here, too, but it's a long way off. Look, what can I do?"

"For one thing, please don't take her to the One-Ways when you go, and don't let George take her either. She's big enough to stay by herself while your mom's at work. That way she won't be around drugs or people who'd coax her to use them. She needs to start sleeping at night so she can learn at school and be active during the day. She's been nocturnal far too long."

There was a derisive snort on the other end of the line. "Good luck! If you can get her to sleep at night and go to school, you're fighting her whole history. I told you, I think she's already fried her brain with snorting shit and taking pills and LSD. I'm not sure if she can learn *anything* now."

"Her teacher, Mrs. Warner, is trying to catch Olivia up as much as she can. Olivia's street-smart and alert in some ways." Kate thought of a suggestion. "And, will you call us if you think Olivia is in danger? We'd come get her if you think we need to."

"I guess so, but I sure can't see why you want to do this. Livie would be the first one to tell you she's not worth it. None of us are."

"She's already told us she's no good, but we don't believe that about *anybody*. She's only a child. We want to at least give Olivia a chance, a choice about her future."

"A choice, hm? Well, I won't get in your way if I can help it. I can't do much, but I'll talk George into leaving her home when we go to the One-Ways, if that's the way she wants it. But if she wants to go, we won't be able to stop her."

"I know, Lynette. I'm hoping she won't want to go."

"What do I do if she gets shaky and sweaty and gets into Mom's stash of pills and booze here at home?"

"Is there anyplace you can hide them?"

"I'm not gonna get hit in my face! It's my ticket out of here."

"Then we'll have to persuade Livie not to use those either."

I can see a long road before us. What changes will Livie make in the lives of my family? And there's not even any certainty of success with her having so many problems.

"Okay, Ma'am, I'll do what I can. But don't expect miracles. They never come. I know! I've waited for one, and nothing ever comes but just more shit."

"Thank you, Lynette. Please keep in touch. Call us anytime. We'll keep her tonight and bring her home before your mom comes so she can get dressed for school."

"School, hm? You can't get her to like school. I sure don't." There was a hard laugh. "But okay, Ma'am. Keep Livie whenever you think she's weak. Let me know, so I can tell Mom that she's over at a girlfriend's."

"I'd rather you not lie. Can't you tell her the truth, that she's with us?"

"You don't want *my* mom knowing where you live. Bye."

"Oh, and Lynette?"

"What?"

"You don't need to 'Ma'am' me. I'll be totally happy just to have you be *honest* with me and call me whatever you like."

A ripple of laughter came through the receiver. For an instant, Kate forgot the hard, heavily made-up girl she'd seen, and pictured a normal teenager like her own kids.

"You noticed? Most people don't. Mom never does. That's how we keep from getting hit, *most* of the time. May I call you

Teacher?"

"If you like, or Kate, or Mrs. Johnson--just not 'Ma'am.' After your Marlboro trick, I'll probably *always* associate the use of 'Ma'am' to be a lie, and I really don't want you to lie to me. I'd prefer that we trust each other."

"Okay, Kate. I won't lie to you, and I won't call you 'Ma'am'--except—unless it's in front of my mom and I want you to know what I'm saying *isn't* true...you know, like a secret code. What do you think?"

"Lynette, you're a genius! Thank you."

Lynette's voice softened. "Thank you too, for at least *trying* to help my sister."

"We'll all try together, Lynette. Good night."

Kate hung up the receiver and turned to her husband. Phil held out his arms, led her back to the living room couch, and she cuddled into his ample lap. "I hope I did the right thing in being honest with Lynette. She seems so hardened."

"Honey, I think you did fine. No matter how hard she *looks*, she's only two years older than Olivia. That's still pretty young. And, she must care about the kid."

"Lynette sounds much smarter than Olivia. Her speech patterns sound pretty normal for her age group, where Livie's are stunted. Lynette said she thought Livie might have already done damage to her brain from the drugs. Is that possible? We have so much to learn. But Lynette might be right because, though Olivia can pick up some things, she's definitely behind other kids her age in developmental awareness."

Phil laughed. "There you go sounding like a teacher again."

"I know...sorry."

"No need to be sorry, my dear. That's who you are. He winked. "Who we *both* are. In case you're having a few fears, you *know* we couldn't have turned her away. And, if you can get all our kids to retire for the night, I'll race you to bed."

"You're on."

Chapter 9

Over the next days and weeks, the kids helped Olivia keep too busy to fall off the wagon during the day, and she stayed over often. But nighttimes were rarely quiet. About midnight, the girl could be heard crying softly on her preferred sectional couch. Kate got up, put on her robe and slippers and went to sit beside her.
"Didn't mean to wake you. It just hurts bad."
"I know." Kate felt Olivia's sweaty palms. "I think it's still some withdrawal. I wish I knew how to make this go faster for you, Olivia. Let me get some ice and the hot water bottle." Kate returned quickly to sit at Livie's side and take her hand

Olivia's whimpers gradually grew to a suppressed scream, with one fist jammed in her mouth in a futile attempt to keep quiet, the other grasping Kate's hand so hard she thought it might break. The girl's whole body stiffened as her cramped legs jerked. Kate slid the ice wrapped in a towel under one of Olivia's calves, and the hot water bottle under the other. "Let's see which helps first, shall we?"

"Nothin's helping," puffed Olivia between clenched teeth.

Kate restrained the girl from biting her own hand to stifle the pain. "Let me try massaging your legs, Livie." Kate kneaded the calf of the girl's right leg, feeling knots that formed under her fingers. Soon Kate was crying, too, just from the frustration of not knowing what to do to help Livie. "Does this help any?"

"I don't know, a little maybe. Heat's better'n cold."

Kate removed the ice and dropped it to the floor, as she pushed the hot water bottle under both calves and massaged firmly.

Another spasm knotted Olivia's mid-section as she grabbed her stomach and rolled into a fetal position. "Oh, shit, I can't stand this...I mean...oh, I can't talk and take this, too. I can't remember the right words."

"It's okay, Livie. The language can wait. You're going to get through withdrawal, Livie, I promise. Then you'll have goals, and a future. What do you want to do first, once you're well?"

"Crap, I don't have any future. Right now, I wish I'd just die and get it over with. I'll be dead before long, anyway."

Kate jerked sharply. "Why would you say such a thing?"

"If Mom doesn't kill me sometime, the drug pushers or the gangs will. Even if I'm clean, there's nothin' ahead of me but runnin' from one or the other."

"Livie, no. You *must* see a future for yourself. That's what keeps us all going."

"Whatever." Olivia knotted her fist into her belly.

Kate had the feeling she was only reassuring herself that things could change. Olivia seemed resigned and not much worried about the future she saw for herself.

"Can't you give me somethin'? Please."

"Livie, you're trying to get over the addictions. It would only be detrimental to take any kind of painkiller now."

"Det...det...there you go again. Big words don't fix this." Olivia rocked back and forth, holding her arms around her knees as Kate rubbed her back.

"Please, please, just let me go back to my gang. They wouldn't be so mean. They'd give me somethin' to get me by."

The girl tried to pull away, but Kate held her tightly. "Livie, you know I can't let you go back now. You've come such a long way, and most times, there's been no backsliding. You can't go back there, again." Kate continued to rock her, much as she had Cori when she was a colicky infant. Livie's sobs continued as she leaned against Kate's bathrobe, dampened by both their tears.

"Can I help?" came a voice from the dark at their side. Ned rubbed his eyes and ran a hand through tousled blonde hair.

"I wish you could, but I don't know what to do for her."

"Livie, suppose you tell me a story about where you want to travel when you grow up," said Ned. "Make it somewhere in space, okay? I'd like to go there someday. What do you think frogs would look like in space?"

Cori padded in from the girls' bedroom. "Yeah, Livie, do you think frogs would have beady eyes and croak in Martian?"

At first, there was little response from Olivia, but as the

two kids sat down on the coffee table facing her and insisted she give an answer, she tried to smile--a feeble start.

"We could play some music for you, Livie." Cori moved to the console, stuck her hand into the record pile, pulled out a 45 rpm and found a plastic circle to put in the middle so it would fit the 78-rpm spindle. She turned the volume knob way down. Soon an Irish jig spun from the machine. Cori laughed, "Sorry, what I can find in the dark is pretty much potluck, but at least it's lively."

Olivia groaned, but she unclenched her body from her fetal position in Kate's arms and tried to sit up alone. She grabbed the hot water bottle and clasped it around her middle to stay the cramping as she rocked herself on the couch.

Ned said, "Hey, I know. Whoever can add something to our 'frogs in space' story can choose the next record blindly in the dark. Each tune will be a brand new surprise."

Cori and Ned always had been on each other's wavelength, much as Phil and Kate had been as children. Cori picked up on his idea and, together, they got Olivia to at least nod.

Kate stretched her sore arms as the three young people put their heads together for the next line of their makeshift story. *Frogs in space, for crying out loud.*

"Why don't you go lie down, Kate," whispered Ned. "Cori and I can sit up with Livie. You've been up for two hours that I could hear. You have to teach tomorrow."

Has it been that long? No wonder my back and arms ache! "Thank you, Ned." Kate patted the teen's broad shoulder gratefully and smiled. The boys were so different--James tall, dark and lean, the football quarterback, while Ned was short, stocky, and blond, the linebacker. But she had watched both develop depths of compassion and devotion to their adopted sisters and to the concept of "family." They had become like her Phil, *both* strong *and* gentle—the best combination—*but perhaps I'm partial.*

"If you need me, call. I'll go rest for a little while." She turned to Olivia. "You seem a little better already, Livie, don't you? Maybe each episode runs its course in a couple of hours."

The girl just nodded, still clutching her hot water bottle.

"Night Mom," said Cori.
Kate brushed her hand by Cori's cheek "Night-night, you guys. Get back to sleep as soon as you can. Love you."
Kate crept between the sheets, hoping not to disturb Phil, but he'd been waiting for her. He wiped her tears gently with his big thumbs and pulled her into his arms.
"You're exhausted, Hon. I'll take a turn tomorrow night, and the kids are great--they won't mind sitting up with her part of the time."
"I feel so helpless just watching Olivia suffer." Kate brushed Phil's neck with a kiss as she snuggled closer. "We've got to find some answers. The libraries have almost nothing about drugs, addiction, how long withdrawal lasts, or what we can do to help her through it. For all we know, it could be like alcoholism-- once an addict, the craving is always there."
"I'm hoping it's not so serious for a young person," said Phil. "Nothing much has been written about a kid. Only about heroin addiction in old men from Skid Row, and that seems to be the only rehabilitation effort as well. Nobody seems to think a kid might get into the drug scene, though everyone mentions the hippies. The only hint I found is that one must talk to kids when they go off to college. I'm thinking that's way too late."
Gradually, words slowed, fatigue took over, and they drifted off to sleep in each other's arms.

A few days later, sunrise found Phil and Kate maneuvering for space in the one tiny bathroom. Phil brought his straight razor up one cheek as he squinted into the mirror.
Kate groped blindly around the shower curtain, her dark hair dribbling in rivulets down her bare shoulders. Phil automatically switched the razor to his left hand and handed her a towel, then gave her a quick kiss and a pat on the rump. They smirked at each other as Kate wiped the shaving foam from her face. It was their morning ritual.
"What do you think, Phil? Olivia's been pretty good lately, We've only gotten phone calls and had to go get her and dry her

out a couple of times in the last weeks, whenever she goes home."

Kate stepped over the rim of the tub, toweling down vigorously as Phil moved closer to the sink to give her room behind him.

"Yes, but her mom still insists she go home after school long enough to clean the kitchen no matter where she is."

"The other girls go in and help her, *if* her mom is deeply asleep. They can finish pretty fast working together. Olivia said her mom almost seems relieved when she offers some excuse why she won't be home for the night."

"It's safer for her to be here so we know what she's doing, at least until she's over this craving and withdrawal stuff," said Phil. "I guess we have to count small steps of progress, though. At least she can now string together a complete sentence without curse words—that's a relief."

Kate snickered. "Her visit to the Cadette Girl Scout Troop probably set scouting back a hundred years, but she enjoyed it."

"Wish we could get her to eat something besides hot dogs and Mars bars."

"I'm not going to bend the budget on Mars bars--no nutrition in candy. But if you've noticed, I try to serve hot dogs a couple of times a week."

Phil took the naked Kate in his arms, kissing her on the neck. "Believe me, I think we've *all* noticed! Cleo now parks under Olivia's chair at every meal. Olivia isn't gaining any weight, but Cleo is. It looks pretty suspicious to me." Phil's warm laugh rippled against her. Phil dangled Kate's bra and panties in two fingers. "Ready for these?"

Kate grinned and grabbed at the items, while Phil playfully held them out of reach. She held out her hand and he kissed its palm and laid the undergarments in it. Phil hooked the back of her bra. She slid into a fluffy blouse and straight skirt, struggling with her side zipper. Phil reached over to help her. She kissed his bare shoulder in thanks just before his white shirt covered it.

"I'll help you with your tie in a second," she said, while sitting on the edge of the tub to don her nylons. "You know, I think

Olivia wants this to work. So do the rest of the kids. God, I hope we're doing this right. Are we too optimistic?"

Kate stood to step into her high-heeled pumps. Phil watched her try to brush some order into her still damp, unruly curls. He leaned against the wall, buttoning his shirt and smiling at her ineffectual struggle. She caught his eyes in the mirror. "The sad part is that we don't know if anything we do as a family can actually help Olivia. Her value system and lifestyle are so messed up. Sometimes Livie just grips my hand and cries. I try to get her to talk about the future. She doesn't seem to think she'll ever have one, yet she acts hard-core and behaves aggressively as though she thinks there is something *wrong* about having normal feelings."

Phil turned Kate to him and his silent hug gave her strength, as though he was sharing his big bull body's force with her. She loved those huge shoulders and neck, his big, gentle hands...*oh those hands*. She could bury herself in that muscular, hairy chest and feel safe and warm.

As she recovered herself and reached for his tie, there was a knock on the door and Cori's voice called out, "Mom, when you finish kissing Dad, could you help me get my hair straightened? Cindi says I look like a lost cause, and Alisa says to use the iron."

"Duty calls," Kate said. "Just when I thought I could get enough hugging, hm?"

"I hope we'll never get enough," joked Phil, stropping his razor, wiping it off, and laying it carefully in the drawer. He took her hand, kissed her palm, and said, "Are you ready to go out and face six teenagers getting ready for school in a small house. I'm sure somebody is waiting for the bathroom."

In spite of Olivia's effort to reinvent herself, her fractured value system frequently caused unforeseeable confusion. The family worked hard to avoid frustration, but sometimes Olivia just seemed to see the world differently.

That afternoon after school, Kate took the four girls to a large discount store for a few items of clothing. Usually, Kate made the family's clothing, but she tried, whenever the budget would allow, letting each of the kids get something store-bought. Alisa, Cindi, and Cori each selected a new skirt, sweater, and socks, in different colors, since they all wore the same size and often mixed and swapped clothes. Olivia had the same items, but could choose a pair of colored jeans for school, rather than the skirt. Three girls were at junior high, where the dress code did not allow pants. Though they would have liked new jeans for *after* school, it wouldn't fly with Kate's budget this month.

    Cori was a tomboy who hated wearing dresses or skirts and vowed someday to do something about the old-fashioned dress code at junior high school. Alisa and Cindi didn't mind dresses at all, preferring more "girly" clothes and dressing up. Kate listened half-heartedly as the discussion raged. She smiled, thinking how many times she had fussed at having to wear a skirt to teach Physical Education when she felt like demonstrating a cartwheel instead of just *telling* the kids how to do it. It also was no fun to sit folded on the floor for an art project in a dress because teachers weren't allowed to wear slacks, either. It was an impractical policy for teachers of young students.

    . At the cashier's stand, her purchases about depleted her cash, but Olivia asked about an additional pair of jeans.

    "I only have enough cash left for groceries for the week. And, I can't afford to buy the other girls a pair to keep things even. I'd have to use household money, and I hate borrowing from Peter to pay Paul."

    "What's that?"

    "Taking cash out of one fund when you run short in another—like if we spent grocery money on clothes."

    "Oh," Olivia said, looking disappointed.

    "You really have been doing better, though, Olivia, and I appreciate your effort. Maybe next time."

    Olivia smiled. They gathered their packages and had started toward the station wagon, when Cindi said, "Wait a minute. Where did Olivia go?"

    "She was here a moment ago." Kate looked around quickly, and then saw Olivia walking toward the car carrying an enormous box with a paper sack pulled down over the top of it. They watched as she approached the car. Kate asked, "What's that?"

"A TV set, a big one, 14" screen and everythin'. Wait'll ya see it!" Olivia's face was shining. "It's a present for you guys for stickin' by me."

"But, I...I don't understand, Olivia," said Kate. "You said you had no money, even for the pants. How did you buy this?"

Olivia looked excited and proud of herself. "I just put the sack over the top and carried it down the aisle. They had stacks of 'em--lots and lots."

"But Olivia, it isn't yours to take out of the store."

Hel...I mean, heck, if they'd a wanted it, they woulda told me to stop, don'tcha think? I carried it right by 'em."

Cindi said, "You have to take it back, Livie. You can't keep that. It isn't yours."

Olivia's grin faded, and she set the box on the ground. "But I brought it as a present for you guys. Your old TV is flaky."

Kate put her hand on Olivia's shoulder. "We can't take a present like that, Livie. We know you meant well, but we can't accept it. It would be stealing for all of us."

"But you didn't take it. I did," Olivia insisted. Her anger bristled in her shoulders and emerged in her narrowing eyes.

"But we know it's stolen, Livie, so it's the same as if we did it," said Cindi. "You have to take it back."

"You 'spect me to walk back into that store carrying something I just lifted?"

"Yes," said Kate. "It's the only thing you can do.

"I never saw anything so dumb. It's already out here. They don't even miss it. What's the matter with you guys?" Olivia's hands stabbed the air with fingers rigid.

Alisa repeated, "You have to take it back, Livie."

"I'm not going back in there. What'll I tell 'em?" Hands went to her hips and her stance became wide and combative. "No."

"We'll go with you. Mom'll think of something to say, won't you, Mom?"

Kate blinked, aware that Cori was convinced she could

solve *any* problem. *I hate to disappoint you, Cori, but this one is a doozy.* She put one hand over her eyes.

"Just take it in the door and set it on the counter," said Alisa. "You got out with it, surely you can get back in with it."

But when they looked at the building a hundred feet away, a burly guard stood between them and the door.

"Where was he when you walked out? Maybe he *did* see you, Livie," said Cindi. "You'll have to go in there and tell them."

"You can do what you want with the thing, but I ain't goin' back." Olivia got into the car and slammed the door, slumping down where only the top of her head presented a target.

Kate opened the door and spoke softly. "Olivia, we'll go with you, but this is a hard lesson you have to learn. We don't take what isn't ours. The TV set has to go back."

"It was a present. You can't send back a present. You didn't send back Cleo when James gave her as a surprise present, and you didn't even want a dog."

"But James mowed lawns to *buy* Cleo for us," said Kate. "He didn't steal her from the pet shop. You need to do this, Olivia. Get out of the car. Let's get it over with."

"I won't, and you can't make me. Leave it in the parking lot for all I care." Olivia folded her arms across her chest and pouted like a three-year-old.

"You're right," said Kate. "I can't *make* you. But I don't think you want Cori, or Cindi, or Alisa to take it in and get blamed for stealing it, do you?"

"But they didn't take it out."

"Livie, the cashier will think they did."

"But I'd tell 'em it wasn't them."

"In other words," said Kate with a sigh, "you'd go back in there to tell the cashier it wasn't the other girls, but you won't go back in to tell them you did it in the first place?"

Livie clicked her tongue against her teeth, then expelled a resigned explosion of air. "Oh, all right! I'll take it back." She climbed out of the back seat, not looking at anyone. She bent to pick up the television set and started walking toward the door. The other three girls fell into step beside her. Kate closed the car door and followed behind them.

"You don't have to come," Olivia said angrily. "Nobody told you to come."

"We're just along so you won't feel lonesome," said Cori.

"I'm not lonesome. I don't need nobody. I don't need you guys." Tears were running down Olivia's cheeks as she walked.

"We're here anyway," said Cindi, as she reached out with a tissue and dabbed Olivia's eyes. "Do you need help carrying it? Are you getting tired?"

"Yeah," said Alisa, "it wouldn't do to drop it now. We'd still have to pay for it, and Kate doesn't have any money left."

"I ain't gonna drop it, and you don't need to come."

"Yes we do, Livie. You belong to us, now. We're here with you." Cori walked closer on Olivia's right, and Kate caught up with the others.

"Oh, shit...I mean shoot, that guard's lookin' right at me. He knows I took it. I'll just drop it and run."

"No, Livie," said Cindi. "Don't you dare drop it! Just hang on. It'll be all right."

As they passed, the guard grew to gargantuan proportions. He came waddling behind them, until Kate turned to ask, "Can you tell us where to return things?"

The guard looked bewildered. "Why, there's a counter just inside on the left."

"Come girls," said Kate. She led the march into the store.

Sure enough, on the left side was a yawning, middle-aged woman in the store's navy blue uniform behind a counter. Her figure had thickened over the years, and she apparently had not changed her uniform size to match. Several bulges drifted over the counter. "May I help you?" she asked.

"We're returning a TV," said Alisa.

Olivia hoisted her box onto the counter.

"What was wrong with it?" the woman asked pleasantly.

"Nothing," said Kate. "It's just that one of the girls must have thought it was paid for...I mean, she was carrying it...I mean, we're just through with it...."

"Holy shit!" Olivia exploded. " Kate, you couldn't tell a lie for nothin'." She turned to the saleslady. "I took it, okay?" Her tone was a dare.

The woman's demeanor changed to a stiff bristle. The bulges lifted from the counter. "You mean you stole it!" She pushed a button to summon the guard.

"Yeah, I stole it, but none of these guys knew."

The guard came through the door sliding on the polished tile floor as he rounded the corner. "What's the matter? Oh, it's you! I *thought* you people looked suspicious."

"The TV was a present for them. This is dumb. I already had it outside, and you didn't even miss it, and they made me bring it back."

"I'll have to take you to Juvenile Hall, lass." As Olivia narrowed her eyes and backed away, the guard added, "You ain't going to fight me over this, are you?"

"Oh, no, not to jail," Kate said, recovering her voice. "You have the TV back, and no harm was done to it. Surely, we can just forget this happened and consider the episode to be Olivia's new lesson for today?"

"Lady, that's not how it's done. This kid steals our newest, most expensive fourteen inch TV set and then calmly walks out."

"Ya didn't even miss it. What's the big deal?" Livie fumed.

"Hush, Livie." Kate turned to the guard. "Sir, you have your TV, the child has learned her lesson, and I'm going to take all my girls home now. Thank you, and good day." She could feel Olivia beside her, bristling for a fight, so she gripped her reluctant hand, pulling her along. With the other girls following after, they trooped toward the door like a row of vagrant ducklings.

"But...Ma'am...."

"That's all right, Officer. Thank you very much for your understanding."

The guard and the bulgy lady just stood there, stunned, as the family covered the distance to the door. As they walked through the parking lot, Kate could see the guard coming out to write something down. *Probably my license number*, she thought ruefully. She whisked the girls into the car. But Olivia stepped back outside.

"I ain't goin'."

"What do you mean?"

"I mean I ain't going with you. I'll hitchhike over to the One-Ways, and you won't hafta worry about me any more, ever."

"Olivia, that's ludicrous. I'm not letting you hitchhike, or to go over there. I brought you here, and I'll take you home."

"I ain't goin' home with you guys. You people don't even *think* like me, and I can't change all the stuff in my head. My other friends aren't like you. They woulda cheered for me bringin' that off--happy to see me get somethin' I wanted. And they *sure* wouldn't make me take back a present, either. Maybe I am lud...lud...whatever you said. I don't even know what you guys are sayin' half the time. I'm outta here!"

She slammed the door and strode across the parking lot.

"Mom, you've got to do something," said Cindi.

"She came to us of her own free will. I can't force her to stay." Kate put her head down on the steering wheel. *Now what do I do?* Then she started the car, looked over her shoulder to back out of her parking space and pulled around to follow Olivia.

"What are you doing, Mom?" Cori asked.

"I'm not sure, but at least I don't want her hitchhiking." They pulled up beside Olivia just as she reached the street. Kate stuck her head out the window.

"We'll give you a ride to the One-Ways, Olivia. I'd rather you not hitchhike."

"What if I don't care what you'd rather?"

"I'd still have to try to persuade you."

"Get in, Livie," said Alisa. "We look pretty silly arguing while cars line up behind us trying to get out of the parking lot."

Kate hadn't noticed she was blocking the driveway. Horns blared sporadically behind her, but her foot stayed on the brake. "Well, Livie?"

The honks grew into a chorus. "This is embarrassing,

Mom," said Cindi.

    Olivia turned and held up her hands at the honking drivers behind. Her middle finger was half way out when she apparently thought better of it and waved at them instead. "Oh, all right, I won't hitch if you take me to the One-Ways. But that's it. I ain't goin' home with you anymore."

    Alisa opened the back door. Livie got in and sat down, slamming the door. She folded her arms tightly. Kate glanced at Livie's facial expression in the rear view mirror. It would have curdled milk. No one spoke as Kate drove toward Norwalk.

    Cori broke the silence. "Livie, won't you think this over? It's Friday, and we have a game tomorrow. We need you there."

    "Nobody needs me. And I don't need nobody. I hate your silly games, and I hate you--all of you!" Olivia's voice rose to a screech. "You keep tryin' to make me change--don't say this word, say that one, don't go here, go there, don't smoke, don't cuss, don't steal, don't breathe. There isn't *anything* that's okay with you people. I try to give you a present, and you make me take it back. I have to do all the changin' and I'm sick of it. At least my One-Ways gang don't try to change me. And if I hurt all night, somebody'll give me somethin' for the pain, not just slap a hot water bottle on me."

    This outburst brought dead silence. Cori slumped down in the front seat with tears in her eyes. Her fingers worked their way around a balled up tissue.

    "Olivia," said Kate, her voice growing soft. "We aren't trying to hurt you. We're trying to help. I know it's hard." She felt tears hovering on the edges of her own lashes, as well. *Why do I have to care about this so much?*

    "But I ache all over, and I shake and sweat, and you guys won't let me go to the One-Ways and get somethin'."

    "More drugs won't help," said Kate. "You knew that when you came to us."

    "I was dumb that day. It's all too hard. I don't belong in your world, and you don't belong in mine." Olivia turned her face to the window.

Cori hung over the seat on her knees. "You don't belong in the drug world, either, Livie. Weren't you having a good time with us? You laughed a lot, and you're not laughing now."
"Oh, cut it out, Cori. I didn't mean that part. I don't hate you. I just...I can't be who you want me to be. Playin' the tambourine in your band ain't my thing. It was fun when we did it on the carnival stage, and everybody said they liked it, but we was different. You played the drums and knew you were a drum player, after. I played the tambourine and after, I just wanted to get outta there and smoke a joint."
Kate asked, "Are we pushing you too fast, Livie?"
"I don't know. I'm just so tired of tryin' all the time that I don't care no more. I just don't care 'bout nothin'."
"But, you quit all drugs cold turkey, Olivia, and it already seems like it doesn't bother you as much as it did before."
"But I still *want* it. I can't stop *wantin'* it. In the One-Ways, I fit in. At least, I did, until you guys wanted me all different and goody-goody. Now, I don't fit there, either"
Kate gripped the steering wheel, wondering how to answer.
Mercifully, Alisa ignored the statement. "Livie, you looked good playing a tambourine, and you sang 'Puff the Magic Dragon' okay, too. Why wouldn't you want to stay with the group?"
Olivia threw up her hands. "You guys don't even know that song's about drugs. You shouldn't be singin' it. You don't know nothin'. And everybody laughed when you said we were sisters, Alisa. I *feel* like a sister, but I don't *look* like any of you."
"You're just shorter, Livie, that's all," said Cori.
Olivia snorted angrily. "Cori, you're somethin' else! Open your damned eyes. I'm an Indian--all war tribes--Chiracahua, Sioux, Apache. You're all pink and blonde. Even Alisa and James have dark hair, but they have pale faces. I don't fit in your tribe."
"Are you prejudiced or something?" Cindi asked. "Why should any of us care if we're different? Cori and I may be blonde and blue-eyed, but Dad's family is Indian, too. Cherokee, isn't it Mom?"

Kate nodded. "*And* Welsh, Irish, and a squeak of French mixed in there, as well."

"So see, Livie, we're all mixed breeds, 'Heinz 57 Varieties,' like Dad always says. We're proud of the Indian we have in us. Lynette looks lighter than you do, and she's your *real* sister, so what do you care?"

"That's not it."

"Then what *is* it?" asked Alisa, impatiently. "Why can't you just stop all this stuff? Are we doing something wrong?"

"Not wrong for you, just wrong for me. We're different." Olivia looked down at her hands. "I don't fit in your band, and your softball team, and your Girl Sprouts. I don't fit no place." She tossed her short, straight, shiny black hair and jutted out her chin as though in defiance to the entire world.

"Olivia, everyone else thinks you fit in fine," Kate said. "Even the teachers have come to trust you around their little kids. You've come too far to go back now."

"Look, I can't do it, okay? Maybe when I'm readier."

"If you stop now, you'll have to go through all that withdrawal again," said Kate. "You're almost over it now, and you're doing so well. Don't throw that away." She turned off the main boulevard and into narrow streets.

Olivia looked out the window and suddenly yelled, "Stop! I don't want you guys in the One-Ways. I'll get out and walk now. You take the girls home."

Kate tightened her grip on the steering wheel and said, "No, Livie, if you think this is where you belong, we'll take you all the way to whichever house you want."

"Stop the car. Turn around," roared Olivia. "I ain't havin' the girls in there. You know I can't. Somebody'll hurt 'em, sure. They don't belong here."

"But I thought you didn't care about any of us, Olivia." Kate kept her voice even.

The other girls were wide-eyed as they drove into the first street of the One-Ways. Alisa found her voice first. "These kids look like they're mad at us. What's wrong with them? We're not doing anything, just driving on a public street."

A group stepped off the curb and jeered at the girls inside, shouting obscenities.

"You can't do this! Turn around and get the girls out of here, now, please." Olivia's face contorted and tears ran down her cheeks. "You don't know. I don't want 'em in here! They could get raped, beaten--Kate, please."

"But you said none of us matters to you, Olivia, and you're not safe in here, either." Kate held tight. "We either all go, or none of us go--your choice."

"I'll jump outta the car."

Alisa quickly rolled over the top of Olivia and held down the back door lock. "No, you won't," she said.

"This is crazy. Get off me. Lemme out."

"No, Olivia, we're all going with you," said Kate.

Olivia swiveled her head around frantically, looking behind the car as a few older kids approached. "Get out of here, now," she screamed. "Okay, okay, I'll go with you. You girls can't be in this barrio." Olivia slumped back against the seat as Kate whipped around the first corner and headed back to Norwalk Boulevard. Alisa shifted back into the middle of the seat and everyone heaved a collective sigh of relief.

"Thank you, Olivia," said Kate.

"You're welcome," came the polite answer she'd learned. But her folded arms and grudging, stoic stare told another story.

The other girls grinned and smacked Olivia on the arm. Finally, she smiled and settled back into her seat.

"Gee Mom," said Cindi, "I was afraid you were going to lose your nerve back there and let her out of the car."

"Not a chance." Kate found she could breathe normally again, once she hit the Boulevard, though her hands shook on the wheel. *I took a risk with the kids in the car!*

She was still shaking when they got to Mayberry Park, so she pulled over and turned around in her seat. "Girls, what I did was wrong, to take you to a place we didn't belong. But Olivia, when push came to shove, you couldn't let our other girls get hurt, either. I didn't think you could. That should tell you something about where you belong and where you truly want to be."

"I could just wait until you guys leave me and then hitch back over there."

"But, you won't do that, Livie," said Cindi.

Cindi sounds more confident than I feel. But Kate spoke firmly, "No, Livie, you won't do that because you know you've already gotten through the toughest part. Yes, you're still craving a bit, but if you go back now, it'll be far too hard to start over. You'll be there forever. Stick with us until you no longer have any urge to do drugs." There was silence from the back seat. "You'll need to let us know when you feel shaky or are craving. We'll make popcorn or something. The important thing is that we need to pull together. We've come to love you, and you must like us too, or you wouldn't have put the girls' safety ahead of your own craving for drugs back there. That's a big first step."

A barely audible "Okay," came from Olivia. She sat up straight and shook her finger at the three girls. "The One-Ways are no place for you. I don't ever want you in there. Understand? I'll beat the crap outta any of you that goes over there again."

Cindi coughed loudly.

"I mean…I'll beat the fire out of you all." She put her hand over her mouth.

"We know," said Cori. "We got your message. And we promise. Don't we?"

Again kneeling and leaning over the front seat, Cori reached out her hand, and the girls all piled their hands on top of hers and cheered the way they did before a game.

Kate started the car and they drove the last six blocks home. She didn't want to think about risking the other girls to save Livie. *And is Olivia right? Are we asking too much for her to fit into our world?*

Chapter 10

The next three weeks passed in a reasonably normal fashion, with Kate giving Olivia's efforts about a C plus. But she did go to the One-Ways a few times. It was hard for the family to understand why Olivia could lapse and cause everyone else such frustration and worry. Phil and Kate sometimes suffered from fatigue when Olivia would unaccountably run off from her mom's house and call in the middle of the night for someone to come get her. She was always contrite afterward, and it seemed even *she* didn't understand why she kept slipping up. "I told you I'm hopeless," she would say, crying and cursing herself. Sometimes one of the kids, or Kate, or Phil would almost feel she was right. *Almost!* But they could never feel that way long enough to stop trying.

One afternoon. Lynette called to say Livie had gotten upset about something while cleaning her mom's kitchen. "Mom woke up mad," said Lynette, "and Livie couldn't handle it. I think she was craving, too. Can you go get her before anything happens?"

When Kate and Phil drove over to find her, the One-Ways kids calmly pointed down the street and escorted Kate into the house sheltering Olivia. They had her back home in two hours, swearing that she hadn't intended to take pills, but she missed her friends and had *only* taken some LSD. Kate wondered if she'd taken money for the drug from her brother or had bartered for it, but it no longer mattered. She'd found a way. She still had the blue paper strip that had held the LSD tablets sticking out of her pocket.

Once out of the car at home, Olivia slumped to the ground, sitting cross-legged on the front lawn. Phil and Kate sat beside her and, one by one, the other kids joined them, sticking together as her LSD wore off. Olivia tried to describe what she was seeing with lazily undulating movements of her hands and slurred words that the curb was "...moving up and down in the sunshine." The others waited and listened as patiently as they could, though they could only see the normal, rigid white concrete and green grass. "I can't even count all the colors I see in the grass. It's going up and down, up and down...." Olivia's voice trailed off in rhythm with the heaving and falling of her vision. It was, according to her, "...ssoooooooooo prettyyyyyyyyyyyyy."

Soon, all the kids and the animals were flat on their backs in the grass. Susan even joined them from across the street. Imaginative Ned pointed out shapes in the clouds to Livie. Each teen told what he or she could see in the clouds. Gradually, Olivia started responding with enthusiasm, and even offered a few observations herself.

"What do you think?" asked Phil, as they went inside. "I guess the kids can handle her for awhile."

"I'm hoping this was an aberration," answered Kate. "She just couldn't handle her mom for that one moment and somehow failed." She wiped a tear from her eyes and smiled up at her husband. "I'm hoping it won't happen again."

Phil put his arm around Kate. "I hope she'll be stronger the next time. But I'm pretty sure she'll be--we'll *all* be--doing three steps forward and two steps back for awhile, until she's more sure of herself, until all cravings are gone, until scars heal. Well, old girl," he added, kissing Kate on the forehead, "we'll go neck."

Kate smiled up at him. "Rain check, Love. Hold that thought. That brood out there will be hungry when they come in. Care to help me peel potatoes?"

But Susan's mother from across the street stepped around the day-dreaming teens in the front yard and knocked on the door. Kate went to the door and let her neighbor in, Gina was angry.

"I'm not the only one mad about this, Kate, but the other neighbors are scared to come tell you to your face."

"What is it, Gina? What's the matter?"

"We don't like your bringing a drug addict into our neighborhood. It's always been a safe place where the kids could run around safely until dinnertime. We're a nice, normal picket-fence neighborhood. And here Olivia is living right inside your house most of the time."

"We've been trying to help her straighten her life out, with mixed results, but she's gradually getting better. What's your concern, Gina?"

Phil walked into the living room where the two women stood. Gina barely acknowledged his presence as she blustered on.

"Well, we don't see the improvement, and we want her out of here, or all of you out of here. You mark my words--she'll get your other kids, or our kids, into drugs too. I won't have it!"

Phil said, "Why don't you sit down, Gina. We can talk as neighbors and friends. We love our neighborhood, too. We won't move, nor do we intend to abandon any of the children who've come to us. I think you're overstating the case."

"I'm not sitting down. If you keep this girl, we're no longer neighbors and friends. I've stated my case, and I'm leaving."

"Gina," said Kate. "We've lived here over ten years, and you know we love you and Donald. Susan has grown up with our girls. We wouldn't want anything different for Susan and other kids in the neighborhood than we would for our own. If we thought there was a threat, we would be the first to say so. If Olivia is destructive with drugs, it's only herself she's destroying. She wouldn't hurt anyone else. She's actually come a long way from when she first came here."

"Not far enough, Kate. People like that don't really change. You think about it and you'll see we're right. That girl is going to get other kids on drugs, too. We want her out of here."

"Olivia promised she wouldn't ever bring drugs here, and we believe her," said Phil. "She faltered today, but she's okay now, and she'll be better for days and weeks. Gina, we're teachers. We can no more turn away Olivia, than we could turn away Susan if she came to us with a problem, or any other child in need. Livie needs a community of support, lots of people who see her as trying and improving. We need your help, not your fear."

Gina sighed and said, "I know you two mean well, but first it was James, and then Ned, and then Paula, now Olivia who is even more dangerous. You're not going to get any support from your neighbors when you take in all these problem kids. We all think Olivia should go, or you should." With that, the woman stomped out and ignored the teens coming in for dinner. "Come, Susan. We're going home," she said.

Susan shrugged at Cindi, and walked across the street with her mother.

"Has it come to the point that we must choose between our friends and the children who need our help? Kate's tears were back, as she and Phil stood by the screen door and watched their neighbor leave.

"I don't think we have a choice, love. Much as I hate to say it, our neighbors can take care of themselves—the kids can't yet. And since we cannot afford to move, we may have to get used to being shunned by our neighbors for awhile."

Olivia had reached the point of reasonable sobriety, and the house filled with hungry teens all trooping inside, followed by Goldie and Cleo.

"What was wrong with Gina?" asked Cindi.

"She thinks we should give up on Olivia if we want to keep our friends and neighbors," said Phil. "What do you think?"

Cindi said with a disgusted snort, "We don't give up that easily, do we?"

"She thinks all you kids and the neighborhood kids will follow Olivia if she fails and takes drugs," added Kate.

Cindi laughed out loud, as James came up behind her. "Livie would be the first one to kill us if we did take anything, wouldn't she, James?"

James said with a sardonic smile, "I don't think we should worry about what other people think. It only counts if it's what we think. And I don't think any of us are ready to give Olivia up. We sort of have to keep trying, don't we?"

"Well, that's the way we feel," said Phil. "But you kids have to tell us if you start thinking differently. We may lose some friends over this, but I don't think we can quit under duress."

Dinner was followed by homework and working on the latest jigsaw puzzle. Cori was champion puzzler, somehow having more spatial orientation talent than the others. She always managed to spot the "lost" piece, to the frustration of Alisa, who was always convinced it was "lost" forever.

But Olivia didn't take part. She sat on a rug on the floor, and fell asleep quite early with her arm curled around Cleo. The dog seemed to know her role and never moved a muscle until Phil picked Olivia up after the others went to bed and put her back on her chosen couch. Kate covered her with a blanket. Livie never woke, and Cleo resumed her vigil on the girl's feet.

In the morning, Alisa asked for pancakes and even Olivia was eager to try them. Kate groaned. "I've already got the laundry started. Can you kids make them for yourselves? Here's the cookbook, and you know how to follow directions."

Kate watched as Alisa and Cindi got out milk and eggs, and Olivia looked at the recipe page of the cookbook. Then she went around the corner to the small room commandeered as a library when they had bought the house. It contained wall to wall, floor to ceiling bookshelves filled to overflowing, but it also had a washer and dryer crammed into its closet. Kate sometimes mused about being probably the only household in the country that had Shakespeare and Tide in the same room. The laundry basket seemed to have a life of its own, though, with so many teens. It multiplied many times over every time Kate looked at it. As she sorted darks and lights and denims, she could hear the girls in the kitchen. She figured they would ask if they needed anything.

She heard Cori sing out, "Hey Livie, how much of this flour do we need?"

Olivia didn't answer.

"Livie? Hurry up before I drop the flour canister!"

Kate stuck her head around the corner to see what was happening.

Olivia stared at the page of Kate's old *Good Housekeeping Cookbook* that had been a wedding present, and said, "This don't make any sense. I don't want pancakes that bad! She slammed the book shut and left the kitchen. Kate captured her arm on the way through the living room. "Come on, Livie. You can help me pull sheets off the beds." They walked together to the girls' bedroom.

Kate could sense Olivia's frustration, and thought she knew what had caused it. Olivia obliged, but tugged roughly on the bed sheets nearest her, balling them up in wads. Her black eyes narrowed as they always did when she was upset or angry.

"If reading is hard for you, Olivia, we can help."

"Don't need help," Livie said sullenly. "I get along. It's no big deal." The next sheet flew angrily at the corner with the first.

"Sometimes it can get to be a big deal, though, because then other subjects seem hard, too. You've been pretending you could read at school, haven't you? That's why your teacher hasn't caught it yet, isn't it?"

Olivia didn't answer, simply whipping the next sheet off the bed.

"Would you like one of us to help you a little after the other kids go to bed?"

The girl paused, holding a sheet. "They don't hafta know?"

"Not unless you want to tell them."

"Maybe. I'll think about it."

The voice was sullen, but Kate recognized the anxiety in the tone. "We'll try it tonight, then," she said. "Our secret."

But surprisingly, at breakfast, Olivia brought it up herself.

"Sorry I got mad when you asked about pancakes, Cori. I couldn't find the word for 'flour'. I don't read so good, but Kate and Phil are gonna help me tonight."

Alisa and James said they could help too, if Livie needed extra time. Cori said, "I'm good at math, in case that spooks you, too. Cindi likes reading better."

Soon Olivia was smiling from the uncritical support offered. "Maybe I can get my grades up if I read better. I never was any good in school, and I never liked it before."

"Reading wasn't my best subject either," admitted Ned. "But Phil helped me get over the hump. Now, I like to read. You will too. I'll show you some good books, whenever you're ready."

Things went well for a few more weeks, and Olivia acted more and more like one of the family. She went home only when her mother demanded her presence. The mother didn't seem to care much where Olivia was, as long as she came home long enough to clean the house.

Kate and Phil both worked with Olivia's reading at night. It became apparent that Holly had been right. Livie was several grades behind, academically, and she could not learn easily. She struggled even with second grade books. They became reluctantly aware that Olivia might have damaged her brain cells with her variant collection of pills, marijuana, LSD, speed, and even occasional heroin. Now that she wasn't using those things, they tried to teach her with love and encouragement. Progress was slow, but it was enough that Olivia was happy with herself and more confident. Certainly no one was ready to give up on her, regardless of the silent disapproval of some of the neighbors.

Then after everyone was asleep, someone knocked at the front door. Kate mentally ticked off her brood, knowing they all were in the house. She could never sleep until the last teen came home. She padded to the door in time to hear a voice calling, "Livie. Livie, please come. Please let me in."

Olivia roused and ran bare-foot to the door. "That's Lynette," she said. "Something must have happened."

Kate opened the door. Lynette staggered in, tripping on the door's baseboard with one four-inch gold, fake alligator heel and one bare foot. She fell sobbing into Olivia's arms. Lynette wore a skirt of indiscriminate color that barely covered her derriere, a low-cut blouse now ripped off in the front with one sleeve dangling around her middle. Her hair was ratted high, as Kate had seen it before, but it was now also disheveled. Her eyes and lips were so heavily made up with smeared mascara and lipstick that Kate couldn't tell what she looked like underneath it all. Her left ear lobe was bleeding where one of her gaudy earrings had been ripped from her ear. She smelled of stale semen and wet cigarettes.

Kate said, "Here, Lynette, come sit on the couch and tell us what happened." She wrapped one of Olivia's blankets around the shivering girl's shoulders, covering her near nakedness.

"I couldn't fight the guy off, and he hurt me, bad. I'm so

scared. What'll I do?"

"Where are you hurt?" asked Kate. "We should report him to the police, so they can catch him. Do you think we should call your mom at work and get you to a hospital?"

"No, you can't call my mother, or anybody," Lynette cried. "He was so big and he jerked me around. It hurts to sit down."

Terrible thoughts went through Kate's mind. "Do you want me to take you home?"

"No. Everybody's gone, and I'm afraid to be alone. I ran away from that guy, but he knows where I live. Can I just crash here a little while and go home later?"

Phil entered, barefoot. "What's going on, ladies? I heard voices." He sat down on the round coffee table next to Kate and looked at her with inquisitive eyebrows raised.

"Phil, this is Lynette. She's Olivia's older sister, and a man hurt her. She's frightened to go home. Lynette, this is my husband, Phil. What can we do to help you? Do you need to clean up?"

Olivia sat next to her sister with her arm around her shoulders, though Lynette was a full head taller than Olivia. "Can Lynette stay here with us and you can help her get off drugs too?"

Kate sharply drew in her breath.

"I don't know where we'd put her," said Phil slowly, looking at Kate. "It could be temporary for tonight, but...what are you thinking, Lynette?"

"I'm so scared to go back. I thought I was safe to work in the One-Ways, but this big black slick was so loaded up--it must have been LSD because he was acting so weird and he kept calling me 'Louise,' and screaming that I was weaving in front of his eyes. When I thought he was too weird and ran away, he chased me and grabbed me from behind, ripped my clothes and threw me on the ground. I can't go back there. What if he finds me?" Her hysteria increased, and she turned again to Olivia's shoulder.

"Lynette," said Olivia, "If you stay here with us, you won't have to go back there, and no one could find you or hurt you here."

Phil interrupted. "Now, wait a minute, Livie. Lynette hasn't *asked* for any help to get off drugs, and she'd have to follow rules in this house she might not like. You can't be making decisions for her, *or* for us." He ran his hand over his crew cut that was now a bit too long, rumpled from sleep, and stuck up in little thistles. He looked at Kate with the unasked question in his eyes. She shrugged, and he turned back to Lynette. "You've been living a lifestyle of which we don't approve. It would mean a lot of changes for you, *and* for us, if you wanted to stay here."

"Like what?" the girl asked, blubbering into a Kleenex.

Kate looked at heavy mascara that ran down Lynette's cheeks, and stale lipstick smeared across the oversized lines around her lips. *So many changes--should we even try?* With Lynette's hair still ratted high, and with the clothing she wore, she looked for all the world like a thirty-year-old street walker on Skid Row, not a fifteen-year-old girl who should be in school. *This may be more than we can handle, but I'd hate to turn her out in the street, either. Kate* tried to answer the girl's question. "For one thing, Lynette, you're not safe running around at night. These people you're hanging out with are dangerous, or you wouldn't be here. That's one pattern that would have to change." Kate paused, wondering how to proceed. "What do *you* truly want to do?"

Lynette sat slumped in her blanket. She seemed to be weighing her words. "I've always planned to get out as soon as I could. I don't do drugs all the time, and I don't do certain kinds."

Phil said, "You mean you don't think you're addicted?"

"I smoke pot pretty often, but no heroin. I only do it so I won't have to think about…think about what I'm doing to make money to get out. Drug dealers always have a lot of money to spend." She blubbered, "It sort of goes round and round, doesn't it? I take dope so the job isn't so bad, and I do the job so I can buy the drugs. I don't know how to break out, and now I'm too scared to do the job." The girl shook her head. "I can't go back there, and I don't know where else to go to earn money."

There was a long pause during which Lynette's sobs and Olivia's soft murmurs to her sister were the only sounds. Again Phil and Kate searched each other's eyes for answers. Finally, Phil said," Lynette, even though we're pretty crowded now, as you can see, I guess you could stay here too, but only…only if you're willing to follow our rules, and that may be hard for you."

"What rules?"

"Well, cleanliness, for one. For tonight, just curl up on the other part of the sectional sofa and get some sleep. But first thing in the morning, you'll take a shower and scrape the gunk off your face. And you'll wash that sticky stuff out of your hair." Phil shook his head. "Frankly, it makes you look unkempt and…."

Kate could see he balked at the logical term, "cheap."

The girl patted the top of her disheveled hairdo and sniffled. "It only looks like that now because I've been running and some of it has come down."

"No, Lynette," he said in a slow, patient voice. "It looks like that because it has that sticky rat's nest stuff in it. It builds up and makes your hair dirty. In this house, kids keep their hair clean and natural. You can too. Next, that clothing has to go. Our girls don't run around with such short skirts that they cover nothing at all. You'll wear longer skirts and sweaters and blouses for school."

"School?"

"Yes, school." He looked to Kate for confirmation. "And, you'll have to do your best to blend in with the other girls. That means your appearance and actions need to be clean, bright, and natural, like other girls your age."

Lynette put her head in her hands. "I'm not one of those nicety-nice girls," she cried. "You probably already know that."

"You'll become one, Lynette," Phil said softly, "*if* you want this to work."

Olivia broke in. "Lynette, you won't be scared here."

Phil scratched his rumpled sideburns and turned to Kate. "Did I miss anything?"

Kate picked up from his cue. "Lynette, I'm afraid your whole pattern of living will have to change." She plunged on. "We don't allow kids to go places without permission, and they're not to stay out overnight. We don't want any men coming here looking for you. There'll be no drugs in this house. Livie knows that."

"Nobody knows I'm here, and I'm afraid of men and drugs

now, anyway."

"Okay then, no problem. We'll keep it that way. There will be no dates or going out for...I'd say about six months, until you're completely stable and confident of what you need to do to live a more comfortable, clean, and fear-free life. At the end of six months, we'll reevaluate to see if you feel ready to go out."

"Six months! That's forever. I'll be sixteen by then...."

"Yes, but sixteen is a good age to start dating. That's what we've told our girls too." Kate put her hand under the girl's chin and lifted it gently to make eye contact. "Look, Lynette. Somebody hurt you and you're scared now, but you're lucky this didn't happen sooner or turn out worse. What might he have done to you, if you hadn't been able to get away? We'll want to know you're safe. One of us will take you to school in the morning, and pick you up afterward. You'll leave this house only when the family is doing something together, and you can take part in those activities. That means some outdoor exercise daily. Most of us like a morning or evening run together."

Lynette turned up her nose and grimaced. "I'm no good at any kind of sports. It's too much trouble, and you get all sweaty."

Kate laughed. "Showers and exercise will help work those drugs out of your system like it helped Livie. Do you understand?"

"Yes, but I don't know if I can handle someone looking over my shoulder all the time. I'm not used to it. Mom is hardly ever there, so we've always done whatever we wanted."

"This will only be until you prove you're as reliable as the other kids--prove it to us, and more importantly, to yourself. You don't trust yourself right now. Am I right?"

The girl looked down at her one dangling shoe, now ruined. "I guess not. I've never been this frightened before--just sort of disgusted sometimes, but not scared."

"Then look at this as a six month rest period--just to try out another lifestyle, get healthy, and get over being disgusted with yourself. Call it a healing time. What do you think?"

Phil broke in. "Don't decide now, Lynette. Get some sleep and think about it. Olivia's just beginning to be comfortable, and we're thinking of starting over with you. But you're her sister. Maybe you can help each other. We'll talk again in the morning."

"They get up really early," said Olivia with a grin.

Lynette rolled her eyes toward the ceiling and sighed.

"You can sleep on the other piece of the sectional for now," said Kate. "We'll arrange something else should you decide you want to stay. It may be hard for you, Lynette, but it'll be a big change for us, too. We keep bumping into each other in this house as it is. We'll have to work together. I can help you make up your bed. Wouldn't you like to clean up a little first?"

Lynette wrapped her blanket more tightly and curled up. "I'm okay like this."

"All right then, we'll talk again in the morning."

Kate couldn't sleep well. She sensed Phil awake as well.

"Dawn came too early," he said, as he stretched, yawned, and rolled over to embrace his wife.

"Probably only because we have decisions this morning, and because we're losing our friends. Did you sleep much?"

"On and off...you?"

"Tossing and worrying a bit."

"Are you troubled that Lynette might decide to stay, or decide to go?"

"I'm not sure. Either way, I'll worry about it. She's had such a hard life and no guidance. I guess one more kid at this stage isn't any worse than one more last time. But perhaps it would be better to get boys. They don't need expensive bras." She laughed.

"We'll make this one the last, then. What do you think?"

"We can't handle any more. We still have the kids who come and go for a few days at a time, too, like Alli and Renee. But this is assuming Lynette even *wants* to clean up her act and stay. She seems so hard--maybe as hard as Olivia has been."

"We set her some pretty stiff standards last night. She may not even be here this morning." He laughed. "She may run."

"I know. But I refuse to have her running around at night with us wondering where she is or whom she's with. If she accepts these parameters, it'll mean she's serious. *We* have to feel comfortable about trying, too, don't we? Worrying about Olivia gives me a stomach ache already." Kate laughed, and hugged her husband. "Guess we'd better get dressed and brace ourselves in case the stork has brought us another package. Hm?"

Phil and Kate thought everyone was still asleep as they walked into the living room, but they met James emerging from the boys' added-on room.

"Another one?" he asked, gesturing at the sofa where Lynette lay sleeping. "She looks pretty hard core. Tsk, tsk, what will the neighbors say now?" He grinned on his way to the kitchen.

Kate followed him and started gathering eggs from the refrigerator to make a really big omelet for breakfast. Eggs were usually the cheapest protein item in the store, so she went through a few dozen every week.

James took out a carton of milk and glanced at Kate with a mischievous grin before taking a glass from the cupboard, pouring it full, and lifting it in a toast to Kate's returned smile. When he had first come to them as a scrappy ten-year-old, one bone of contention was that he thought it was okay to drink right out of the carton. He had learned, though, and now it was a running joke between them. He scarfed down the glass of milk. "Gotta go. I've got an early class this morning and work after."

"Will you be home for dinner? We're having spaghetti tonight."

"Now, would I ever miss any of your spaghetti? I've never seen anybody feed so many people with a quarter pound of hamburger in the sauce."

"It's all those finely chopped veggies I put in it. You kids eat a ton of it, and it's better for both you and the grocery bill if it's more vegetarian than carnivorous."

James grinned again. "You're a miracle worker, you know. Do you remember--that's the first meal I ever had in this house?"

Kate smiled at the eldest of their brood. James had been the first of the "bonus" children who had come to them when he was ten and their own girls were only six and seven. Actually, he had followed Kate home. Kids at Sunnyside were always asking her, "Are you James's mother? You sure look like him. He's always in trouble." Kate had no idea who this trouble-making James might be until one day there was a fight while she was on yard duty, and she found two small-for-their-age fifth graders from another class rolling in the dirt, slugging it out. She hoisted them from the ground, and ordered twenty-five pushups, and benched them until they could talk. This day, it didn't work well, as one boy, with a scraggly mop of black hair and freckles sprinkled over his nose, kept getting back up and scrapping with the blond boy all over again. He got up to sixty pushups before he finally was tired enough to quit hitting.

She looked into the face of this boy and felt she was looking in a mirror. *This must be James. Maybe the kid was trying to prove something. A Napoleonic complex about being small, perhaps*?

But James followed her home the next three days in a row. On the third day, he pulled his bike over and sat on the curb in front of the house. Kate got out of her car and asked him if she could help him with anything. He said he was just resting.

When her little girls, Cindi and Cori, came home, they talked with him at the curb, and then came into the house. "Who's that big boy out on the curb?" Cori asked.

Kate laughed to think that small James could seem like a *big* boy to Cori, and answered, "His name is James, but I don't know why he's out there."

"I asked if he wanted to come in and play," said Cori, "and he said he was just resting. He's sure resting a long time. And he has freckles like you." Cori giggled over her mother's freckles since she was lucky enough not to have any. Kate remembered once, as a five-year-old, trying to grind them off with wet sand, but it hadn't worked. "Yes, he has freckles like me, and like Cindi."

The girls set out knives and forks while Kate fixed dinner. Phil arrived, and Cindi, looking out the window said, "Now, Daddy's talking to that James boy. Come see."

Kate walked to the living room door and peered out

through the screen. Her husband sat on the curb with James as they fiddled with something on the bicycle. Soon, they got a wrench and went back to the curb to work on the bike.

"Dinner's on in about five minutes, Honey," she called out. Phil waved to show he'd heard. But she stayed at the screen, fascinated that her husband and this strange, scrappy, pint-sized little boy hovered over the bike as though it were a pot of gold. They wheeled the bike up to the front door.

" Kate," Phil said. "I invited James to have dinner with us. We just fixed his bike."

"Fine. He can call his mother and tell her he's here."

"She don't care where I eat," said the little boy.

"Well, call her anyway," said Kate. "She needs to know where you are."

James dialed from their phone on the kitchen wall, spoke briefly, then said, "Told you she didn't care."

Kate set an extra plate on the table and served spaghetti, her favorite old recipe.

Friday nights they usually went to the drive-in movie where the cost was only one dollar per carload. When the boy made no attempt to leave, Kate asked if he'd like to go to the movies with them. With his affirmative nod, she again told him to call his mother for permission.

Again, he said, "She won't care." He called. She didn't.

They returned from the movie with Cori asleep. Phil carried her in to bed, and still James made no move to leave. "Let me take you home now," Phil suggested.

"Do I have to go home?"

Phil and Kate looked at each other, puzzled. *Was the child lonely? Scared? What?*

"Do you want to stay overnight and go to the game with us tomorrow? When there was no answer but an eager grin, Kate said for the third time, "Call your mother."

"She don't...."

"I know, but call her anyway."

His mother didn't care, and over the next week his clothes

seemed miraculously to find their way to the Johnson house. He and the girls shared their swimming lessons and sports activities, and Phil brought home a second-hand bunk bed that James helped him sand and paint. While it stood in the living room, Phil closed in the back porch to make a combination bedroom/dining/TV room, saying, "We sort of needed the extra space anyway." Phil plastered the walls with James mimicking his every move.

While no one could remember exactly why this lonely little boy had become a member of the family, Cori summed it up best when she introduced him to a neighbor as her brand new big brother. "He followed Mom home and we just kept him." James had made no attempt to disagree with her statement.

Now, Kate smiled up at this strapping six-foot, handsome young man with his seventeenth birthday just around the corner...the one who had followed her home and who still loved her spaghetti. If he ever had issues about no one caring if he left home, they never again surfaced. *What would we do without him now? He's so much a part of us.* James hugged her goodbye.

He was still smiling when he walked back through the living room, almost colliding with Lynette.

"Pardon me," he said, as he looked at the freaky-looking girl wrapped in a dragging blanket. "I'm James."

"I'm Lynette. Sorry, I look a mess."

"No problem, I'm leaving. We're having my favorite spaghetti for dinner tonight."

"I love Spysgetti. But I don't know if I'll be here then."

"Not in that get-up, you won't." James smiled, shook his head and mumbled, "Gotta go."

Lynette limped to the archway followed by Olivia, just as Phil arrived. He kissed Kate on the back of her neck as she scrambled eggs, and turned to face Lynette.

"Well, young lady, I hope you slept well. What have you decided?"

Lynette leaned against the side of the archway and said very softly, "I think I'd like to stay awhile, if you don't mind. Are you sure I have to do all those things?"

"Yep," said Phil. He waited. One could almost *see* the wheels turning inside Lynette's head. Kate held her breath in the momentary silence.

"Okay, I'll try it your way, for a while."

"Doesn't work that way, Lynette. It's not just for a while. It's yes or no."

"Okay. Yes. What do I do now?"

"That part's easy, said Phil. "First, you get cleaned up. Get yourself showered, and we'll see what we have to work with."

"Shampoo, soap, and an extra toothbrush are in the bathroom--the new one in the top drawer wrapped in cellophane," said Kate.

Lynette grimaced. "But, my hair--if I wash it, I'll never get it back up again."

Phil smiled. "I think that's what we're hoping for, Lynette. There's a new hairbrush under the sink, again in cellophane. We always keep extras for overnight guests. Just brush your hair all out and we'll see how you look."

"I'll help you, Lynette," volunteered Olivia. "I know where everything is."

"Lynette," Phil said, "you're a year older, but about the same size as Alisa and Cindi. They can lend you some clothes and tennis shoes. You can't run in those big heels you had on last night, or rather, in one of them."

"But…."

"No buts, Lynette. After you get cleaned up, we'll have breakfast."

"I never eat breakfast."

"Your choice, but lunch isn't until noon."

"I can go down to 7-11 and get something later."

"No, actually you can't. You'll be with the family, and we'll run this morning and go to the ball game after breakfast."

"Oh, shit! I can't--what have I gotten into?"

"Oh, shoot," corrected Olivia.

Chapter 11

When Lynette emerged from her scrub down after two hours jammed in the house's one tiny bathroom with the other girls, the remainder of the crew gasped in surprise.

A lovely, fifteen-year-old girl stood before them with glorious blue-black hair curling loosely to her waist, olive skin, and eyes that certainly had no need of fake eyelashes or mascara. The girls had chosen a white wool skirt Kate had originally made for Cindi, and a pink angora sweater belonging to Alisa. Cori had contributed her scarf at the neckline to accent the ensemble. Olivia stood barefoot, as she had given Lynette her sandals to replace the one torn high-heeled shoe.

"Why, Lynette, you're beautiful!" said Phil.

"Wow," said Ned. "Who would have known you were hiding all that under that frazzled hair and sloppy mascara?"

Lynette winced. "Was it really...." she fell silent.

"I did her hair," interrupted Alisa, proudly.

"I chose her clothes," said Cindi.

"We got her makeup off..." Cori began.

"...with what I found under the sink," finished Olivia.

Phil gasped. "What was it?"

Lynette rubbed her cheeks. "It said 'Boraxo' on the can."

Ned sputtered with laughter. "That's what we use on our hands when we work on the car. You don't put that on your face."

"Well, it worked, didn't it?" Olivia boasted.

Cori steered Lynette in front of the full-length mirror, while Cindi dropped each piece of old, sexy clothing dramatically into a trash basket between thumb and forefinger.

Lynette's eyes widened as she saw her reflection. She turned slowly, looking over her shoulder at Alisa's work on her hair, and at her body in the classic shape of an A-line skirt.

Ned emitted a long wolf-whistle. Kate grinned and nudged him with her elbow. "Watch it, kid," she said.

He grinned back. "You have to admit she turned out pretty spectacular for a …." Again, Kate nudged him, and he covered his mouth with his hand.

Lynette turned to Ned. "You know, you're right. I did look really bad. And I was doing things really mixed up, too. But I want to do better now." She turned back around to the mirror. "I can't believe *that* girl is really me."

"Oh, it's you, all right," said Cori. "Wait 'til Mom sees the drain with your black mascara and phony eyelashes in it. They looked like something alive wriggling down."

"No problem," Phil said. I have a twenty foot snake in case they plugged the plumbing." The vision evoked laughter.

Lynette turned to Kate. "Do you think it's too late for me?"

Kate wondered about that, too. *Is it this easy to change a young girl's life, or will this turn out to be purely superficial? But, Lynette must have hope, or everything is for nothing.* Kate spoke slowly, somewhat in awe of the transformation herself. "I see a lovely young woman in front of me with unlimited opportunities to remake her life any way she chooses. We've seen two girls named Lynette this morning. It's up to you to decide which one you'll live with for the rest of your life."

Lynette looked back into the mirror. Then, she said with a quiet smile, "I'm a little scared right now—this is so different. But I think I like *this* one."

Kate put an arm around the girl. "Then welcome to the family."

Applause from all in the room made Lynette blush.

Both rules and transportation arrangements turned out to be scratchy at first, since they made a hectic time schedule for everyone. Because part of the agreement was that Lynette could not be alone, Kate had to adjust her schedule to pick her up, or have Phil or James do so. Olivia usually stayed near Kate, and Kate dropped the two girls off at their mom's house to do their mandatory housework, while she drove back the three blocks to her own classroom to do lesson plans for the next day and correct papers. Then, she picked the girls up in about an hour, when she went home to fix dinner. If anyone else had a medical appointment or other event, someone had to pick up the slack. It wasn't easy, but after a few preliminary miscues, they established the pattern.

Though Olivia wasn't yet *completely* dependable, meaning someone usually had to be with her, too, Lynette made no attempt to steal away from the family, always waiting in the agreed-upon spot for Kate. Lynette didn't seem to have near the flashbacks, cravings, or withdrawal symptoms that Olivia had, either, so Kate realized she had, indeed, held herself aloof from actual addiction. During ensuing weeks, Lynette made giant strides in school, in her language, and in her everyday behavior. She didn't seem to mind the restriction that she could only go out with the family. Their schedule was full of activities, and Lynette learned to fit in.

It was almost as though Lynette had been waiting for the right moment to start afresh, and the right opportunity to do a changeover inside herself. Kate quickly lost the fear that Lynette's sudden change was superficial, or just *too* easy. The girl seemed genuinely eager to learn the proper way to conduct her life.

On Wednesdays after school, Lynette played volleyball with Kate and her colleagues, something the teachers had done for several years. Olivia preferred to stay in Kate's classroom for that hour and help correct papers for either Kate or Holly.

However, even when Livie *wanted* to help, she couldn't correct papers unless she was given a clear-cut key to follow with specific instructions. Phil still had her reading every night, but anything requiring independent thinking was impossible for the girl. In talking this over with Holly, they agreed that though Olivia might have been low average in ability to start with, her long-term exposure to drugs might have "scrambled her brain cells," as Lynette had put it. So Kate gave specific instructions on how to grade math papers, while Holly spent several evenings in the library trying to find information on how to handle brain damage caused by drugs. Did such a thing exist? Once again, the teachers were frustrated by lack of knowledge and research on the topic.

The teachers' lunchroom was still a daily forum, and

several teachers took an interest in trying to find more information. Fred visited the local police station to ask for "information" on what services were available for young drug addicts, while Andrea Torneo, a fourth grade teacher, tried to talk to her doctor about treatment options and withdrawal. Most results were quite limited, but they discussed them at length.

"Why isn't there a social program for rehabilitation and some kind of protection for a kid that's physically abused?" Marcia was frustrated with her visit to the Social Welfare Office. "Their biggest concern was whether or not the family was getting their welfare check on time, as though money was the *only* problem."

"Well, at least they didn't surreptitiously glance at *your* arms for needle marks like my doctor did," said Andrea. She laughed as she described her doctor's sudden switch in attitude and questioning style, when she had asked about drug rehab programs.

"I didn't know you were going outside the building to ask questions," said Mr. Marken, the principal, as he walked through the lunchroom with a cup of coffee. "We need to keep this in-house, don't you think?"

"Sir, we need help," said Fred firmly. He turned again to Andrea and the other teachers. "It was the same for me at the police station. I'm sure they thought it was me with the 'hypothetical drug addiction' since I wouldn't name names. We need rehabilitation programs for children. We may have to lobby the governor. It will probably come too late for Livie, but maybe it'll help the next kid. I'll write him and see if there is anything he or the California legislature can do. They probably don't realize there could be a problem in this early age group."

"*We* certainly didn't!" Holly said, shaking her head.

The principal remained standing with his coffee, but offered no more comments.

"What if we asked our school district superintendent to find some training for us?" asked Kate. "We should be able to recognize the signs of drug use in our students, and know whom to call, or what to do. I hate flying blind like this."

"I have to call him this afternoon on another matter, so I'll tell him how lost we feel," said Andrea. "He can set up an in-service program. He's a good egg. She lowered her voice in stern imitation. He's the one that always says, "I hire the best teachers I can find and then leave them free to teach."

Everyone laughed, recognizing Dr. Whitson's favorite phrase. "That kind of academic freedom helps us do whatever our kids need," said Fred. "I think he'll want to make it easier for us teachers on this problem, too. He supports us on everything else."

Kate felt a little better, knowing she wasn't alone in trying to find answers. Settling on a course of action to involve the district and the lawmakers lifted her spirits. It was good to know she still had the support of her colleagues, even though her neighbors had deserted her.

Mr. Marken didn't agree. "District will think we can't handle our own problems and skin our own skunks," he protested.

"With something like drugs, we can't," said Holly, matter-of-factly, as the teachers gathered up their things to go back to their classrooms. They left the principal muttering to himself.

Though the situation in the Johnson house certainly wasn't easy, the logistics of it flowed more smoothly as the weeks passed. Then Kate found her husband sitting on the floor by the bathroom door one morning, with his straight razor in his hand and only one side of his face shaved. The girls, one by one, breezed into and out of the bathroom, using the mirror for putting on their lipstick and brushing their hair.

"Thanks, Dad," said Cindi as she stepped over his feet. "We're in a rush this morning."

"*Every* morning," Phil grumbled, "Ah, the challenge of living in a one-bathroom house with five teen-aged girls," he said philosophically with a sigh. "I'm in the middle of a train wreck."

Phil was late getting home that night—something that never happened. Everyone watched as he arrived carrying a stack of flat boxes up to his chin, disappeared into the girls' bedroom, and made lots of hammering and banging noises.

"What's he doing in there?" asked Alisa.

All speculated, but no one in the Johnson house ventured

into a room if a door was closed. It was an unwritten understanding to allow a measure of privacy. They couldn't peek.

Finally, Phil emerged, with his hammer in his hand. "From now on," he announced firmly, "the bathroom is only to be used for its specific purpose or our usual three-minute showers. All lipstick and hair-do things," he swirled his hand loosely around his head with a "you know what I mean, are to be done in your bedroom." He strode into the dining room and sat down for dinner.

The girls couldn't stand the suspense and rushed into the bedroom to have a look. Ripples of laughter could be heard into the dining room, and they came back still smiling.

"I guess Dad got tired of us taking up his shaving time," said Cindi. "We now have five mirrors along the wall of our bedroom." It's great! Just like a back-stage dressing room." She bent to kiss him on the cheek as she slid into her seat at the table.

Phil shrugged sheepishly, as the rest of the family giggled. "Well, Ned, James, and I *are* outnumbered, you know."

Though Olivia had overcome withdrawal symptoms, she still woke with occasional nightmares. Kate still got up with her.

"I feel shaky sometimes, and I miss my old friends," Olivia confided one night. "This'll sound dumb to you, but I miss havin' a boyfriend, you know, to have sex."

Kate's usual talk about a nice girl waiting for marriage was already too late for Lynette and Olivia. Instead, trying to keep condemnation out of her voice, she said that perhaps such interest would diminish with time.

"Do you think so?" asked Olivia, matter-of-factly. "I just feel horny *all* the time."

Kate tried not to flinch. "You can stay busy enough not to think about it. You'll be happier in the long run, if you can grow up and wait for someone to truly love you. You need someone who'll take responsibility and make a life for you, rather than just take advantage of your body while you're knocked out on drugs."

"But it isn't just for *them*. I like it too. And how else can you thank someone for buyin' you a hamburger or somethin'?"

Kate tried hard not to groan or cross her eyes. *Now, how do I answer that? A hamburger, for goodness sake!*

"You like it too. Phil keeps his arm around you all the time, and I'll bet..." Olivia grinned mischievously, "...you two are goin' at it whenever us kids aren't underfoot."

"That's different, and it's private."

"I knew you'd say it was 'different,' but I don't think so."

"Well, it *is* different, Livie. Phil loves me and makes a life for all of us, and he takes responsibility for all of our well-being. Marriage is a partnership where both sides contribute, and neither party 'pays.' Our love for each other is freely given. He doesn't expect me to 'pay him back' for his putting food on the table."

Olivia looked thoughtful for a moment. "Do you mean that I'll find someone I love enough, and he'll love me enough, that we'll do it for free?"

Oh, Lord! Sometimes it feels like Livie is from another planet. Kate paused to take a deep breath and think. "That's one way of putting it. Now that you're beginning to gain control of your own life, Olivia--stopping drugs, making better choices, and not hanging out with addicts, you can be proud of yourself. Your life will be easier, and you'll feel more confident. When you respect yourself as an individual, and you get older, you'll find someone who'll be proud of you and respect you, too. You deserve a good life, Livie. That's what you should choose for yourself. And *no one, ever*, has the right to control your body because they buy you a hamburger or anything else. You're the only one who owns your body and your reputation. No one else can take that self-respect from you, if you guard it well. Do you understand?"

"I guess so. You want me to keep busy and try to forget about sex until I get older and find someone like Phil who'd be good to me."

"That's what I hope for all our girls, Livie." She hugged the girl. "Now, get some sleep and let me get some, too. Good night."

"Night, Kate...and thanks for being here."

Kate climbed into bed and into her husband's arms. "I don't even know where to begin on this one," she whispered.

A couple of months later, when the family had felt particularly good about Olivia's progress, and Lynette seemed as comfortable in the house as Alisa, Cindi, Cori and the boys, someone pounded on their front door at three in the morning. Phil went to the door, and Kate quickly joined him when she heard Olivia's mother screaming obscenities. Mrs. Gonzaga barged past Kate and Phil, staggering and almost falling. Phil caught her before she hit the floor. But when he lifted her to her feet, her hair straggling over her face and smelling of alcohol, she savagely pushed him away and began screaming again. "Livie, where are you? You get yourself out here right now."
    Kate said, "Shh, the children are sleeping. Please calm down." But the woman stumbled right into the small hallway leading to the couple's bedroom, the bath between, and the girls' bedroom. With no one in the front bedroom, she hurled herself from wall to wall past the bath and slung open the girls' door.
    Cori immediately jumped up, startled.
    Phil followed into the room. "See here, Mrs. Gonzaga, we can't have you waking the kids. What is it you want?" Phil grasped her arm to turn her back into the hall, but she jerked free.
    "My baby. I want my baby back. You can't keep my baby. Livie, Livie," the woman screamed. She stumbled against the new bunk bed Phil and the boys had bought at the swap meet and refinished. Lynette slept on the bunk above and Olivia was below. Cori had chosen the bottom of the older bunk bed, leaving the top for Renee or Alli, or other sleepover friends. Alisa and Cindi had opted for two army cots Ned put up for them in the laundry room/library. They folded them away during the day.
    Mrs. Gonzaga continued screaming for "her baby." Soon the whole household stood in the hall or bedroom in a colorful assortment of pajamas, yawning and grumbling at the intrusion. Goldie found a safe perch on the top bunk. Cleo couldn't bark, so she didn't add to the din, but she rushed anxiously from person to person, licking hands and pulling on pajamas in an apparent attempt at rescue from this crazy intruder. She added to the confusion and frenetic activity.

Lynette roused from the top bunk, quickly slid down the ladder at its foot and said, "Mama, what are you doing here? If you needed us, you should have called."

"You're not my daughter anymore," the mother said sullenly, pushing the girl away. The motion upset Mrs. Gonzaga's equilibrium, and Cori yelped as the woman stumbled into her bed, knocking over her four-foot, stuffed green dog and breaking a music box that stood on the nightstand.

"I came for my baby," Mrs. Gonzaga said, loudly, "and you ain't stoppin' me."

Livie woke from the ruckus, too, or perhaps she'd only pretended to be asleep, hiding. She peeked out, saw her mother, and pulled the covers over her head.

Mrs. Gonzaga staggered to the lower bunk, stuck her hand under the covers and grabbed Olivia by the hair. "Get out of there, you pig," she shouted. "You're coming home with me right now."

Olivia screeched, "No, Mama, no...."

"Here, Mrs. Gonzaga, please stop," said Kate, struggling to maintain a reasonable tone while trying to pry the woman's grip from Livie's hair. "Let Livie and the other children sleep now, and we'll bring her over in the morning."

"Get away from me," screamed the woman. Olivia's squeals of pain as her mother dragged her from bed joined the chaotic noise level.

"No, please, don't do that to her, " cried Kate.

Phil moved Kate gently aside and took the woman by the shoulder, even as she stumbled again. Olivia's head hit the floor with a resounding thud. The woman immediately swung at Phil's head with one hand, reaching to grab Olivia's hair again with the other. "You shit-heads can't have my baby. I'll kill her first."

"Mama, please, stop," cried Lynette.

"Get away from me, you slut! You don't tell me what to do." She jerked her arm out of Phil's grasp and backhanded Lynette across the face. The girl fell to the floor.

"No!" screamed Alisa, holding her hands over her ears in the hall. As the bedlam persisted, Kate knew Alisa had lived in an abusive household once, and this horrible scene must be bringing back bad memories. James put his arm protectively around Alisa. Cleo ran between Phil's feet to get to Lynette, stood in front of her and bared her whole long muzzle of teeth at Mrs. Gonzaga, while Ned quickly helped Lynette to her feet.

"Phil, can I do anything?" James yelled above the fray.

"I don't know," shouted Phil. "She's gone crazy." To the incoherent woman, he spoke more quietly. "Ma'am, you can't come into our home and create panic like this. Look around you. The kids are crying, Olivia's hurt, and you've been drinking. I can't believe you drove here without hitting something. Why don't you have a cup of tea and calm down, and let the kids get back to bed." He again turned the woman away from Olivia.

Mrs. Gonzaga screeched, "God damn you to Hell," and swung her free arm at Phil's head.

He ducked, but grabbed her wrist to hold it away. "This is completely out of line. You will not come into my house and use profanity or violence."

"They've all left me, Betsy, Gail, Rita, Carol, Denise, George and Lynette. Lynette isn't even the same girl after what you've done to her. You can't have Olivia, too. She's my baby." She continued incoherent muttering, jerking Livie from the floor, again by her hair. Olivia had been letting her hair grow out. It looked more feminine on her, but now, Kate thought it a mistake.

Cleo frantically jumped at the woman. Mrs. Gonzaga kicked the dog away.

Olivia cried out, begging, "Don't let her take me, please...please! Mama, don't make me go back there...please."

Cori said, "Please Ma'am, Mrs. Gonzaga. Livie's doing so well with us, and she wants to stay. Please don't take her away."

The woman drew back her hand as though to strike Cori, but apparently thought better of it when she noticed Cleo's "smile" of bared teeth. She aimed at Olivia, instead, but Cleo moved to Olivia. Phil grabbed Mrs. Gonzaga's hand and said, "Madame, you will *not* hit these children in our house. You are to get out, *now*." With that, he turned the woman around and began steering her toward the door of the bedroom.

She bit his forearm and wrenched free, rushed back to Olivia and again grabbed her by the hair. "Come on, Baby. I'm not leaving you here."

"You mustn't take her--not like *this*," cried Kate. Even while trying to calm this insane woman, Kate could hear her own voice edge several octaves higher with anxiety. It was a mob scene in her own home with all the kids yelling and crying, and trying to help Livie. "Please let her go," Kate cried, reaching out to the girl, tears running down her face. "Please, you can't take her like this, not with violence."

Olivia grabbed at Kate's bathrobe, begging, "Don't let her take me! Can you call the police or somethin'?"

Cindi was already running from the room.

Kate struggled to hang on to Livie's hands, but her mother dragged them apart. *If I keep hanging on, this woman will tear her in two.* She reluctantly let go.

The woman slurred her words with drunken laughter. "The police? That's rich. You never wanted police seeing what you did before. These shitty people have no right to keep you. I already called the police and assed...axed...asked. *I'm* your mother, and you have to do as I say and go where I say. Your silly police already said so."

"Is that true?" Lynette looked helplessly at Phil. "Isn't there any way to stop this?" The girl was shivering.

Mrs. Gonzaga dragged a struggling Olivia toward the door with hands reaching to stop her, only to have Livie yanked away. Phil and Kate tried to reason with the woman, while Livie kicked and screamed, almost outdoing her mother's shrieks.

"At least, let go of her," said Phil again. "This doesn't need to be a tug-of-war with her hair. The child can walk by herself."

But as soon as Olivia got her hair free, she ran to Kate, and her mother grabbed her by the hair again.

"Shit—see what you've done to her? Now, she'll run away from her own mother. You've taken my baby. You're ruining her."

Kate could see that any effort they made to stop this scene

of madness would make it even worse for Livie. She quietly spoke to the child. "Livie, we'll try to help tomorrow. But we don't want to hurt her or let her hurt you any more now. Maybe she'll be more reasonable in the morning. Do you understand?"

"Stop talking to my girl like I'm not even here. She's not going to liss...listen to you anymore. I'll see to it!" She literally spat out the words.

Ned moved back perceptibly and wiped her spittle from his face with disgust.

Cindi came running back from the phone, crying. Kate read the answer in Cindi's face immediately. She announced, "The police said we couldn't do anything to stop her from taking Olivia, if the woman was her own mother. He said we didn't have any rights at all." She fell into Kate's arms, sobbing.

"See! Didn't I tell you?" Mrs. Gonzaga pulled the sobbing Olivia to the front door. The girl cried openly, while the whole group gathered around her. Cleo stood on her hind legs, leaning her long body against Olivia's to lick her hand.

Mrs. Gonzaga shook her finger in Kate's face. "You don't have any rights at all. She's my kid...mine!"

"Mrs. Gonzaga please," said Phil. "Calm down so we can talk rationally. No one's trying to take your baby. We can work something out." He rubbed his bitten and bleeding arm.

"No fucking way! Livie's coming with me. Damned if you'll ever see her again."

"At least, let me drive you home," Phil persisted. "You're in no shape to drive."

Mrs. Gonzaga said with a note of triumph, "Doesn't matter--borrowed car." She charged out of the house, dragging the girl by her shirt, upsetting the flowerpots on the porch. They heard Olivia sobbing all the way to the car, "Please, Mama, please...."

Doors slammed and the car roared away, narrowly missing James's van as Mrs. Gonzaga dropped over the curb and rammed the garbage can.

Silence replaced mayhem as realization set in. They were helpless against a law that couldn't, or wouldn't, help Olivia.

Kate buried her face in Phil's neck as Cindi leaned against his side. Alisa sobbed against James's shoulder. Cleo paced the floor, her claws clicking on the tile, back and forth in front of the door. Scaredy-cat Goldie still hid.

Lynette angrily blamed herself for everything. "Why didn't we fight her? Cleo should have bitten her. You could have hit her, Phil. I should've gone with her. Maybe I could've protected Livie or fought Mom off. But Mom didn't want me, just Livie."

James said, "I suppose we could have all piled on to give Livie a chance to get away, but where could she go? Nothing you could have done would have changed the outcome."

Phil said quietly, "Lynette, your mother isn't able to listen to reason right now, and hitting others is not the way we do things. Had any of us resorted to violence, we could only have made her even more out of control and made things worse for Livie. Maybe we can try to talk to her in the morning after she's calmed down."

"Mama thinks I don't love her any more because I came here," said Lynette, her chin quivering. "Did I do wrong in trying to save myself? Was I being selfish?"

Immediately, everyone rallied around the teen. "No matter what happens with Livie," said Phil, "you have to keep trying for yourself. You can't go back to where you were before. You're a different person now."

"Isn't there anyone we can call, like the police, or the hospital, or welfare, or *somebody*?" asked James. If her mom kept pulling her by the hair like that in front of us, I can just imagine what she'll do to Olivia once she has her alone."

Phil said to the anxious young man, "There's nothing they can do to help now, maybe someday. We need another way."

Cori and Ned had climbed to their semi-secret perch for comfort, up the walls to the opening into the attic where they sat together with their feet dangling down into the hall. Kate could hear them above her, both blubbering about why they hadn't found a way to keep Mrs. Gonzaga from taking Livie away.

"Okay, gang," Kate said, amid all the moaning and self-recriminations. "There's nothing we can do for now. We tried to reason with her, but she would only have hurt Livie more, had we continued. She was in no condition to listen, and the police couldn't help. So, for now, let's just calm down. I'll bandage Phil's arm while Cindi and James start breakfast. It's still early, but we're all wide-awake, anyway. We can put our heads together around the table and think of how we can help Livie later today."

The disruption within the household was a palpable thing, and it almost seemed a relief to have a decision made and have something to do besides cry. One by one the kids drifted into the kitchen and dining room, setting the table or fixing toast or scrambling eggs. Cori and Ned were the last to arrive, after closing up the attic opening and sliding down the door jam. By the time the family was seated around the table, early even for the normally early-rising Johnsons, the kids and adults were a little calmer, though still torn over such trauma happening in their home and worried about what would happen to Olivia.

Cori asked, "Could we drive by after school today? Maybe we can catch Livie outside and see if she's okay."

Kate sighed tiredly, shaking her head. "I've been told by every agency I've called that anything that happens in the home is a family matter, and the school is to 'butt out.' I'm not sure where we could go to get help."

"But this happened here in *our* home," said Cindi. "Doesn't that make it different, like breaking and entering? I should have thought of telling the police she intended to drive drunk."

"You did your best, Cindi," said Phil. "They told you we have no rights if Livie is with her mother. We can't get Livie back, not by force, and not by law. It only worked so far because her mom didn't seem to want her, anyway. Now, she says she does. The law can't help us."

"I'm to blame," Lynette said. "I'm the one she should be hitting, but Livie gets it most." She looked into Kate's eyes. "You know, Livie won't last three days alone with Mom. And Mom will be tired of her by that time, too."

"You mean this has happened before?" Kate's tears were not far from the surface, every time she thought of the ugly scene in their home. "This was such an invasion."

"Sure. Whenever Mom gets drunk, she wants us around, especially Livie, 'her baby,' but all the rest of the time, she says she doesn't want us and doesn't know why she had us 'good-for-nothings.'" Lynette looked down at her hands, as though trying to decide if she should continue. "Livie gets it harder, I think...no, I'm *sure*, because she had a different father. My dad died way before Olivia was born, and she looks darker and different from the rest of us. No one has a pregnancy that lasts eleven months. I didn't understand that when we were little, but now, I think mom secretly hates Livie."

There was silence while the family took in this bit of news.

"Then why does she want Livie back?" asked Cindi.

"I don't know," said Lynette, pushing away her plate of scrambled eggs. Tears ran down her cheeks. "But I don't think Mom's getting pregnant was Livie's fault. She shouldn't be punished forever."

Kate patted Lynette's hand and struggled for some logical explanation. "It's hard to say what motivates your mother. Perhaps it's guilt or revenge, or recrimination."

"What do you think will happen next, Lynette?" Phil waited quietly for the girl to regain composure to answer.

"Same as usual. After about three days, Livie will get sick of it, or scared, or Mom will really hurt her bad, and she'll take off."

"Will she come here, now that she knows she has some place to go?" asked Cori.

"She'd better not! Mom knows where to find her now, so she can't come back here until things quiet down again."

"But...." Cindi's chin was quivering too much to get the words out. "But, she's got no place else to go except back--back to the One-Ways."

Chapter 12

Four worry-filled days went by until the phone rang. Ned, being closest to the kitchen, answered it, listened for a moment, and then turned to Kate. "It's for you. Some girl who talks sort of like Olivia." As Kate ran to the phone he added, "But it isn't her."

Kate took the phone and said, "This is Kate Johnson. Who is this, please?"

"I still had your phone number from when you gave it to me--you know, in case I needed help."

"Bettina, is that you?"

"Yes. It's me. I just wanted you to know that Livie is here in the One-Ways and she's real bad. She said somethin' about not lettin' her mother find her, but she's real bad, and I'm afraid she'll die, if *somebody* doesn't come." The girl was crying.

"Thank you for letting us know, Bettina. We'll be right there. Can you keep her with you for about twenty minutes until Phil and I can get there?"

"I'll try, but she's real bad, and I couldn't keep the guys away from her. My old man hit me and said I had to git home and stay there. She was tryin' to run away when I saw her last time, but she's so loaded, she kept passin' out. I don't think...."

"We're coming right now, Bettina. Just protect yourself, and we'll come get Livie. Thank you for having the courage to call. You're a good girl, Bettina. Thank you."

Phil was already grabbing jackets and car keys, instructing James to use his judgment for anything the other kids needed. James nodded, and held the door open as Kate and Phil ran out.

The kids in the One-Ways quickly passed the word that 'the teachers' were there to find Livie, and several simply pointed down one street and then a new group pointed to the next. Phil and Kate didn't see Bettina anywhere. Kate worried that perhaps her "old man" had, indeed, made her "git" home. *What a life these kids lead...it's heartbreaking. How can they ever break the cycle? All these babies they're having will grow up the same way.*

Olivia was, indeed, "bad." They found her unconscious in the bushes in front of a house on the fourth street in, surrounded by several young people in various stages of drug-induced inebriation.

When Phil and Kate parked and ran up onto the lawn, one of the young men said, "Boy, Livie sure can't maintain like she used to. She's been goody goody too long. She ain't gonna get outta this one." He shook his head as though she were only a sick animal.

"I'll get a blanket from the car," said Phil. "You check her pulse."

"Did anyone see what she took, or how much?" Kate knew better than to ask who had given Livie drugs. These kids were pretty stoned, but she hoped one might know.

The teens looked at each other and shrugged. "We was just tryin' to keep her in one place," said one tall girl who peered out from under half-mast false eyelashes. "You know, man, so she wouldn't run into the street or somethin'. She won't run anywhere now." The group of young people looked down at the outstretched Olivia with no particular anxiety or action, too loaded to care.

"Thank you for watching her, kids. We'll take her now."

Phil wrapped Olivia in the blanket he'd brought from the car and knelt with his ear to her mouth to see if she was breathing. He shook his head at Kate. "I don't like this," he said. "Let's go." He picked up the unconscious girl, and carried her to the car, placing her in Kate's lap. They sped off to the nearest hospital.

At the emergency room, Phil took Olivia from Kate and ran inside. A nurse met him and wheeled a gurney under Olivia, where he placed her down gently. The nurse began a preliminary examination.

"What happened?" asked the nurse, a tall blonde in starched white.

"We think a drug overdose. But we don't know what kind or how much of the drugs she took. We found her unconscious."

The nurse took Olivia's pulse, lifted her eyelids, and poked and prodded her quickly. "We'll need you parents to sign for us to pump her stomach. We'd better make it fast." The nurse was already wheeling the gurney down the hall as Phil and Kate jogged along beside her.

"We're not her parents. We take care of her sometimes."

The nurse came to a halt so suddenly that Kate bumped into the now stationary gurney. "Then we can't pump her stomach. We can't treat her without her legal guardian or parent's signature. Are you her legal guardian?" The nurse glared at Phil. When he shook his head, she abruptly shoved the gurney to the side of the hall and folded her arms. "We cannot treat this child, then. We can do nothing for her here. You'll have to take her to General Hospital."

"But General's an hour away--two hours in evening traffic...." began Kate. "Would you call an ambulance to transport her there faster?"

"Not without a parental signature."

"I'll go get her mother," said Phil. He glanced anxiously at Olivia. "For God's sake, start work on Livie, and I'll get her mother here by the time you finish. She could die if you wait."

The woman's blue eyes doused all light as she squinted suspiciously at Phil and Kate. "The legal guardian or parent must sign *before* we begin treatment. Pumping is an invasive procedure. We don't know who will pay the bill without a parent's signature."

"The mother is on welfare anyway, but I'll pay, if she won't. You can't just stand there and let the girl die. You must treat her quickly, or transport her."

"But you're not her parent, and you're not my supervisor." The woman, with an air of finality, walked to her desk, sat down, and shuffled papers behind her glass wall.

Phil motioned Kate to stay with Olivia, then ran down the hall and burst out the exit door. A moment later, his car roared away, tires screeching. Kate remained by Olivia, holding the girl's hand and talking softly to her. "Hold on, Livie. Stay with us. Phil will get your mom here as soon as he can. Think about the ball game. Talk to me, Livie...."

There was no response. Kate bent her cheek to Olivia's lips and felt the warmth of her breath. She was at least breathing, but her breaths were so shallow. Kate rubbed the child's wrists rapidly, as much to convince herself she could do something, when she really knew in her heart she could do nothing until Phil returned with Olivia's mother. She prayed, she worried, and then suddenly prayed for more than Olivia's survival. *What if Mrs. Gonzaga's at work? What if there's no way to find her? Tell me what to do.*

Kate noticed the sickly green of hospital walls, the skewed curtains that were supposed to provide privacy inside the examining rooms, and the sour smell of disinfectant and urine. A machine hooked to a patient in the next room, beeped in metronome rhythm—the only sound in the silent room. Kate could stand it no longer. Olivia was deathly pale, and had not moved for a long time.

She carefully laid Olivia's hand on the gurney and marched over to the nurse. "Miss," she said firmly, "I demand to see the doctor on duty."

Miss Starched White bored a hole straight through Kate with her blue-eyed stare. "It won't do you any good. We have rules, and I'm following them."

"Please let me see the doctor. I'm feeling quite faint, and I need help." She gripped the desk for support.

"You mean *you* are the patient?"

"Yes, and I do believe I'm responsible enough to sign my own paperwork."

The nurse grumbled, but she moved into the depths of the building to find the doctor. After a few minutes, a gangly young man about her own age entered the ER hallway and asked if Kate was the patient. She nodded.

When the doctor adjusted his horn-rimmed glasses and peered at her, she blushed, but hurriedly pointed at Olivia, lying pale and rigid on the gurney.

"What happened to her?" He glared across the desk at the nurse. "How long has this child been here? Why wasn't I called?" Without waiting for an answer from the nurse, who had suddenly become attentive, he felt for a pulse in Olivia's wrist. When it proved weak, he went to her carotid artery and touched it deeply with a scowl on his face.

Kate explained in rapid words spurred by fear. "I'm not her mother, but she stays with us most of the time. My husband went to get her mother, but she works nights sometimes, and she may not be there, and we can't just let Livie OD because we can't find her mother." Her words tumbled out fast in panic that the doctor might not listen. "This is an emergency room. Won't you please do something for her *now*, and I guarantee we'll pay whatever it takes once she's been treated." Kate dissolved into tears, her carefully controlled composure shattered. "I'm scared she'll die like a friend of hers did...please...please...."

The doctor nodded curtly, spoke sharp commands to the nurse. They wheeled Olivia down the hall and disappeared.

Kate paced for ten minutes until Phil rushed in with Mrs. Gonzaga. The woman was still grumbling about being hauled off in the middle of the night, without her permission. "I didn't want to come with this madman, but he yelled and grabbed me by my arm. I should press charges. He forced me to come with him."

Phil looked down at the floor. Kate knew it was to stifle his own emotions. "You should have been eager to come help your 'Baby,' don't you think?"

"Where is she?" demanded the mother.

"They took her inside," said Kate.

"What are they doing to her?" Mrs. Gonzaga's voice became louder, and Kate feared she would start a screaming session again.

"They probably had to pump her stomach." Kate stopped pacing and sat in an ugly, gray plastic chair in the adjacent waiting room. *Phil and Olivia's mother are here now. Phil will take charge.* Her defiant lie to the bureaucratic nurse caught up with her, and she cried. She rationalized this lie as a necessary evil.

Phil said to Mrs. Gonzaga, "They'll have some papers for you to fill out when the nurse comes back, but for now, you probably can sit down. He walked over and bent to look in his wife's eyes. "Are you okay?"

Kate nodded.

He asked, "How did you get them to take Olivia in?"

"Later. Long story. It's enough that she's getting some help now. I've been praying so hard that the help is in time." Kate reached out to squeeze his hand.

"Stay here, ladies. I'll go get some coffee from the machine in the hall."

Phil strode out confidently, but Kate could see him pause in the hall and lean his head against the coffee machine. *He's as scared as I am. We've both come to love Olivia. God, please help her fight this one more time. Help us fight for her one more time.*

She could think of nothing to say to Mrs. Gonzaga who was still muttering about being kidnapped on some stupid snipe hunt.

Though the stale, bitter coffee didn't help the atmosphere of gloom, it did appear to penetrate Mrs. Gonzaga's drunken consciousness. She seemed more sober.

Olivia was gone a long time. Kate's thoughts ran the gamut from praying for Olivia, to hoping the girl's mother would realize that her actions could be life-threatening for her child, to wondering how to bridge wide barriers of difference in values.

"When's the doctor coming back?" asked Mrs. Gonzaga angrily. "What did he say was wrong with her?"

The Johnsons answered carefully, not wanting to give the woman more ammunition to throw at Olivia.

"We found her unconscious and brought her here," said Phil. "We'll have to wait for the doctor to tell us what happened."

They sat in strained silence, with Phil's arm around Kate, warming her and giving her hope. It must have been a slow night, as no sound of entering patients or sirens broke the eerie quiet-- only the continued beeping of the machine in the next room.

After what seemed like forever, the doctor entered the waiting room, his green scrubs matching the ugly green walls. All three of the adults in the waiting room jumped up and surrounded him for news.

"We pumped her stomach and her heart stopped twice, but she's stabilized now."

"What happened to my baby?" asked Mrs. Gonzaga. Her

whining, cloying voice grated on Kate like the screeching of fingernails on a chalkboard.

The doctor looked surprised. "Why, she overdosed on barbiturates."

The woman put her hand to her breast with a relieved sigh. "Oh, thank goodness. I was so afraid it might be drugs!"

In the dead silence that followed, the doctor looked bewildered as he searched the faces from the mother to Kate and Phil. It was obvious Mrs. Gonzaga really had no clue what he was talking about.

The doctor rolled his eyes and turned to the Johnsons with his directions about what had happened and what would be done next. Kate and Phil listened to the doctor intently, while Mrs. Gonzaga stared off into the distance, relieved of any responsibility.

The doctor added, "You realize that after Olivia rests here in the hospital overnight, the police will take her to Juvenile Hall in the morning, don't you?"

Kate caught her breath, and even Mrs. Gonzaga popped to attention.

"Oh, no!" Kate cried. "Surely you won't do that to her after the pain of this whole ordeal. Surely we can take her home to recover and get back on her feet."

"This is all your fault," Mrs. Gonzaga screamed at Phil. "You brought me and my girl here to this shitty hospital against our will."

"If they hadn't brought Olivia here when they did, the girl would be dead!" The doctor's harsh comment silenced the mother, and he turned again to the Johnsons. "I'm afraid this is out of my hands. It rarely happens with one so young, but we're required to notify the police whenever an illegal substance is used. They may have some questions for you about where you found her and how she got the drugs."

"We don't know who gives her the drugs," said Phil, lowering his voice, "but we do know she has difficulty getting along at home with her mother. If there is a hearing, is there any chance they'll let Olivia go where she wants to go?"

"I doubt it. The courts decide how long to keep the children in Juvenile Hall, and they send them back to their mothers, afterward. There really isn't another choice. Certainly the child will have no say in the matter."

Kate' hand flew to cover her mouth. She feared to imagine what would happen to Olivia in Juvenile Hall. She had heard so many stories from Olivia and Lynette about some of their friends who had been sent to 'juvie.'

Kate heard Phil's voice as from down a long, echoing hall asking, "How long?"

"Oh," said the doctor, pulling off his hospital gown, "they usually get to a juvenile hearing in about six to eight weeks. They have a heavy backlog these days."

The doctor seemed so nonchalant about their losing six to eight weeks of recovery time with Olivia that Kate felt angry. But she realized he was only handling this case the same as he would have handled any other and, after all, he had saved Olivia's life when the nurse could have let her die while waiting for help.

"Will someone explain this to Olivia, so she understands that it's temporary?" Kate couldn't believe the police would take Livie straight from the hospital to jail.

"You can be here in the morning before they take her, about ten, and you can talk to her then, if you like."

"We'll be here," said Phil gruffly. Kate knew they'd both have to get substitutes for the morning hours of school, but they couldn't let Olivia be taken away in a police car, still sick, and angry, and frightened.

Chapter 13

The family visited Olivia once a week, all the court would allow. Livie wrote plaintive, practically illegible letters almost daily, with 1-4-3 under the return address. "That's jailhouse talk for 'I love you,'" said Olivia at one of their weekly visits.

A guard showed the family to an open, bare room. They gathered around Olivia, full of hugs, news, and forced, bubbly encouragement to assuage the gloom of this home for wayward juveniles. The guard stood a few feet away, as though he thought someone might try to spirit Olivia out through the barred windows.

Livie had questions about the start of school, the track team, the Scouts-- everything from which she was now excluded. Kate mentioned that Olivia's language was holding up well. "You don't even slip up anymore with bad words. We'll be able to start on grammar when you get out."

Olivia laughed with a short burst of air. "That's just for you guys, you know. If I talked like this with the other gals in here, they'd stick me, sure."

"Oh," said Kate, realizing the other girls might use street talk and be pretty rough.

Olivia smiled and squeezed Kate's hand. "Don't worry, I won't forget. Like you said, it's where and when."

"What's appropriate?"

"Yeah, like that."

When the guard walked to the end of the room, Olivia lowered her voice. "I couldn't tell you in letters, 'cause the guards read 'em. But, there are all kinds of drugs and weapons stashed in here—more than in the One-Ways. Everyone has 'em."

Kate said, "Olivia, stay away from the people with drugs or weapons. You can't let them mess up what you're trying to do."

Olivia looked away for a moment, and then said, "It's really hard, guys. I'm tryin', but if you don't take 'em, the others think you're a loner or stuck up or somethin'. It's hard to be an outsider, cuz they gang up on ya. I tried."

Cori took Olivia's hand and looked in her eyes. "You have to ignore them, Livie." She stressed every word. "You can do it. If you can stay away from drugs in here, you can do it anywhere."

"I know, Cori." She looked at the others and held out her arms in a gesture of frustration. "Honest, I'm tryin' but I'm not good at fightin' like I used to be--out of practice, I guess. And I take hits when I don't go along. I'm not even any good anymore at defendin' myself. Wish I had a bar or a chain. I'd show 'em."

Kate winced, noticing for the first time the bruises on Livie's neck and arms with some alarm. "Did this happen to you in here, Olivia?" She pointed to Livie's neck.

"It's nothin'. Don't go gettin' all worried. I can handle it. Don't say anythin'."

"Why didn't you tell the guards, so they could stop others from hurting you? No one should be fighting. They're here to get better training than that."

"Boy, you don't know nothin', do ya?" Olivia brushed her hands over her face as though clearing cobwebs. "The guards don't do nothin', and the others would jump me, sure. You don't tell guards nothin' in here."

"Olivia," asked Phil. "Are you in danger?"

She looked down at her hands, which were also bruised. "A little. But, not if I go with the flow." She hunched her shoulders and squirmed her ear to her shoulder. "I'll be startin' all over when I get out of here, but you gotta know I'm doin' the best I can...."

"...To survive," finished Lynette, putting her hand on Livie's shoulder. "I know."

Kate started to say something, but Phil squeezed her arm.

"Don't anybody do anythin' about this, okay? You'd only make it worse for me in here. I gotta get along somehow. I'll tell ya all of it, after I get out."

Cindi asked, "Has your mom been to see you?"

"Only that one time when you guys sorta made her come. She don't care. She says I did it to myself. She's sorta right. I guess I did, but I couldn't stay there with her no more."

Olivia brushed her jailhouse slippers against the floor, and then kicked up one leg. "Look, no shoestrings. They don't want anybody to hang themselves, like you could really *do* that with a shoestring." She laughed with a contemptuous sound they had not heard from her in a long time. "Guess it wouldn't be a bad idea though. Things here are so bad. Can anybody get me out?"

Kate thought of the school's efforts. "Several of the teachers at Sunnyside have written letters about how hard you'd been trying last semester and how they felt you should be let out." She didn't offer further information. She didn't want to bring up the results of their effort to draw attention to child abuse at the Sacramento Statehouse. The teachers had only been reminded again that what happened in the home, stayed in the home. They had no right to disagree with the parents or take action themselves. They were told such anti-abuse legislation was not a high priority, but they were determined to keep writing.

Instead, Kate said, "We haven't heard anything yet. I think the judge has something to do with it, but we'll keep trying." She tried to smile, for Olivia's sake, but her effort was interrupted when the guard announced visiting time was over, and they all had to leave. He took Olivia by the arm. No time for goodbye hugs.

They drove home in silence. All had been startled to find that Olivia was definitely losing some of the ground she'd gained on the outside with the family. There were noticeably negative influences at work in that place. Cindi finally broke the stupor as they pulled into their driveway. "I can't believe drugs and weapons can get into juvie. You'd think that would be impossible, wouldn't you? What's Livie supposed to do?"

Phil said, "I think we're all shocked by that, Cindi." Kate noticed his set jaw and tight grip on the steering wheel.

"I'm scared for Livie," said Cori. She squeezed up her face to a pinched look.

Ned patted her hand and said, "It'll be all right."

Kate wondered. *Would anything ever really be all right?*

Once they were alone for the night, Phil said, "We're going to be starting all over with her after this stint in juvie is done."

"I know. And that's assuming the court or her mother will

even let us see her, much less help her direct her activities." Kate was more depressed than optimistic, and she had terrible stomach pain much of the time. She didn't know of any cause, yet the pain persisted. She unconsciously rubbed her cramping mid-section.

"Are you thinking we should even try again, or give it up?" Phil asked.

"I don't know. Do you think it's hopeless? I don't want to believe that, though it's really hard to worry so much about someone, especially when you feel as though your hands are tied by legislators that won't listen, a lack of counseling facilities for children, and a Juvenile Hall more intent upon punishment than rehabilitation. I could go on all night. I suppose it will depend on what the judge says."

"If we could have Olivia all the time, I think she'd be okay. She's learning a normal value system and to fit into it like the rest of the kids. But this back and forth thing has her trapped. She just gets comfortable with us and starts behaving well, then her mother drags her home, abuses her, and she runs back to the familiar--the safety of old gang friends and drugs. I'm not sure what we can do if they send her back to her mom and the same old cycle."

"She bears scars we don't even understand," said Kate.

Phil wrapped his arms around her and sighed. They both were discouraged. What would happen once Olivia was free again?

But six weeks extended to almost ten before the judge was willing to hear Olivia's case, and summer events kept Phil and Kate involved with the other kids in their care. Alisa, Ned, and Cindi graduated from junior high, ready to enter high school with James and Lynette in September. The girls raced through track season after softball finished.

Though Kate and Phil coached the track teams as usual, their biggest surprise for the summer was Lynette's learning to high jump. They insisted that she join the team, but mere participation was all they had really expected. It became a joy to watch one who had seemed so worldly grow excited about a sport totally new to her. She became quickly involved, and the final local track meet thrilled everyone.

After watching other events, the crowd gathered around the high jump pit and watched as competitor after competitor was eliminated. Finally, only Lynette and a girl from Huntington Park were left. The other girl grazed the bar on her first try, and missed it again on her second, leaving Lynette to have to clear this height, or sustain a tie. She was visibly nervous, reaching out often for a hand touch from one of the family members. But as she lined up for her final jump, the crowd started cheering, "Lyn-nette, Lyn-nette and, as she began her run, they shouted, "Go, go, go" until she cleared the bar with a monumental scissor leap on her first try, and came down on her feet.

She ran to where the family watched and leaped into Phil's arms as he lifted her from the ground. "They were cheering for me," she said with wonder in her voice. "For *me*! Nobody's ever done that before."

"There'll be lots more cheers for you, Lynette. You did a great job!"

"I did it, Coach, didn't I?"

"You sure did, Lynette. We're so proud of you."

"On every count, Lynette," added Kate, as the girl stepped to the ground and turned to the rest of the family. "You can be good at anything you try. Your world is filled with opportunity."

"You've worked hard for this, 'Nette," said Cindi with a hug.

Not only the family, but also the crowd of spectators cheered as Lynette stood on the podium and accepted the simple blue satin ribbon for first place in high jump--the first prize she had ever won in a lifetime of disappointment. Tears ran down her cheeks, as she turned to hug the girls at second and third place in a spirit of sportsmanship that was entirely new for her. The crowd erupted in more cheers, and a breathless Lynette joined the family. The relay team of Cori, Cindi, Barbara and Renee, who had outpaced all the local competitive teams, went all the way to the state finals that year, having won every race. But everyone agreed that watching Lynette win her first blue ribbon at little Mayberry Park, and her excitement to have accomplished a goal, *any* goal, was the most exciting event of the whole summer.

"I wish Olivia were here to see me." She said at their celebratory dinner of "Spysghetti," her favorite food. The whole family had laughingly picked up Lynette's warped pronunciation of Spysghetti and Hangabers.

As the family chatted and made plans around the dinner table for when Olivia would again be with them, a phone call came for James. He spoke a few minutes in the kitchen, and then returned to the dinner table clenching his fists.

"What is it?" asked Kate, instantly alert to the look in his eyes.

"My dad--he had a heart attack--a bad one, and no one even called me. My mom moved out and left him alone when he got out of the hospital. He can't do anything for himself. I don't understand why she didn't call, or why she'd leave him there."

Kate and Phil moved to his side.

"If he's still at home, now," said Phil, "we can take you there to see him."

Kate put her arms around James. "I'm so sorry. Didn't your mother tell him why she was leaving?"

"She told him she didn't want to take care of any weak old man, and she just walked out with her suitcases. My dad was crying when he told me. I've never heard him cry before. He's at that house they bought out in the desert all alone, with no one to help him." James put his head in his hands, his normal composure collapsing in the face of shock. "I guess she never cared about *him, either*," James said, between gasps of air.

"What do you want to do?" asked Phil. "How can we help?"

"I'll have to go take care of him. There's no one else, and she took the money...." His voice was swept away with emotion.

Kate glanced at the stunned faces around the table. *Losing James is losing one of our own. We just celebrated his seventeenth birthday. It's too soon for him to go.*

James's voice rasped as he spoke. "I don't want to leave you guys. You're my family, and you cared about me when no one else did." He brushed back the black hair that had fallen into his eyes. "But my dad sounds really bad, and he's alone. I feel like I barely know him." James shook his head. The words seemed to come hard, as though from great depths. "I used to be scared of him, but I think I have to go." He looked around the table at the kids and pleaded, "You guys understand, don't you?"

"Of course, we do," said Phil, answering amid many nodding heads. "You can't leave him alone when she already has."

Ned came around the table to put his hand on James's shoulder. Ned wasn't as tall, nor nearly so muscular, yet he took the lead in saying, "Do you want help to pack?"

On top of losing Olivia, James's imminent departure grated hard on Kate. She rose and cleared the table to get control of her emotion. *I say I understand, when I really don't*, she thought. *How could his mother just walk out the door and expect James to cope with a gravely ill father alone?* Out loud, she tried to be practical. "We'll mail your school transcripts to you. Don't worry about anything. We can bring whatever you need."

Cindi mopped her eyes with her napkin. "We don't want you to go, James."

"Lynette will be a junior," said Alisa, "and Ned, Cindi and I were looking forward to being at Sierra High with you still there...our big time senior brother. And Livie will miss you when she gets out of juvie."

"Yeah," said James. "I was looking forward to having you all there, too, and I wanted to graduate from Sierra, but the desert is too far for me to drive every day. I don't even know if there's a high school near my dad's house." He looked at Kate as he promised, "But I promise I'll try to stay in school. I might have to get a GED, if Dad needs more care during the day."

"You know we'll help, if you need anything," said Phil. "Do you need to borrow the van to get to school and work."

"Thanks for offering, but my dad said he can't drive anymore, so I'm assuming I'll be able to use his old car. Besides, Ned has his license now, and Alisa and Cindi should get their licenses soon, so they can drive everyone else. They'll drive the van." His voice broke. "You won't need me."

Cori jumped up and ran to hug James around the waist. "We'll *always* need you. You're our big brother. You have to promise to come back as soon as you can." There was a chorus of protests with everyone talking at once, as reality set in.

Kate realized they were discussing the end of an era for her family. But she understood the compassion in James's heart. *He's right. There really isn't anything else he can do.* Kate stifled her tears and babbled on about calling home, and staying in school, and remembering how to cook everything.

James interrupted. "Don't worry, Kate. You'll know if anything goes wrong with me--you always have. Like when I got my tonsils out." He smiled and put one arm around the woman he'd depended upon for a long time. "You remember?"

Kate stopped abruptly, suddenly realizing that the boy who had followed her home as a small-for-his-age ten-year-old was now much taller than her. James was nearly grown. She smiled. "Yes, I remember. That *was* weird, wasn't it?

Alisa said, "Okay, you two, what was that all about? Was it before I came?"

Cori broke in with part of the story. "Mom was at the hospital with James's mom and us when James was only ten and Cindi and I were little, and he got his tonsils out. His mom was there to sign the papers, so Mom dropped his mother off at her house after the surgery. We were going back in the evening for visiting hours, but...."

Cindi interrupted with her own recollections. "Mom pulled into The Corner Store to get something fast for dinner, but she didn't even go inside. She just backed right out again and sped back to the hospital. We were scared. She left us in the car...."

"Yes, it was the strangest thing," said Kate. "Something just wouldn't let me go into the market. I left the motor running in front of the hospital, and ran down the hall to James's room. The staff looked at me like I was crazy."

"Why'd you do that?" Lynette asked. She cocked her head to one side and wrinkled up her nose, a mannerism they had discovered whenever she was curious.

"I just felt *something*...I can't explain it. But when I got into James's room, he was lying on his back, bleeding profusely, choking on his own blood and unconscious. I grabbed him up and flipped him over so the blood could run out his throat, and started screaming for the nurse."

"Gosh," said Ned. "What happened to him?"

"He was hemorrhaging and no one had checked on him soon enough, or turned him to his side. He was bloody all over and coughing up even more blood. When the nurse and doctor came running in, they saw that the choking was almost gone. The doctor checked his heart while I held him, and the nurse cleaned up and changed sheets. When James opened his eyes, I thought he'd be scared, so I said, 'It's okay, James, I'm here.'"

"And I said, 'I *know*. I *called* you,'" said James with a grin. "And, boy, did everyone freak out!"

Kate laughed. "That part was funny because the nurse, the doctor, and I looked at each other, and all of us had the hair standing up on the back of our necks. It was more than any of us could figure out. James said it so nonchalantly, as though he could just send me a message through the air whenever he wanted to...even when unconscious. I never could explain how that happened. It *still* gives me cold chills."

James smiled again, and hugged Kate. "Well, I *did* send it through the air, didn't I? And you *got* the message, didn't you? So see, no matter where I am, you'll know if I'm in trouble, so you shouldn't worry. Just trust our mutual ESP. I'll call as often as I can, but I doubt if I can leave my dad much. I'll do the best I can."

Kate struggled to stay composed, knowing James had enough to deal with. She was determined not to cry and make it harder on him to leave.

Phil said, "We know you'll do your best at everything, son. You always have. We're proud of you. Just let us know if you need us, and you're always welcome to come home when you're ready."

Kate watched as James and the kids packed up his clothes and favorite items he had accumulated in his seven years with the family. With tears and hugs, and Cori's parting gift of her big green dog "to remind him of home" stuffed into the front seat of the van, Phil and Ned set off to drive James to his father's house in the desert.

Kate retreated to her bedroom, closed the door, and sat down in the dark on the crazy quilt bedspread. She wanted to cry alone. With heightened senses, she could hear the branches outside her bedroom scraping against the house with each breath of wind. It was too quiet. In spite of the good things that had happened during the summer, it had also been a summer of loss, first her neighbors, then Olivia, and now yet another. *I always knew in my heart that James wasn't ours to keep, that someday we'd have to let him go, but I never dreamed it would be so soon.* Kate had pictured his senior year, his graduation, eventually perhaps his military service and his wedding as being a family affair for those who truly cared about him. Now, she wondered if any of that would still be possible. James's reminding her of their ESP connection had made her think, too. They could nearly always read each other's thoughts, almost as much as she could trade thoughts with Phil and Cindi. She wondered why she couldn't feel that connection to understand Olivia's thoughts and actions as easily. *I wish I could predict her. What is it about Olivia that somehow escapes us all?*

    Soft rapping sounded on the door, and Cindi called out, "Are you okay, Mom?"

    Kate quickly wiped her tears with both hands and said as cheerfully as she could, "Sure, honey. Come on in."

    Cindi opened the door tentatively at first, then wider, and slipped in, followed by the other girls. Lynette asked, "Is it okay to turn on the light? At Kate's nod, she did so. The four girls arranged themselves cross-legged around Kate on the big bed.

    Kate tried to joke. "Looks like it's Ladies Night, since the guys will be late getting back, doesn't it?" The girls smiled weakly, because one of their "ladies," Olivia, was still in Juvenile Hall, and now one of their "guys" would be missing indefinitely.

    Cori put her arms around her mother. "It's hard to imagine

things without James here in our family."

"Let's make some popcorn, Mom," suggested Cindi. "We need to get up and *do* something, like you and Dad always tell us to do whenever we feel bad."

Kate nodded and slid off the bed. "Good idea. No moping allowed. Come on, girls."

The next day, they got another letter from Olivia. It was hard for her to write letters, and Kate was aware that her writing and spelling were as far behind grade level as her reading, but the family ignored the misspelled words just to hear that she was still all right. Livie was, for a change, enthusiastic. "They tole me I culd chuz wher I want to liv. I want to liv with you gys. Can you writ a leter to cort and tell that you wil tak me? 1-4-3"

Phil and Kate feared that there would be no such choice, but Olivia's hopeful enthusiasm lifted everyone's spirits a little. The whole family helped write the letter.

In September, they went to court, not so much that they thought Olivia would really be allowed to choose where she would live, as just to be present in the courtroom to give her confidence.

There was no time to talk, however, as the court officer called for attention, and the judge entered the courtroom. He was an over-sized, middle-aged man, and the sparsely furnished room echoed with his heavy footsteps on the bare tile floor. Even whispers seemed to echo into the room and bounce off the plain white walls. Only the judge's bench was burnished with heavily waxed mahogany, while the rest of the hard wooden seats lacked both style and comfort. The bailiff brought Olivia into the courtroom at that moment, and all eyes turned to their lost girl.

Olivia looked small and frightened. Her hair was uncombed, as though they had roused her from sleep. She wore the Juvenile Hall prison uniform of dull blue, faded from many years of washings in hot, sterilized water. The institutional, baggy look, in contrast to Livie's usual preference for wild, multicolor outfits, made Kate wince.

The girl stared blankly, slowly searching faces, until Phil stood and waved. Then she smiled at each of the family members in turn and lifted her arms joined in the "winner's" salute, as though she had won the first round just by having them with her.

But Olivia's expression soon changed when she saw her mother walk in, almost pushed ahead by the public advocate who had been appointed for her. Mrs. Gonzaga frowned from under heavy eyelids. Her rouged cheeks reminded Kate of a circus clown, but even the woman's face seemed tame when compared with the low-cut neckline of her see-through lace bodice and the mini skirt stretched over her bulky body. *No wonder the girls have no sense of what's appropriate. What an example!*

Olivia avoided her mother's gaze, staring instead at the wall above the judge's head. The bailiff steered Olivia to the front of the room. The witness chair dwarfed her small stature, her short legs swinging helplessly. Phil took Kate's hand in his two big ones. She looked down the row and saw all of their kids sitting on the edge of their seats and, apparently, holding their breath as well.

The hearing was perfunctory and short.

The judge asked, "Is Olivia Gonzaga's parent present?"

The public defender nudged Mrs. Gonzaga to stand up.

The judge raised his bushy eyebrows, moved his glasses down his nose, and pronounced, "Then it is my order that Olivia Gonzaga go home with her mother and behave herself." He banged his gavel and started to rise, shuffling papers together.

A silence ensued while his statement soaked in. Olivia stood. "Is that it? Can I go home with the Johnsons now?"

The judge leaned his hands on his desk and peered over his bifocals at the diminutive girl he considered an addict. "Not at all. You're going home with your mother where you belong."

"You can't do that! The social lady told me I could choose. My mom doesn't want me, and I won't stay there. Just you wait, I won't stay!" Olivia broke into sobs.

Phil held Kate's s hand tightly to keep her in her seat.

The judge rapped the gavel loudly. "Young lady, there will be no hysterics in my courtroom. Dry it up! You have two choices. You can go home with your mother and stay off drugs, or I'll send you back to Juvenile Hall, and you won't get out for two years.

And that will be only with good behavior, which..." He looked at papers in front of him. "...has so far not been apparent."

"I'd rather go back to jail," said Olivia, with her old defiance, betrayed only by the quivering of her chin.

Cori shouted out, "No, Livie! We'd never see you again."

Phil hugged Cori to calm her tears as the judge banged his gavel, and the whole room fell apart. Olivia's mother shouted and pounded on the table. The public defender was on his feet objecting, and the bailiff didn't seem to know whether he should restrain the hysterical Olivia or move to defend the judge.

Olivia looked shaken and indecisive. "I don't know what to do," she screamed, turning in circles. "Somebody listen to me. Help me! I can't go back to her."

Tears rolled down Kate's cheeks unabashedly.

The judge's gavel restored order. He frowned down at Olivia. With his bushy eyebrows, he seemed formidable. "You, young lady, will do as I say, or you'll be in Juvenile Hall a *very* long time. You go home and mind your mother. You hear?"

Olivia looked down, punctuating her sobs with hiccups. She mumbled, "Yes, Sir."

"I couldn't hear you, young lady."

"Yes, Sir," Olivia said, somewhat louder.

"All right, then. You go with the bailiff and change your clothes. Your mother will be waiting when you're finished. Make sure I don't see you again in this courtroom."

With her head still down, defiance in every line of her body, Olivia jerked away from the bailiff with her fists clenched.

Kate looked at Phil for solace. He shrugged and took her hand as they gathered up their brood and headed out to the hall.

Mrs. Gonzaga stood far down the hall, smoking a cigarette with her arms folded, her back to the Johnsons, her lace bodice bulging in rolls down her back.

Cori left the family and made her way down the hall timidly. She asked Mrs. Gonzaga, "Please, may Olivia still come to track practice and Cadette Girl Scouts?"

The woman gave Cori a withering stare and brayed loudly,

"You keep away from my girl. She's not going anyplace with the likes of you. I'll bet *you* gave her the drugs."

Cori walked back with slumped shoulders and buried her face in Phil's side, as he put his arm around her from one side, while Ned held her hand on the other.

"At least you tried," said Lynette, trying to comfort Cori. "My mom wouldn't even look at me." The older girl looked down, tears in her eyes.

Kate put an arm around Lynette. "Do you want to try to talk to your mother?"

"No. It wouldn't do any good. I'm not even trying. I'm not crying about that. I'm more worried what will happen to Olivia when she can't handle life at home, as usual."

Olivia emerged from a door down the hall in her street clothes. They were the same muddy ones she had on when the Johnsons had found her in the One Ways. "Her mother didn't even bring her any clean clothes," said Kate.

Lynette sighed. "Did you expect anything different?"

Alisa and Cindi moved toward Olivia in the push of the crowd, with Cindi calling, "Livie, meet us at the house to talk."

"I'll be there," Olivia shouted, but her mother grabbed her arm and jerked her toward the revolving glass door. "You're not going anyplace, you fucking brat." Olivia held up her hand against her mother's slap. "And you stay away from her," Mrs. Gonzaga growled at Cindi, as she pushed Olivia through the door and half-dragged her down the courthouse steps.

The family watched from the door as the public defender opened his car door, and Mrs. Gonzaga shoved Olivia inside. The girl fell into the back seat in front of her mother, and the door slammed after them.

"Well, that does it," said Lynette with a wooden tone. "Livie won't stay. She'll be gone by the end of the week, and she'll wind up back in juvie or out on the streets."

They all stood huddled together long after the public defender's car turned the corner and disappeared. Neither Kate nor Phil could think of any words of encouragement.

Chapter 14

To Kate's surprise, Olivia lasted longer at her mother's home than Lynette had predicted. School started, and Olivia attended every day. She drew encouragement from long phone conversations to the Johnsons at night, after her mom went to work. She tried to meet them at The Corner Store after school, when she could. The Johnson kids advised her to stay clean, so the courts would forget about her after a few weeks, and hoped her mother would forget about her soon, too, so she could come visit.

Now that Olivia was in junior high school, she saw Cori every day. Though Cori was a year ahead, she made a point of seeking Olivia out at lunchtime and for a few moments after school. Cori updated the family on Olivia's progress, or lack of it, and reported with some glee that Olivia hated wearing skirts to school as much as she did. Cori still vowed to find a way to change the dress code, and Livie was her vocal supporter. Cori decided that if she ran for Student Body President in the spring, she would have a platform for change.

One afternoon only a few weeks into the start of school, Kate heard Cori duck under the bougainvillea vine that screened the front porch. While everyone else walked in by the actual entrance, behind the bougainvillea, Cori always took a short cut, bending under the vines, scraping by their dangling blossoms, and then banging the screened door as she entered. Kate smiled. The familiar sound of Cori's homecoming was at least distinctive.

"I'm in the sewing room," Kate sang out. Since Alisa and Cindi had moved back into the girls' room with Lynette and Cori, utilizing both sets of bunk beds, Kate could again open up her sewing machine that stood in the library/laundry room. A lesson in sewing stretch materials at the fabric store turned Kate into a t-shirt "maniac." But the kids liked the results--t-shirts in every size and pattern to go with all their pants and skirts.

"Oh, so now it's the sewing room, huh?" Cori teased. "It's still the laundry room and the library, though, isn't it?" As Kate smiled, Cori pulled up a chair and sobered. "I need to talk to you, Mom."

Kate turned to her daughter, the sleeve of a purpley-pink t-shirt she'd been making in Lynette's favorite colors still lying in her lap. "So my youngest has something heavy on her mind, hm? Shoot, Hon, I'm all ears."

"Mom, what do you do if someone in authority does something sort of mean?"

"Maybe define 'mean' and determine if it was some type of misunderstanding."

Cori shook her head. "I don't think it's a misunderstanding. Mr. Carleton made it pretty plain. He called me into his office today and said I shouldn't hang around with Livie. He said I'd get a bad reputation, she'd get me on drugs, and you and Dad would be ashamed of me." She put her books down on the floor and faced her mother. "I thought my reputation was about what *I* did, not about what someone *else* did. Am I wrong?"

Kate said slowly. "No, you're not wrong. In the first place, you've never done anything in your life that could make us ashamed of you."

"Except when I was three and my friend and I threw bricks over the back wall to hear them go 'splash?'" Cori laughed. "Dad was pretty mad when he had to dive in again and again in January to fish the bricks out of the neighbor's new swimming pool."

"Well, it was rather cold. We were lucky there was no damage because we sure couldn't afford to fix anything broken."

"That's the only spanking I remember. Dad said I should always look to see what I was doing, instead of launching into some action without thinking it through."

"Well, you and Danny were just curious, but it was a lesson well learned."

"Yeah. I guess that's what I'm doing now--trying to see if I'm doing things in the right way. Have you and Dad ever had any second thoughts about Livie?"

Kate thought about Olivia's role in their lives. *Was it a wise decision to bring such a troubled child into our home? Have I been wrong to expose my family to a girl with such a problematic background?*

"Of course, sometimes. I know it's been hard for Livie, and for the rest of us, since her whole value system has had to change in order to be with us, and you kids have had to be so very patient. Let's face it—our lives are much more strict and conservative than she's used to. We're neither like her family nor like the One-Ways, and that's all she *knew* until she came to us. Yet, I can't imagine not trying to help after she stumbled into my arms that day. Your dad and I are teachers. How could we have turned a child away?"

Kate had, herself, been a "throwaway child" that others took in from age three until age five, when her father found her and brought her to California. There were never any explanations, so she had never known why she was left alone, but it had definitely influenced her shy teen years. She wondered if such an old memory could still be *that* much a part of her own psyche?

"Most of the time, Livie's doing pretty well—not exactly what we'd expect from you girls raised in a loving home, but with her background, she's doing pretty well. I can't believe Mr. Carleton thinks you should abandon Olivia for her past actions, instead of encouraging her present efforts."

"Mom, I know some of our nosy neighbors think we shouldn't help any of the other kids, Olivia especially. They think she'll get all the kids in town to use drugs. Does that bother you?"

"I suppose bringing Olivia and Lynette into a different milieu has seemed risky to them. Olivia scares people with her rather rough mannerisms, even though she's improved and rarely loses her temper anymore. Even when she's being good, though, she somehow attracts attention, not all of it positive. I don't know why. Of course, it bothers me that our friends don't understand."

"But it bothers me more that the principal should put such a dilemma at the feet of my daughter. Dad and I can handle it, but you shouldn't have to."

"I don't know why, Mom. Maybe Juvenile Hall put something on her record. Maybe he's afraid she'll bring drugs into the school. I told him Livie had promised never to do that, or to bring them into our house, either. But I don't think he listened. I hate to say this, Mom, but I think he just doesn't like her. And you know Livie. When she thinks someone doesn't like or trust her, she gets all feisty and defensive. I'm afraid if he does ever call her in, she'll say something she shouldn't."

—— Cori's wrinkled brow showed her concern. "Livie's lonely at school. Her mom still won't let her come to our house, so she goes home and is tempted to go to the One Ways, where at least she has friends. She says she hasn't used any drugs over there, but she *is* hitching rides back with weird people."

Kate shook her head slowly. "And that's troubling, too, isn't it? I wish she would stay totally away from the One-Ways."

Cori looked down, alternately pointing and flexing one foot. "She has a hard time making friends, and I don't know what to do to help her. I take her along with me when I go to lunch with my friends, but some of them say their mothers don't want them hanging around with Livie, or me, for that matter. They think I might be taking drugs, too, though I thought they knew me better than that." She laughed in a bitter way. "And Livie doesn't seem comfortable with them, either. She says she just doesn't fit in with anybody--like she's gone too straight for her druggie friends, and she has too much past hanging over her for any of our friends. I think she's sort of stuck in the middle, sort of torn both ways."

"Does it bother you that some people criticize us for trying to help Livie?"

"Sometimes. But I don't worry about what other people think that much. They don't understand her at all. But Livie *was* using drugs in Juvie. She was afraid of the other girls if she acted differently. The trouble is, I think she still wants the drugs, a little bit, anyway, since juvie." Cori slumped against her mother. "She's not using them now, but I know she still wants them, sometimes. It must be a constant fight for her. I'm afraid every day something bad will happen. I couldn't think of anything else to do except advise her to stay busy, but she won't take part at school. She says she feels like an outsider there, too. What should I do, Mom? I don't want Livie to mess up and get in trouble again. I just get so frustrated with her. It all seems so easy to me and so hard for her."

Kate put her arm around Cori and said, "Honey, you have a huge heart, and I don't ever want you to change, but I don't want you to worry so much. Regardless of what Mr. Carleton thinks, sometimes Livie just needs a friend to listen. You're good at both listening and guiding her. But it certainly isn't your fault, or anyone else's, should Livie not make it. We've all tried our best, but it's not up to you to carry her on your back. She must stand up to some of these pressures herself, and make her own choices."

"I don't think she's strong enough to make good choices; being pulled back and forth like she's on a swing or a yo-yo all the time. Maybe she really can't make it. Change is hard for her."

"Perhaps others will mellow out in time, when thy see Livie is trying to change her life."

"Mom, everyone is wrong when they think Cindi or I would ever take drugs with Livie. You know that, don't you?" She looked at her mother, waiting for an answer.

"Hon, it never entered my mind. You've seen first-hand how troubled Olivia is, and you and Cindi both think for yourselves, not like the herd. You'd never abandon your own independence." Kate couldn't help smiling at her youngest child, knowing Cori was the most conservative young girl she'd ever known, and she did everything her own unique way. She would never be a follower—of Livie--or anyone else.

"You and Cindi are rocks in dealing with Olivia and Lynette, and your dad and I count on you. We couldn't have tried to help them, let alone James, Alisa and Ned, if you girls hadn't been willing sisters. You two are as bad as your father and I about not being able to turn anyone away. But, I think you both know that you couldn't help Olivia if you joined her in the drug culture." She smiled at Cori and hugged her hard. "I'll talk to Mr. Carleton tomorrow and explain what we're trying to do, so perhaps he'll help. In the meantime, just do what you feel is right. I've never been disappointed in your good judgment."

"Except about throwing bricks into a swimming pool."
"Except about throwing bricks into a swimming pool."

They laughed together, and Cori went off to tackle her homework. Kate put aside her sewing to start dinner.

Kate was just leaving after school for the junior high the next day to talk to the principal, when she was startled by Lynette and Ned's bursting in shouting the news, "Olivia's missing again!" Alisa and Cindi followed closely behind. Ned was so flustered, he started wheezing from his asthma, so everyone followed Kate to the kitchen to boil water to ease his breathing with the steam. The kitchen became a Tower of Babel until Phil entered and held up his hand for silence. "Stop, all of you! Take a deep breath, and then *one* of you talk at a time, please."

Alisa spoke first, still breathless. "Brenda's in Livie's classes, and she said she and Livie were called into the office for arguing in class. It was just words, but Mr. Carleton seemed to want to make an example of Livie and he called their mothers."

"Mom, Cori told you Mr. Carleton was just waiting for Livie to do something to get her in trouble," added Cindi.

Alisa filled in the details. "Brenda said Livie's mother slapped Livie and dragged her out of the school. Livie screamed that she'd run away where no one would ever find her."

"And we know this because…."

"Ned was driving us home," Cindi said, "and we stopped at The Corner Store to talk to Renee and Brenda."

The Corner Store was where most of the kids stopped for cokes and message exchanges on the way home from school. It was actually a liquor store, but because of its location across the street from the park and the junior high and near two elementary schools, the proprietor stocked plenty of jujubes, candy bars, sodas, and sunflower seeds. He knew the kids by name, and he enjoyed the influx of business immediately after each school day. Any events of the day would be discussed at The Corner Store.

"Mom," resumed Cindi, "If Livie runs away, her mom will put her back in juvie. She can't go back there! Can you and Dad stop her?"

"Please," said Lynette. Kate noted that Lynette was as pale as her cream-colored t-shirt. She reached out to squeeze her hand.

Phil looked at Kate. "Any ideas, honey?"

Kate asked, "Are you sure Brenda got the story straight? This is second-hand information, isn't it?"

Ned recovered his breath enough to say, "Brenda told everyone at The Corner Store she was mad because it was too little a thing for the principal to have called parents. She said she and Livie just argued a little bit, and the teacher got mad and sent them both to the principal. Brenda's mother told Mr. Carleton it was a minor infraction, and she would take care of it. But Mr. Carleton expelled Olivia, even though he didn't expel Brenda."

"That wasn't even fair!" Cindi was indignant.

"Okay, gang, let's slow down a minute," said Phil. "Are we sure Olivia meant this about running away, or could Brenda have been over-reacting?"

Lynette slumped in the nearest chair. "She meant it." The girl fumbled in the pocket of her jacket, pulled out a wadded up piece of paper, and spread it out in her lap. "Livie wrote a note while the moms were in the principal's office and passed it to Brenda. She knew we'd be at The Corner Store, so she brought it to us. I can't make it out. Livie writes so sloppy." Tearfully, Lynette held out the paper to Kate.

Kate read the note aloud. "No tim. Lenet Im goin. I gonna be aright. Don look fur me. 1-4-3"

"I knew it!" Lynette sobbed, while Cindi encircled her with a comforting arm.

Cori walked in from the garage, carrying bags of Cleo and Goldie's pet food, and shadowed by the animals. "What happened? What's wrong with everybody?"

Ned and Alisa immediately filled her in. Soon all the kids were hatching plans to find Livie, and Phil and Kate looked at each other, helplessly. "Okay," said Phil, addressing Lynette. "Do you really think Olivia could get out of the house?"

"Yes," whispered Lynette. "You can bet after this, Mom will hurt her bad, and Livie will leave as soon as she gets a chance. I'll bet she's gone already."

"Why don't you call your house? asked Phil. "Maybe

Olivia is still there, or your mom will say what happened, or where she thinks Olivia might have gone."

Lynette moved to the phone, picked up the receiver and dialed. The whole crew followed her every move since they could do nothing else. They listened as the phone rang twice, and then Mrs. Gonzaga's voice came on the line.

When Lynette asked for Livie, the loud oaths and expletives sputtering on the other end of the line bombarded everyone like scattered shards of broken glass. Lynette moved the receiver further from her ear. "Mom, please tell me what happened?"

"Whadda you care? That fucking kid ran off again. She gets into trouble with some dumb teacher and the principal calls me. I had to walk down to that shitty school, and there she was, expelled. I told her she was a fucking nuisance and that I'd give her what for when we got home. You shoulda seen her trying to talk to that other little bitch and her mother in the room. I just dragged her out of there...."

"Mama, did she actually leave?" Lynette's voice was teary, tentative.

"What's it to ya, you whore? She tore away from me and ran down the street. I sure wasn't gonna chase after her. She'll be home when she gets hungry, and I'll be a-waitin' for her with the toaster cord."

"Mama, please. Did she say where she was going?"

"No, and I wouldn't tell you if she did. You've got nothin' to do with me, or her, so you can just fuck off, and I'll take care of her when she comes home. I already called the po-lice. I better not see the likes of you round here buttin' in."

"No, Mama. I just thought maybe I could try to find her."

"Fuck you, Lynette. Your name means nothin' to me. Fuck off." They could hear the phone slam down. The line went dead.

For a moment there was silence, as Lynette stared at the receiver in her hand. Her shoulders slumped as she drew into herself. Kate wrapped her in a hug, as Ned pried the receiver from her hand and hung it up on the wall.

"Well, so much for positive parental example," Phil muttered. "But, we at least know Brenda's message was accurate," Brenda did get the note, it's in Olivia's handwriting, and your mother doesn't know where she is or when she'll be back. That confirms what we feared." He turned to Lynette and added, "I guess the police will be looking for her, too. But, Lynette, I'm sorry your mom said such ugly things to you. Surely she should realize you're only trying to help Livie."

"It's all right. I'm used to it. I'm just scared of where Livie might go. She has no money, no clothes--and I know she won't go back home to Mom. What should we do?"

Alisa said, "Maybe we should just wait a while and hope she comes here. She's run off before."

"She wouldn't come here," said Lynette. "She knows this is the first place my mom would tell the police to look. I bet they're on their way here, already."

"Should you go to the One Ways and look for her?" Cori sounded hopeful.

"I'll drive over and ask around," said Kate. "I'll find Bettina. I know she'll tell me the truth, if she knows anything."

"I'm coming with you," said Lynette.

"If you two are staying together over there, I'll stay here to talk to the police, in case Mrs. Gonzaga told them to search here," said Phil. "I don't want the other kids having to deal with that."

"And if she's not in the One Ways, and the police can't find her?" Cindi let the question hang in the air.

"Then, we may have to wait until Olivia decides to contact us," said Kate. "And I think she will, eventually. She always does. I only hope it's before she gets messed up again. We'll have to decide what to do when the time comes."

From that night onward, each Grace before meals included a plea for Olivia. Ned always added, "Please God, keep her safe, and bring her home to us."

Chapter 15

Kate had no luck in the One-Ways the first week, but then she found Bettina.

"I saw Livie the first day or two," the girl said. "She even refused pot, so I think she's stronger about leavin' the drugs alone. But I could tell she's still tempted."

"Did you see her anytime after that?"

"No, just those first couple of days. She said the cops were lookin' for her. She didn't want to bring down the whole barrio, so she said she'd have to leave. None of us saw her go. She knew you'd come lookin'. I'm sorry I don't know anythin' more, but I'll call you if I hear somethin'." Bettina looked down sadly. "I still have your number."

"Thanks so much, Bettina." Kate put her hand on the girl's arm. "How are *you* doing these days, and how's your baby?"

"I'm pregnant again." She sighed heavily. "My old man swears he'll keep me knocked up so I can never try to get away from him again."

Kate felt sad that Bettina showed none of the spark of independence she had shown on previous visits. She seemed to have accepted her fate. "I'm so sorry, Bettina. If there's anything I can do...."

"You can't." Bettina rubbed her belly and said, "I'll show soon, and the old man will be all glad. He thinks I can't ever get out of here without him, and he's right. I can't even hope for that-- not anymore. Maybe none of us can change."

"Don't give up hope, Bettina." Kate hugged the girl and repeated, "Call me if you ever change your mind."

Bettina smiled. "I'll call you if I hear anything about Livie, too. It's been a long time we've been tryin', but maybe she still has a little chance left. None of us can change easy. Even Alice has an old man, now." Bettina shrugged with hands outstretched.

Almost weekly, Bettina called Kate with what she hoped

were leads on Olivia's whereabouts. One of their gang said he saw her with some Thai people around Echo Park in downtown L.A. Another said he thought he saw her out at Redondo Beach, and yet another girl said Livie had mentioned going far north. Phil and Ned cruised all of the suggested neighborhoods, all quite shoddy and crime-ridden, knowing it would be a miracle if they could spot the teen. But none of the leads panned out.

Six weeks passed with no word. During that time, though the neighbors were full of gloating "I told you so" comments, the family went through their daily lives hanging on to the hope that somehow, somewhere, Olivia could stay safe. Kate and Phil talked quietly about all options in bed at night, the only time they were ever alone, but they had no answers. "I can't bear to think of Olivia out there by herself," said Kate.

"I know," comforted Phil, as he held his wife to him. "But we have to remember she's survived pretty much on her own for most of her life. She's a tough kid. We'll all just keep hoping and praying, and waiting. She'll turn up."

"But no one should have to feel so alone. We've tried to make her feel she belongs, but she doesn't have the confidence to make that break from her old life, and she has no opportunity to break with her mother. Cori's right. Livie's swinging somewhere in between two worlds. Where will she end up?"

Kate cried a lot, and suffered more stomach pains in silence. She called the police so often, to see what they'd heard, that she memorized the number. Detective Fredrick recognized her voice, greeting her by name. The detective said he'd call the Johnsons if the police heard anything at all about the runaway.

The kids asked everyone who knew Olivia if they had seen her, but all leads turned out to be mere rumors. Cori blamed Mr. Carleton. Cindi blamed Livie's mother.

Whenever the phone rang, someone jumped to answer, hoping it would be Olivia. Twice, Kate answered the phone, but no one spoke. She felt sure it must be Olivia trying to reach them. Each time, she only heard noises before the line went dead.

Waiting grated on nerves, and each family member worked

hard not to take their frustrations out on each other. Alisa even snapped at Kate when she suggested she shouldn't stay so long out in the car with Bruce after a date. "You're not my mother, and you can't tell me what to do!"

Kate was crushed, and Phil speculated whether it was time to find Alisa's mother and send her to live with her mother's rules a while. Alisa apologized, but both Kate and Phil hated the tension Livie's disappearance had caused. Everyone was on pins and needles, while Livie seemed to have dropped off face of the Earth.

The family was as much on a swing as Olivia, since they had come to love her, and couldn't bear to let her go to what they truly believed was the darker side of her nature, and they couldn't seem to find the way to pull her permanently to the light.

Finally, about eleven o'clock one night, as Kate and Phil completed their rounds of the house and were about to crawl into bed, the phone rang. Kate ran through the living room to the kitchen to grab the phone's receiver. She couldn't quite make out the distant and muddled voice, but she felt it must be Olivia.

"Hello, Hello, Olivia, is that you?"

"Hm?...I...."

"Olivia, where are you?"

"I dunno...someplace...."

"Are you in downtown Los Angeles, Olivia?"

By this time, Phil had joined Kate in the kitchen, bringing her slippers and robe against the nighttime chill.

"No...'nother one." Livie's voice was slow, groggy, stumbling over every word, with long pauses in between. Kate could barely make out her mumbling. *Oh, God, she's loaded on something—if it's downers, it'll be hard to get information.*

Kate fought to keep her voice steady. "Okay, Livie, if it's not Los Angeles, could it be San Diego?"

"Where? Doon know where...too close...a big city. Far...a big red...."

"Try to listen, Olivia. We'll find you, but you have to maintain, at least enough to tell me where you are. How about San Francisco? Is that the other big city you mean?"

"Yeah…I think…my head hurts…hurts…all fuzzy…."

"Olivia, listen to me. Don't hang up." The urgency in Kate's voice brought Phil closer, encircling her with his arm for support. She leaned against him, grateful for his strength.

"Livie, I can hear cars. Are you on the street?"

"Cars evywhere…evywhere…yeah…two…two streets."

"Are you in a phone booth, like on a corner or something?"

"Yeah…sort of…it's the red thing…so big…."

"Okay, Livie. Look outside the phone booth and try to see the street sign on the corner. Can you read the letters to me?"

It grew quiet. She couldn't hear Livie's heavy breathing—only bumping noises. Kate held her breath, hoping the bumping was only the door of the phone booth.

Olivia's voice returned. "Yeah…street sign…says H…A…and has a T…I dunno…somethin' after the A…."

"Is it Haight, Livie? That's a big street. Does it look like two words or one?"

"Yeah…one and S…T…please…come...get me, Kate. Everthin's shakin'…."

"We'll come, Livie, as soon as we know where you are." There was a long pause during which Kate could only hear Livie's breathing and muffled sobs.

"Livie," she called again and again, fearing the girl would hang up. "Livie, honey, talk to me. Stay awake. Answer me, maintain, please, Livie."

"I miss…I wanna …I'm so messed up…."

"Please, Livie, what's the cross street on Haight? What else was on the sign? Can you see it? Can you tell me what it says?"

"It's all jumbly…but the red one… big…red…word…."

Kate sighed. "Okay, Livie, what does the big red one say?"

"S….T….somethin'…I can't…S…T…red…big…."

"Are the big red S and T part of a sign, a street, or a business name…like the Texaco Star?"

Phil nudged Kate and whispered, "If you put in too many choices, she'll get more confused. Try one at a time."

She nodded. Phil grabbed a notepad and was busily writing

down all he overheard. There was no such thing as privacy with their phone being on the wall in the kitchen, anyway.

"Livie, how big are the letters?"

"Jus big...S and T...you see 'em?...big, red...."

Kate shook her head and whispered to Phil, "I don't seem to be getting anywhere on the street or the sign. I'll try something else." Into the receiver, she said, "Olivia, where are you staying?"

"Right here...by the S...T...so ya can fine me...."

"I mean a house, Livie, not the phone booth. Is your house near the big S and T?"

"No...but sorta...."

"Can you give me the address?"

"Dunno...left...and then...left one more ...left...big house...three floors...fifth one over, ...no...third...no...I dunno, Kate... please....come...."

Kate repeated the words as Phil wrote them down. "Yes, Livie, we'll come get you, but please try to give us more information. We need an address, or something."

Ned entered the kitchen. "I heard the phone. Is it Livie?"

Phil nodded.

From the other bedroom came Lynette and Cindi, joining the three in the kitchen. "It's Livie," repeated Ned.

Lynette broke in excitedly, "Where is she?"

Kate covered the receiver with her hand long enough to say, "I think San Francisco, maybe. She's not coherent."

Lynette squealed. "Rita! If she's in San Francisco, she must have found our sister, Rita. I never thought about her going there. Is she there? Ask her, please?"

Kate spoke again, urgently, "Olivia, are you at Rita's house in San Francisco?"

Livie's frightened voice came back. "I heard Lynette. Come...alone...Rita will kill me...if you bring...anyone...if she knows I called...."

"Lynette," whispered Kate. "Do you know Rita's address?"

"No, she never tells us anything--only that she's in San Francisco and she goes to the park every day about three in the afternoon. If Livie's with Rita, she's using drugs because I know Rita's dealing." Lynette started to cry. "I'd hoped so much...."

"We'll worry about that later, Lynette. Let's just try to find her for now."

Into the receiver, Kate said, "Olivia, please try to tell me where Rita lives?"

"Left...left again...thas all...left...."

"From where you are standing now, in the phone booth?"

"Yeah...left."

"The police may make us bring your mother because...."

The terrified voice rang out for all to hear. "No, no...I'll hang up...no one...not Mama...not Lynette...Rita can see from...upstairs...if you...bring anybody...I run...."

Kate could hear Olivia fumbling around with the receiver...*Oh God, don't let me lose her now.* "Okay, Livie, we'll come alone. Just don't hang up, Livie. Don't hang up."

A long silence ensued before they heard Olivia's voice and could breathe easily again. "Are you...comin' to get...me? I'm sooooooo dizzy...sooooo tired...."

"We're coming, Olivia. Just try to help us find you. San Francisco is a big town. Please look again at the street sign for the other cross street."

"I can't...see it...jus the big...

"Red S and T, I know," Kate finished with a frustrated sigh.

"Yeah...jus that...it fills my eyes...hurts. You'll find...me, won't you? Maybe at the park."

"Which Park, Olivia? Don't fade out on me. I need you to maintain. Which park?" Kate searched her brain for the names of any parks she could think of in the unfamiliar city of San Francisco. "Is it Presidio Park?" She'd heard of the park, but she wasn't sure. It might just be a military base.

Olivia said, "No... 'nother...my stomach, everthin' hurts."

"How about Golden Gate Park?"

"Huh? ...maybe...I dunno...I gotta go...now...everthin's shaky and Rita's mad. She can't know...I called. Hurry. Come...you and Phil and Cindi...and Cori...and big brother,

James...I miss everbody...hurry...I gotta...."

Olivia's voice trailed off with no sound of a receiver being hung up, but there was no longer her breathing, either. Olivia was gone. Kate reluctantly hung up.

"Well," said Phil, fumbling with his notes, "This is all we have. Not much to go on. And it'll take us eight or nine hours to get there. She could be anywhere by then."

Kate turned to see that Alisa and Cindi had joined the group huddling over Phil's scribbled notes trying to make sense out of them. Had the event not been so traumatic, the collection of brightly colored pajamas, robes, and mussed hair would have been comic for their usually well-groomed brood. Alisa's perennial hair curlers dangled loosely, unheeded, under the bright overhead light.

Ned spread open the street atlas, looked at the blow up of San Francisco, found Haight Street, and gasped. "It goes almost all through the city. Without a cross street, it'll be impossible."

"Try looking for a district, like Haight Ashbury—isn't that where all the Hippies and druggies hang out?" Phil waited as Ned and Alisa poured over the map.

"That might narrow it down. It looks like about 20-25 blocks in that area."

Phil snorted. "Figuring left and left again when we don't know where we're starting from, or which direction she was facing in the phone booth, that would be an area of 80 to 100 blocks we'll have to scour."

Lynette stifled a sour chuckle, "Don't forget Livie and I mix up left and right."

"Oh, great!" said Phil, shaking his head with a huge sigh. "That doubles the area, and we don't have much to go on. This may take awhile. We'd better take blankets and snacks. We can't afford a motel or restaurants--just the gas to get us there and back will be bad enough." Lynette, Alisa, and Cindi scurried to grab the items, fix sandwiches and fruit for a big bag lunch. Ned trundled out the picnic ice chest and loaded it.

"Tomorrow is a school day," Phil added. We'll have to call for substitutes. Alisa, can you....?"

"I'll do it first thing in the morning," the teen said. "Are your lesson plans on your desks, as usual?"

"Yeah," said Phil. Kate nodded. "Tell them it's an emergency, and we'll be back in a day or two," said Phil.

Kate called Detective Fredrick and came back with news. "He said to check in with the police in San Francisco as soon as we get there. I told him Olivia said not to bring her mother, because Rita might take it out on Olivia if she thought her family knew where she was. First, he said that legally, we *had* to take her mother. But then he said not to, because Olivia might really run, and she wouldn't call us or trust our word again. We're apparently her *only* link." Kate thought a moment and then added, "He said to be sure to bring her straight to him when we get back, so *he* can deal with the mother's anger himself."

"Well," said Phil, scratching his fuzzy flattop, "let's go right away. I'm glad I filled up the gas tank on the way home today. There won't be many stations open at this hour."

"You haven't had any sleep yet. Will you be able to drive all night?"

Phil laughed. "You may have to spell me off, if I feel a nap coming on."

Cindi went to wake Cori, who could always manage to sleep, even through the noisy excitement. Cori emerged from the girls' bedroom, rubbing her eyes and grumbling, until the task was explained. "Then, what are we waiting for?" she asked.

"I got the impression Livie may be afraid of Rita." Kate turned to Lynette. "Is that possible?"

Lynette nodded. "Rita can be as mean as Mom. I don't know if Rita will let you take Livie, even if you find her. Rita's dangerous, especially when she's on heroin or speed." She paused a moment. "She has some nasty, big friends that hang out with her when she's dealing. I don't know what they'll do. Be careful."

"We'll have to *find* her first, before we can worry about that, and it doesn't seem like that's going to be easy." Phil shuffled through his sparse notes. "Not many clues."

Cindi and Cori disappeared and were back in minutes,

dressed in flowery jeans, sloppy loose-fitting old shirts and trailing three long bead necklaces each. "We'll blend in with the hippies who live in Haight Ashbury so we can ask questions," said Cindi.

"Maybe we should take some bougainvillea flowers for our hair," said Cori. "What do you guys think? Could we get away with standing on a street corner looking 'stoned,' while asking for Rita like if we wanted to buy drugs?"

Lynette laughed. "You two are priceless! But you might have a point because everyone in the area would know Rita, if she's pushing, and I think she is." Lynette walked slowly around the two sisters, and tugged Cindi's blonde hair down to its full length. "Brush it out as straight and long as you can," she advised. "You look about right. Take my two beaded Indian vests, too. But, I wonder if you know how to look stoned?"

Cindi slipped on a headband and struck a pose, slouching and leaning against the door jam, her eyes half-closed, slurring her words as she said, "I ain't takin' drama at high school for nothin'."

"Besides", added Cori, "we've watched Olivia lots of times when she was desperate to get a fix of something and when we've kept her busy enough to talk her out of it, so we sort of know how she acts when she's craving, too."

Lynette nodded. "I think you can do it. You could pass."

Phil broke in. "Wait a cotton-picking minute, you guys. I don't want our girls hanging out on street corners asking strangers for drugs. We'll think of another way."

"Dad, listen. I think this is a good idea," said Cindi. "If we can find Rita, Livie might be with her, or at least she'd know where Livie is. Please let us help, too."

Phil still looked unconvinced, but Lynette said, "I think they're right, Phil. That's probably how Livie found Rita, too. Rita will keep Livie in her sight so she won't run or talk to anyone else to give away the location of her drug business or her pad."

"I've got an idea." Alisa ran to her room and returned with two photos of Olivia. One was of a time she had come home drugged from the One-Ways. Phil had taken the photo to show her how bad she looked when stoned. It had shocked her all right!

Olivia hated the photo, but she kept it to remind herself what drugs did to her. The second photo was of Livie all bright-eyed in her Cadette uniform, hat set at a jaunty angle, and sporting her sash with her first earned badge on it. Alisa handed the photos to Kate. "You can show these when you ask people about having seen her. "She'll look like one photo or the other, so people may have seen her either alone, or with her older sister."

Kate looked at the two photos--so different, yet so representative of both their good times and bad times since Olivia had entered their lives. "Good idea, Alisa. I'll go to the shops on Haight Street. Someone may have seen her come for groceries."

"Or cigarettes," said Ned. "If it's a shop on the street near her house, she'll always ask for the same things, so someone might have noticed her—a speedy, dark little girl buying Marlboro cigarettes, Mars candy bars, and maybe hot dogs."

"I think we're getting somewhere," said Kate. "Your ideas just might help us find her. What do you think, Phil?"

Phil looked from his two dressed-up-for-Halloween daughters to the other three eager-with-ideas teens, and his wife holding the photos. He finally shook his head and said, "I think I'm outnumbered. You know, I'll be zonked by the time we get there, so maybe if I pretended to sleep like a homeless person in whichever park the police tell us the hippies gather in for the afternoon, maybe I'll see Rita and Olivia before you guys do." He laughed again. "Are we crazy, or what?"

"Hey, that's getting with the program, Dad," said Cori. She giggled. "Imagine my straight-laced, upstanding father hanging out with the stoned hippies."

Kate put her hand over his, "I feel a glimmer of hope of finding her now." She stretched up to kiss Phil on the nose. "I love you, but I don't think your pajamas will quite do, even for a homeless person. Let's put on some old clothes."

Within the hour, a packed car hummed in the driveway. Kate sat in her usual place in the center of the front seat, snuggled up against Phil. She leaned across him to give last-minute instructions to the rest of the kids gathered by the car.

"You guys get some sleep for school tomorrow, and take care of each other," ordered Kate. "Alisa, set your alarm. You know you have a hard time waking up, and don't forget to call for subs for us. The district numbers are by the telephone. Lynette, you check that she and Ned are up on time, too. Lynette, there's leftover spaghetti sauce in the fridge, so you can fix everyone your favorite 'spysghetti' for dinner." She smiled at the teen. "Ned, don't forget your asthma medicine, and, if you have any problems, call Susan's mom across the street for advice. Gina's not being friendly these days, but I know she'd help you in a crisis. I just don't want to wake her now, at midnight. And don't forget your homework when you get home from school. Ned, drive safely. You guys be careful. I love you. We'll get home soon as we can."

"Quit worrying, Kate. We're fine," said Ned, with a grin. "Just find Livie." They all waved goodbye.

Phil backed out of the driveway and drove across the darkened city to 101 Highway North, while the girls in the back seat dozed off.

Phil turned to his wife. "You realize we're setting off for a large unfamiliar city, to find a little girl among people who don't want to be found, with only one street name, and a hundred blocks of left and left again. Or maybe right, and right again, depending which way Olivia was facing and if she had her lefts and rights straight. We're looking for a three-story house in a city, as I remember from only a few short visits there, had *all* three-story houses, and a phone booth, when one is on every corner." He sighed. "Realistically, maybe we shouldn't get our expectations up too high. We might be on a wild goose chase."

"Don't forget about the big red letters, S and T. I wonder if those are a gas station, or a street sign, or a billboard--could be anything. Will we know it when we see it? Was Olivia even seeing colors correctly?"

"We must be out of our minds."

Kate laid her head on his shoulder as he drove. "We probably are crazy, my love, but Livie *wants* us to find her, and at least we've got hope on our side. It's all we've *ever* had."

Chapter 16

Sunlight burned through the dawn's coastal fog when Kate and Phil maneuvered through the San Jose to San Francisco segment of 101 Highway nicknamed "Bloody Bayshore" for its multiple fatal accidents.

"Remember when you were stationed at Moffett Field in the Navy, and the kids were babies? All the so-called improvements on this highway haven't kept up with the increased traffic and wild driving, have they? I still feel a little edgy, especially with our girls sleeping in the back seat."

Phil patted her hand. "And I suppose our exhaustion after an urgent eight-hour drive isn't helping the edgy feeling, either. Any more gum to help me stay awake?"

She fumbled in her purse to hand him a stick, as Phil pulled up in front of the first police station they found within San Francisco's city limits. He went in while Kate waited in the car with the girls. After a few minutes, he returned, sliding back into the driver's seat with a sigh. "Well, that was a waste of time."

"Why?" said Kate. "Detective Fredrick promised the San Francisco police would help us. He said to come here first."

"These guys gave us city maps and said the hippies hang out in Golden Gate Park, but beyond that, they offered nothing. They don't go into the area much now that the hippies have overrun the city, not for mere runaways, anyway. He said they're *all* runaways, and it's hopeless to try to find anyone. They advised us to give up and go home."

"We're not giving up! We drove all night to get here. Livie is out there, alone."

Phil took Kate's fluttering hands in his. "Dear, we don't know for sure that she's here. But we're not giving up. This is a leap of faith, but we're here, so let's go find Livie."

"Are we there yet?" asked Cindi, rubbing sleep from her eyes and running fingers through her long, tangled hair.

Cori yawned loudly. Early rising was not part of her

repertoire, but this time, she was already bright-eyed.

"We're here," said Phil. "Let's have a sandwich for breakfast and make plans."

The car bounced as Cori climbed over the back seat to open the ice chest in the rear compartment of the station wagon and passed forward sandwiches and drinks. She kept one of the peanut butter sandwiches for herself and grinned mischievously as she handed the other to her mother. They both liked the same kind--PB with no J.

"What did the police say, Dad?" asked Cindi.

"They don't think we've got a chance. They say if we get in trouble in Haight Ashbury, we're on our own. I can't believe this area could be *that* much worse than the One Ways, but we don't know anything about the hippie culture, either." He yawned and stretched his neck, as both fatigue and concern creased his face. "We'll leave you girls here at the police station until we get back. You'll be safer here."

"Not on your life, Dad," said Cindi. "We'll be fine. Cori and I can run fast if we have to. We're here, Livie's here, and we're going to find her. I just know it."

"We don't need the police," added Cori. "Livie will be watching for *us*, too. She knows we'll come."

If she even has us in the right city, Kate thought. But, she smiled brightly at her husband and patted his shoulder. "Eat up, darling, it's going to be a long day."

"I'm surrounded by bloody optimists." Phil grinned and unwrapped his sandwich.

An hour later, after finding gas station restrooms, they parked the station wagon on a side street near the Haight Ashbury perimeter, and marked its position on the four maps Phil had wangled from the S.F.P.D., so everyone would know its location.

"We can't just drive all over San Francisco looking for a red sign when we don't even know what it is, we have no idea where Rita lives, and phone booths are on *every* street corner. So, we need to think this through to maximize our effectiveness. I'm going to Golden Gate Park, here by the band shell." Phil showed the others on his map. "And you girls can find a spot about here." He circled a four-block area not far from the park. "Should you have funny reactions to your questions about Rita, or be uncomfortable on the street, run straight to the park and find me. Promise! I'll be pretending to be asleep"

Cindi laughed. "Or *really* asleep. How do you know there's a band shell, Dad?"

"There's always a band shell in a park that has concerts." He smiled. "Call it a calculated guess or something I saw on TV."

"Okay, Dad. We know where the car is, and where you'll be," Cori said. "It's Mom that we won't have any way to find."

"But I'll know where *you* are," said Kate. "We'll all meet back at the car at five if we haven't found anything by then. If you girls find Livie, or get a lead on Rita, go straight to your dad at the park, first, and then meet me back at the car at five. I'll be checking stores along Haight Street. If I find her, I'll do the same. Any questions?"

Cori snickered. "You and Dad both sound like teachers. We're not little kids."

They grinned, and Phil stuck out his hand like they always did before a game. One by one, the other three hands piled on top, and they gave a half cheer, half prayer, "Livie, Livie, rah!" threw their hands up high, and set off in different directions.

Though the plan had seemed feasible while together, later, alone, Kate felt panic creep in. Half her family was split up all over a strange town, while the other half waited 650 miles away. *I can't believe my two little girls are standing on a street corner looking for a drug dealer, my husband is in a hippie hangout, and I'm looking for businesses in an area known for so much crime the police won't even come if we need them. This is not exactly the straight-laced life we'd planned for our family--before Livie.*

She sighed and started walking from one side of Haight Street to the other, ferreting out grocery stores or filling stations that carried candy bars and cigarette machines, and accosting strangers on the street. She stopped the first man she saw and showed him the photos, asking if he'd seen a small, dark girl who looked drugged or lost. His gaunt face registered no emotion as he barely looked at the photos and said, "We're *all* drugged or lost." He pushed past Kate and disappeared into an alley.

"Well, that went well," she muttered to herself, with only a hint of sarcasm.

Kate stopped a woman emerging from a row house. The woman's rolled down stockings and sloppy shoes seemed out of place on someone of her middle-aged status.

"I'm looking for this young girl," Kate said, proffering the photos.

"You from the police?"

"Oh, no, ma'am," Kate was startled that the woman's tone was so distrustful and angry. "I was hoping you might have seen this girl. We think she's lost here somewhere."

The woman shoved away the photos and shook her head, a tight smirk on her face. "I don't see nothin'—don't hear nothin'—don't know nothin'."

Kate watched the woman hurry down the street, her muddy shoes leaving tracks on the already dirty sidewalk. It took only a few more encounters where suspicious or hostile people shrugged and moved away to make Kate feel she had some medieval contagious disease. A couple of times she sensed a hesitation, or perhaps a glimmer of recognition, but nobody would trust her enough to talk. She yearned for a friendly face.

One gas station owner turned his weathered, wrinkled face to Kate when she approached. He was at least interested, though he didn't think he had seen Olivia. "We get lots of runaways in here, but nobody tries to find them. Is this kid someone special?"

Kate answered carefully, "She's special to us. Our family has been trying to help her get off drugs."

The man snorted, "That's impossible around here, lady. Drugs flow down this street like soda pop." He wiped the grease from his hands onto his overalls and shook his head. "I've run some of the pushers off my property when I actually see 'em dealing, but they gang up on anyone trying to stop 'em. They've threatened me, and I don't relish my filling station going up with a boom, so I've been pretty quiet about it. I don't know where all that 'peace and love' is supposed to be with these hippies. There's a fight on this street corner nearly every night."

"We were told the police don't come in here much. Is that true?"

He laughed bitterly. "Dunno, but I'd get no help if these kids torched my place. The cops have given up on The Haight. They're just waiting for all the kids to grow up or move away to some other place. I guess that's what I'm holding out for, too."

"Do you see any signs of the fad wearing off?"

"Not yet. But sooner or later, these hippies with all their love children named 'Sun' and 'Butterfly' are gonna have to grow up and get real, like the rest of us."

"We can hope," said Kate. "It feels as though our whole value system is being attacked. You know; what made the nation great in the first place. It scares me. But for now, I just need to find our lost little girl. Do you have any suggestions?"

"Well," he said slowly, pulling off his hat and examining the greasy ring around its inner band. "These kids meet in pretty much the same places every day, so if you find where her gang hangs out, you'll find someone who knows her. But, most of 'em are so loaded from the night before, I'm not sure they even know where they've landed in between times. You won't see 'em on the street until after noon, and then they'll surface, looking to buy or beg for food. They'll come down this street in groups on their way to the Park to get their drugs from the pushers for another night."

"So they'll go by here later this afternoon?"

"Yeah. It's like a bloody parade. They walk down the middle of the street like the cars can't touch 'em. Sometimes they block my driveways so cars can't get in at all, or they beat on the hoods, singing and laughing. Damn, it hurts business." He shook his head and then clamped his hat back on it. "Most people go to some other gas station now--out of the district. I can't blame 'em."

"I may come back this afternoon if I don't get a lead on Olivia before then. Thank you for the information."

"You're welcome, lady. Hope you find her."

Kate moved forward, entering every little store. Sure enough, there were few young people on the streets at this hour of the morning. She wondered if Olivia was sleeping off her drugs someplace, too. *What will I say to Rita to get her to let me take Olivia with me? What if Rita really is violent?* For the first time, Kate faltered in thinking they might be successful in finding Olivia. They'd been so reckless and optimistic in trying, against all advice and odds. *What if we really can't find her? She'll think we abandoned her.* She pushed the negative thoughts out of her mind.

After stops at several little stores and stations, along with seedy little places selling tie-dyes and bongs and roach clips or psychedelic posters of half-dressed entertainers, Kate still had no leads. No one admitted to having seen Livie. The street itself mocked her forced optimism. Boarded up windows and iron grates in front of doors reflected the state of fear in the district—even worse than the One-Ways. Kate felt eyes follow her as she picked her way past yet another junkyard. Several people lay asleep or passed out amid the twisted car bodies, tarps, and broken glass. Dirty papers blew in stale gusts of wind, and cigarette butts littered the ground. Perhaps they weren't cigarettes. Kate assumed the sharp, burning hay odor rising from the litter was marijuana. She hurried past an alley where a young man was relieving himself against a pole with no more shame than a stray dog.

Kate was sickened to think young people could live like this, with no values, no responsibility, lost in a haze of drugs. Where were their parents? Wasn't anyone searching for them, crying for their loss—wondering where they, as parents, might have gone wrong, or what they might have left undone? She recognized that this was the kind of world from which Olivia had come, and this was an inside look. Livie always called she and Phil "her *Bridge Over Troubled Waters*," but neither had understood what troubled waters they were. The thought depressed her.

As noon rolled around, Kate grew aware of a rumbling stomach and munched on the peanuts in her pocket. They didn't help. The rumbling seemed somehow deeper and more painful than mere hunger. She didn't know what was wrong, and she didn't want to speculate, but something deep inside her wasn't right. She hadn't told Phil about it. They really couldn't afford a doctor right now and, like most teachers, she had a tendency to avoid illness because she was "too busy to get sick." It was never convenient to get sick when you had a classroom full of kids to worry about. But lately, the pain came more violently and frequently. *I'll deal with this when we get Olivia home.* Kate pressed her forearm hard against her mid-section and walked on.

A few young people were beginning to appear—shambling, emaciated, filthy, with bloodshot, brooding eyes peering out at surroundings they barely acknowledged—like zombies. *What a waste of precious national treasure,* she thought—*losing our young people—our next generation.*

A dark young man brushed by her and whirled around, stumbling against the wall. Recovering his precarious balance, he screamed at her, "What are ya doin,' bitch?"

Kate quickly excused herself, though the accidental encounter had not been her fault. But from his slack jaw and wide-open pupils, he had no idea what he was doing.

Ahead, Kate noticed another small store on the corner. She ducked into it quickly, welcoming the dark, cool atmosphere as preferable to the warped people with apparent death wishes on the outside. She prepared for yet another disappointment, but pulled out one last smile to approach the saleslady behind the counter. The smile was wasted.

The older woman lazily moved aside boxes on the counter, making room to open the first one. She only looked at Kate peripherally, as though a customer might disappear if she just ignored her long enough. Uncombed, frizzy gray hair protruded impudently through a holey hairnet. An apron of grungy brown overwhelmed her faded, once-upon-a-time-flowered print dress.

Kate pulled an orange soda from the cooler, pried off the cap in the opener on the side, and set the bottle on the counter with a thump to attract the woman's attention.

The woman sighed at the bother and turned to take Kate's dollar bill and give her seventy-five cents change. She looked more aggravated at being disturbed than anxious to make a sale, but Kate was determined to break through the woman's indifference.

"I'm looking for a young girl."

"There's a lot of them around," the woman said. She continued moving dual cupcake packages from the boxes to shelves behind the counter.

"Please look at these pictures and see if you might've seen her." Kate held out the photos. The woman ignored her.

"Please, ma'am, if you'd just look at the photos. Our little girl has been missing for over six weeks, and we have reason to believe she's being kept here against her will."

"How would *you* know? These kids come here from all over. None of 'em ever wants to go home. Why should they? They're living in la la land." She stopped shelving stock long enough to glance at the two photos. "Are you sure this is the same kid?"

"I'm afraid so. She's had some good times and some bad ones."

"Well, she cleans up well," the woman said, handing back the Girl Scout photo. "I wouldn't see any like *that* one around here." She squinted at the old photo Phil took of Olivia on drugs. She adjusted her glasses further down on her nose and seemed to study the lop-sided grin, heavy-lidded eyes, and Olivia's slouch on the divan with a pair of fingers held up in a peace sign. "This one looks a little familiar."

Kate leaned forward, fueled by sudden hope. "Do you think so? I've looked everywhere, and no one else has seen her."

"I could be wrong, lady. They all look wasted like this." She started to hand the photo back with a shrug.

Kate said, "Please look again, ma'am. We're desperate to find her before something bad happens to her. She called us late last night from a corner phone booth, we think on Haight Street-- maybe a gas station. She sounded scared. She wanted us to come get her, and we drove all night to get here." Kate took a deep breath realizing she was rambling. She groped for some detail about Olivia that would set her apart from the legions of wasted kids this woman probably saw every day. "If she came in here, it was probably for Marlboro cigarettes and Mars candy bars--a small kid, sort of stunted for her age, with straight black hair, Indian complexion. Please tell me you've seen her."

The woman's expression softened in the face of Kate's eagerness. "Let me look at it again." She peered at the photo closely, moving her glasses down the bridge of her nose. "Does this kid remind you of a grasshopper, sort of leaping into everything, all jumpy and active? She sort of sticks out in a crowd? I'm pretty sure she's been in here."

Kate laughed. "That sounds like Olivia, all right, at least when she's not doped up. When she's on drugs, she can be slow, and she doesn't think well, so her speech gets funny. She's apt to cuss a lot then, too." Kate was excited—at last, a possible lead.

The woman shook her head. "The people she was with, I don't think they called her 'Olivia.' It was something else...something funny, with an L, like 'Lovey' or...."

"Was it 'Livie'? People call her Livie, short for Olivia."

"That was it!" Suddenly, the woman seemed eager. "I think you're right that she's in danger. She tried to use our phone once, and an older girl slapped her and pushed her to the floor. I wanted to say something, but there was this big bearded man with them. He ordered the kid around too, and a couple of others. All of them were high. I was afraid to do anything." The woman shook her head, "tsk tsking" as she did. "When you said Marlboros and Mars bars, it rang a bell. She comes in sometimes, and that's all she buys. I thought maybe she didn't have money for anything else."

"That's got to be Livie. If left to herself, Mars bars and hot dogs are all she'd eat. I can't thank you enough for helping me. Do you have any idea where this group lives?"

The woman shook her head. "Lots of kids come in. I don't see where they go."

"Livie gave me some confusing directions over the phone last night," said Kate, desperately trying to jog the woman's memory for further information. "She sounded pretty uncertain, maybe sick. She didn't make much sense. She said something about living around the block to the left and then left again in a three-story house, three, four, maybe five houses down. Does that help any? I see that the gas station catty-wampus across from you has a phone booth on its corner. Maybe she called from there. She kept saying something about seeing a big red S and T, but that isn't the name of the gas station." Kate swept her eyes across the street again, straining for a red sign.

The woman mulled over the vague information. "S-T? No, that's Gary's station over there, no S-T." After a long pause, she scratched her frizzy head and brightened. "You don't think it's the 'State Street Band,' do you? There's a big billboard on the side of the junkyard straight across the street. You can't see it from here, but it's real big, and the background has red and black lettering."

The door slammed as Kate sped out. Unmindful of cars, she dodged across the intersection to the phone booth and turned to face the junkyard. There on the side, at least ten feet high and twenty feet long, was a red billboard advertising the "State Street Band," appearing at the band shell at Golden Gate Park on Friday night. Kate raced back across the street and into the store. "That's it! That has to be it! The phone booth faces it." Kate grabbed the woman's hands and laughed, "She was there. We must be close."

The woman grinned and pried her hands from Kate's tight grasp. "Sorry, arthritis. Okay, you're close, so now what?"

"I could wait here and hope Olivia comes in, but...."

"She doesn't come in every day. It's been maybe two days, and she had all those violent people with her. She didn't bounce around like she usually does. She was quiet—looked a little sick."

"Okay, so waiting here would be my last resort. But if she comes in, you could tell her to wait here as long as she can, and I'll come back for her before five p.m."

The woman nodded. Kate felt her eyes watching every move as she stood near the doorway and moved her hands in left and left again patterns from the way the phone booth faced the red and black sign. She asked the woman, "It could be either way. If she had her rights and lefts okay, that might be down that street and a left turn down a block."

"I don't think she came from that way. I'm trying to remember, but I think she came in from that way," the woman said, pointing in the opposite direction. "I usually couldn't see her until she bounced in the door, and if she had come from that other direction, I would have seen her through the glass."

"Okay," said Kate trying to reverse her thinking, right for left. "Do you know if there are three story houses one street down that way from here?"

"Lady, I hate to tell you this, but practically every house in the area, except for new ones, are three stories--two real floors and an attic. They were mostly built after the earthquake and fire of 1906. They're all old and dilapidated."

"I was afraid of that." Kate was anxious to find the house before the group went out to the park in the afternoons. She looked at her watch. It was almost one. She turned again to the woman, excited to go--*but where first?*

"Maybe you should take a breath," the woman said, kindly. "Finish your soda pop and then decide which way to go. There are lots of houses down there, and they all look alike. And these kids crowd just *any* old body into these pads to stay with them."

"Let me think. If I go the way you said, a block down and turn, and try the third to the fifth houses in both directions, I might get lucky and find her."

"And if you don't?"

"Then I'll knock on every door, on both sides of the street in both directions. I really need to work on Livie's sense of right and left when we get her home."

"Look, lady, I understand your hurry, but things around here are crazy. None of these people take kindly to strangers just knocking on doors and asking questions."

"But Livie's only a teen. You'd think they'd want to help me find her."

"You're kidding yourself. Just be careful approaching any doors. Go slowly and keep your hands out front so they don't think you're a cop or something. The houses all have these buzzers, so they don't have to open the door to anyone. They only buzz you in, *if* they know you. They probably won't let you in to ask any questions."

"Really? It seems so odd to me. These are mostly just kids."

"Yeah, but they're *strung out* kids, either catatonic or hyper or dangerous, depending on what they're taking today and how long it's been since they had a fix." She spread out her gnarled, rough hands. "They hate cops and parents, and they won't give you any information, if they can help it. You need to know that." She paused and then added, almost as an afterthought, "And when you get done checking around for the day, come back to let me know if you found her or not. Somebody needs to know if you're going in there after her, in case you don't come back out."

Kate had a hard time believing such precautions were necessary. As a teacher, her perception of kids, even *these* kids, was simply as troubled, not dangerous. But remembering her first trip to the One-Ways, she realized she might have underestimated hostility she had neither perceived nor understood. She thanked the woman for her kindness and promised to come back before five.

Kate started off in the direction the woman had indicated, on the blind side of the store, down one block, then what? Left or right? Rows of dilapidated old three-story houses marched in long lines over the hills, with identical spaces where lawns had once been. Now, they were plain old dirt, with multi-colored Volkswagen vans painted with big enough eyes to be those of God, or with rainbows enough for all spring showers. It was overwhelming. *Where do I start?*

After pondering a few moments, Kate felt conspicuous standing still. So she plunged off to her left, going down one side of the street and planning to go back up the other and then try to the right, in case Olivia had her directions backwards.

At the first house, Kate did as the saleswoman had told her--approaching slowly with her hands in plain sight. Nevertheless, when she rang the doorbell, no one buzzed her into the entryway. She waited, aware of movement on the other side of the stained glass door. Finally, the door opened a crack, with a sturdy chain holding it.

A young woman peered out. She was unkempt, half-dressed, with her long hair and loose housecoat scrambled in all directions. In response to what Kate hoped was a pleasant smile, the woman said, "What do you want?"

Kate held out the photos of Olivia and said, "I'm looking for this little girl, and I'm hoping you might have seen her in this area."

"She's not here!" The door slammed.

Does that mean she is there, and no one will tell me, or that she really isn't there, or that they won't talk to anybody about anything?

Kate tried another door. The next two houses yielded much the same result--uncaring people with no desire to find a missing kid. At the fourth house, no one would answer the door or buzz her in, though she could hear people scurrying around within and the unmistakable sound of flushing toilets. *They probably think this is a drug bust and they're flushing down their stash.* She snickered to think she had picked up some jargon from Lynette and Olivia in spite of herself. Laughing at herself relieved tension, and it made her feel closer to the girls.

By the sixth and seventh house with no result, Kate was beginning to think she was wasting precious time, and perhaps she should join Cindi and Cori on the street, or Phil in the park. Yet, she couldn't escape the gut feeling that she was close…but where?

On a whim, she crossed the street, thinking perhaps Livie meant a house on the other side. The first and second houses also drew blanks. At the third, she knew she was in plain sight of the frosted glass door, and she could hear voices, though she couldn't make them out. She squared her shoulders and rang the bell.

Suddenly the buzzer sounded, and she found herself pushing inside, having no idea what she would find on the other side of the door. As her eyes adjusted from the sunlight outside, she noticed the foyer was papered with psychedelic paintings and posters that barely covered the cracks in the plaster. A water drug pipe lay overturned. The large room was empty of furniture except for a dirty mattresses on the floor. One was, to Kate's embarrassment, occupied, by a completely naked young lady and a huge, hairy man who merely looked up, grinned, and flashed her a finger. The young lady was oblivious to any concerns of privacy. With relief, Kate realized it was *not* Olivia.

She looked away quickly. The store lady had said the old houses were actually informal apartments sharing facilities, "pads," the kids called them. Several others would be living here—perhaps Olivia, too. The acrid stench of garbage, marijuana, and musky body odors, infrequently washed, all melded into an almost unbearable assault on her senses. Clutter dominated the foyer, with sweaters, soiled underclothing, dirty needles, old sandals, and wastepaper all lying where they fell. It looked as though nothing had been put away or cleaned since the houses were built. Grime coated every surface, with multiple smudges and watermarks on walls of indeterminate hue. Bare mattresses and sleeping bags lay in every corner of the entry. *How many people live here?*

Kate heard a screech, a crash, and someone cursing loudly at the top of the staircase. She looked up to see a woman grabbing Olivia, screaming, "You little shit! You buzzed someone in here. I've warned you again and again. She could be a pig!"

Rita, for with the resemblance it could be no one else, yanked Olivia's head back by the hair, and put her free hand around the girl's throat. Livie squirmed and tried to duck under her sister's arm. Rita blocked her way, tripping her with one leg.

Kate ran up the stairs, dodging trash scattered on the decrepit stair treads, and reached out to Olivia.

Rita pushed Olivia toward the railing until she hung half over the edge.

"Come one step closer and she's wearing a broken neck," Rita said.

Chapter 17

Kate halted abruptly, three steps down from the pair, desperately gauging if she could grab Livie before Rita could push her over the banister. Prospects didn't look good. She spoke quietly, hoping she could calm the hysterical big sister, "I'm so glad to have found you. You must be Rita. I'm a friend of Olivia's, and I've come to take her home."

Rita bent Livie further over the railing. Livie squirmed wildly, her feet kicking out to try to find a footing, and her arms trying to wrap around the railing, but she couldn't break her sister's grasp. "She ain't goin' nowhere except down. You can pick up the pieces. You're a pig, ain't you?"

Words stuck in her throat, but Kate shook her head vigorously. For such a small girl, perhaps five foot one, Rita was strong. Livie was wiry, but the younger girl was a rag doll in Rita's grip. Except for her wild and frizzy long hair, Rita resembled Olivia more than Lynette. She looked middle aged, though Kate knew she was only a few years older than Lynette--probably about 22. *Could drugs do that?* If Lynette had originally looked like a hooker, Rita looked, in addition, emaciated, grasping, and sick to the very soul. *There's no hope for this one. I have to get Livie out of here.*

"She called you, didn't she?" Rita's eyes burned with fury, as though they could pierce right through Kate.

God, what is this girl on? Kate evaded Rita's question, feeling it might make things worse for Olivia. Instead, she broke into the bubbly, breathless, fast-talking mode she found in the One-Ways had seemed to confuse those who were addled on drugs. "You don't know how hard it's been to find you. Lots of people on the street told me where you might be. I've been knocking on doors all morning. I'm so glad to find you before you left for Golden Gate Park. I'll just take Livie with me, and we'll get her home to her mother in no time." Kate regretted the words as soon as she said them.

Rita's grip tightened. Old bruises were visible on Livie's throat. "You brought my *mother*? I'll kill Livie, sure. She's no fuckin' nothin' to me."

"Oh, no, Rita, it's just me, as you can see. No mother, no police, no one. There's *no* threat to you. Just let me take Livie, please!" Kate held her breath, trying hard not to raise her voice, not sure what Rita would do. But her body was poised to spring, as she adjusted her left foot more firmly on the step. She hoped she could upset Rita and grab for Livie before Rita could push her over the edge.

Olivia's eyes pleaded with Kate. *Expecting me to do what? What can I say or do to get you out of here? I'm just winging it, Livie, blindly trying.*

Kate moved her eyes away from Olivia and kept Rita riveted in her gaze, desperately trying to hold her vagrant attention. "Gee, Rita, a kid like Livie, looking so young, probably cramps your lifestyle. Why would you want to keep her here? You can get rid of her and have your old life back? I'm sure she costs money and causes you problems." She took a deep breath, trying to think of an argument that would make sense to this strange young woman. "Aren't you afraid, with Livie underfoot, the cops will think you're dealing to little kids? Her being here could probably get you in a lot of trouble."

Rita didn't answer, but Kate could tell she was listening, in a distracted, confused way. Kate quickly resumed, waving a finger peripherally at Olivia, who had started to protest her words, and keeping her eyes focused on Rita's. "Why, if I take her out of here, your operation will be much safer. What do you think? Wouldn't getting rid of Olivia now be better than having someone come back later with the pigs?" The word grated on Kate, but she said it firmly. Livie was at stake, and she had to make the most of Rita's attention, at least until she could inch forward enough to get a hand on Olivia.

The subject of this strange conversation had stopped struggling in response to Kate's s finger wave. Livie managed to sneak one hand onto the banister, though the rest of her still leaned far over the edge, on her back, with one of Rita's hands on her throat.

Kate felt Olivia's eyes on her, probably trying to read her next move. *God, I wish I knew what it would be, myself!* She kept up the chatter. Perhaps she could irritate Rita enough that she would let go of Olivia to take a swing at her. Livie might hold on.

"You're a cop, or you'll bring back the pigs. I can't let either of you out of here." Rita shouted to someone up the stairs, "Dink, come here, quick."

"Honest, Rita, I'm not a cop, and I really don't care what you do with your life. All I want is Olivia. She can't possibly do you any good. I promise neither of us will be telling anyone, even your mother, where you are." She added in desperation, "When we go out that door, we don't know you."

"I can't trust you! I can't trust nobody! I can't let her out of here to rat me out."

Kate heard footsteps running down the upstairs hall. A huge black man with skuzzy, long dreadlocks stumbled toward the women. "What's up, Rita? You woke me again."

"Nothin' I shouldn't a done a long time ago." With that, Rita suddenly shoved Olivia. Kate lunged over the railing, grabbing Livie by the arm. The wiry young girl frantically clung to Kate's arm and shoulder, until she could get a leg over the railing and hang on. It was a fortunate move because Kate had little strength left to hold Olivia's full weight on her arm.

"Get her out of here," screamed Rita, ripping Olivia's legs from the banister and pushing her hard against Kate. "I never want to see her again! She's no sister of mine."

The sudden weight and change of tactic dislodged Kate. She and Livie both fell backwards down several steps. Kate flailed, grabbing at anything, and finally caught the railing to stop their fall and absorb Olivia's weight. While Rita screamed obscenities, Kate set Livie on her feet, and they raced down the stairs to the foyer.

Before Kate could get the unfamiliar door open, Rita shrieked, "Livie, stop!"

No! Not another change in this woman's moves. She's

crazy. Kate continued struggling with the door that locked automatically behind everyone who entered, looking for a knob to turn. Livie reached out and undid the secret lock Kate couldn't find, hidden within the framing around the oval window. Kate wrenched the door open and tried to shove Livie through it, but Rita was already upon them.

Rita grabbed Livie by the hair, pulled her head back sharply, and kissed her hard, long, and forcibly on the mouth. Livie struggled to turn her head to escape her sister's mouth and saliva.

This scene horrified Kate, but she couldn't get Livie free, though she beat wildly on Rita's arms. Rita didn't seem to even feel the blows.

Rita ended her horrible assault and let go of Olivia with a shove to the floor. Olivia's purple lips dripped blood from where she'd been bitten. Ignoring Kate, Rita sauntered halfway back up the steps and said coldly to Olivia, "Don't you dare forget! I can always find you, *and* anyone you're with."

The woman placed her hand on a knife half hidden in her belt, half drawn. *No mistaking the implied threat.*

Kate bent to help a stunned Olivia to her feet, and Rita screamed, "You! Get her out of here, and she knows what'll happen if anyone finds me or narcs on me."

Kate pushed Olivia through the door, grabbed her hand, and they stumbled down the steps, not stopping until they reached the corner. Both were sobbing, faces wet with exertion and shock, and gulping in fresh air. Kate fished in her pocket for a handkerchief to wipe the blood from Livie's mouth. Livie winced when she touched the wound.

"What was that all about, Livie? Why did she do that to you?"

"A warning," Livie panted. "I heard of a death kiss, but I never thought...my own sister...and the knife...." Livie shook her head as though to rid herself of the image, and spit blood. "I never did anythin' to her. Honest. Let's get out of here."

Olivia held tightly to Kate's hand like a small child. Her knees kept buckling under her. Kate asked no more questions.

Olivia finally got her breath and said, "I can't tell you how bad.... All I can think of are cuss words. I'm sorry." She turned to bury her face in Kate's middle with her arms wrapped around. Kate had no words either, but just held the girl quietly, wondering if all Olivia had survived in this awful place could ever be undone.

"It's okay, Livie. What matters is getting you out of here." Olivia brightened a bit as Kate steered her into the comparative safety of the little store. The proprietress immediately came over. "Well, I see you found your little runaway. I have to say I'm surprised. I didn't really think you had a chance."

To Olivia, she smiled and said, "Hello, Miss Mars bar." She handed Olivia a candy bar and said, "This is for you to take with you, so you'll remember how this lady found you." She shook her finger at the girl. "It looks like you've been hurt. I hope you know you're darned lucky today. Don't come back here again."

Livie thanked the woman, then looked up at Kate and said, "I know. It was pretty stupid of me. But I knew you'd come. I was watching for you and saw you through the door. I dived across Rita to hit the buzzer before she saw you." All of a sudden, Livie jumped. "Where's Phil and everybody? You didn't come by yourself, did you?"

"No, we're going to meet them now. Phil's at the park, and Cindi and Cori are out on the streets asking druggies where to find Rita for a fix. They figured sooner or later, someone would tell them, and you might be with Rita."

Olivia was surprised. "They'd do that for me? They're crazy. You're *all* crazy. But we gotta find 'em quick, before lots of kids get into the street. They'll get busted, sure. Druggies will know they don't belong. Somethin' bad'll happen. How far?"

"A few blocks down. Why?"

"Hurry." Olivia took off down Haight Street at a stumbling run, grabbing often at brick walls and fences for support.

Realizing Livie must know something about the street that she didn't, apprehension dawned for her own young daughters. Kate jogged after Olivia.

Chapter 18

They ran two blocks before Olivia staggered and stopped, panting, and leaning against a dirty brick wall full of graffiti.

Kate was glad to slow down. She had a stitch in her side, and that mysterious something deep in her belly stabbed sharply. She stopped, hands on her knees, breathing hard. "Let's rest a minute." She looked closer at Olivia. The girl was shaking, and her dark complexion had faded several shades. Beads of sweat dotted her forehead. "What is it, Livie?"

"I shoulda knowed this'd get me before I got far. I'm gonna be sick." She slid down the wall to a sitting position on the sidewalk, helpless as the papers blowing in the wind. "I don't know...she gave me somethin' in a needle. It's gettin' inta me now." Olivia started to cry again, her body went limp in a little huddle against the building. "I can't...." She turned sideways and vomited onto the sidewalk. Kate reached into her pocket for more Kleenex and bent beside the girl, wiping her face.

"Come on, Olivia, you must get up. It's so dirty--you mustn't lie here." Kate reached down to help the girl to her feet. Half way up, Olivia slid back into a little heap.

"I can't, Kate. It's not just dirty here. Don't you see? *I'm* what's dirty. I'll never be free of all this." She put her face in her hands, cried out, and then grabbed her stomach. "Get to the girls, quick! I'll just lay here until ya get back."

"Not on your life, Livie. I'm not letting you disappear again. I'll help you up, and we'll find the girls together."

Weakly, leaning heavily on Kate, Olivia got to her feet, staggering, holding a hand against the wall for support on the other side. "Kate, this is gonna get worse. I don't know how long. I shoulda known she'd shoot me up with some bad stuff."

"Don't worry. Once we find the girls, they'll help us get to Phil. Hang on."

Obediently, Olivia struggled along, supported by Kate's arm and the walls of stained brick or chain link fences.

As Kate pulled Livie along, the streets were filling up with young people, the "parade" the garage owner had described. But no one seemed surprised that a young girl was doubled up and obviously in pain—no particularly curious or sympathetic looks, and no one offered to help. Kate had the eerie feeling of being among people with all expression only a façade, like paper dolls. Life in this place seemed totally devoid of compassion and humanity. *Are Livie and I the only people alive and aware here?*

When she glanced at Livie, she saw the same blank expression. *Don't give up now*, she scolded herself. *Find the girls. Get out safely before Rita joins the "parade."*

The two made a little headway. One block, two, with rest periods in between. Four blocks, five. *She's getting heavier all the time. I can't carry her alone.*

Suddenly Cindi ran up to Kate's side, and Cori pulled Olivia's other arm over her own shoulder.

Cindi hugged the limp Olivia and got a weak grin in return.

"I knew...I knew...we gotta get outta...before Rita...comes."

"It's okay," said Cindi. "We're going to go get Dad."

Olivia gave herself up to being half-dragged, half-carried to Golden Gate Park.

Within a half hour, Kate unlocked the car door and Phil deposited the limp Olivia he'd carried from the park onto the seat beside her. Kate wanted the girl up front where she could watch her vital signs, in case the narcotic Rita had injected got worse and they'd have to stop at a police station along the way to get them to take Livie to a hospital. Cindi and Cori piled into the back, as Phil hurried around to the driver's side.

Olivia lay in some kind of stupor—leaning against Kate, half awake, but vague and partially incoherent again—the way she had sounded on the phone the night before. As Phil started the car and pulled away from the curb, she cried, "Wait—go back."

"Go back where?"

"To the house...I want ya'all to see..."

Kate couldn't believe her ears. "Livie, we almost didn't get you out of there. If you've forgotten something, don't worry about it—you don't need it. Why would you want to go back there? What about Rita and those other people?"

"I forgot...I want...Cori and Cindi need to see...where I've been." The words were in slow motion, with long pauses. "'Sides, I gotta get somethin' important."

She's delirious, Kate thought.

"Olivia," said Phil. "The people in that house kept you in semi-captivity, and you've been hurt there. We're not going back in there. We're going back to L.A."

"Please...I forgot...."

"What did you forget, Livie?" asked Cindi.

"I had a picture...of the family. The one...I had my fingers... like horns over James's head...and...he was grinnin' and didn't know." Olivia started to cry. "It was in my pocket when I ran."

Kate gently touched the girl's tearful face and said, "Livie, we have the negatives at home. We can always get another copy printed for you. Don't worry."

"But, I can't...leave it here. It has your...address and stuff on it. If I don't get it...she's got it...I don't want her coming after...you guys."

"Olivia," said Phil, "We aren't going to worry about that. Your sister, Rita, has no reason to try to find us. Let it go."

Blubbering dazedly into her sleeve, Olivia said, "You just...don't know...."

Once in the car and moving toward the highway, silence gave way to a tension-relieving rush of questions and garbled answers.

"How...did you...find me, Kate? Was it...really Mars... bars?"

"Pretty much." Kate asked Cindi for a blanket from the back seat and tucked it around the shaking Olivia sitting beside her. "How were you girls doing on the streets, Cindi? Livie seemed to think that wasn't a good idea, that you'd get 'busted.'"

"Nobody was out there until about noon, and we were

bored. But, then weirdo characters came out of the woodwork. Nobody would answer questions."

"A few did," said Cori.

"Yeah, but they acted strange, and a couple of times we almost decided to run to find Dad. They'd ask us where we came from, and who sent us, and if we were narcs. It got spooky."

"But lots of them seemed to know Rita. They twitched when we said her name."

Laughter came from Cindi. "Oh, was *that* what they were doing? It looked to me like they were trying to find her, too, and they looked pretty desperate for a fix."

"Well, probably--that, too. What was it like for you, Dad?"

Cori's question called for highlights of Phil's long "nap" on the grass near the bandstand. "Lots of kids were just sleeping where they fell, I think, all sprawled out. I wondered if they were dead or just sleeping off their drugs from the night before."

"Mostly…just sleepin' off," volunteered Olivia, nodding her head side to side.

"Probably, since they occasionally groaned or shifted position. But this one couple came over near me and laid down on the grass and proceeded to get naked."

"Oh, my gosh, Dad, what did you do?" Cori covered her face with her hands. "They'd just do that in front of God and everybody?"

"It…don't matter," volunteered Olivia. "Make…love…not…war…."

"I don't think it was love, Livie. More like lust. One even had to ask the other his name. I got up and moved away, but this young man says, "Hope we ain't bothering' you Old Timer." Phil laughed. "Old Timer? Me? I'm thirty-four and I'm already an Old Timer?"

The girls laughed. Kate could picture Phil's discomfort in such a situation. Their lives together had been lived so conservatively, always trying to make up for the dysfunctional homes from which they had both come. They'd worked hard together to create a sanctuary where their children could live happily. Olivia had certainly brought new experiences into their lives, and Kate wondered if they would ever be so naïve again.

"They sure don't seem to care about themselves or each other," said Cindi.

Olivia roused again and said, "I needed that…picture, but that's what I wanted ya to see at the pad…don't want ya two ever…try…drugs, or anythin'."

Cori reached over the seat to pat Olivia on the head. "You don't need to worry, Livie. We've seen all the garbage dope has put you through."

"That's what I….wanted ya to know," Olivia repeated. "My little sister, Cori…." Olivia climbed into Kate's lap, laid her head on Kate's shoulder, and fell sleep.

Kate looked at Phil. He smiled at her and whispered, "Good job, Love, I somehow knew it would be you who found her, if anyone could."

Kate was near tears with fatigue. Whatever had to be talked about could wait. In spite of a small flash of concern about this photo that worried Olivia so, Kate laid her head on her husband's shoulder, snuggled the sleeping Olivia in her arms and nodded off.

Both Kate and Olivia awoke at about Santa Barbara, at a pit stop for all to refresh themselves a bit. It was a slow trip with frequent walkabouts to stay awake. Olivia was feeling better, and she haltingly told the girls of their encounter with Rita, their flight, and what she could remember of her six weeks in the pad. She was pretty hazy, and she admitted to almost continuous drug use. Most of the time she had not known where, or with whom, she had slept. She remembered waking up one night with a needle dangling out of her arm. "Dink said I'd been like that for days. They all had just been steppin' over me, doin' their thing. And there I was stuck with a needle on the floor."

"I couldn't handle them fallin' around, drugged out, so I tried to stay off the stuff and clean the kitchen. I'm used to cleanin' my mom's kitchen. There never was much in the fridge, but I tried fixin' 'em sandwiches from whatever was there. But they wouldn't eat until they got the munchies. I got so lonely. The only way I could live in there was to take whatever they were taking."

"What were they taking, Livie?" asked Cori.

"I don't even know—nobody cares? Uppers, downers, heroin, hash, speed, goof balls, mostly pot. There was stuff all over the house. The cops woulda loved comin'. I thought about tellin' a couple of times, after I had the needle stickin' out, 'cause I *know* I didn't do that to myself, 'cause I hate needles. But I was too high to know who did it...mighta been Rita. She laughed about it, after, and said if she kept me high, I couldn't run out and tell on her."

"Why didn't you tell the cops or someone?" Cindi's expression was curious. "I'm trying to figure how you got yourself into such a place. I know you didn't mean to, but it's hard to understand why."

"Couldn't find a cop anyplace--didn't know who to tell or call without it gettin' back to the pad, and anyways, I was scared I'd get caught."

"By whom?" Phil asked.

"Everybody, I guess, but mostly Rita. When I hitched to San Francisco, I thought she'd help me stay away from Mom, 'cause she hates her too. It was easy to find Rita. Everybody knows where she hangs out. She wasn't happy to see me. Told me I had to tough it out with mom and not drag in anybody else. She scared me when she threatened you guys for knowing about me. Said I already told you too much. And she was mad that I led Lynette to you. Now, I know Rita's worse than anybody. Even Dink pulled her off me when she beat me. 'Course, they fought big time when I woke up on his mattress. I didn't go there on purpose, Kate, honest. I don't know how I got there, just woke up, and there he was."

"You were drugged, Livie. It wasn't right of him to molest you."

"Honest, I tried to stay off the pills and junk, but I didn't have anyplace else to go, and everybody there was high. If I'da told anyone, they woulda told Rita I ratted her out." Olivia's voice remained fearful. " Rita has spies everywhere. After a while, bein' wasted was the only way I coulda stayed there…nobody cared about nothin'."

"It must have been horrible for you," said Cori. "Why didn't you call us sooner?"

"I tried a couple a times, but Rita caught me and dragged me back to the house. I heard Kate answer, once, but with Rita there, I couldn't say nothin'."

Olivia looked across the front seat at Phil and Kate. "I'm messed up again. I know ya gotta be mad at me. But it was so lonely with everyone else loaded up and all happy on drugs. I didn't know where to go, if I left. I'm sorta hangin' again, ain't I?"

Kate thought carefully before answering. "You kicked drugs before, Livie, and now, you'll have to kick them all over again. But you *know* you can do it because you've already done it a few times. There'll be flashbacks and withdrawal again."

"Oh, God. I forgot about that. Will you….?"

"Of course, we will, Livie," said Phil, in a husky, choked up voice. "You simply must choose what you want to do, and we'll try to help you, however we can."

Kate knew her husband hated to lose his objectivity, and that it so rarely happened. *This trip has been a strain—I can see it in all their faces. We're all wondering if Livie has any chance of putting this trip to the ugly side behind her, or if any of us can?*

It was dark as they neared home, cresting over the pass. The lights of L.A. looked inviting. Kate was again at the wheel, and Cindi and Cori slept peacefully in the back seat--Cori curled up on the seat with her head in Cindi's lap. Olivia was awake and much more alert, now that the drugs were gradually wearing off.

Olivia rose from her blanket with the stretch of a cat, her arms high. "I can't wait to get home. I got a monster headache."

"We'll be glad, too," said Phil, "but we have to stop first at the police station."

Olivia bristled. "What police station? I thought we were going home."

"It doesn't work quite like that, Livie," said Kate, bracing her arms against the steering wheel for what she knew was coming. "Your mother was given custody by the courts. We didn't have any right to come get you. She would have wanted to come, too, if we'd told her you called, and we wouldn't have had any choice by law, but to bring her."

"But I called you. I didn't call her. Why are we going to the police station?"

Patiently, Phil explained, while Kate made her way through the wee-hours crowd of cars still in Hollywood. "Olivia, there's nothing we'd like better than to take you home with us, but your mom called the police to look for you. They had a bulletin out to confine you in juvie, because you violated the conditions of your release by running away from your mom. She let them do an arrest warrant on you. One police detective has been trying to help us find a way...."

"No way! She knew I was leaving *her,* not runnin' away from any court."

"But, that's how it stands with the law right now, Livie. The police have orders to act on her declaration. So when you called, we talked to Detective Fredrick first. He said the only way we could go get you *without* taking your mother along was if we brought you straight to him, so he could deal with her, himself."

"But he's a cop! He'll give me right back to her or send me back to juvie."

"Livie, he thought he could help you best by not telling your mom we'd gone to San Francisco until *after* we left, but sooner or later, he'll have to confront her. She'll be angry. Detective Fredrick promised he'd try to help you choose where you could go, but we don't know how your mom took the news that we'd gone north without her." Phil gripped Olivia's hand. "The detective said for us to just *go* because we feared you'd run again, if we had your mom with us. That's what you said, anyway, and we couldn't take the chance of losing you completely."

Olivia put Phil's hand against her cheek and said, "But you won't let Mom take me, will you?" Big, husky Phil was totally without words.

"Olivia," said Kate as gently as she could. "We won't be the ones making the decision. But we had to *find* you before anything else could be decided. Hopefully, by the time we get there, Detective Fredrick will have worked something out with the court and with your mother, so we can take you home with us."

Phil said, "Detective Fredrick assumed your mother would be happy to know we'd heard from you, you were alive, and that we might be able to find you and bring you back. If that's the case, he thought he could persuade your mother to let you stay with us on a trial basis, depending on how well you recovered—your condition. If that's not the case, then, we'll have to play it by ear."

"You trust this guy--the detective?"

"Yes, Livie. He's been trying to help us find you and to find a way to keep you with us. He understands that you have problems at home, and he feels sending you there, again, would be wrong. Whether he, or we, can influence the court, may be another matter. Kate reached for Olivia's hand. "We were so scared you were lost, and we needed to *find* you. You can't imagine how worried everyone has been, and we just wanted you home safe, any way we could get you back."

"I know." Livie grew quiet. "I just didn't know where else I could go. My fault."

Kate turned her attention to the early morning traffic going through the City of Commerce, with its many industries always changing shifts. She dodged a delivery van crossing Washington Boulevard and turned southeast.

They finally pulled up at Norwalk Police Station. Six in the morning, and sunrise was slow at this season. Kate asked, "What should we do if Detective Fredrick isn't on duty yet?"

Phil squeezed her hand. "I imagine he left orders for what to do, since he knew we might be coming in during the night-- whenever we found Livie."

The silenced motor woke Cindi and Cori, and the whole group stumbled sleepily together into the station with Olivia holding both Kate and Phil's hands.

Only the night shift sergeant was at the desk. They asked

for Detective Fredrick and were told he wasn't coming in until 8 a.m., so they sat down to wait.

"Can I help you?" asked the desk sergeant.

"No, thank you," said Phil. "We'll wait for the detective. He's been helping us."

The man looked them over and nervously thumbed through papers at the side of his desk. He walked over to look more closely at Olivia where she sat flanked by Cindi and Cori. She raised her eyes, still a bit hazy and blood shot, to stare back at the man.

"You're that missing girl, Olivia Gonzaga, aren't you?"

"Yeah, so?"

Cori touched Olivia's hand to remind her.

Livie corrected her rude words. "Sorry, I forgot. Yes, I'm Olivia Gonzaga. Why?"

The policeman backed away, drew his gun, and pointed it at Phil and Kate. "There's a warrant on my desk for your arrest."

Phil looked up in surprise. "Arrest? For what?"

"Kidnapping. You're both under arrest."

"Kidnapping? You're joking. We went to San Francisco with Detective Fredrick's permission to try to find Olivia. He knows all about it. He *told* us to go."

The desk sergeant hit a buzzer on the wall, and three other policemen entered the waiting room. They spread out, separating Phil and Kate.

"Please call Detective Fredrick," said Kate. "He'll tell you this is a mistake."

"Lady, this is no mistake. This," he waved some papers, "says that Mrs. Gonzaga, this girl's mother, swore an affidavit on grounds you kidnapped her daughter and knew all along where she was. It says you withheld information on the whereabouts of her missing child, went to kidnap her, without informing her or offering to take her own mother along. What do you have to say to that?"

The man took Olivia's arm. She screamed and tried to evade his grasp, but he corralled her and asked one of the other officers to hold her back.

"Hold still, Livie," Phil admonished. Olivia quieted and stood with the officer's hand around her arm, waiting. "Look," said Phil, "It should be apparent that Olivia ran away from her mother. She called us yesterday to come get her. We went to San Francisco on very limited clues in hopes we could find her and bring her home. Finding her safely was *all* we were thinking about. Detective Fredrick said to bring her straight here so he could arrange with her mother for us to keep her until she felt better again. Ask Detective Fredrick. No one has committed any crime."

"Detective Fredrick doesn't have any say-so anymore. Mrs. Gonzaga wanted him off the case when he didn't contact her until *after* you were gone." The man spoke the words as though they gave him great pleasure--an officious gesture.

"We aren't kidnappers, " said Kate. "This whole thing is ridiculous. Livie called us to come get her."

"But you knew where she was all along, according to the mother's affidavit." With that, the sergeant turned to Olivia. "Did you call them before yesterday?"

Olivia was startled by the question, frightened and confused. She said, "Well, yes, a couple of times, but...."

"See, you folks knew where she was all along. She called you before."

Olivia screamed out, "You didn't let me finish." She lurched forward, battering weakly at the man with her hands. "You didn't...I didn't get to talk...you don't know."

"No, Livie," said Phil sharply. Again, she stood still, responding to his voice.

"My mom and dad didn't know where Livie was," said Cindi, indignantly. "We had to hunt for her in San Francisco, and the police there wouldn't even help us."

"We stood on a street corner all day," added Cori. "If we knew where Olivia was, don't you think we'd have just gone there to get her?"

The desk sergeant looked confused. "The affidavit says...."

"That's inaccurate," said Phil. "If we kidnapped her, why would we bring her here?" Kate saw Phil struggle to remain calm.

It was a good thing because she was about to lose her own control.

"We demand that you wait for Detective Fredrick," said Kate. "He'll tell you that Olivia called us, and we went. We didn't stop to consult her mother when that's who is responsible for her running away in the first place. None of this makes any sense."

The sergeant said, "Even if we wait regarding you two, the girl goes back to Juvenile Hall until her mother can pick her up."

"No!" It was a joint chorus, from Olivia and the whole Johnson family.

"That's not fair," said Cindi.

"She can wait here with us for the detective," said Kate. "You can watch us. We're not going anywhere. You can decide what to do with us once Detective Fredrick gets here."

"Well…" wavered the desk sergeant, "it's only for an hour or so. I guess we can at least hear what Detective Fredrick has to say about you folks."

The officer asked, "What about this one?"

"We'll call Juvenile Hall and see what to do," said the desk sergeant. "This is above my pay grade. If she was kidnapped, like the affidavit says, then she was taken against her will and isn't responsible, so we'll return her to her mother. If you didn't kidnap her, then she's a runaway and she'll have violated the instructions of the judge. She'll go to Juvenile Hall. The judge's paperwork seems pretty clear on this issue."

"Well, she can't be *both* kidnapped *and* a runaway," said Phil with his usual dry humor. Kate shot him a warning glance.

Olivia stood up straight and said, "Either way, I'm screwed. But you ain't gonna screw them, too. They didn't do nothin'. I wasn't kidnapped. I just left, and they came to find me when I called. I'd rather go back to juvie than home with my mother."

"No, Livie. Let's wait this out and try to find a better solution," said Phil.

Kate moved toward the girl, but the officer stepped menacingly in front of her to block her from contact.

"You can't get near her, ma'am. The paperwork accuses you of kidnapping her."

Kate threw her hands in the air. "This is the most ludicrous situation I've ever seen in my whole life." She reached out for Phil's hand and he moved to her side, careful not to look as though he was heading for the door.

"Please," said Phil. "Don't take Livie away from us like this. She's been through far too much in recent weeks. Let the detective explain this whole mess."

The desk sergeant scratched his head and said to the officer holding Livie, "Oh, let the girl sit with the family until Fredrick gets here. But we have to notify her mother that she's safe here with us." He returned to his desk, leaving an officer posted at the door. Olivia and the Johnsons sat quietly together on the bench, waiting, holding each other to reassure themselves. Surely, nothing bad could happen when they had only tried to do the best they could for Livie.

But long before Detective Fredrick arrived, a taxi deposited Mrs. Gonzaga in front of the station. She burst in, yelling, "You gotta send Olivia right back to Juvenile Hall. She's a delinquent, and I won't put up with her anymore. I want this whole fucking bunch of people held on charges of kidnapping."

Olivia protested loudly to her mother that the whole thing was "…a fucking crock of shit," before she was dragged away kicking and screaming. Even Cori didn't bother to correct her choice of words.

Chapter 19

When Detective Fredrick arrived, he cleared up the matter concerning "the kidnappers," and charges were quickly dropped. Mrs. Gonzaga's outbursts worked to convince the desk sergeant that to take the mother along to San Francisco would have been disastrous. However, the damage was done. Olivia was sent back to juvie pending another hearing, so the Johnsons dragged home at mid-morning, exhausted and heavy-hearted.

A note from Alisa greeted them on the bulletin board. "I hope you found Livie. Cleo had nine puppies this morning. They're in the laundry basket. Sorry, I didn't realize she was in labor, and I guess she picked the only soft spot she could find. I'll help you clean up after school. Goldie's with her."

They rushed in to find the little guys, or girls--Cindi laughed that Kate could never tell which was which--in the basket. Though seven of them were marked in tan and white like Cleo, there were two tattletale black ones, silently naming the black cocker spaniel down the street. Cleo rested on the cool floor in the living room while Goldie "babysat," looking a little more addled than usual. As he rounded up one little miscreant that squirmed to the edge of the basket, another would crawl in a different direction, and the old cat would go bring it back. This distraction brought bubbles of laughter for a moment. But as Phil went out to get a clean box and some old towels to transplant the puppies, the jubilant laughter died when Cindi sat down abruptly. "I just can't believe Olivia has to face another hearing.

In answer to requests from the teachers of Sunnyside, the school superintendent, Dr. Whitson, had become interested in Olivia's case and frequently called on Holly and Kate to help out with in-service training he now required for teachers of the district. He brought in experts on drug abuse to explain the differences between speed and hallucinogens and other needed knowledge. When Kate called the superintendent to tell him Olivia was again locked up, he exerted his influence to get the hearing within three days, and he testified at the hearing to support Kate and Holly's efforts to rehabilitate Olivia. He had even rushed through a new plan to help them.

Dr. Whitson announced the news to the judge. "We've set up maybe California's first alternative school in an old warehouse the district owns, with volunteers who painted and scrubbed, and teachers who contributed games and bulletin boards. It's a new and quite controversial concept, an experiment to keep so-called 'incorrigible kids' in the neighborhood, instead of sending them away to Juvenile Hall. It will allow Olivia, and other kids like her, to go to school half day, with intensive counseling and individualized study to catch up with her erratic educational history, and still participate in outside activities with her peers."

Kate put her hands over her mouth, excitedly hoping the judge would buy into the new plan. Phil squeezed her arm.

After considerable discussion between the superintendent and the judge on the feasibility and accountability of the project, it was agreed that Olivia could be one of the school's first students.

The superintendent added, "I'd like to stress the importance of Olivia's continued participation in Scouting and sporting events to keep her busy after school. The Johnsons have been one of the few stable influences in Olivia's life, and I'm asking you to stipulate that they supervise her extracurricular activities."

Olivia sat up straight in her seat and sent a big smile toward the superintendent.

"Mrs. Gonzaga," said the judge, "you'll have Olivia at home, conditionally, but she'll be monitored for her attendance at school. In light of the superintendent's interest in the case, she will be allowed activities with the Johnson family."

Olivia bubbled over into a grin, turning around to give the Johnsons an eager wave.

But Mrs. Gonzaga screeched, "You can't do that!"

The judge said, "Yes, Mrs. Gonzaga, I can. And I'm warning you that Juvenile Hall is still on the table, should Olivia get into trouble again. Be sure she gets guidance from the Johnsons, and you need to support her in those activities." He banged his gavel. The Johnsons still couldn't legally keep Mrs. Gonzaga from dragging Livie out of their home whenever she wanted, but Livie could now be a part of family outings and games during the day. It was an uneasy compromise of sorts.

The alternative school, aptly called "The Warehouse," was an easy block from Sunnyside Elementary, so Olivia came after her half day there for homework help from Kate and Holly. One afternoon Kate put her to work helping Cyrus, the slowest child in her class, to read short passages. She whispered to Livie, "While you're at it, see if you can get him to pronounce the 'g' on the end of words spelled 'ing.' He tends to leave them off."

Olivia sat with Cyrus and had him repeat a whole list Kate gave her, but she had to repeat the words, too, in order to help him. "Singing, running, playing, doing, saying…." Kate watched from across the room to see what would happen.

Suddenly Olivia realized what she was doing, looked up, and smirked across the room at Kate. Kate grinned back and waved her fingers—their secret. Though still a bit sporadic, Livie began remembering most of her own "g"s after that. She also picked up interest and ability in reading and math skills by having to organize her thoughts to "tutor" someone slower than herself.

Most nights her mother demanded that the Johnsons take her home, but she would be right back the next day to spend her daylight hours with the Johnsons. Life with Olivia seemed *almost* back to normal as she breezed in and out of their family montage.

Soon after Olivia's return, Phil and Kate sat with her on the back porch one evening. "You're doing well now, Livie," said Phil, "quitting again cold turkey, and getting through withdrawal better this time. Do you feel you've moved past San Francisco?"

Olivia took a deep puff on her cigarette and let it out slowly, the one remaining vice she had left that had slowed, but not stopped. Phil waited quietly for her answer. Kate glanced from one to the other.

"I hated bein' lonely. I hated the dirt. I hated them beatin' on me. But I'd be lying if I didn't say that when we was sitting around at night, smokin' and dopin,' and feeling all mellow, listening to the music, and the strobe lights flickering on the psychedelic wall paintings, it seemed weird, like it was all pulling me into the scene--like bein' in a dream, just floating to whoever happened to come to you. I didn't feel lonely then. I liked that part a lot, being part of something. But inside me, I knew you guys wouldn't like it, that you'd want me to be a part of something else, *your* kind of life, so I tried to stay out of it. Sometimes I could. Sometimes I couldn't. It was confusing."

"Why do you suppose you had such mixed feelings, Olivia?" asked Kate. "You do understand the confusion is because of the drugs, don't you?"

"Yeah, and I guess I knew I shouldn't, but it was like my mind was swinging back and forth—who was right, who was wrong? I felt sorta in the middle of it all. When they talked about the good things they were doing, I wanted to be a part of it."

"Like what?" Phil asked, with skepticism rising like a smoke ring.

"Like protesting war and having peace and loving everybody. They sang when they burned a flag, and their draft cards. They beat a soldier in the park one day with a tire iron. I heard he died later."

Kate was startled. "And you saw that? Didn't anyone try to stop it or help him?"

"He was a baby killer," Olivia said calmly, *too* calmly. "Everybody said so. Americans killed women and children and bombed hospitals. Hippies had to stop 'em."

"Olivia! Our soldiers are *not* baby killers!" Phil's voice rose in a rare display of anger. "Why would you believe such nonsense? They're in Vietnam to help the South Vietnamese people who were overrun by Northern communist forces. The communists are the killers, trying to take over helpless people. Our soldiers went there to help."

At Olivia's startled expression, Phil softened his tone, "Livie, these political things are part of a power struggle going on all over the world. The Soviet Union has enslaved half of Europe and the Chinese have done the same in Asia. Don't you know what happens to people who protest against the government in communist countries? Those people are shot! They're killed if they try to leave communist-controlled countries."

Phil stomped out his cigarette. "I have friends in Vietnam and in Europe. Do you have any idea what our lives would be like under communism without our freedoms? And yes, that means your hippie friends' freedom of speech to protest, too? They're herding each other like so many sheep with no knowledge of the world situation."

Olivia looked from Kate to Phil. "I don't know what you're talkin' about. I'm mixed up. Who are communists? Nobody in The Haight said soldiers was helping anybody."

"Olivia, that's why you should educate yourself about things and not just go blindly believing anyone who drugs himself and protests for the sake of protest. You have so much to learn! Your hippie friends tune the whole world out, yet they claim to have the market cornered on peace and free love and brotherhood. They don't even know what they're talking about." Phil sighed and reached for Kate's hand. She recognized his anger and let it subside in the warmth of her palm.

Olivia was silent a moment, and then she reached out her hand shyly to Phil and Kate's joined ones. "Okay, I know I messed up, big time. I promise I won't go back there. But I 'member a lot of the dream stuff in my head. Too much, especially at night."

Kate put an arm around the girl. "You're safe now. You can let those memories fade and concentrate on getting your drug cravings under control again. We know it's not easy, but we do want you to keep trying."

Olivia laughed bitterly. "You know I'm trying, but I don't know if I can *ever* be what you guys think is normal. I've got weird flashbacks in my head that scare me all the time. And Rita's havin' that picture you wouldn't let me go back to get gives me the willies, too. You don't worry about what she'll do, but I do. I know her. She still has that gang mind, and...I guess I do, too. At least I think about being with 'em." Olivia heaved a great sigh, and finally smiled. "But I promise I'll try again, for you guys."

"It has to be what *you* want, too, Livie," said Kate. "Deep down, you know that. It's your way out of this dead-end lifestyle."

Olivia nodded. With hugs and promises, they began the adventure all over again, but with a little less hope than in the beginning when, naively, all things seemed possible.

Kate snuggled in Phil's arms later that night and finally was able to say what bothered her. "Olivia's mom will lose interest in Livie soon, and then she'll be with us day and night. She tries harder then. But we can't stop her mom taking her back. And when Livie fails, we're the ones getting the phone call in the middle of the night to go find her and dry her out, again. We've started over *so* many times." She rubbed her eyes. "Can Livie make permanent changes swinging back and forth from one value system to another? Maybe we're asking too much. She has so much to overcome: her mother's hatred, the orgies of San Francisco, her sister's malice, her gang connections, not to mention a flare-up of her old addictions. Will she eventually hurt herself? Sometimes I think it would've been kinder to let her stay in the One-Ways, where she at least felt she belonged?"

Phil gave her a gentle squeeze. "Maybe, but on the other hand, when she's here, she's happier, more active, healthier, and *not* on drugs," said Phil. "So she belongs here for a chance at a real life. Think what her life would be back in the One-Ways forever, like Bettina and Alice, or in San Francisco like Rita. I don't think we can give up--not until she's mature enough to decide which side of the fence she's on. We have to keep trying, even with the setbacks. Olivia could very well be dead by now, had we not intervened. We can't abandon her."

But there were others to be considered, as well, and lately it seemed the tension caused by one crisis often led to yet another that required complete attention.

One night at dinner, Alisa asked why Phil and Kate hadn't adopted her.

"We tried adoption when you first came to us," answered Phil. "We passed the background checks, but when they measured the house, they said if we adopted you, we would have to send

James and Ned away. We could never have done that. They're ours, too."

"But some people have lots of kids in a small house."

"Only biological kids, Alisa," said Kate. "You could have a child every year and live in a ten foot shack, and the courts wouldn't care. But they have rules on square footage per child for adoptive or foster homes. We couldn't qualify for either. Your mother would have to agree, too. We don't know where she is."

The other kids sat quietly as Alisa shed a dramatic tear or two.

"We'd like nothing better than to adopt you," said Phil, looking around the table, "*all* of you. You all feel like our own kids. For you, Alisa, we have no power of attorney, no legal documents, and no way to find your mom or dad should you need medical care. We've learned with Olivia that they won't even treat a child if the parent isn't present to sign. Thank goodness you've been healthy, so far, but we live in mortal fear that you could have an accident, especially now that you're driving and dating."

Alisa's normally pale face grew red. "I think you just prefer to keep everyone else in the world instead of adopting me. Livie gets all the attention around here."

Kate gasped. "Alisa, that's not fair, and it's not like you to be so unkind. You needed a lot of attention when you first came, too, and we gave it to you. Livie is having problems now, so attention goes where it's needed most. Don't you understand that?"

"Well, we all got better, and she never will. You've just wasted two years of all our lives on her." Alisa ran from the table and disappeared into the bedroom.

Kate sat with her head in her hands and couldn't eat another thing. Phil moved to her side and wrapped his arms around her shoulders, laying his head against the back of her neck.

"Honey, she couldn't have meant that."

Kate found her voice, finally. "Do the rest of you feel neglected, or that we're giving Olivia too much of our attention and ignoring you?"

Ned was quick to answer. "Look, I was a wreck when I

came here too, from my step-dad's beatings and my mom's illnesses. You guys give us what we need, when we need it. Alisa's just ga-ga over Bruce right now. That's what's bugging her."

"Sure, we all get irritated with Livie when she lies, or disappears, or does something stupid," said Cindi. "We're all trying hard to help her get over these bad things and have a happy life, then sometimes she blows it all off like our love for her doesn't matter. Maybe she doesn't want a happy life for herself as much as we want it *for* her."

Ned and Cori nodded. Lynette had been quiet, but now she spoke up. "Alisa has been here longer than I have, so maybe I should be the one to leave."

"No way," Phil said. "You're one of us now, and you've turned around completely, while Livie's still having problems. You don't miss the drugs, the gangs, or One-Ways any more, do you?"

Lynette shook her head. "All I wanted was a chance to get out. I'll never go back. But Livie's torn both ways. She doesn't fit anyplace. And she's not smart, so she wastes chances. She can't seem to completely shed all her background, no matter how hard we all try." She began to cry. "I don't know what to do for her, either."

Ned threw an arm around the girl and said, "We have to work together, Lynette. Even Alisa, when she's not on her high horse. And Livie, when she's able to be with us."

Cori nodded. "Alisa isn't always sweetness and light, either. If she had to go to her real mom, she'd be back here on the next plane."

"I guess we've all been so worried about Livie that maybe we didn't notice Alisa was getting to these difficult years," said Kate. "I don't want to neglect any of you. I just want Livie to be safe, too."

Alisa sulked an hour before coming to talk privately with Kate and Phil. "I'm sorry, you guys. I know I have to solve the problem before sundown. It isn't really Olivia. I guess I just wanted somebody to blame. It's about Bruce."

Kate smiled at her. "We've long since learned that what

teens *say* is wrong isn't necessarily what's *really* bothering them. So what's going on with Bruce?"

"He's only the most popular guy in drama, and all the other girls like him too, so when he wants to spend more time alone with me, I'm afraid he'll find someone else if I go running in the house the minute we get home, like you want me to do."

"Examine that big, long sentence again, Alisa. What's your dominant thought—fear, insecurity, jealousy? *None* of it sounds like you're sure you like him, or he likes you--only that you're afraid someone *else* might get him. If you do what he wants only to keep him with you and away from others, that makes you pretty vulnerable, doesn't it?"

Alisa looked down. "Maybe." She thought a moment and then said, "I really do like him and I think he likes me, but I'm scared I'll lose him, if we can't be alone more."

"Why does he want you to be alone, Alisa?" asked Kate. "Have you asked yourself, or him? It's a good thing sometimes to see how your date acts around others, like your friends and family. Almost anyone can seem charming alone."

"Oh, he's charming all right. On stage, when we're acting, when he kisses me."

"If he really likes you that much, I don't think you'll lose him by asking him in to spend a little time getting to know your family when you get home from a date. He might feel better knowing he's welcome. And that would make us more comfortable with his dating you--more so than your sitting out in the car, necking. Can you see why that makes us uncomfortable? We love you, and we feel responsible for your safety."

She pouted a bit. "We weren't doing anything much, just lots of kissing. The girls in my classes all say...."

Phil took over. "Alisa, we don't think you're doing anything wrong, now, and we know you don't *intend* to do anything wrong. If you really wanted to do anything, you could certainly do it anyplace else as well. And the other girls aren't you. You are a unique individual. Bruce or any other boy won't remember you because you are *like* all the other girls. A boy will remember you for what makes you *different* from others." Phil looked over at Kate and smiled. "I sure did." He turned again to Alisa. "Bruce is a couple of years older, and his hormones are kicking in. You're just learning about guys and dating. If you fear losing him, as you admit you do, then you'll be in danger of making mistakes, should he ever ask more from you. Fear of losing someone isn't a good reason to give in to his passions. If he cares about you, he'll let *you* set the limits, and he'll respect you more for doing so."

"Coming from a guy, I guess I should believe you, hm?" Alisa was quiet a moment. "I guess I could try inviting him in, since you guys are always waiting up, anyway. But what if he doesn't want to come and threatens to find another girlfriend."

Kate smiled. "Much as you might not like that scenario, I think it might tell you something about whether or not he really cares for you, if he threatens anything at all."

"I hadn't thought of it that way, and it scares me."

Phil put his arm around the girl as she sat between them. "Alisa, remember when you were a little ten-year-old, and you were so insecure you stuttered if anyone even spoke to you. You've grown into a lovely, smart, talented young woman who can be anything she wants to be and love whomever she chooses. You are no longer that insecure little girl, so you mustn't let her come back into your life as fear of losing someone if you don't play 'follow the leader.' You deserve a guy who will appreciate your best qualities and honor your standards. Maybe Bruce is that guy, and he'll be glad to have you set your own limits. If he's not...."

"Then, I don't need him, right?"

"Just invite him in next time, and we'll see what he's made of," said Kate, with a big grin. "If he can handle *this* bizarre family, he might be the greatest guy in the world."

"Okay, and guys, I didn't mean it about Olivia. She *has* improved--a lot. I just don't know if she can improve all the way"

"Neither do we," said Phil. "But we can't give up on her as long as she's trying. Just like we couldn't give up on you."

One problem was resolved for the moment. But the drama

made Kate and Phil wonder where the tension had come from. Why had it not surfaced before? Was it really Olivia that fostered cracks in the castle, or normal teen angst in a family of growing teens? "I guess we don't have all the answers," said Phil with a laugh, as they retired for the night. "All anyone can do is try."

Then, James came home. His father had succumbed to his weak heart, and his mother took the house. Now eighteen, James immediately sat down with Phil and made plans to complete the year of school he'd missed, go into the service, and go to college afterward on the G.I. Bill. It was great having him home again. Olivia, especially, missed her buddy. She and James and Phil sat on the back stoop whenever she could come over, talking out problems, their cigarette stubs glowing in the dark.

At the following week's Sunnyside's volleyball game, a new challenge emerged. A son of one of the teachers home on college break spotted Lynette and asked if he could take her to his fraternity's formal dinner-dance. She had completed her six months of restriction, but she'd shown no inclination to go out or date anyone. When the young man approached Kate and Lynette during a rest period, Kate could see he was already smitten.

Lynette's hands shook as she touched Kate on the arm and whispered, "Do you think it's all right for me to go someplace like that with him?"

Looking from Lynette's tentative smile to the young man's eager grin, Kate nodded, and Lynette said shyly to the young man, "I've never been to a formal dance before, but I think it sounds wonderful." The girls giggled together all the way home.

Lynette was lovely, but still a little rough around the edges, so the family began a crash course on social skills--how to walk, talk, and behave at a formal event. Kate dug out a long slip and high heels so Lynette could practice rising and sitting gracefully instead of plopping into a seat with no concern for poise. Alisa insisted Lynette set the table with books balanced on her head, and Cindi unscrambled the mysteries of which fork came first. Often panic set in and Lynette would cry, "I just can't be a lady." But Phil gave his pep talk about how "If you behave like a lady, people will treat you like one." It always worked, coming from this gentle man, at least with everyone except Olivia.

"Hey, don't look at me," said Livie to her sister, as she watched the proceedings while clowning with Goldie and Cleo on the floor. "You all know it's too late for me."

The excitement of Lynette's first *real* date meant it was a total family trip to a department store to find her the proper dress. Though Lynette tried on a dozen or more dresses, one or another was rejected as too revealing, too gaudy, or too "frou frou." Kate feared that because the girl had a nice figure, the sales lady was pushing the more sexy types of dresses, and said so. Finally, however, Lynette walked out of the dressing room in an ivory-colored lace gown with a sweetheart neckline that framed her smooth, tawny complexion, and the whole shopping crew, including the saleslady, gasped in unison.

"That's it!" James said with enthusiasm, gathering a unanimous decision.

The dress was more than the Johnsons could really afford, but after conferring, Phil and Kate decided it was the perfect investment for Lynette's self-confidence. Phil said, "The dress is as important as the good shoes and good bras we consider necessary expenditures on our tight budget, so we'll just eat more hot dogs." The deal was done.

On date night, it was hard to tell who was more excited, since the whole family waited up for Lynette's return. Cori said, "I'm just praying she'll have a good time and not catch her heel in her dress and strangle herself, or some equal catastrophe."

A little after midnight, Kate heard footsteps under the bougainvillea. After a brief pause, Lynette entered the house as though in a trance, holding her right hand out in front of her the way Cleo did when she wanted someone to shake her paw. Though the dreamy expression in her eyes immediately signaled to everyone that the evening went well, Lynette's first words revealed the importance of the occasion in her own eyes.

"All he wanted to do was kiss my hand!" she said, breathlessly. She leaned against the closed front door. "He bought me flowers and dinner, we danced all evening, he introduced me to his friends, and he didn't even expect me to pay him back with sex, or anything. He just kissed my hand and said he had a wonderful time. There must be something to this 'lady' stuff."

Phil caught Kate's eyes and grinned. "I told you this would be a good investment."

From that point on, there was never the slightest question that Lynette would emerge as a success story. She studied hard, planned for college, and happily dated the young man whenever he was home from school. Her new respect for herself as a human being with rights and responsibilities never again wavered.

But, in a normal family, the 'ups' are sometimes offset by unexpected 'downs.' The next day, while driving a carload of kids to a softball game, Kate fainted at the wheel. With girls in the back seat screaming, Cori, who was sitting next to her mother in the front, steered to the side, wormed her foot in to the brake and stopped the car. Cindi went to the nearest house to call the operator for help, while Cori and Olivia stayed with Kate, and the rest of the team ran to nearby Mayberry Park to tell Phil. At the hospital, they found a particularly dangerous attack of bleeding ulcers, so the secret of the mysterious stomach pain was out.

The doctor told Phil and Kate, "Some think ulcers are brought on by spicy foods, but this comes not from what you eat. This comes from what's eating you. Will you tell me about it?"

Phil looked into his wife's eyes and said, "Olivia is the only one who gives us agonizing concern and frets you to death. I can't lose you. Should we give up on her?"

"No way," said Kate. "I'll just be more aware and try to relax about things."

The doctor shook his head and walked from the room.

Though trying hard and doing well most of the time, Olivia was still "on the swing," as Cori called it. She would be fine while with the Johnsons, but when her mother demanded the girl go home, Olivia would seek solace with a rougher element of friends. She was not using drugs, but many of her friends were, and she couldn't seem to stay away from those friends if she didn't have the Johnsons nearby to keep her busy and happy. Phil and Kate warned Olivia about this dangerous type of fraternization.

"You have to take responsibility for yourself, Livie, with or without us, whether anyone is watching or not," explained Kate. "It has to come from inside *you*."

"I try," Livie said, turning her gaze from Kate to Phil. "But I sorta promise one day and get weak the next, I guess. They just all need someone to care about 'em, like you cared about me and got me off drugs. They all need someone, too. Some of 'em are friends I can't say 'no' to, like Bettina and Alice."

"You may be too fresh from your own difficulties to be able to help anyone else just yet."

But that idea proved not to be quite true, either. Olivia was nothing if not full of surprises.

On a Scout trip to sing for an old folks' home, they found a boy of thirteen living at the same facility. Since there were no rehabilitation or custodial care facilities for young people, such children were sprinkled in among the old and hopeless.

"It's so sad for him to be here where life already smells like death," said Cindi.

Strapped into his wheelchair, the boy was unresponsive except for his eyes, which followed the girls' movements as they sang folk songs. Olivia stopped singing to wipe the drool from his mouth. It was apparent that the boy's brain was gone.

When Kate and the Scouts asked an attendant about the boy, after their program, he said, "Oh, him? He sniffed glue two years ago. Got to be a habit. Sniffing any substance goes directly to the brain, right through the nasal passages." He pointed up his nose to his brain. "It's like sticking a gun up your nose. Boom!"

While all the girls were shaken by the young boy's vegetative state, Olivia was particularly devastated. "I never knew sniffing things could do that. Maybe that's why I have trouble learning. We gotta tell your little kids."

Olivia began giving pep talks to Kate and Holly's classes, and other teachers who trusted her, about the danger of taking drugs by any means, but especially by sniffing them. Since it had become an increasing fad to sniff something in a little brown bag, the teachers felt the kids listened to Olivia when they might not listen to others. "She's been there, and she knows," said one fifth grader. She enlisted the aid of other alternative school "problem kids" to help watch for drug problems and talk individually with children they felt were susceptible. "Early detection," she called it, having picked up a little jargon from all her teacher friends.

Olivia took her new mission seriously; convinced she could help prevent such tragedy as the boy they'd seen. As Kate watched her talk about avoiding drugs in front of student groups and noticed how verbal she had become and how protective she was of the elementary children, she began to feel Olivia had found a niche where she felt confident. The superintendent gave her a certificate for her dedication, and she proudly pinned it on the bedroom wall. Her mother had again lost interest, so Livie was with the Johnsons day and night and doing well. Kate hoped that this success so much appreciated by the teachers would bolster her defenses.

Even Alisa said, "Livie, you've done a lot better lately."

Though Phil and Kate had agreed that Lynette would be their last "bonus" child, Phil brought home seventeen-year-old Roger for dinner one night. He told Kate he was sure Roger hadn't eaten for some time. So the cheese was augmented with more macaroni, and they all sat down to eat.

At the dinner table, Phil told how he had handed a nearby young man he didn't know ten dollars to walk across the street from his high school during a smoking break and bring back a newspaper to use in his history class.

Roger broke in, "I thought he was a dumb sucker, giving me a ten spot. I figured I'd walk right out the back door of that store and keep going with ten dollars in my pocket."

"Why didn't you?" asked Alisa.

Roger grinned. "I almost did. But then I looked across the street, and there he stood, talking to one of the other teachers like he wasn't even worried about me coming back. He's the first person who ever trusted me, and I didn't want to disappoint him for some stupid reason." He grinned again at Phil. "You really shouldn't trust people like me. *Nobody* should be trusted. You're too gullible."

"Well," said Phil with a laugh. "You came back with the change, didn't you? To me, that means you *can* be trusted, so get used to it."

"Yeah, I did come back--dumb me. And what did you do? You took me into your class like I belonged there, and I'd been ditching school when you sent me for the paper." He glanced around the table. "It wasn't even *my* class. He got me back in the school I'd just left, and I kept showing up all week. Damn, if I didn't think he was stupid. Then, I thought about it, and it was me that was damn stupid."

"Darn," corrected Lynette and Olivia in unison. Olivia added, "You use drugs, don't you? You can't do that here, either. Do you have a problem with that?"

"For *you*, I just this very minute swore them off for a lifetime," said Roger.

Laughter surrounded him, and he joined in.

"Wait until our biggest brother, James, gets home and sees you," said Olivia. "He's getting really big and handsome, too, but he used to be a scrawny little kid."

"Where is he?" asked Roger.

"At work right now," answered Ned. "He was with his dad for a while, but he's back now. We all keep coming back home."

Roger scanned the group with a puzzled look and asked, "You mean you can just *stay* here? I've never been anywhere I could *stay*. I've knocked around the streets since I was thirteen. My mom got a new boyfriend younger than her. I was already over six feet, and she didn't want me hanging around because this guy might leave her. So I left."

Cori cocked her head and asked, "But where could you go? Your father?"

"I guess he didn't want me either. My old man's black and Mom's Apache Indian. He got himself a black woman when I was about two. My folks never married. Mom didn't like me much. I guess I reminded her of him. So I just hit the streets."

Olivia got up to serve dessert, her favorite chore, and said to Roger, "Can I get you some of Kate's s Devils food cake?"

"Wow! Beautiful ladies, and I get waited on, too? Did I fall into heaven?"

With that, and another bunk bed building session, Roger became a part of the family. Olivia made it her special mission to help him feel at home. He, too, had to stay in school, do homework, help with chores, and even join in on water fights or evening singing of "What the World Needs Now" or dancing to "I Heard it Through the Grapevine" amid the noisy laughter of the Johnson living room. It was his idea to stop scolding Cleo for digging holes in the back yard and turn it into a miniature golf course. He and Phil went to a second hand store to get golf clubs.

The young man thrived in his new home, proudly introducing "his beautiful sisters" to everyone he met. As usual, with the multi-ethnic Johnson family, a few eyebrows raised as people tried to figure out how a mixed race young man with long, dark hair and an ever-present, leather, slouch cowboy hat could claim family ties ranging from Nordic blondes to Japanese, to combinations of Indian and Irish. He never lost his enthusiasm for being part of a family who could love him. Olivia usually managed to be his teammate for chores, and he learned to laugh. Who had more influence on whom, was never established, but several months went by in relative calm.

Then Cori rushed home with news that she was running for Student Body President for the coming year because she wanted to get dress code rules changed to allow girls to wear slacks. She appointed Olivia her campaign manager. "It'll keep her too busy to go to the One-Ways, in case her mom comes."

Kate put her arm around her youngest child and smiled. "You realize that if Olivia lets you down, you could lose the election?"

"Yeah, I know, but Fran, Margo and Susan will be co-chairmen and anyway, Olivia needs to feel needed." Cori snickered. "The principal's mad at me for running on the pants vs. skirt issue, and he still thinks Olivia will get me into drugs. He never understands that Livie isn't using anymore. She can sniff out a drug user or gang wannabe like Cleo does a mouse, and we go talk to them. Livie keeps them from bringing anything on campus. You'd think Mr. Carleton would see that his drug problem goes down when she's around, not up. He's so clueless--constantly giving me dire warnings, that even if I should *accidentally* win the election, he'll refuse to change the dress code. So, I'll have to take it to the School Board." Cori lowered her voice to a barreling bass to imitate the pompous man. "'They'll never listen to you two, a softball catcher and a drug addict.'" Cori smiled. "I *have* to do this, Mom."

Kate nodded, knowing her daughter was determined, and probably right.

"You want a laugh? Livie said she'd get some of her old gang to 'strong-arm' kids to vote for me. I told her we wouldn't use that kind of 'help.' We'd just tell the truth about the issues and make posters, and we'd win fair and square, or not at all."

Kate laughed with her daughter. "That must have been *quite* a conversation."

The election became an event, with Cori playing on the practicality of the issue, especially when slacks were beginning to be acceptable everywhere else, *except* school.

Kate and Phil wondered how much of the enthusiasm was because the principal so much opposed Cori's candidacy.

Livie couldn't spell well enough to make posters, but the campaign team of Fran, Margo, and Susan painted poster board on the living room floor, while Livie diligently hung them all over campus. It was the usual teamwork, laughter, and optimistic dreams that had always fueled Johnson family activities. Collectively, everyone in the extended family had been more upbeat, feeling all unsettling changes were now behind them.

But, the night before the election, Olivia's mother came to "rescue" Olivia once again. The scene of Livie's fierce objections, and Mrs. Gonzaga's drunken cruelty, never presaged anything positive.

Chapter 20

The big day dawned California warm. Cori won by a landslide over a boy who said girls should wear feminine dresses, "especially mini-skirts." To celebrate, a flag football game was scheduled after school, and the girls changed into slacks they'd brought along. Kids swarmed out of the school's back gate, across to The Corner Store to buy their stash of candy, pop, Cracker Jacks, and Cori's favorite, sunflower seeds, before the game. "Cori's crowning," as Livie called it, would be at halftime. Cori now feared Livie's mother wouldn't even let her come.

Kate drove her usual route home after school, down Meyer Road and past The Corner Store. Meyer Road had one lane in each direction, with no curbs or sidewalks. Instead, there was a thirty-foot dirt easement on each side of the street that some forward-thinking councilman must have thought would keep the property open to later curbs, sidewalks, and two more lanes of traffic. The kids walked on this wide easement as though it were a real sidewalk. In front of The Corner Store, Max, the proprietor, installed a little island--a wide sidewalk, a parking lot at the east end, and several diagonal parking spaces that faced into his personal little strip of sidewalk. Max knew his handiwork would most likely be torn out by the city if and when the expansion took place. "That could take thirty years," he'd say. "My customers need paved parking space now."

But as Kate approached The Corner Store, there seemed unusual motion and dust in front of her. Her peripheral vision was drawn to the easement on her right, where she spotted Margo writhing in the dirt, and a woman rushing out of a nearby house with a blanket to cover the fourteen year old. *My God, Margo! What could have happened?*

Cars normally parked in nice diagonal rows in front of the store seemed mixed up, turned every which way. Frantic for Margo's safety, Kate steered around the tangled cars into the parking lot, realizing she was driving over crunchy little boxes. She parked and ran back down the sidewalk to get to Margo, whom she'd seen at the west end of the commotion. Mass confusion, screams, and running feet created chaos all around her. But Kate forged straight ahead through the milling people with her mind on Margo.

She heard a voice call her name from the ground to her right, and looked down to find Fran lying quietly beneath a van that was turned the wrong way. Its open double doors flapped over the girl's prone position. *How could she get under there? How could a van get turned around facing backwards?*

Kate dropped to her knees, ducking the swinging van doors. Fran was coherent, talking slowly. "I can't seem to move, Mrs. Johnson," she said. "Isn't that weird?" Her red satin blouse looked disjointed at the shoulder, as though the arm was not attached, but the blouse still was. Kate bent down, putting her ear close to hear Fran's words.

"Will you get my mother?" the girl asked, far too calmly.

"Of course, honey. We'll get her here right away."

"She's going to be scared."

"Don't worry. We'll help you and your mom." Kate touched the girl's cheek gently. "What happened, Fran?"

"Some guy plowed into us girls with his car. He didn't even stop. I was stuck on his hood. I don't know how I got over here." Fran looked bewildered, but not frightened. Her lips quivered. "I'm so cold, Mrs. Johnson."

Kate shouted at the people milling around the crash site, "Has anybody called the operator to get an ambulance? Margo and Fran are hurt." She looked up at one junior high boy who stood crying nearby. "Make sure Max already called the operator."

"He did already," came the reply. "I saw him. I was just in there...there's lots of people...we all saw it...lots of the kids...." He didn't finish, but ran back inside the store.

If Max called, Kate knew somewhere a telephone operator was frantically looking up and calling every ambulance company in the book to find one with available personnel in the area that could be dispatched. If one couldn't come, the operator would have to call another until she found someone.

She stood and grabbed the arm of the next kid she saw, one of her former students, and sent him to Fran's house a few blocks away on Studebaker Road to bring her mother back. "Run!" He seemed stunned, so Kate gave him a shove, and the boy took off. Another kid she sent for Margo's father. She sent someone to get the blanket out of the back of her car, and he ran off to do so. She scanned the pile of cars, trying to sort out what might have happened, and realized she still hadn't checked on Margo.

"That driver did it on purpose," shouted a man running onto the sidewalk to whoever would listen. "The old guy from the gas station across the street saw him running from his car, and he chased him down and tackled him. He's got him at the gas station until the police come. It's some druggie. He should be lynched!"

A shiver went through Kate's confused senses. *Where are the police? That old man can't hold onto a young kid long. And what might these angry, scared people do?*

Shouts, screams, mangled bumpers and hoods--all was a mess scrambled in a giant Mixmaster. The child returned with the blanket and together, they put it around Fran's form, being careful not to move that strange configuration of her unhinged shoulder. While tucking the blanket under Fran, Kate realized that the crunching sounds she had felt under both her car and her footsteps were hundreds of broken cigar boxes, apparently being unloaded from this van. They were over and around Fran, scattered over the van's floor and crumbling out the open double doors, clear down the sidewalk and parking lot. Now that she noticed, even the air smelled of tobacco.

Something was mixed in with the boxes and crushed cigars. Kate picked up pieces and recognized what they were—sunflower seeds—loose--everywhere.

An agitated man she didn't know took her by the arm and said, "The kids said you know a child on the other side of this pile-up, and he's in a bad way. Can you come help us hold him still?" The man wiped blood from his face and smeared it on his jacket. "We think he's hurt internally. If you know him, maybe he'll respond to your voice, at least until the ambulance crews arrive.

Will you come with me…please, ma'am?"

Kate spotted Barbara and motioned her to sit with Fran until she got back. She couldn't take it all in. *Are there still more kids? He said ambulance crews—plural.*

The man led her around the massive pileup to the street side. She could see people tending to Margo on the west end as she passed. He threaded his way between several crumpled cars adjacent to the street and into the heart of the pile. Kate followed the man and knelt where he pointed. She had to squirm under, as two cars were locked together. She felt glass shards slicing into her nylons and her knees, but she crawled until she reached the boy writhing in pain under a front bumper. It was Ron Rolfini, a boy she'd had in class only two years before.

"Can you reach him?" shouted the man.

Another man passed a blanket down to her. "I hope you know this kid. He's thrashing around. He'll be hurt even worse."

"I know him." She pulled the blanket under the car with her and did her best to wrap it around the boy, pulling herself forward to hold him more still. "Ronnie, it's me, Mrs. Johnson. I'm here to help you. Try to rest." Ronnie's new bicycle with the banana seat lay twisted near his legs. Kate's heart plummeted. Though the outside of his body didn't look bloody, she felt a mushy, moving fluid when her fingers touched his back, in the kidney area.

At that moment, she knew Ronnie, the smallest boy in his class, could not survive. Her insides wrenched at the knowledge, but holding it in produced a physical pain in her throat. She wanted to scream to get it out, but instead, she spoke to the boy in low, soothing tones, hoping against hope. "Hold still, Ronnie. Don't move, dear. Hold as still as you can until the ambulance comes. Don't kick…try to rest. Hang on." Her words seemed to calm him a little, but he didn't open his eyes. Kate held him firmly and pleaded again. "Please try to stay still, Ronnie."

His anguished cry tore her heart. "I can't, Mrs. J. I can't…I can't…."

There was nothing she could do except hold him. She fought back her tears and cradled his shoulders, trying not to touch the telltale mushy spot again. In a moment, he was unconscious.

Someone nearby spoke her name. Lifting her head, she saw Cole leaning against the car above her. He took desperate gulps of air, breathed out in raspy puffs, and spewed blood from the corner of his mouth each time he coughed. His friend Steve stood beside him, holding him steady.

Immediately, she called one of the men remaining nearby. "Please, check out this boy, too. Something's wrong with him. Cole, tell us what happened. What hurts?

Cole kept holding on to the car's hood above her and crying, "Is Ron all right? Is he all right?"

Kate had no comforting words. "Cole, do you know what hit you and Ron?"

"We were double on Ron's bike coming out between the parked cars and all of a sudden the cars pushed together and smushed us in the middle. I went up in the air, and Ron went under. I woke up on top of that car." He pointed two cars away from the one Kate crouched under. "Steve helped me get down."

The man put his arm around Cole, steadying him. "Where are you hurt, son?"

Cole wrapped his arms around his chest and said, "It hurts to breathe. I feel all squished up in the middle."

With Steve's help, the man made Cole lie down nearby on a tarp and stayed by him. "The ambulances will be here soon. Lie still until we see what got squished, okay?" Kate recognized the attempt to make Cole relax and appreciated the man's compassion.

From the corner of her eye, she saw Jonah, a Korean former student with paralyzed legs. He balanced on his crutches through the rubble to get to her. "What can I do, Mrs. J.?"

Tears filled her eyes. Though Jonah had initially needed help to even sit in his desk, her class of kids had pushed him to strengthen his arms with push-ups and monkey bars, even as he dragged thirty extra pounds of leg braces. And now, here was Jonah, wanting to help.

"Be careful of all this debris," she called out to him, turning her face from Ronnie's unconscious form, so she could hear

Jonah's voice.

"It's Ronnie, isn't it? Let me go get his mom. I know where she lives."

Kate could see the determination in his set jaw, in spite of his handicap.

"I can do it, Mrs. J.!"

"All right, Jonah, I know you can. Ron's mother works nights so she'll be asleep now. Just keep banging on the right front window until she hears you, and then bring her back here. And ask one of the other kids to go find Cole's mom, too, will you?"

Jonah nodded, and picked his way through the rubble, out to the street, and out of her sight. *God, are we all doing the right things?*

Kate tried to shift her knees a little in the glass shards. The coppery odor of Ron's breath and blood was joined by a gassy smell. Fluid dripped from the tank of the car above her into an increasing puddle on the ground. She called to a man nearby to look. "Do we need to move Ron, or do you think it's okay?"

"Uh, oh," the man said, as he crawled around Kate and Ron to get his finger under the drip and smell it. "We're going to have to move him." He stood and yelled to a dark woman on the other side of the pile, "Have Max call the fire department, too. We have leaking gasoline over here." The woman moved quickly inside the building.

"Can you slide him out the way you're already holding him," suggested the man. "He doesn't look very heavy."

"He's not." Kate scrabbled crabwise backward as best she could in a dress, while holding Ron up from the ground with elbows and forearms to keep from bumping or scraping him against anything.

The man reached down and picked up the limp boy from her arms. Another stranger helped her to her feet.

Kate nodded her thanks, tears running down her face. "I hear sirens now." But when the noise rounded the corner from Carmenita onto Meyer Road, they could see it was only the police. Frustrated cries rose from the crowd.

"I'll take him over to the house next door where the first girl was, and I'll try to keep him still."

She shook her head. "I don't know if it will matter. You won't lay him down?" She sobbed as she touched the boy's face with one finger, tracing the line where his usual dimpled smile lay.

The man nodded, and cradling Ronnie, he picked his way around the cars and headed for the neighbor's porch.

Kate turned to ask the other man to move Cole back further from the gas leak, when she saw Holly driving slowly by the scrambled cars. Holly stopped when she saw Kate and yelled out, "Olivia ran to school to tell us you were first to get here, and you needed help. What can I do?"

Kate' fuzzy brain tried to take in that statement. *How would Livie know?*

Before Kate could answer, Olivia jumped from the car, flailing wildly, grabbing her around the middle and almost knocking her off her feet.

"Please, don't die, Kate. Everyone's going to die!" Sobbing, Olivia frantically searched up and down Kate's bloody arms and legs. Susan followed Olivia, looking dazed.

"Look, I just found Susan shivering over there," said Olivia. "She's all shaky, because the car sliced her nylons right off her when it hit Fran and Margo." Olivia's voice rose to a screech that made Kate wince. "We gotta get you to a hospital. You're bleeding all over."

"Olivia," said Kate, trying to keep her voice calm, tilting Livie's chin in her hands. "I'm okay. My cuts are only from glass on the street. I need to stay here to help get the kids to the hospital. I want you and Susan to go home with Mrs. Warner."

Holly had joined them, leaving her car idling in the street. It didn't matter. Meyer Road had become a parking lot. She laid a hand on Olivia's arm.

"No!" Livie screamed, hysterically. " Kate, you don't understand. I shoulda known this would happen. It's all my fault."

"Olivia, we don't *know* what happened. There's no way it could be your fault. A car hit them. Now calm down and go with

Mrs. Warner. That's best for now."

"Kate," Olivia cried out, leaning her full weight on Kate's arm. "Listen to me. There's somethin' I gotta tell you...."

"Not now, Livie. The older kids should be home. I need you to stay with them until Phil comes. Tell him to come get me at the hospital. Do you understand?" Kate turned to the other girl.

"Susan, you have get calm so you can tell the police what happened. I need you both to go home safely, so I can concentrate on what's happening here. No arguments."

Kate nodded at Holly. Ignoring Olivia's pleas, Holly took the two girls by their arms and escorted them to her car. Kate's heart went out to Susan, who had just seen two of her friends carried away by a car right next to her. Kate called out to Holly, "When you get Livie to our house and Susan to her mom, please bring Cindi back. She's the practical one who can help most."

Holly nodded.

" Kate, you gotta listen to me. I have somethin' important to tell you." Olivia still screamed at Kate as Holly pushed her into the car and drove away, picking her way through the pile up.

Kate's knees buckled and she sat down hard on the pavement between two crushed fenders. Moments later, she remembered the car dripping gasoline and hoped to find someone in charge. There was only chaos. Everyone seemed overwhelmed by the scene, even the police.

Kate wiped at the sweat and blood from her face with the sleeve of her dress and stared at the blood, Ronnie's blood. The dress didn't matter. Nothing mattered.

As Kate sat there, Renee came to find her. She was crying. "Fran's mom got here, and she's acting funny, but that's not why I came. Cori's on the other side, by The Corner Store. She needs you."

"Oh, is she here helping, too? I can come with you now." Kate got shakily to her feet and turned toward the teen.

Renee covered her face with her hands and blubbered, "Cori's not helping. She's hurt, too."

Chapter 21

The idea of sunny Cori getting hurt didn't even make sense. *It's Cindi who's accident-prone like me. Cori is the climber, the adventurer, the one who never even falls down.*

Kate followed Renee through the rubble, out into the street, threading their way through piles of cars and frantic people. Finally, in the distance, Kate thought she could hear more sirens--the ambulances at long last. Mind-numbed, she stumbled, and Renee took her hand, leading her onto Max's sidewalk, almost back to where she had heard Fran's voice in the first place.

Propped up against the wall of The Corner Store was a limp, unconscious Cori, her head bleeding down on her shirt. Two unknown adults held her neck and head in an upright, rigid position using rolled up clothing against each side, bracing Cori against the bricks. Kate gasped. She must have run right by her own daughter in her hurry to get to Margo and stopped not fifteen feet away to kneel by Fran. *Sunflower seeds everywhere? I should have known Cori had to be here.*

Kate knelt beside her daughter, fearing to dislodge the grasp of the two people patiently holding her neck. *She's breathing, thank God.* The man nodded at her and the woman tried to smile. "How long have you been holding Cori rigid?"

"She hasn't stirred for a while. I think that's a good thing. If she's out, maybe she's not hurting so bad. Max said we should just stay here, in case she wakes up and tries to move. We saw her hit her head and neck--we're not sure what else she got hurt."

Kate nodded. "Thank you both. I'm her mother, but I was helping on the other side. I didn't even know she was here. I'm so sorry." Her shaking hands gently touched Cori's hand, warm, but unresponsive. "I hope she didn't see me run past her. How could I not have seen her?" Guilt made the tears bitter, and Kate held her stomach and rocked back and forth on her knees.

"Has anyone figured out what happened?" Renee knelt beside Kate, putting an arm around her former teacher's shoulders.

"There were probably thirty kids inside the store," said the woman. "We all saw Cori flying through the air and thought she was coming right through the big picture windows. Instead, she hit the wall in the middle and slid down here. It was that van when it flipped around backwards from the impact that just knocked her through the air."

"I'd guess she flew about sixteen feet before hitting the wall," said the man."

Kate couldn't speak. She watched Cori's breathing. *Sixteen feet?*

"She must be one tough cookie," continued the man. "Don't you worry none." He looked up as a roar came from the milling crowd. "Two ambulances are here now. We'll get these kids to the hospital, and they'll be just fine."

Holly returned with Cindi. They quickly knelt next to Kate. At first, Cindi couldn't quite take in the sight of her sister in such a state. "Oh, my God," she said. "What can we do to help her?"

"Just be here with her, Cindi. We'll just stay with her."

Cori didn't move, though Kate noticed her breathing quicken. She touched a torn place on Cori's slacks. Something about it didn't seem right. Just above the knee the leg was cut deeply, but there was no blood. "Cori, can you hear me?" She said the words softly, hoping Cori would wake up. Something from First Aid nagged at her brain. *What was it? Don't let a person with brain injury go to sleep.* When Cori raised her fingers in Kate's hand, she knew Cori could hear her. She touched the leg below the cut. "Does your leg hurt, honey?"

Cori spoke slowly, not opening her eyes. "I can't feel anything down there, Mama. I can't move my legs." Tears were on her eyelashes, so very long, like her father's.

Kate caught her breath and exchanged glances with Cindi and Renee. Cori hadn't called her "Mama" since she was two! Kate could only pat her daughter's hand and murmur, "We're here with you. It'll be okay, Cori."

"The others? They were waiting for me."

"They'll be okay, too, Cori. Just rest."

"My new pants, Mama." Kate's little girl gritted her teeth and didn't make another sound. Kate prayed for her daughter, the athlete, who couldn't feel her legs or move her neck.

"Now that one over there," said the man, nodding in Fran's direction, as though the silence in Kate's mind needed to be filled. "She was on the hood of the driver's car until he hit the van, and the impact tossed her under its side, somehow. It was the darndest thing. These kids were just minding their own business getting ready for the game, and then they see their friends get hurt. But there are a lot of eyewitnesses to what happened. We'll lynch this guy, sure."

It was the second time Kate had heard someone suggest lynching, and she didn't even know who was responsible.

Jonah returned with Ronnie's frantic mother, still in her chenille bathrobe.

"Good work, Jonah," Kate called to him.

The boy nodded and moved the woman up to the first ambulance so the crew would load Ron inside. "This is his mother. You can take him in this ambulance, now," he said to the driver, as though he had the authority to speak for her. They loaded Ron into the back compartment. Jonah switched his crutches to one side and used his freed up hand to help Mrs. Rolfini up the steps next to Ronnie. Then he closed the doors and the vehicle pulled away.

Fran's mother suddenly began screaming hysterically at the ambulance crew moving her daughter toward the second ambulance with Margo. "She's going to die. My baby's going to die." She beat the man's shoulders, as he carried Fran's stretcher with his colleague. They almost dropped the girl while trying to ward off the mother's blows.

Kate found herself rising and moving to the mother, maneuvering between her and the stretcher. The woman turned her fury on Kate. "She's going to die, I tell you. Somebody do something. My baby's going to die."

Kate heard the slap of her hand against the woman's face above the din. Nearby observers gasped.

"Stop! Fran will hear you. She'll go into shock. Keep quiet

and let these people help her. Everybody is doing their best."

Kate suddenly realized she had actually *hit* someone, the mother of one of her daughter's friends. Her voice softened. "I'm sorry. We're all scared. Let's just get the kids to the hospital. Fran was alert and talking to me before you got here. She was doing fine. Don't scare her, now!"

The woman was silent as the ambulance crew finished loading the two girls. A couple of kids steered her and Margo's father into the front cab while the aide worked with both girls inside the ambulance.

Numbly, Kate walked back to kneel at her daughter's side. "There isn't another ambulance yet. We'll have to wait." *Oh, God, please let them hurry.*

Cindi whispered, "Good save, Mom."

The woman holding Cori's head said, "My kids would say that was 'far out.'"

Kate was embarrassed. "I didn't mean to hit her. But I know people who are unconscious can still hear. If Fran heard her mother say that, we'll lose her too."

She noticed Cole was also still waiting for another ambulance. "Holly, since Cole can still walk a little, can you take him and his mom to the hospital in your car so they can look at him sooner? We don't know how long...."

"But Cori?"

"We can't move her. We'll wait here. If you get to the hospital fast, maybe you can ask one of these first ambulances to come back for her."

Holly loaded Cole and his mother into her car, and Steve climbed in beside his friend. As they left, people quieted. Cori was gritting her teeth, but Kate knew she would not cry. Bystanders gathered around, as though in a circle of prayer.

Finally, one of the ambulances returned, and after what seemed like hours later, all five children were in operating rooms. The hospital had called in all available staff, plus several doctors and nurses had heard of the accident on the radio and came in answer to a call for volunteers. A quiet group of parents and friends sat solemnly holding hands in the waiting room. The room filled as car after car drove up, dropping off kids who had witnessed the accident. All were solemn and quiet--not knowing what they could do to help, but not wanting to leave, until there was some news of their friends. They gathered in small groups, comforting each other.

Ronnie's older brother, Rick, was in drama class with Cindi and Alisa. Though Rick had asked often to date Cindi, Phil and Kate refused because Rick was a senior, and Cindi was only a freshman. But Kate now wondered if their decision had been a mistake, as she watched Cindi giving Rick the support he needed. At this moment, life seemed short and tenuous.

The sliding doors opened and Phil strode in, followed by the rest of the family. Roger held tightly to Olivia, who was shaking so much she could barely walk. Phil came to Kate and took her in his arms. Tears in his eyes asked the question.

Kate shook her head. "Nothing yet. They're all in there."

"How bad is Cori?"

"I don't know. She regained consciousness, but she couldn't feel her lower leg or move anything except her hands. Two people kept her head and neck braced without moving until the ambulance finally returned to put her on a backboard. She was thrown quite a distance, Phil. I'm scared." She lowered her voice and whispered into Phil's embrace, "I don't think Ronnie will make it. He was...."

"We'll keep hoping and praying they'll *all* be okay, Katie. Hang on."

Time dragged by. Margo's doctor came out to talk to her father. He was a divorced man raising three girls alone while working the graveyard shift. His sideburns were grimy, and his hands shook, as the doctor told him Margo would survive. But her leg was broken in such a way that it would take several surgeries to fix. "She might always walk with a limp. We'll do what we can," said the doctor.

"A limp is nothing. She can handle a limp. Will she live?"

"Yes. All the damage was confined to one leg. Thanks to

the people who helped her right away, there was no shock."

Margo's dad erupted into nervous laughter and pumped the doctor's hand up and down. The doctor smiled. "We were lucky."

A nurse came to announce that Cole was admitted with a punctured lung, but he should make a fair recovery in a few weeks. His mom and Steve followed the nurse down the hall to be with Cole. *Two living, three to go.*

But then, two doctors in scrubs came out together. Those in the waiting room stood up expecting more good news. The first doctor went to Fran's mother, who stopped pacing.

"She didn't make it," the doctor said. "We thought she was going to be all right once we restructured her shoulder and stopped some minor bleeding. But then she went into shock, and we couldn't save her. It was sudden and unexpected. I'm sorry."

The mother turned against the doctor, cursing and hitting him. He merely held her hands still, apparently accustomed to misdirected anger and grief.

Kate found herself talking earnestly to the doctor. "No, that can't be right! Not Fran. It must be a mistake. I talked to her. She wasn't even scared. She was calm and coherent. I was sure she'd be fine." Then suddenly, she remembered, and turned toward Phil whispering into his embrace. "It's her! Fran *heard* her say she'd die. She heard her, and if *her mother* thought Fran would die, she did. She believed her mother and just died. How could she?"

Phil took Kate in his arms and all her grief for Fran poured out. She was shocked by her own bitterness toward this woman. She couldn't find any sympathy for a woman who'd given up on her own child. *But didn't I run right past my own daughter, and I didn't even see her lying there?*

Within minutes, word came that Ronnie died during surgery. Though Kate had tried to prepare herself for this news as inevitable, she still hurt to see Ron's mother collapse into her chair, sobbing and holding her eight-year-old twins. She'd been widowed when the twins were babies. Rick and Ron had been her strength through all those years. Kate and Phil immediately went to her and Kate held her in a long hug. Across the room she could see

Cindi holding Rick as he cried for his little brother. Cindi stroked his dark hair, her own eyes red and puffy.

The devastating news paralyzed the group of students, but few left. They waited for word on their new Student Body President. Even the candidate who had run against Cori was there.

Another hour passed before the doctors came to say Cori was stabilized. She had massive head and neck injuries, and her right leg from the knee down seemed paralyzed. "Because her neck was immobilized, we could save her," said the lead surgeon, "but she took a terrible blow that should have killed her. She must have been in excellent physical shape because her body absorbed tremendous force. She'll survive, but we won't know for a while what the permanent damage will be. We'll keep her here in the hospital until we do more tests to know if the paralysis is permanent or not."

Kate collapsed in Phil's arms. "She'll be okay, she'll be okay, Katie, dear," he kept repeating.

James came to embrace Phil and Kate. "Don't you guys worry. Cori is Cori, and she has more determination than anybody I know. She'll get over this."

One by one, people came over to offer hugs, encouragement, and promises to come visit the kids remaining in the hospital. Cindi hugged her mom and dad and said she was going with Rick and his mother to make arrangements for Ron's funeral. Cindi whispered, "Mom, I don't think Rick can handle this alone. Right now he's not feeling much like the 'man of the family.' I'll be back to see Cori at visiting hours. You understand?"

Kate nodded, and they left the hospital. Kate could see Olivia sobbing across the room and Roger holding her still. Ned and Lynette were trying to reason with her over something. Soon, the whole group came over.

Roger said, "You'd better sit down."

They did. Kate didn't know what to expect. Olivia climbed into Kate's lap and buried her head on her shoulder. Kate held her, while Phil patted her on the back and said, "Come on, Livie. We're all doing the best we can here."

Olivia blubbered her way through a few unintelligible words and finally lifted her head. "Kate, I tried to tell you, it's all my fault…all this mess. He was there at Mayberry before the crash. He wanted me to go with him and I wouldn't. I knew he was messed up and shouldn't be driving. He said he knew a way to scare girls and have fun, and he was going out to do it, and did I want to come along and see? I told him no because you always said no one should ride with somebody…."

Kate shook her head in confusion. "Who, Livie? Who are we talking about? My mind is going every which way, and I'm not thinking clearly right now. Slow down and make some sense for me, please."

Olivia closed her eyes tightly. "This is so hard. I snuck away from Mom when she started hitting me and wouldn't let me go to school or Cori's coronation. I went to Mayberry Park to wait for the game. It was Ernesto. He's a drug dealer and old gang guy from the One-Ways. He saw me, and we talked. He was smokin' joints one after another and saying how he was gonna drive his car out and have some fun scaring girls."

"You *know* that he was smoking pot before he drove into those kids? Are you sure?"

Olivia hung her head and cried. "I'm sure. I had one puff from his joint. Just one, Kate, honest, and I'll bet there are still a lot of his stubs on the sidewalk there. I tried to tell him not to drive, but he wouldn't listen. I shoulda gone with him and maybe I coulda steered the car away. I think he aimed at the girls and thought he could turn away at the last minute and just scare 'em. It's the way Susan sounded when she told about it. She could see his face through the windshield. He was that close."

Roger reached out and touched Olivia's shoulder. "Tell them the rest, Livie—why you didn't go with him."

"I was scared. I was stupid. If I was caught in a stolen car with Ernesto. He said he didn't steal it because the keys were in it, but I remembered what you said that if it isn't yours, you can't touch it, and I knew, with him being a drug dealer and all, they'd haul me off to juvie again, so I told him I wouldn't go. He got mad and drove off, all wild. It was only just a little bit down Meyer Road that I saw him swerve toward the girls at The Corner Store, and all the crashes started. I was so scared I just stood there not knowing what to do, and then I saw your car go by, so I ran to Sunnyside to tell the secretary to send someone--that you were there already and needed help. I knew it'd be bad. See, it's all my fault. I shoulda found a way to stop him, or gone with him to steer away from the girls, but I was so scared of juvie. Now, Ronnie, Fran, and even Cori...." She broke into uncontrollable sobs.

Phil put his arm around Olivia and said, "Livie, there's probably no way you could have stopped him. He was already down the street and hitting the cars before anyone could've stopped him. It wasn't your fault. Your not going with him didn't *make* him do it. He already *planned* to do it."

Ned broke in, "Everybody is pretty mad about this. I heard some people talk about lynching Ernesto, after what he did. And now to find out he did it on purpose, just to scare the girls. The guy's evil and deserves lynching or worse."

"But," said Phil slowly, "this is America, and bad as I hate to say it, even Ernesto needs a fair trial. We'll have to see that the law takes care of him--not an angry mob. Violence doesn't help anyone. Olivia will testify against Ernesto when his trial comes up. With her testimony, the courts should put him away for a long time. It won't bring Fran and Ronnie back, or get the other three back to normal, but he'll be punished.

And since you feel bad about this, Livie, and you were there, this is your chance to help. You're the one who can testify in court to ensure Ernesto goes to jail."

Olivia's eyebrows rose in shock and she let out a yelp. "You people are crazy! I can't tell! He's part of the gang!"

Chapter 22

It had been an eight-week nightmare. Two funerals, and Cori in an induced coma, the arrest with many people either saying Ernesto should be hung, or blaming the Johnsons for bringing Olivia, Lynette, and Roger, known as previous "problem kids" into their community. Additionally, Olivia was blamed for not having somehow stopped the carnage, and for knowing Ernesto as a drug dealer and a gang member without having turned him in.

Olivia blamed herself as well. She was terrified of testifying in court. "Don't you know what he or his gang brothers will do to me, to all of us, if I narc on him?" Kate hoped sanity would return to the street as people returned to business as usual, but for weeks before the trial, life was difficult for the family.

Conscious of the criticism on his new home, Roger sacrificed his shoulder-length wavy hair to the barber to look "more All-American Mr. Clean" for the upcoming trial. Under his battered leather cowboy hat, he had looked like a B-movie outlaw, though he had turned out to be a gentle soul, careful of his sisters, and especially protective of Olivia. She pronounced him "ever so much more handsome" without the long hair. He kept the Fu-Manchu mustache of which he was so proud.

Ironically, the neighbors were less critical after the haircut, and they accepted Lynette, because she adapted to fit with their middle class morés. But much blame for the accident and Ernesto's drugged presence in Whittier was directed at Olivia, who never quite looked like anyone else. Kate remembered what Fred, her teaching colleague, had said once, that even if you had a hundred kids lined up, Olivia would stand out as potential trouble. Even when she was on her best behavior, this still seemed to be true. It was a mystery as to why. Kate still thought it might be something in her body language, her combative stance that never went away.

Olivia was a frequent visitor to the three students remaining in the hospital, often hitchhiking there after school in spite of Kate and Phil's promises to take her later when the rest of the family got home. She spent afternoons with Cole and Margo and Cori, when Cori was awake. The doctors kept Cori knocked out for several days, as her concussion and brain swelling improved, and until they determined how much of the damage was permanent. They also studied the lack of feeling in her right leg, sticking needles into it at random, like a pincushion. Cori felt nothing. They explained that the surgery team was so worried about her head and neck trauma, that no one noticed the cut above her knee until after surgery when it was too late to save the feeling. After all, they said, the wound hadn't bled, so it seemed less dangerous. Cole was released from the hospital first, but with residual damage to the lung that would cause a lifetime of pain and depression. Eventually, he got lost in drugs, too. Margo recovered with a stiff right leg, but she had strong arms and was quite good on crutches. Cori was last of the three to go home.

Cori, after the initial fear for brain damage was passed, had so much pain that sleep was impossible. Doctors tried braces, shots into the neck and into the bone, which were followed by another three-day coma. Cleo and Goldie were her constant companions, lying on her bed, with Cleo coming to fetch a family member every time Cori even stirred. But eventually, she was able to use crutches to hobble around providing she wore her neck brace, to the delight of everyone in the Johnson family.

Immediately, she insisted on being taken to school, though getting her in and out of a car with casts, crutches and braces was more than an ordeal. James's van was easiest, so he took on the job of carting her to school and picking her up.

Her Vice President had done nothing while Cori was out of school. A malaise hung over the place with much depression. So Cori's first act as President was to persuade fifty kids to go with her to the School Board meeting. There, she made her case for changing the dress code to allow slacks or pant suits for both students *and* teachers. She cited her mother's difficulty in assisting children in the recent accident while crawling under cars wearing a dress. In spite of the principal's objections, the school board approved changes unanimously. Cheers erupted in the boardroom.

Cori's next plan was for a school dance to lift spirits of those who'd lost two good friends. Olivia joined her in feeling something needed to be done to bring everyone back together and lift spirits of those who had witnessed the accident.

The principal vetoed that idea, too, but he made one mistake. He said, "I won't allow a dance *on* school property." The girls took that to mean that they could have a dance, as long as it was *elsewhere*. Cori coaxed the Mayberry Park supervisor to allow use of the park building, called every parent to get plenty of chaperones and food, while Livie and Susan recruited kids to make decorations. The committee was wrapped up in the project.

One of the nosey neighbors, who had been so critical, told Kate she wouldn't allow her girl to go. "Some kids will smuggle in booze or drugs, and Cori won't be able to stop them," she said. Kate told the girls, and Cori made more phone calls to assure rule compliance, while Olivia was sure she had a plan.

Kate was surprised when Olivia said, "Will you take us to the police station?" Cori and Susan convinced the officers that police presence at the dance was welcome. They invited the officers to pop in frequently to eat, look around, check kids loitering outside, or dance. This was Olivia's idea. The fact that she actually thought the officers would *enjoy* dancing to *Sugar Pie, Honey Bunch* brought their smiles and promises to help the kids keep their dance trouble free, if only to prove that it could be done--that not all kids were thugs, as Mr. Carleton seemed to believe.

Kate noticed that while Susan and Cori worked their enthusiastic magic on some of the officers for good supervision, Olivia took aside a couple of other officers and worked another type of magic. She heard Olivia volunteer to stand at the door, if they would. She would identify any kids that used or sold drugs. "I can tell you who they are, and we can tell them they have to give their drugs to you before they'll be allowed in. If they do that and go in, maybe they'll have a good time *without* the drugs, and they won't think they have to use them all the time. Just promise not to narc on them, if they do good by turning the drugs in, okay?"

One officer turned to look at Kate and she simply shrugged,

unable to hide a smile. Olivia continued to the officers, "Look, anything Cori organizes has to be on the up and up, ya know? She won't want dope in there." Livie begged the officers so sincerely that they got tickled. "We'll give your method a try," one volunteered, barely suppressing a grin.

The dance was a packed house with no problems. Cori and Margo couldn't dance, so they served as disc jockeys and changed to something fast, if couples got too cozy and too close. *Tell it Like it Is* would become *Put a Little Love in your Heart* in a heartbeat.

The principal hid in his office for a week afterward and refused to allow a write-up of the event in the school newspaper. The kids didn't care. They'd engendered laughter again.

Though Kate and Phil felt sure it was too soon, it wasn't long until they caught Cindi, Reneé, Alisa and Olivia behind the garage pitching practice balls to Cori who squatted in catcher's stance on her left leg, with her unfeeling right one stuck straight out at the side. Though she couldn't yet jump up on one leg, she could still throw down to second from a squat position to trap a base runner. Running was a problem because she couldn't feel anything below the knee, and she couldn't feel if or when she was about to take a fall. It didn't seem to matter to her, though. She just got back up. The kids began to make plans for softball season.

The parents shook their heads in wonder. Cori was, indeed, Cori, and the other kids backed her up. As for Olivia, she only talked about Cori's recovery, school, or Cleo's latest puppies. She refused to discuss the upcoming trial. Her mother had not wanted her back since the accident, and that suited her just fine.

"Hear ye, hear ye, hear ye. The court is now in session."

The courtroom was so packed, people spilled out into the corridors. Teens who had witnessed the "Slaughter at The Corner Store," as the press called it, parents, local business owners who helped corral the defendant--all were present. It rivaled a murder trial for the length of the witness list. Proceedings dragged on, with witness after witness describing the crash. The old man from the filling station described the young man who had jumped from the car and run, and how he was forced to tackle him to hold him for the police. Countless police officers measured widths, lengths, and angles to determine if the driver could have swerved and missed the girls, or not. Kate cringed when the diagrams depicted child victims as little stick figures lying in different places.

Susan's testimony was critical since she was the only person who saw the defendant's face up close who had not been swept away and injured. The prosecutor asked her to tell the sequence of events in her own words.

"Margo, Cori, Fran and I were walking along the side of the road...."

"You mean the easement on this chart?" He pointed.

"Yes. Cori forgot sunflower seeds, so she ran back in the store to get them. We said we'd wait for her, and we did, just standing on the...the easement."

"Please point out where you were at that time and show where Cori ran back?"

Susan's hands shook. Kate knew this ordeal was hard for her young neighbor. The children had played together back and forth across the street since they were three. Susan was a delicate strawberry blonde with more interest in painting than in sports.

"Cori went back, and she'd just come out of the store with sunflower seed jumbo packs when Ernesto came down the street from Mayberry Park, and he aimed his car at us." Her voice broke.

"Take your time, young lady. Everything's all right."

"Ernesto had this gleeful, mean smile on his face, like he was happy to hit us." She glanced at the defendant, who glared back at her until the gallery could see Susan shiver noticeably.

"Maybe he thought he could turn away at the last minute, but he must have hit the gas instead of the brake, because he came faster, and his face looked different after he hit Fran and Margo." Susan also described what the officers had said was a sub-sized custom steering wheel that didn't offer much control over a car's steering. It was, according to the officers, illegal.

Susan said, " I was facing Ernesto when he hit Margo and Fran, sliced off my nylons, and Margo flew in the air to the side.

Then I saw Fran carried away draped over his hood and I turned in time to see Fran until he crunched into all the parked cars. They squeezed together with such a hard bang that the cigar van flipped around the other way."

Susan was crying, and the prosecutor handed her a tissue. He said, "And then what happened, Susan. What did you see?"

Susan gulped back her sobs and continued. "Fran got thrown off the hood and under the van, and as the van spun, the doors caught Cori coming out of the store and down Mr. Max's sidewalk. It threw her into the air and against the store."

"Did you see what happened to Ronnie and Cole on their bike?" asked the prosecutor.

"No. I saw them go between the parked cars earlier, but not after that. I don't think I can forget what I saw and how Cori flew through the air. And poor Fran."

Susan was released from the witness chair and cried against her mother's shoulder in the audience.

Cole was able to pick up the story from there, telling how he and Ronnie hadn't seen anything coming at all, until they heard engine gunning noise and were scrunched between the parked cars.

On the witness stand, kids who'd been inside the store described their fear that Cori would come flying through the glass windows and how everyone was screaming and running. One boy even described the sound of the thud when Cori hit the brick wall. Kate felt bile rise in her throat. Phil put his arm around her tightly. Tears were in his eyes, too.

Olivia fidgeted, nervously rubbing her hands together and leaning against Kate, as witness after witness described what they saw. Soon, she would be called to testify about Ernesto's intention, drug habits, and mental and physical condition before the accident. Each time the bailiff rose, Livie crouched in her seat in case it would be her turn. Phil had explained to her that all she needed to do was tell the truth, exactly--only what she knew to be true. That she didn't have to tell anything except the answers to the questions she was asked. But since all the other witnesses were asked to tell their story in their own words, they might expect the same of her.

"How will I know what's important?" she whispered. "What will Ernesto do to me?"

"It's going to be all right, Olivia," Kate whispered back. "You testify, the court sends Ernesto away for a long time, and it's all over. You won't have to be scared, then."

"You don't know that. You just don't know. Maybe that's the way it is in your world, but that's not the way it is in mine."

Kate put her arm around the girl, who was shaking. "Olivia, you've been with us for three years. You're part of our world now, too."

"I wish I believed that, but you just don't know."

But, before Olivia was called to testify, when it seemed there were no witnesses left *except* her, the defense lawyer requested a sidebar, and he and the prosecutor approached the bench. The judge said, "Conference in my chambers." The bailiff escorted both lawyers and Ernesto into the judge's chambers.

They went in with serious expressions, leaving all spectators and witnesses to mumble and wonder and buzz among themselves, in spite of the bailiff's ever-present admonitions to keep the noise down. The buzz grew louder with frustration and anger at the delay.

"What could they be doing in there?" said Margo's father.

Another man shouted out, "I told you we shoulda lynched the guy. They're in there making some kind of deal."

Voices rattled around as folks wondered if this was true.

Olivia leaned across Kate's s lap to ask Phil. "What's it mean? What're they gonna do? What's taking so long?" Phil simply shrugged, as mystified as everyone else.

Cori was uncomfortable sitting for so long and begged to remove her hot neck brace. Kate wouldn't allow it, but Lynette fanned Cori's face with her slim purse.

Down the rows, restlessness grew, and it didn't seem as though anything good could be going on. After forty-five minutes, the chamber doors opened and Ernesto and his lawyer came out, followed by the judge and the prosecutor. They were all laughing!

The crowd roared angrily to see Ernesto, who had killed

and maimed children, laughing at his trial. The judge banged his gavel to restore order. Two men shouted out their frustration. The judge had one man removed from the courtroom and continued banging his gavel until the room quiet, but tense with rage.

"The sentence in this unfortunate *accident,* and for joy-riding in a car with a substandard steering wheel, is three years of probation for Richard Ernesto. During that time, he shall not be allowed to drive a car." He banged the gavel. "Case dismissed."

Ernesto and his lawyer were hustled out the side door by the bailiff, the judge disappeared back into his chambers, and the spectators sat in stunned silence for a heartbeat before bedlam broke out.

"What happened?" spectators asked their seatmates. "I don't understand."

"How could the judge give him probation? He killed two kids and injured three more, not to mention all the cars he wrecked. 'Accident?' It was no accident. It was deliberate murder!"

"He's damaged this community so it'll never forget. How could the judge let him off with no punishment."

"I told you we shoulda lynched him."

It was as though all sanity left the courtroom with Ernesto-- and he was out, free and clear. No one could accept or understand the verdict. The court hadn't even called the one witness, Olivia, who could testify he was high on drugs. Officers shoved everyone out of the courtroom. Doors were locked when everyone was out.

In the foyer, Olivia leaned against Kate and asked, "Does that mean I don't have to talk up there? Is it all over? Will they put Ernesto in jail now?"

"It's over, Livie. But Ernesto isn't going to jail." Kate's attention was on Cori. The look on her face was one step before explosion. Kate moved quickly to her daughter's side.

"He killed Ron and Fran, Mom. He killed them. Everybody knows he killed them! Old Mr. Winslow at the station caught him red-handed. Susan could see the happy look on his face when he aimed at them. Livie knows he was on drugs. I don't understand how they could let him go. You know he'll be right back out there driving again, and no one will catch him. How many people does he have to kill before they lock him up? What about Fran and Ron's murder? This isn't fair to anyone!"

Kate let the storm run its course, even though she could echo every one of Cori's words. "I don't know, Honey. The lawyers apparently wanted to stop the witness list before they got to his drug history, and they came to some kind of a deal to give him probation, instead of a jail sentence. I don't know why any more than you do. And I'm just as sick over it as you are."

Cori buried her face in her mother's arms.

"What do we do to a judge?" asked Roger. With head down and hands clenching and unclenching he put an arm around the shaken Olivia. "Will the judge protect Livie now?"

"I think all we can do is vote him out at the next election, but I've never seen a judge get voted out, no matter how incompetent," said Phil. "Livie should be in no danger. She didn't even have to get on the stand."

Roger and Olivia looked at each other and Roger shook his head. "You don't know how it is in gangs, do you?"

The stunned crowd could not seem to disperse. Little clusters formed over the courthouse steps and the sidewalk, as the Johnsons walked into the sunshine. Olivia was frightened. Some of the people in the crowd seemed to take out their frustration with the verdict on her.

"How do we know you didn't give him the drugs?" yelled one person. "How do we know you didn't incite him to do this?" "Why didn't you stop him?" Two high school kids started to grab her arms, but James, Roger and Rick beat them to it and pushed the others aside. Ned raced ahead to start the van. The five drove off.

The crowd parted to let the rest of the family through. Cori struggled with the steps on her crutches, with Alisa, Cindi, and Lynette helping her. It was a slow walk down, and they all felt the hostile atmosphere. By the time they reached the station wagon, Cori was exhausted from the exertion. Lynette and Alisa cried. Cindi stared straight ahead, unable to even speak her anger.

When Kate, Phil and the girls got home, the boys and

Olivia were sitting around the dining room table, silently. All looked seriously worried, and Livie was confused.

"I don't get it," she said to Phil. "I thought I was supposed to testify to send Ernesto to prison. That's the only way I could survive this, *maybe*. You promised he'd go to jail for a long time. Now he's walking around free and everyone's blaming me. But they didn't even call me to testify. Does that mean Ernesto doesn't know I was supposed to narc on him?"

"Livie, your name was on the witness list, and Ernesto's lawyer would have had the list," said Phil. "That was probably why his lawyer stopped the trial before it got to you. You could've put Ernesto in that car and on drugs. Once you testified to his drug use and his *intent* to aim at girls, he'd be convicted."

"So does that mean Ernesto knows I ratted him out...or at least, that I meant to, before they stopped his court thing?"

"Probably. But he'll be on probation, so he'd be stupid to try anything, especially when you didn't actually testify. Why should he bother you now?"

"Hmph!" Livie shook her head and sighed. "Sometimes I feel so close to you guys, that you're the only ones who love and understand me, and sometimes we are so far apart I don't even understand what you're thinking."

"What does that mean?" asked Phil.

"That you know all about the world, but you don't know nothing about gangs. Ernesto will be coming after me just for *agreeing* to testify against him. Yes, he's that stupid. He knows where I live. I won't be safe anywhere. I'm gonna be looking over my shoulder--forever."

"Oh, Livie," said Kate, trying to calm the girl's fears. "Surely you're exaggerating. He'll just be glad to have gotten off so easily. I'm sure you're safe here. Why would anyone want to hurt you? You didn't actually testify or do *him* any damage. He got off scot free."

"I broke the code."

Chapter 23

Reacting to Olivia's fear, family members made sure someone was with her at all times. She stayed pretty close to home, hoping she wouldn't run into Ernesto or his brothers.

The summer brought the usual track and field season, and fall brought a new school year. With everyone in high school, football, cheerleading, drama, band, and homework brought the usual household chaos. These all existed along with Cori's efforts at recovery.

"It's purely by determination and cussedness," said Ned, laughing with James. They watched Cori leaning down, using her hand to push her foot against the pedals of her bass drum before her seven-man band group would arrive to rehearse in their living room. Kate and Phil leaned against the kitchen arch to watch.

"What do you think you can do *that* way," asked Ned?"

"I figure if I can bypass the dead part of that knee, I can train my lower leg and foot to do what my *mind* tells them to do, even if the doctor says the messages won't go through the knee's nerve. I don't believe him. I believe in mind over matter."

"You're crazy, Cori," said James, "but if determination can bypass *anything*, you'll probably manage it. Here, let me help. James folded himself into a ball at the foot pedal of the drum set and moved Cori's foot up and down on the pedal. After a while, she grinned and pushed down the pedal herself. "We're still not on the right rhythm, but I can move it, if I concentrate hard enough. This is going to work, guys, I just know it."

Cori worked every day with the foot pedal, with various family members moving the foot when her "mind" got tired. Within a short time, she was again playing the drums and running. She couldn't feel anything below the knee, but if a fall surprised her, she just got up again and ran the bases, always with Kate's fear that she would reinjure her neck. They knew she was in pain, but she never complained and continued doing the things she normally did. Both Kate and Phil felt she would somehow come out on top of her injury. Cori only had one way to look at life—the way things *should* be, and she usually managed to make them so. The other kids were always at her side and at Livie's.

"What are they doing, always together?" a neighbor asked.

Roger answered, "Protecting our sisters.

As months went by, Rick hung out with the family more often, finding companionship with all the guys, and waiting patiently for Cindi to become of age.

Then, Olivia and Cindi saw Ernesto driving down Meyer Road one day. They ran home to tell Kate and Phil. "I think he saw me," said Olivia. "I think he knows I'm here."

"Can't the police arrest him now that he's violating his parole by driving?" asked Lynette. "Livie's been terrified for months. Now we can put him in jail and quit worrying."

Kate called the Whittier and the Norwalk police. Their comments were the same. They didn't have anyone in the area, and Ernesto would be gone by the time any officers arrived.

"Can't you pick him up at his house?"

"Well, he wouldn't be driving then, would he, Ma'am?" drawled the officer. "And we can't take hearsay evidence. We must catch him in the act before we can do anything about him."

"But he's threatened one of our girls, a sixteen year old."

"Has he actually hurt her?"

"Not yet, but he's threatened."

"We cannot, by law, do anything to him until he actually does something."

Kate slammed down the phone. *That may be too late.*

And it was too late. Only a few nights later, from the entry hall came the sound of a banging door and shattering glass. Kate jumped at the sound and dropped the papers she'd been grading. She recovered quickly, rushing to investigate just as Olivia lurched into the living room and collapsed to the floor in a bloody mass.

"Don't let 'em get me again," the teen shrieked. "Don't let 'em get me."

"Who? Olivia? What happened?" Kate knelt by the terrified

girl, tracing a bloody trail up Olivia's jacket and neck to find its source. She probed gingerly with her fingertips, found an oozing gash on the girl's head, grabbed a sofa pillow, and pushed it tightly against the wound to staunch the bleeding. "Hold still, honey." Kate wrapped her arms around the wildly thrashing girl and rocked her back and forth. "Phil, wake up--come help me!" she screamed.

"Don't let 'em get me," Olivia repeated. She shut her eyes tightly and stiffened, clenching her teeth, her body still jerking spasmodically.

Phil shuffled into the room in his ratty old bathrobe and even more ancient flip-flops. He rubbed sleep from his eyes, yawning and mumbling, "What's all the ruckus, Hon? It's almost midnight."

The scene in the middle of his living room floor quickly brought him to wide-awake status. He knelt by his wife and took Olivia's wrist. "Pulse is still strong. Olivia, can you hear me? Can you tell us what happened? Where does it hurt?"

The girl couldn't speak through her tightly clamped jaws, but she kicked her heels on the floor and held on to Kate.

Phil turned to his wife. "Where's she been or how did she get hurt?"

"I don't know. I didn't expect her tonight. She said she had to go to her mom's. She just now stumbled in the door and collapsed, saying somebody's after her. There's a bad wound on her head. We've got to get her to a hospital."

"You know the local hospital won't take her without her mother. Last time, the doctors wouldn't even look at her. They said we had no right...."

"I know, but I think she'll need stitches."

Livie jerked in Kate's arms.

"Hold her head still so she won't bang it again," Phil cautioned. "I'll go get her mom. I can probably be back before the police or ambulance will get here, anyway."

"What'll we do if Mrs. Gonzaga won't come?"

Phil spoke softly. "Don't worry, hon. I'll get her here, if I have to drag her. General Hospital's two hours away. If I get her mom, we can be at Southside Regional in a half hour."

"I'll go with you, Phil," said Lynette, entering the room and turning white at her younger sister's condition. "If Mom won't come out, I can get in through the window."

Phil disappeared around the bedroom door and returned in mere seconds, zipping his jeans and hopping on one bare foot to get into his tennis shoes at the same time. That accomplished, he pulled a sweatshirt down over his dark crew cut.

One by one, the other teens entered the living room, alarmed when they saw Olivia. Kate directed Alisa to the telephone to dial the operator to find an ambulance. Cindi brought a washcloth filled with ice from the kitchen that Kate placed between the bloody pillow and Olivia's head wound. Cori raided the linen closet for a blanket that Roger wrapped around the injured girl. Livie's legs jerked in spastic movements Kate had never seen in First Aid class.

James knelt silently, holding Olivia's ankles to keep her from banging them on the floor. Cindi also knelt beside her mother. "What's wrong with Livie this time, Mom?"

Kate could hear the fear in Cindi's voice, and wondered if it echoed her own. "It's not a drug overdose. It's a head injury. She said someone's trying to get her." She held Olivia tightly, but the girl was now unconscious.

Phil snorted. "Kate, honey, as bad as I hate to say so, Livie has several people who might want to hurt her—Ernesto, or even her sister Rita, and maybe some of those gang people."

"My money's on Ernesto," said Cindi. "He saw us."

Phil quietly laid his old Smith and Wesson on the floor at his wife's side.

"Phil, put that away. I could never shoot anyone."

"I hope you don't have to, love, but we have a houseful of kids to protect. You watch that door and shoot anyone that walks through it until I get back with Livie's mom. I'll call out to you." His eyes held hers. "Do you understand?"

Kate looked from the face of her determined husband to the damp face of the moaning teenager in her arms and nodded.

She whispered one unnecessary word, "Hurry."

Phil grabbed a set of car keys from the stack where the teenagers always dropped them on the piano and bolted from the house, followed by Lynette. Kate heard a car rumble into motion and drive away.

A frenzy of activity ensued, as everyone who'd been quietly staring at the gun suddenly realized they should act. Cindi rushed through rooms closing and locking all doors and windows, while Ned and James ran to stand guard by the kitchen door that went out to the back yard, barricading it with a kitchen chair and dragging the bag of baseball bats with them. Cori turned out the lights, so they could see outside, but no one could see in. Kate could hear Alisa in the kitchen struggling to talk with the Operator. In a crisis, her long-gone, childhood stutter returned with her attempts to ask, "Wh...what do I d...d..do n..n..now?" Roger stared white-faced, kneeling by the side of his young friend, rubbing her hand and calling out to her, as though sure she could hear him. "Livie, Livie, we love you. Hang on...."

"I'll take care of the glass, Mom," whispered Cori. She was now fifteen and recovering more every day. She quietly swept up the broken glass in the entry hall by the moonlight that came streaming in.

Had it been Olivia who banged the door open hard enough to break the mirror on the wall, or had it been her attacker, maybe Ernesto and his gang, now waiting in the yard? The kids hunkered down on the floor near Kate, who still rocked Olivia in her arms.

Silence overtook them all, and they waited, not sure if their Dad would come first with Olivia's mother so they could hurry to the hospital's emergency room, or if someone else would come first—whoever was trying to "get" Olivia.

Looking at the young teen's face in the moonlight and waiting in the darkened house, Kate thought of all the times she had seen Olivia hurt. It was always something, and she could never figure out why Livie couldn't seem to see the "common sense route" that would avoid these catastrophes. Why hadn't she stayed home, for instance? But though life would certainly have been more normal and much easier without Olivia, Kate felt her heart torn by yet another injury to this child of the streets. There had been as much heartache during the time she'd been in their lives, as there had been fun and laughter. Lately there had been the joy of her progress toward a safe maturity...and now this.

The only sound was the clicking of Cleo's claws across the tile floor, and Olivia's occasional moan. The dog licked Livie's hand and curled up beside it where it dangled outside Kate's arms.

The rest of the family listened carefully for any movement outside. Finally, they heard a car and Cleo ran to the front door wagging her tail. Almost simultaneously, Phil's voice could be heard as well. "Kate, it's me."

Gratefully, Kate put aside the gun Phil had given her, and Cindi unlocked the front door to greet Phil and Lynette. Olivia's mother was grumbling, drunk, and barely seemed to realize it was Olivia, "her baby," bleeding on the floor.

"She wouldn't answer the door," said Lynette. "I had to climb in our old 'getaway window' and let Phil in so he could drag her to the car. She didn't want to come."

"I see an ambulance isn't here yet, anyway," said Phil, "so let's get Olivia to the hospital. We called the police from her mom's and asked them to meet us there. No matter how drunk this woman is, surely, she can make her X on the paperwork."

At his words, all filed out to the cars except James and Ned. "We'll stay here in case they try to vandalize the house, or something," said James, still holding a baseball bat.

"It's the 'or something' that worries me," said Phil. "I'd feel better if we were all together. It's only a house—you guys need to come with us."

The hospital hadn't changed since their last visit, but the nurse's station had. A younger, more eager nurse was on duty, and when Mrs. Gonzaga was indicated as the "real" mother, the staff immediately took Livie to the emergency room.

Police showed up shortly after to interview everyone, but no one really knew what had happened to Livie. Cindi volunteered that Olivia had seen Ernesto driving and was afraid he had seen her, and that he had threatened Livie for agreeing to testify against him the previous summer. She also mentioned with some rancor that they had called the police to request help *before* this happened. The policemen ignored that statement.

"Oh, you're the family involved in The Corner Store thing...that's right. This Ernesto was the one who got probation. We need to talk to Olivia Gonzaga."

"You'll have to wait until they're through with her," said Phil.

An hour later, Olivia lay in her hospital bed with her head wrapped in multiple bandages and an IV tube trailing from her arm. "And I *hate* needles," she said.

Mrs. Gonzaga fussed around aiming barbs of anger at everyone in the room. Phil offered to send her home in a taxi, and she took him up on the offer. Olivia breathed a little easier once her mother was gone.

"Was it Ernesto?" asked Cindi. "Do you know what happened?"

"I'll ask the questions, young lady," said one of the uniformed officers, a young one, brimming with self-importance.

Cindi backed away from the bed to let him go forward.

"Was it Ernesto?" he repeated verbatim. "Do you know what happened?"

Even Livie had to laugh with the family and the older officer, though she immediately grabbed her head with pain.

"The doctor said her head injury bled a lot--a blunt force trauma," said Kate to the officers. Trying to lift Olivia's spirits, she added, "She always has had a hard head." The two exchanged a grin and Livie waved her fingers.

"It was a bar," said Livie. "He hit me from behind with a crowbar."

"I thought you were going straight to your mom's," said Kate. "Ned dropped you off there. Why didn't you stay put?"

"She was drunk and didn't remember she told me to come home anyway, so I hitched over to see Bettina. She called and wanted me to see her newest little girl. I thought it would be okay, but Ernesto and his brothers spotted me walking home. They started following me in their car. I was running, and Ernesto got out and chased me, and he hit me with the bar. I dodged as best I could, but one hit was really hard." She paused to hold her head still.

"It hurts if I shake it," she said, resuming her story. "I was a few blocks from your house and a long ways from my mom's, so I rolled into the bushes when a car came by and Ernesto got scared and ran to the car. I tried to get to your house, but the last part I don't even remember how I found you. It hurt so bad and I got so scared and dizzy."

"What drugs did you take over at the One-Ways?" asked the younger officer.

"Hey, man, I'm not doing that any more, not for a long time. But Ernesto and his gang were loaded. He has needle tracks, too—probably why he ran off when he saw the car. And I'm not fighting or carrying a weapon anymore, so I didn't have anything to defend myself with." She looked at Kate, almost accusingly. "At least I could have fought back when they jumped me."

When all the pieces were put together, the policemen went off to find Ernesto, and the Johnsons were allowed to take Olivia home with a prescribed painkiller that she said she wouldn't take. "It looks too much like downers," she said. "I'll just hold my head still so it doesn't rattle so much."

Roger carried Olivia to the car and held her in his lap all the way home. "You know I'm going to marry this girl when she gets well again, he said with surety."

Olivia didn't argue.

"You're too young," said Kate, automatically.

"How old were you and Phil?"

Phil and Kate exchanged glances and grinned, sheepishly. "A little older than Livie," Kate answered. "You know you'll have to get her mom's signature?"

"She never knows what she's signing, anyway," said Lynette, smiling.

"Then it's settled," said Roger. I was going to tell you at

breakfast, but then all this happened. I signed up for the Air Force yesterday. When I finish basic, we'll get married and then they'll send us someplace far away, so I can take Livie and protect her. I should have been with her this time."

"I know, it was probably stupid to go by myself," said Olivia, "but I always think I can take care of myself. I just thought I could sneak over to help Bettina and hurry right back. Guess I was wrong. There doesn't seem to be any way to leave the One-Ways behind, does there?" She laid her bandaged head on Roger's shoulder. "You know you'll have nothing but trouble trying to keep me straight, don't you, Roger? It's hard for me to be good *all* the time, even when I'm trying hard."

"I'm not worried," said Roger, and he kissed her soundly. Somehow no one was surprised.

The police stopped by later that day to tell them they had found Ernesto—dead. They now had a murder case to investigate. They were pretty sure his brothers had knifed him over a drug deal gone bad. "One less druggie, and we can lock up the others," said one of the officers as they walked away. "So much for that, just one less druggie, and that's all he was."

"I see him as a murderer," said Cindi. "But I guess this is a case of 'what goes around, comes around.' Ernesto or his brothers won't be here to hurt Olivia, and Ernesto finally got his justice."

"Perhaps we can get on with life, now," commented Alisa.

But things never stayed calm long in the Johnson home.

The next week, with no warning, Ned's mother came to get him. She had finally decided to go to New York to get away from her abusive boyfriend, and demanded that Ned go with her. She didn't want to go alone, though she had been without Ned most of the time for several years. She said that, in case the boyfriend came after her, she'd have "…her big, strong linebacker to protect her." Being barely underage, Ned had to go with her, and the Johnsons could do nothing but say goodbye.

It was tragic to the family, another huge loss. Ned was the one everyone depended upon for his imaginative way of seeing the funny side of things. Also, he had been a supportive good friend to Cori and Cindi for years, and they were devastated. Ned hugged everyone, including Cleo and Goldie. "This is hard," he said, "Thank you guys for being my family. I love you all. His tears joined those of the whole crew.

"We're proud of you, Ned," said Phil, choking back his feelings. "Have a good life, son." Kate couldn't even speak.

Ned promised to come back when he got older, but the Johnsons mourned as he drove away with the mom he hardly knew. New York was far away, and the house felt empty.

Phil comforted Kate by reminding her that they had no right to keep any of the bonus children, or even their own girls, for that matter. "They're merely on loan from God for whatever time they can stay, for whatever purpose they need to be here with us. All *any* parent can do is give them as much love and guidance as we can and try to instill a value system until the children are on their own. Then we must let them go. Ned's ready, and he'll make his way just fine, regardless of his mom's lifestyle."

Alisa and Cindi were already investigating what college they would attend, and Lynette had started junior college classes concurrently with those in high school. Soon, Roger was off to Air Force basic training. James chose the Army, and Cindi's friend, Rick, joined the Marines.

"Hey, what happened to the Navy?" complained Phil. But the house had become increasingly quiet with all the boys gone for basic and MOS training. Of course, all would get leave for the wedding. James and Rick already knew they would probably be going to the winding down war in Vietnam, while Roger planned on taking his new bride with him to his hoped-for assignment in England.

"That should be far enough away that Olivia can start our married life in a safe place, don't you think?" Roger worried a lot about Livie's safety, though everyone tried to reassure him that with Ernesto and his gang out of the picture, things should go just fine.

Wedding fever took over the house full of girls as plans progressed.

The girls made several forays of bridal shops all over town. "They just don't make anything but flower girl dresses in size zero," complained Cindi.

"She's never gonna grow unless we stretch her," chimed in Cori, while Alisa took off her shoes and rubbed her sore feet.

"We went just everywhere today, and nobody had anything Livie's size. The prices, even for bridesmaid dresses in normal sizes, were ridiculous, too," added Lynette.

The object of conversation, Olivia, leaned against the wall. "Kate, am I ever going to grow bigger?"

"I doubt it, Livie," answered Kate with a chuckle. "If you were going to grow any more, you would have done it by now."

"You mean I'm stunted?" Livie stretched tall to her best four-foot seven inches, as the rest of the girls giggled. "All the rest of you are well over five feet. What happened to me?"

"You stunted your growth by smoking," said Cori. "I told you that you should stop four years ago, and you wouldn't listen."

Lynette said, "I think somebody just chopped her off at the knees a long time ago." She laughed, as Livie warmed to the subject.

"Mom," said Cindi. "Is there any chance you could make the dresses, if we all helped you?"

Alisa said, "We could take on the cooking to leave you free to take up residence in the sewing room for the next month."

"I'll correct your papers," said Olivia.

Oh, boy, thought Kate. "I suppose that's our only option, since the prices are scary too. Let's dig out the box of patterns and see if there are any styles you like." Cindi brought the box into the living room, and very soon they rushed out to the fabric store for an hour.

When Phil got home to his "gaggle of girls," he found them sitting in the middle of the floor surrounded by billows of dotted swiss in white and five different pastel colors. Kate was on her knees cutting out in alterations for the tiniest wedding dress and five bridesmaid dresses.

"Don't tell me. Let me guess," Phil said, when the girls didn't even notice his arrival. "We have turned the house into a manufacturer of rainbows."

"I'm glad you noticed, Phil," said Olivia. "That's *just* what I want--a rainbow of colors. Isn't this gorgeous?" She ran to greet him with a hug.

"Is this paid for?" he asked. "Or am I getting a night job?"

Kate rose to kiss him and said, "Paid for, from Peter to Paul. No night job, but we'll be eating Lynette's 'spysghetti' for the next six weeks."

Phil groaned and nodded pontifically, which made the girls laugh. "Who's going to be which band of the rainbow?"

"I'm the lavender, naturally," said Lynette.

"I'm yellow," said Alisa.

"Pink for me, and blue for Cindi," said Cori.

"Okay, I know Livie will be the bride, but who's the pale green for?"

"Susan," said Olivia. "I asked her to be a bridesmaid, too"

Phil threw a glance at Kate and she nodded.

"Yeah, I know Gina hasn't been happy about my being here, and I was afraid she wouldn't let Susan be in the wedding. But Susan is a good friend, and she begged her mom, and Gina finally said it was okay."

Livie was so excited, Kate figured she'd tell Phil later about the encounter that produced that result. Kate was surprised, too, that Gina allowed Susan to participate, but their neighbor seemed to have mellowed a bit over time.

The next weeks went fast, while Kate made Olivia's wedding dress in empire style with triple smocked bands on the upper part of the long sleeves embroidered in tiny pink rosebuds. The pastel dresses were the same empire-waisted style only with short sleeves and a scooped neckline. Almost every evening after school, there were fitting sessions because, though the five bridesmaids were all the same basic size six, they varied in bustlines and shoulder lines, and no one could stand still long enough to get an accurate hemline.

"I swear you guys are holding something in or puffing it out, or standing on a different leg every time I try these dresses on you. We're going to be changing things right down to the night before the wedding."

The girls only giggled until Kate had to smile as well.

Kate's most often used phrase was, "Hold still, Livie," as she pinned in seams with pins sticking from her pursed mouth, maneuvering for a nice fit in spite of Olivia's hyperactive fidgeting. The veil of illusion netting was pinned with a miniature tiara to her much longer dark hair, since she had again let it grow out past the little boy bob she had worn when Kate and the family had first met her. It brought Kate near tears at every fitting to see how beautiful their littlest girl looked in the dress. Her tomboy image all but disappeared for a few moments. But then she would shatter the illusion by wriggling out of the dress and rolling around on the floor wrestling with an ecstatic Cleo.

At a final fitting only a week before, standing on a box so Kate could sit on the floor and pin the hem more accurately, Olivia grinned and said, "You know I hate dresses. This is the prettiest one I've ever seen, but you can't even run in one of these if someone was chasing you." She laughed. "I'll only wear this dress once to get married in, and once to be buried in."

Kate faltered, as the pins clattered to the floor. She felt a distinct pain in her throat, and struggled to maintain her equilibrium and stifle the cry. The vision that flashed through her mind was like other times, when Phil had fallen from the deck of a navy ship, when Cindi had been badly bitten by a dog, when James had nearly hemorrhaged in the hospital... Each time she had known...she had known....

"What's wrong, Kate?" Olivia had scrambled down from the box and now had her arms around Kate on the floor. "Do you need some water? Is it the ulcer again?"

Kate pulled herself together enough to say sharply, "Get back up on that box before you get your wedding dress all dirty!"

Chapter 24

Cori helped her father plan flower bouquets and boutonnières they would make the last day. Cindi went to the bakery to order a cake, and Olivia went with Kate to make arrangements with the church for the big day. Lynette and Alisa were assigned to figure out the veil pattern from the sheer netting and attach it to the tiny tiara they made of pink rosebuds to match the dress. Since all of the girls had part time jobs now, they were also planning their wedding gifts and giggling over them whenever Olivia was elsewhere engaged.

Roger wrote that he was saving his money to take Olivia with him to his next assignment since his rank would be so low she would be unsponsored. He would be home in a matter of days, and everyone was in a high state of excitement as the hours clicked by.

Olivia sat in the evening with Phil and Kate and pondered her future. "Maybe I have one after all," she said wistfully.

Kate had forced away her fearful vision as quite "silly" and probably only a cramp. Now, she smiled and said, "Told ya so. You only had to choose what you wanted your life to be."

"Roger's a good guy, isn't he? I hope we'll have that bond like we talked about, Kate—the one where no one ever has to pay anyone else for sharing." She looked at Phil, "And if he's half as good to me as you've been, Coach, I know things will work out."

Phil grinned. "Yes, I think it was one of my better decisions when I brought Roger home from Norwalk High that day."

"Do you feel ready, Olivia?" asked Kate. "You're barely seventeen, and that's still pretty young."

"Ready as I'll ever be, I guess." She sighed. "I'm a little scared wondering if I can stay good enough to make him happy, but I'm going to try as hard as I can. Have I changed enough? Will I be able to stay away from people who get me messed up?"

"You both will need to try hard for a lifetime," said Phil, quietly. "You've come a long way, Livie, and you're definitely a different person. Now, you can look forward as long as you keep making smart choices. Roger has turned into a fine young man, and he'd do anything for you. And remember that his loyalty deserves your loyalty as well."

"Yeah, I think I sorta understand what you've been telling me. Having someone to care about me is a really good thing. And we'll soon go far away, England, if he gets his wish. Gee, I never dreamed I'd get out of the One-Ways, much less see another country. Will the English speak English?"

She grabbed both Kate and Phil's hands in her excitement, as they laughed at her question. "I'll get you a book about the British Isles from the laundry room, Livie," said Kate.

"With lots of pictures?"

"Yes, with lots of pictures."

Late at night Kate and Phil talked over the ups and downs of their years with Livie and the other kids, wondering if they had helped or hurt their chances of making it in the "real world." Phil was optimistic all the kids would be okay, wherever they landed. "There wasn't any reason to talk Livie and Roger out of getting married, I guess," he added. "He'll at least take care of her because he genuinely loves her, and I know love in someone's eyes when I see it." He smiled at his wife.

Kate nestled in his arms. "I'm not sure if Livie really understands what love is. But three years away will help them learn to depend on each other. If she can last all that time and still stay clean and away from temptation, I pray she'll be just fine."

"I think we'll all rest easier having Olivia safe with Roger in another country. She'll always have to work hard to overcome her scars and abuses, but Roger will take good care of her."

"The one thing I feel we may have made a mistake on was the Cindi and Rick thing," said Kate. "They seemed to have something special, and we wouldn't let them date because of the age difference. Watching how excited Cindi is that Rick will be coming home to be in the wedding, I've wondered."

"But Cindi was so young, then," insisted Phil. "We did what we thought was right." He snorted. "Famous last words."

"I know, but I worry about all the kids, and it seems like their separation while Rick goes to Vietnam with the Marines will be difficult for Cindi Will they ever get together again?"

"We'll see. All we can do is our best, and like probably every other parent in the universe, we're going to make some mistakes. We'll hope that wasn't one of them."

Only days later, the day before Roger was scheduled to arrive for the wedding, Kate came home from work to find Livie and Cori arguing in the living room. She could hear their raised voices as she walked behind the bougainvillea bush to the front door. It was unusual to hear friction between any of the kids, and something in their heated argument made her stop and listen without interrupting.

"You promised, Livie," said Cori. "You promised you'd never do this, and a promise is a promise."

"But it wasn't mine! I told you. I was only holding it for someone else--only 'til tomorrow. How'd you find it, anyway?"

"It was in a stupidly obvious place, Livie--Mom's nylon drawer. You know that's where she keeps the bank roll of quarters for us to take for lunch money when we need it." Cori shook her head sadly. "It's like you *wanted* it to be found. I'm so disappointed. We loved you. We trusted you." Cori pounded a raucous chord on the piano and Kate could hear Cleo whine. Even the dog was unused to harsh voices from any family member

"Who are you holding it for? And why would you do that, since you told us you were staying away from those kinds of people? I can't believe you'd let everybody down like this, and right before your wedding, too. Roger will arrive tomorrow, and you pull something like this at the last minute. Don't you even *care* what you do to everybody?"

Cori's not one to become easily angered. This has to be big, thought Kate.

"Cori, I'm so sorry, but I didn't dare tell her no. She threatened everybody here. I didn't know what else to do. There wasn't any time to think...." Olivia started to cry.

The anger in Cori's voice softened only slightly. "I asked you whose it is?"

"It's Rita's. She came down to L.A. on some drug deal and she had the picture and knew where I was, so she called to have me meet her at the park. I knew you'd have a fit if I saw her, so I didn't tell you. I figured the park was safer."

"You'd see that woman behind everyone's back, after all the grief she gave you?"

"But she *is* still my sister, and I couldn't refuse. You know how she is. She'd come here, if I didn't go meet her."

"Livie, you know she's bad news. And if you tell her you're marrying Roger, she could hurt his military career, too."

"I didn't take anything, or smoke anything, or tell her anything. We just talked. She said she had a big network to organize, and she'd cut me in, if I wanted to be a dealer down here. I told her no, Cori. I told her no, and she got mad. She said the cops were after her and she didn't have a place to stash her samples for the gangs in East L.A and the One-Ways. She thought she was being watched. When we saw police cars going up and down the street by Mayberry, she shoved the bundle to me to hide. I told her no, again, but she had this funny look on her face, and she said, 'Are you still friends with those teachers?' Cori, I knew it was a threat. I took the package, and she ran away. She'd said she was sure the police would search Mom's house, so I hid it here. No one would ever look for it here. You guys are all so straight."

"You shouldn't have done that, Livie. You promised us, and you knew I wouldn't have that stuff in our house."

"I promised I wouldn't bring *my* drugs into your house, and I never did. I told you these aren't *mine*. Rita will pick up the package tomorrow, and then we'll be rid of her again."

"Only until the next time she wants something from you. And no, she won't pick it up! I flushed it all down the toilet."

Livie shrieked, "No, no, no, Cori! Rita said it was worth over thirty thousand dollars. She'll kill me. What did you do?" Livie sounded unbelieving. Kate heard her run to the bathroom, coming back holding a handful of small little cellophane bags and the outside brown wrapping paper. She threw them to the floor.

Kate made her presence known as Livie crumpled on the floor, in fetal position, sobbing. Cori stood angrily over her with tears running down her face as well.

"What's going on, you two? This sounds serious."

"It is, Mom. Livie broke her promise and brought a bundle of white powder here."

"I keep telling you, it wasn't mine," Livie blubbered, curling her body more tightly. "It was Rita's, and she threatened you guys if I didn't hide it for her. I didn't know what else to do. I'm sorry, Cori. I'm sorry." The girl sat up with her head cradled in her arms on her bent knees. "Cori, you shouldn't have flushed it. I don't have the money. Rita will kill me."

Kate sat heavily on the sofa. "You guys had better tell me the whole story." They did, and it seemed the situation was a worse mess than she could have imagined.

"Why did you flush it, Cori?" wailed Olivia. "Why didn't you wait 'til I could explain?"

"Livie, if the police found that here, our whole family would be involved. Mom and Dad are teachers, and they'd lose their credentials. You'd be arrested, and Roger would be kicked out of the Air Force, all because of you. You had no right to bring drugs into our home." She sighed and reached down a hand to help Livie up. "Get over it, Livie. If it wasn't yours, you don't need to worry. Just call the police and tell them what happened."

"Oh, Cori," she said. "You make it all sound so easy. Just 'always do what's right, and everything will be okay.' You and your mom go around in a little sweet place that everyone protects. You never see anything bad in the world. That's your way, and I love you for it, and I know you're trying to help, but…." Olivia mopped her eyes with a tissue Kate handed her. "…but sometimes I don't see the right so good. It's hard to know what's better or what's worse when other people are in gangs and make threats. You don't understand. Where I come from, just doing what's right is *never* enough. Loyalty is all that counts. Somebody will hate you for thinking you're better than them, or they'll be mad at you because you won't take LSD with them or smoke a joint with them, and they think you might rat them out if you try to be good, so they don't trust you anymore."

Kate said, "You've come too far to go back to that life."

"I don't want to go back to that life, but look at all of you!" Olivia spread her arms wide to include the whole world, though only Cori and Kate were within her sight. "Look at you so shocked if I have just one little puff of a joint, or forget to use the 'g' on the end of singin', or get angry too easy, or the neighbors think I look too rough, or I'm too noisy, or they're afraid I might corrupt their little kids. It's like none of the *good* things I've tried to do matter to anybody but you. I'll never be good enough to fit in with the people around here. I'm still that piece of trash you wagged home, Kate, no matter how hard I try to be different, or how hard you try to make me different."

"But Livie," said Cori, "you have loyalties here, too. Even the school superintendent appreciated what you've done, and Roger loves you, and we do too. I don't understand how you get yourself into these things. To me, it seems so logical for you to just walk away."

"But I'm not you, Cori. I don't belong anywhere. Not with those hoity-toity people who do everything perfect. Even my dancing along the street with Roger, sorta skipping to keep up with his long legs, the neighbors turn up their noses and don't talk to us. I don't fit in the One-Ways because I won't do drugs with them anymore, and I don't fit in here because everybody remembers when I *did* do drugs. I'm no good to Roger because I'm always getting him in trouble, just being me. He says he doesn't care, but I think he needs somebody better than me. I just cause everybody trouble. I can't make it, you guys. I just can't. It's always gonna be this way, with me hurting those I love the best. And now I've broken the code again, messing up with my own sister."

"But Lynette is your sister too, and the rest of us have treated both of you as our sisters," said Cori. "Doesn't that count?"

"It counted, big time, when I took Rita's package to keep her from coming after you guys. I know my loyalty is to this family, too. But now, since I don't have the package *or* the money for it, she'll be coming after me."

"I'll call to tell the police what's happened," said Kate.

Olivia threw her hands in the air. "When are you guys gonna get it? The police will never believe someone like me. Don't you remember what the brothers did with Ernesto? You were raised to think the police were your friends, but that's not my way. 'The police can't arrest someone that threatens you until they actually do it, and then it's too late. We found that out with Ernesto, and I still have headaches from that crowbar."

"We could try to get a restraining order," ventured Kate. "Maybe she'd...."

Olivia snorted. "That's just a piece of paper, isn't it? Do you think Rita would pay any attention to a bloody piece of paper? If I don't give her back her stash, and I don't have the money, she'll take me out, Kate. You remember her kiss threat, don't you—'me and anyone I'm with,' so I gotta get out of here now, and I gotta get away from Roger, too."

"Livie, can't you just explain to Rita and offer to pay her back a little at a time and get a job or something?" asked Cori. "I'll help you with the money I make part-time at the flower shop."

"Cori, you'll never get it!" Livie said "The *only* way I can pay back that kind of money is if I go into her drug ring and sell dope for her. You guys taught me too much for me to do that now. I'd keep thinking of the little kids in Kate's class that I talked *out* of doing drugs. I can't work for her, and Rita wouldn't want me helping her very long, anyway. She wants those drugs now to start her action down here. How long could I push drugs before I got caught, and Roger wouldn't understand why—no one would." Olivia broke into heart-wrenching sobs and Kate put her arms around her. "I mess up everyone I care about," she blubbered.

Cori said softly, "I'm sorry if I got you into trouble, Livie. It's just that I saw the package and realized that junk shouldn't be in our house. Too many people would be hurt by it, and I was so disappointed in you, so I flushed it. It didn't belong here, and you knew that when you brought it."

Olivia raised her head and reached out to Cori. "It's not your fault. You're just Cori being straight up Cori. I shouldn't have expected anything different. It was my fault. I just didn't know where else to take it, and I didn't want Rita to come here."

She broke out a short, bitter laugh. "Would you guys listen to me? I've gotten too good to do drugs or want to sell 'em, but I'm not smart enough to know what to do with a stash. I bring it to the place I feel safest, and it's the wrong thing. I don't get what's right or wrong. I thought I was taking care of *everyone* by not letting Rita come after you guys, *and* not letting her get caught with drugs, or narc on her, *or* risk Roger's career, but it wasn't the right thing at all. Now everybody's mad at me. I'm gonna get killed by my own sister, and there's nothing anyone can do to stop her." She flopped on the couch and Goldie immediately hopped up.

Kate moved to the phone. She dialed Norwalk Police station and asked for Detective Fredrick. They said he was on leave, but another officer took her call. "What can you do to protect a young person who's been threatened for disposing of drugs from a dealer?" she asked.

"Give me names, Ma'am."

"I can't do that until you tell me you can protect her."

"Ma'am, these drug dealers are all alike. There isn't anything you, or we, can do. They kill each other all the time. They have their own private laws in their own corners of town. It's an epidemic." He sighed and said, "Okay, tell me when and where this is going down, and I'll try to have officers there."

Kate was offended at his tone, and his philosophy of thinking everyone was alike, but she turned to Olivia. "Where and when did Rita say she'd meet you?"

"Who wants to know? I don't think this is a good idea. The cops won't help."

"I think it may be our only option to try to protect you, Livie," said Kate, "and that's all I'm worried about right now."

"Mayberry Park, near the tennis courts because nobody plays tennis at six in the morning, tomorrow--but this isn't going to do any good, Kate."

Kate said into the telephone, "Can you have people at Mayberry Park before six tomorrow morning, invisible, yet able to protect the young girl who's scared for her life?"

"Lady, I can't guarantee anything, but we'll do our best. We'll send some of our undercover people there if you think this is a big enough bust. What drug is it?"

"What was it, Livie?"

"I didn't open it, but I think it was probably cocaine or maybe heroin because I know she deals that, too."

"Which would have a value of $30,000?" Kate asked.

Olivia shrugged her shoulders. "I don't really know."

Cori said, "It was a lot of little clear envelopes with white powder, if that helps any."

Kate repeated the information. "It won't actually be a bust, because one daughter flushed the drugs. It's only that the dealer will hurt this girl when she shows up without the drugs."

The officer seemed to lose interest. "Well, if the stuff is already gone, and we aren't sure what it was, anyway, what's the point of us going to Mayberry? We'll have no evidence."

"You should go to protect the young girl who has been threatened by the dealer." Kate felt angry with this man.

"Who's the dealer?"

Kate looked at Livie, shrugged and said, "It's one you wouldn't know, from San Francisco."

The officer's tone changed. "We have an APB out on a drug dealer from one of our informants. She's from The Haight, and she's down here to spread the joy and start a new network in the gangs. A woman. Rita Gon....something. Could it be her?"

Kate blew out her breath and contemplated what would be the safest course for Livie and the best way to get Rita off the streets. "I think that may be her," she said.

Olivia was on her feet. "Did you just narc on my sister?"

Kate again covered the phone and said to Olivia, "They're already looking for her anyway, and it's the only way we can help you stay safe." Olivia sat back down hard on the couch, arms folded.

"We'll be there, said the officer. We almost got her the other day, but when we stopped her, she had nothing on her, so we couldn't make an arrest. Will she come to meet this kid?"

"She will, but there may be no drugs. They're gone."

"Wrap up newspapers in a similar package so the dealer won't see the kid empty-handed. We'll hope the woman makes some kind of move or has other drugs in her possession, so we can nab her. We don't want her distributing here. We already have enough drug problems without importing more from Frisco."

"Would it be possible for the girl not to show up and you'd take in the dealer alone?"

"If the kid didn't show up, the dealer would disappear, she'd be wise, and we'd have no cause for arrest. She wants that package. Let her think the drugs are in it."

"I want this young girl protected."

"Ma'am, I can only tell you we'll try. What does she look like? Could you bring her in to talk to us?"

Livie shook her head forcefully. "I can't go to the police station. What about Roger?"

"She's afraid to come in," said Kate. "She's dark, Indian, and quite bouncy, and she looks a lot like the dealer, only smaller."

"A relative?"

"Yes, but this dealer could hurt somebody. Ours won't."

"Ma'am, you must realize that these kids, once they're in it, will always have more loyalty to their gang and their relatives, even if they're in jail, than they will to anyone else. They've got two ways out of the gang, in the back of a police car, or in the back of a hearse. Don't get your hopes up."

"That's not true in this case. This one's clean. Can you please help us keep her safe?"

"Names?"

"I don't think I can do that, Officer. Please understand how frightened she is. Besides, I think you already know the names."

"Okay, Ma'am, we'll try to have someone there, but if this is a wild goose chase, we're not responsible for the outcome."

"Thank you, officer." Kate hung up.

"So, what's going down?" mumbled Olivia, slumped on the couch, absent-mindedly scratching Goldie's ears.

"He says they'll try to have someone there, and we must wrap up a similar package so she won't see you walking through the park empty-handed."

"I thought about that."

Cori said, "Why don't you just not go, Livie? If Rita's there all by herself, she'll just go away."

"Cori, if I don't show up, she'll come *here*. She has that picture you wouldn't let me get back in San Francisco with your address and phone number--remember? How do you think she knew where to call me? She *knows* where you live. She knows she can get to me through you. I won't let that happen. I have to go."

"Then we'll all go with you. You can tell her what happened. She couldn't do anything to you in front of everybody."

"She'd leave and come back later with her gang and deal more trouble to us all." Livie sighed and squared her shoulders. "I got myself into this. I have to go meet with Rita. This isn't going to go away unless I deal drugs for her, or produce the dope, or the money. She's gonna be really mad, when I can't do any of that."

"We can't let you go, Livie," said Kate. "I've seen how vicious Rita is. You made a mistake taking that stuff from her in the first place, but we can't give in to her threats.

Olivia shook her head. "You saw only a little piece of her, and she has her gang who'll back her up. I need to get out of here before Roger comes. Just tell him I tried to love him, and I do, but I'm no good for him or anyone else. He needs somebody better."

"We'll tell him no such thing. There's no place safe you can go," said Kate. "Besides, Roger loves you, and you'll be better off here, with him and with us, where someone can help you."

"Kate, listen to me." The girl took both of Kate's hands and held them tightly. "You guys tried hard for years. I talk mostly like you now. I'm not using drugs. I'm not running with a gang or doing anything really illegal or immoral, just like you wanted. I was even a bloody Girl Sprout. You tried, and I tried hard because I love you all. But the gang always knows where to find you, even if you try to quit. They always think you owe them something. I broke the code, twice--once with Ernesto, and the only thing that saved me, then, was that his brothers killed him, and they got sent up for it. But no one can save me with Rita. She's further up the chain, and I don't even *know* all the people that work for her. Now, she's gonna know I narc'ed on her, and if any of those cops try to take her tomorrow, she'll get away and come back later, and it'll just be worse. I doubt the cops will even come help me, anyway."

"No, Livie. Wait until Phil gets home," said Kate. "We'll try to sort this all out. Maybe we can come up with an answer working together, like we usually do." Kate and Cori both tried to reason with Livie. It was no use.

"Livie, we can't let you go without settling on a plan."

Olivia smiled at Kate. "Plans don't always work."

Cori added, "I'll get the wrapping paper and string and we'll stuff it, so Rita won't know the junk is gone." She gathered newspapers from the table and wadded them up while Livie wrapped the paper around the bundle with some of the glassine envelopes inside. Together, they tied it up as best they could in nearly the same size, and Livie laid it on the piano.

She grabbed her jacket, hugged Cori and then Kate, and said, "Tell the others I love them. Don't look for me tonight. I want this settled before Roger gets home. I don't want him to know or get caught up in it."

Olivia put the bundle under her arm. "And I'm sorry I couldn't be better. There's just too many old ties that won't break for me to make it in your world."

She grinned for a moment. "But, at least I tried. Phil always says that's the most important thing, right? Just like stealing home plate. You don't always win, but you can always try."

Chapter 25

"What if the police don't come? asked Cindi.

The family played a languid game of tennis at the Mayberry Park courts. It was very early, and steam still rose up from the dew-drenched grass. It would no doubt become a hot day.

Phil hit a soft backhand toward Alisa. "I figure if there are people in the park, like us, Rita won't be stupid enough to hurt Livie in front of witnesses. I hope she's smarter than that."

"But Livie said Rita would come back later to get even," said Cori. Her voice quavered. She leaned against the fence around the courts, supposedly keeping score, but really watching and waiting for the arrival of Olivia and her sister.

"If we can get Livie out of here in one piece, with or without the police, we'll have a little more time to figure out a better plan for next time," reassured Phil.

"I'm scared, said Alisa. "I wish all the guys were here."

"So do I," said Cori. "They'll be in later today."

"Roger will be in this morning from basic training. Why didn't Livie wait for him?" Alisa seemed particularly nervous.

Cindi asked, "How will he know where we are?"

"I told Susan to watch for him," said Kate. "When he arrives, she'll fill him in on the details, and he'll come join us as soon as he gets in. We just have to get through this morning's encounter. Then we still have lots more to do before the wedding."

"But what's the plan, Dad?" asked Cori.

"As soon as Livie hands Rita the package, I'll tell her we're all leaving together to play tennis, or some such thing. I'll think of something when the time comes."

"If the police are here, maybe you won't need to do that," suggested Kate. "Maybe Olivia can walk to us and let the police take Rita and search her. I hope Rita has cocaine or heroin on her, so they can get her off the streets."

"The police may already be here, Kate," said Phil. "I doubt

they'll be in plain sight--not if they want to catch Rita in the act."

Alisa punctuated her protest with her racket. "You mean we're playing tennis only as a crowd scene to make Rita back off a drug exchange." Alisa saw everything in terms of the theatre.

Phil nodded. "We hope that's *exactly* what she'll do—back off."

"She might leave when she sees us. And what if Rita recognizes Lynette?"

"I doubt it," said Lynette. "I don't look like I did the last time she saw me. But, if she wants to establish a network down here like she has in San Francisco, she'll want those drugs. She won't just leave. I think she'll try to hurt Livie or make a fight of it. I wonder if she'll be alone or have someone with her?"

"Let's assume she's alone," said Kate. "I think we'll have a better chance of distracting her, if she's by herself."

The tennis game had become a desultory, half-hearted effort, with even Cindi hitting slow balls into the net. *We're all too nervous to really play.* Alisa was right. We are, indeed, simply stage props for this event--a crowd scene for the opening curtain. *And how will it close?* Kate anxiously touched Phil's arm.

He patted her hand and faked a confident smile.

"We may be forgetting something," said Lynette, giving up all pretense at playing. "Soon as Rita realizes those aren't drugs in the package, she'll know we interfered. Where can Livie go to be safe then, if the police aren't here to get Rita, and she gets away?"

"It means we have to get Olivia away *before* Rita opens the package," said Phil. "If Rita sees the contents, there's no telling what she'll do. We can't let Olivia do this alone. We'll just pray that Rita doesn't open the package immediately, and that we can get Livie away quickly. We have to help Olivia face down her sister. Anybody have any better ideas?"

There were no comments. They saw Olivia approach the park bench, perhaps fifty feet away, sitting down with her package to wait. She swung her short legs impatiently under the seat.

"She doesn't see us yet," said Cindi. "Play ball, you guys. Let's hope she doesn't notice it's us until it's too late for her to do anything drastic." They obligingly picked up their game again. The crack of the balls on rackets was the only sound.

Soon, a faded red van went around the block twice before coming to a halt near Olivia.

Rita and a man got out and walked across the wet grass.

Kate recognized Dink from their San Francisco pad where she had found Olivia. She wondered fleetingly if he would be part of Rita's new drug network in Southern California. Maybe he just came to help out, or maybe he was part of " Rita's protection team" that Livie had described.

"I'm going now," said Phil. "Stay here and play until we see Rita's reaction. I don't want any of you too near, in case these two get violent. If so, you run. I'll grab Olivia." Phil strode purposefully toward Olivia.

Kate fell in step beside him. "You're not going alone."

Dink spotted them first and nudged Rita to look.

She continued moving toward Olivia with a scowl on her face. She didn't even utter a greeting.

Phil stood beside Olivia with Kate close behind..

Olivia stuck one arm up stiffly and wriggled her fingers at the girls on the tennis courts. She smiled, not at all surprised the family had come to help her. "I knew you'd come," she whispered.

Rita screamed just like her angry mother did, gesturing wildly. "Are you crazy, Livie? Who are all these people?"

"Just my friends. I told them not to come, but they don't listen much." Livie grinned. "They came anyway. I'm sure they just wanted to meet you. We're going to play tennis afterward." She called out loudly, "Isn't that right, Cindi?"

Cindi waved back at her.

Livie was now smiling broadly as she handed the package to her sister. "You've got your package. We're leaving now. Bye." She grabbed Phil's hand and pulled

"Wait!" said Rita. The authority in her voice froze Olivia to the spot. Her confident smile evaporated. "You don't go any damn place 'til I tell you." Rita squeezed the package and said to Olivia as though the others weren't even there, "Stand still, Livie. I don't give a fuck who you brought with you. This deal's between you and me, and this package feels light. You took some out for yourself, didn't you?"

"Nope. I don't use that stuff anymore." Livie lifted her arms above her head, entwining her fingers in a languid stretch.

"Like I really believe *that*," said Rita.. What about the deal I offered you? You'll make more money working for me than you ever will with a factory job like Mom. You don't have the smarts to ever do anything better, now do you?"

Livie shook her head.

Dink moved closer and said in a warning voice, " Rita, shut up, now. You're saying too much." Rita ignored him

She spat on the ground and said, "You're so stupid, Livie. But, I've got something here for you that will change your mind." Rita put the package on the ground at her feet and reached into her backpack, bringing out a syringe, already filled. "Just fixed this up only for you. This is high quality stuff." Her features changed to a slow, cajoling smile. "Make you feel gooooooood, baby sister."

She moved toward Olivia.

Livie shook her head and backed away a little.

Phil stepped in front of Livie. "You know we won't let you force anything on Livie. She's been clean a long while now. Why don't you pack up and leave her alone?"

Rita said curtly, "No one asked you. This is between me and my sister."

"Then I'll tell you again myself, Rita," said Olivia, smiling at Phil as she moved to his side. "No, way will I help you pedal drugs to kids, and no way do I want your needle. I don't do that stuff anymore. I don't even want it. I don't even like needles."

"You *always* want it, Livie. You know you can't stay away. Hooked once is hooked for life." Rita spoke in a soothing, hypnotic voice. Her seductive smile dripped with malice. "Here, let me give you this good stuff. It's the stuff I use for samples to my new network. You need to become one of my runners and help me set this up down here. You know all the people in the One-Ways, and you could set me up good. With you managing down here, and me up in Frisco, we could make a killing. Money to the hilt. Take the shot, Livie. Then send away these people, and we'll talk seriously, sister to sister."

"I think you've said enough, Rita, and you already have your answer from Olivia," said Phil.

Dink broke in. " Rita, don't be stupid talking like that in front of all these outsiders." He kept looking around and behind him, knowing a needle in plain sight was dangerous.

"These people don't mean shit to me," Rita countered. "This is between me and Livie."

" Rita," said Livie slowly. "*They're* not the outsiders. They've been my family, too. I'm not sure what I am, but I *do* know I don't want to be with you, on this or anything else. And I wouldn't be good at selling dope for you, since you say I don't have any smarts, now, would I?" Olivia grinned at echoing Rita's mean comment.

"Besides, I'm getting married to a nice guy and we're not using drugs or hanging out with the old gang in the One-Ways anymore. We're going far away, so I'll tell you goodbye now." Olivia moved away from her sister, reaching out for Phil's hand.

" Rita stared angrily from face to face. "I tell you this package is too light. What are you gonna do about it?" She stomped on the package, catching everyone by surprise. When only newsprint and clear, little glassine bags fell out, she screamed at Livie. "I knew it. You'd backstab your own sister. You'll not get away with this. I'll get you good."

Dink moved toward his van, trying to pull the angry Rita with him. "Shut up, Rita. Come on. We'll get 'em later. I don't have a good feeling about this. Too many people."

He tried again to grab Rita's arm. She yanked her arm away screaming, "Livie, don't think you're getting off just because you brought people with you. If this is a set-up, and if I don't get you now, I'll be back. You know I will. Look over your shoulder, girl, because you're already dead!"

Rita punctuated her bitter words with jerky motions of her closed fist. Suddenly, she pulled something out of her belt and the closed fist was no longer empty. Something gleamed in the sun.

Phil grabbed Livie's shoulder and herded her away, as other family members ran toward them from the tennis courts.

Two police cruisers appeared from behind the park building and drove right across the grass in seconds, blocking Dink and Rita's retreat to their van.

Kate saw Rita's arm draw back and she hurled something away. She wasn't sure if it was the knife or the vial of drugs. She tried to follow the trajectory, but she was more intent on knowing Phil and Livie far enough away from Rita and keeping her yelling girls from coming any closer. "Stop where you are, girls," she screamed. Alisa stopped in her tracks, but the other three came on, Lynette and Cindi running, Cori running stiff-legged behind them..

The four officers came out with guns drawn.

Then it dawned on Kate. *Oh no, Rita's too smart for us. I'll bet that was the needle she threw. She won't have anything on her.*

Rita almost smiled as the police approached her. Dink didn't move, and the pair was surrounded.

Kate watched as a policeman patted down Dink, removed a gun from his pocket, and dropped it to the ground.

One officer immediately grabbed Rita's backpack from her shoulder. "What you got in here, Miss?" he asked, while dumping out its contents on the grass.

"Nothing, officer," said Rita, looking him up and down seductively. "Just my hairbrush and lipstick. You like the color?"

The officer ignored her sly smile and continued separating out the contents until he stood, shook his head at the others. "She's clean," he announced angrily.

"What's this, though," asked another policeman who picked up the package stomped onto the ground. "I think this must have had cocaine or heroin in it, to judge from the glassines."

"But there's nothing in it, now, is there, officer?" Rita smirked at Olivia, who stood quivering beside Phil, her hand firmly clasped in his.

"There *were* drugs in it, officer," Olivia spoke up. "But they were flushed down the toilet yesterday."

"Well, Missy, we can't hold this woman on drugs that aren't here, now can we?"

Kate said, "She threw away a vial when you came?" Kate walked toward the place she thought she had seen the needle land.

"Do you see it?" asked the first officer.

"Not yet. But it was this way. Can't you help me look for it? It must be here somewhere. I think she threw it pretty far out."

"Lady, we're not rummaging through a whole park full of wet grass looking literally for a needle in a haystack. Maybe you only *thought* you saw her throw it. We can't link it to her anyway, even if we found it, so we'll have to let her go."

"But when I called you, I told you there might not be any drugs on her, but she was dangerous to her sister. You came."

"Can't you do *something*?" Phil said. "You can't leave it at this. Olivia will be at risk if you let this woman go."

Throughout this exchange, Rita gloated at the family standing before her. "They can't arrest Dink and me without evidence, no matter what you people say," she echoed the officer.

"But I saw the drugs," said Cori. "I'm the one who flushed them. They really were there."

"But they aren't now, young lady," said the officer. "My hands are tied. Let them go, Andy."

"But the guy had a gun."

"Licensed," said Dink, calmly. "You officers don't think I'd run around carrying an unlicensed gun, now do you?"

"Has it been fired?" asked the first officer.

Andy sniffed the barrel. "No, sir."

"Let them go." But as Andy did so, the officer in charge turned to Rita and said, "But I'll be watching you, Miss. If anything goes down, it'll be you on the suspect list."

Rita smiled coyly at the officer and said, "And I'll be watching for you, too," then she screamed, "So fuck you!"

She and Dink walked triumphantly back to the van. The family and police officers watched helplessly. As they drove away, Rita held her thumb and forefinger out the window toward Livie like a gun. "You know," she shouted out, and the two were gone.

Chapter 26

The family continued to search the grass, unsuccessfully, hoping to find the needle, more because they felt some kid might find it and get hurt than with any hope the police would, use it.

"I guess they're right that they can't link it to Rita," said Lynnette. "They'll have to catch her with the goods on her to get her off the street. How are we going to protect Livie?"

Olivia was still shaking. She said, "You know she meant those fingers pointed at me. She'll get me sooner or later. She never gives up on threats."

"We won't let her get you, Livie," said Phil. Let's go home. We need to think about how to take care of you."

The group moved to the car.

Cori said, "I probably shouldn't have flushed down the stuff in the drug package because then the police would have had the drugs and could have arrested her."

"No, Cori," said Lynette. "Rita's smart. She would've made sure the drugs were in Livie's hands, not hers. She probably suspected a set up and that's why she dropped the package on the ground. That way she could claim it was Livie's."

"Besides, Cori," said Olivia. "You just did what you thought was right. I should've remembered that. I knew Rita might pull something. I should've known better from the start."

As the family sat around the kitchen table, Roger drove into the driveway with a noisy old fliver that seemed to gasp for breath. They all ran out to greet him. Olivia hurled herself through the air and into his arms, kissing him so soundly his uniform hat fell from his head. Cindi retrieved it, and all collected their hugs, while Roger carried Olivia on one hip like he would a four-year-old.

For the moment, they forgot the threat hanging over her head, and perhaps Cori's too, since she had admitted to flushing the drugs down the toilet in front of Rita. Their joy in having Roger home again overtook them, and they walked into the house laughing and clapping him on the back.

"Are the other guys back yet?"

"No," answered Kate. "You're the first one in. James and Rick are due in later this afternoon."

"How was basic training?" asked Alisa, on her way to start hot chocolate, as everyone gathered around the table.

"Hard at first," said Roger. "I had a little trouble taking orders from this sergeant who only knew how to yell at me, and I tried yelling back. That didn't work very well," he said sheepishly. "Yeah, Phil. I remember you told me about that." He grinned at Phil. "But then I got the hang of it and came out with pretty good honors."

Olivia sat on his lap as he told of his adventures in Air Force basic training. "My MOS will be as a fireman, and I get to go to advanced training and wear those shiny silver suits to get pilots out of crashed airplanes."

Lynette said, "Doesn't that sound kind of dangerous?"

"I don't like the sound of it," echoed Livie, wrapping her arms around Roger's neck.

He spoke proudly, something good in his voice, more manly, more grown up than Kate had seen him before his departure.

"Oh, nothing to worry about, Honey. Those silver suits can stand very high temperatures, and I'll have all the training I need to do the job. I think I've found my real career. It's more exciting than sitting at a desk or handing out supplies." He grinned. "Besides, I have a surprise. I got the assignment I wanted in Bentwaters." He gleefully pulled Olivia closer. "We're going to England, baby. Can't you just see yourself watching the Changing of the Guard and Big Ben?"

Olivia grinned back. "I've been listening to everybody talking about England and yes, I'm ready to go." She suddenly sobered and added, "I sure wish we could go right now, like tonight."

"But Honey, our wedding is in two days, and this is our leave and vacation. When James and Rick get here, we'll have our rehearsal, and we're going to live it up. We'll have a great wedding, and honeymoon big time when we get to England."

Roger then noticed the sober looks that had appeared around the room at Olivia's comment. "Okay, you guys. What's going on? What's happened?"

" Rita's here," blurted out Olivia. "The police didn't have any evidence to hold her, so she's out, and she is planning to do me in 'cause I ratted her out in front of the police. I was just trying to do the right thing, but I could tell she was mad." Olivia started to cry and buried her head in Roger's neck. He held her tightly.

"I think you all need to fill me in," he said. And they did.

"We'll make sure Livie isn't alone anywhere she goes," said Phil. "We'll hope Rita leaves town before Livie is seen anywhere without us. Once you get Livie away to England for three years, she should be safe for good."

"What about the wedding?" Lynette asked the question on everyone's mind.

"It's at a church your sister doesn't know. She doesn't know exactly when the wedding is, unless your mom told her," said Kate. "All the preparations are made. I don't think we should change our plans since someone will be with Livie all the time."

"I want this wedding so much," said Roger holding Olivia's hand gently. "I want to marry this girl the right way." He grinned. "It may be the first thing either of us has ever done the right way. I know she'll be beautiful in that wedding gown you described in your letters, Kate."

"I sort of wish my mom would come," said Olivia sadly. "I'm only doing this once, and I'd like for her to be glad for me."

Lynette said, "What do you care, Livie? She signed the papers, and that's all you need from her to go away and live a good life on your own."

"I just feel bad that no one from my old family is happy for me and Roger."

"You know *we* are," said Phil, kissing Olivia on the cheek. "It's going to be beautiful, you're going to be a beautiful bride, and then you'll be safely away from here. You mustn't worry, Livie."

"But I know Rita. She's not leaving town until she gets her

network set up and gets me. I told you she's crazy."

Roger tapped Livie's nose with his forefinger and said, "Honey, anybody that tries to hurt you has to get through me first, and I don't think even Rita can do that. Leave it to me, and just don't worry about this stuff. We have a wedding to celebrate, and I want to see you smile. I've been waiting weeks just for that smile."

Olivia smiled at Roger and then the whole group. "Okay, gang, what do we still have to do before the wedding?"

Cori jumped up. "Dad and I are going to get the flowers and do all the bouquets tomorrow, and everyone else has a job too. This is going to be fun." Cori's normal exuberance on conducting a "project" formed everyone into an enthusiastic team.

By the time James and Rick arrived at dinnertime, the excitement in the house drowned out most of Kate's anxiety.

"To our missing man, Ned, wherever he is," toasted James with his lemonade. "To Ned," they all echoed.

"And to doing weddings right," said Rick. Roger smiled and kissed Olivia's hand.

Laughter and dinnertime chatter continued. "Hey man," said James. "Where'd you get that old jalopy out front?"

"Don't make fun of my jalopy," said Roger in mock insult. "A guy at the base sold it to me for $50 bucks, and it got me home, didn't it?"

"I think James and I need to overhaul it a little before you lovebirds take off for a honeymoon. We'll check it over in the morning—your last day of freedom, old man. Enjoy it."

They were interrupted by a phone call from Olivia's mother. Olivia talked quietly in the kitchen as the family finished up dinner.

When she returned to the table, Kate asked, "What did she want, Livie? Has she decided to come to the wedding after all?"

"If she does, I'll have to make her a corsage," said Cori.

Olivia was surprisingly quiet. "She wants me to come see her before the wedding. She said she might come if we could solve our family problems. She thinks I should spend my last night alone with her before I go off with 'some man.'" Livie touched Roger's face with her fingers. "She sounds like it's really important to her."

Phil said, "I don't know, Livie. That might not be a good idea with Rita out there somewhere. Did your mom say anything about seeing her?"

"No. Rita wouldn't go to Mom's 'cause they really don't like each other. I think she and Dink would stay with their old friends in the One-Ways. But I'm not sure I want to spend that last night with Mom, anyway. I never know what kind of mood she'll be in. If she's had anything to drink...."

"It's a trick, Livie," said Lynette. "You know she doesn't care. She just wants a chance to hit you in the face so you'll be all ugly and bruised for the wedding."

"I don't know, Olivia," said Kate, anxiously. "You've never been able to stay with her without problems, and you don't want to mess up your wedding plans."

"She didn't sound drunk, and she kept saying she wanted 'her baby' at least under her roof one more time before the wedding so we could solve all our anger with each other." Olivia looked at Roger, thoughtfully. "I might be happier if I knew she wasn't mad at me anymore. What do you think?"

"I'm not a good one to ask about mothers," answered Roger slowly. "I'm just afraid for you to be out of our sight to go visit *anybody*."

"But what if she really does want to be nice for once. I'd be happy if I just knew she wasn't mad at me anymore."

"I'll go with you," said Roger.

"She said she wants to be with me alone—a mother-daughter thing. You know. One part of me is still afraid of her, and one part of me would like to get rid of the anger. I feel in the middle again. I guess I'd just like to be able to trust her for *one* time in my life."

"I think we're all worried about your going there for any purpose, Livie," said Kate. "Perhaps you could get her to come over here to talk to you. Phil could go get her. and we'd all go out back and leave you two alone."

"She kept saying how much it meant to her to have me

under her roof one more night as 'her child' before I 'became a woman.' Maybe she means it this time, and maybe she'd come to the wedding and be happy for me just this once. I just wish, before I start my new life...." Her words died away.

Phil spoke up firmly. "I don't want you to go anywhere, Olivia, even there, without some of us with you. Rita might show up unannounced, and you'd be alone."

"I don't think Rita would go there even if Mom begged her, but you're probably right. I won't go." I'll call Mom tomorrow and tell her." Olivia seemed almost relieved to have the matter settled.

Roger came running into the living room in the late afternoon the next day.

"She's gone! I laid down for just a minute after the wedding rehearsal and fell asleep while she was talking to her mom on the phone. When I woke up, I found her note."

He handed the piece of paper to a surprised Kate, who was busy sewing the final hem in Alisa's bridesmaid gown.

"I don't understand. She was here just a while ago working with Cori and Phil on the flowers. When did she go? She didn't say anything at all." Kate ironed the note flat on her knee.

"Dear Roger. Mom sunds so sad on the fone she was crying. I went to see her just for a few minuts. Don wurry, Ill be rite back, and Ill call when I need a ride. I hate having bad feeling abot her or her abot me. She seys this tim she means it and will be good. That this will fix everthing. I lov you and Mom seys you aren't suppose to see me in my wedding dres anyway...Mom might come to the wedding, if I see her tonight. I can hop...I'm ok for just a little while.... 1-4-3."

"What should I do?" Roger fidgeted from one foot to the other. "Should I believe that she's okay, or go after her?"

A honking horn interrupted them. Rick and James had been messing around with Roger's old car all afternoon and claimed excitedly that they had it running without galloping. They wanted the whole family to admire their handiwork.

"Hey Pal," said James. "It's running good now. You and

Livie won't have to hitch a ride to your honeymoon."

He and Rick stopped short when they saw the look on Roger's face, and Kate's somber one.

When the matter was explained, Rick asked, "Where's Phil? He'll have an idea."

"Phil just left to to talk to the minister and get everything at the church squared away for the reception," said Kate.. It's getting dark now, but he probably won't be home for another hour. What do you boys want to do?"

James quickly moved into high gear. "The three of us will go get Livie at her mom's. We'll just tell her mom we're worried about her and want her at home, since Rick and I haven't seen her in eight weeks of boot camp. We'll just *make* her understand. Let's go." All three swung into the car and thundered out of the driveway.

They were back in half an hour.

"We're not staying, Kate," said Roger. "We just wanted you to know what happened before we left." His hands shook as he explained. "We have to go look for her. Livie had been there, and her mom said she left with Rita and Dink!"

Kate reeled. "Oh, no! How did that happen?"

James said, "That woman said she wanted Olivia and Rita to settle their differences. It seems Rita came and asked her to call Livie. It was all a trick to get Olivia over there!"

Kate could hear the disgust in the young man's voice.

"She said Rita told her not to mention that she was there because then, Livie wouldn't come."

"She was all tickled with herself that she'd arranged a *surprise* reunion," added Rick. "Didn't she *know* Rita had threatened Olivia?"

"I think she knew there was bad blood between them, and that Livie didn't want to see Rita," said Roger. "But I doubt Livie ever explained any of the reasons to her. They never talked anyway, and Livie didn't trust her mother." He exploded then, pounding his fist on the car roof. "Damn, and Livie really wanted to trust her own mother and have her at the wedding. How could that woman trick my Livie by pretending to be nice to her?"

"Mrs. Gonzaga said that Olivia tried to leave when she saw Rita," said Rick, "but that Rita said she and Livie were going out for the evening to talk things over. She let them go! She didn't even know where they were going. She thought it funny that Olivia kept saying no, and she was crying all the way out to their van."

"Yeah, she just thought they needed to argue it out and settle their differences," said James, shaking his head. "Time's wasting, guys," he said. "Let's go. Should we split up or go together?"

"Wait, guys. Did you tell her Olivia was in danger and to keep her there and call us if she came back?" Kate was frightened. "Wouldn't you think her mother would've noticed if Rita took Livie without her wanting to go?"

"She wouldn't believe us that one sister would hurt another," said James. "She denied the possibility."

Rick said, "She even laughed when she said Rita twisted Olivia's arm and kept her in front of her all the way to the car."

"It's the knife," said Kate. "She used the knife in her belt to make Livie go in front of her. Oh, my God." She rushed to the kitchen to call the police, and she asked for the officer who had said he would be watching for infractions by Rita.

Phil drove up just as the boys were loading in the car. He jumped in the back and said to Rick, "Fill me in on the way, guys."

The girls returned from cake decorating and were frightened by the turn of events.

Lynette said, "If Rita takes her to the One-Ways, maybe Livie can get away and find Bettina or Alice or one of her friends." The tone of hope in her voice broke Kate's heart. She feared the vision she'd seen. What should they do?

Cindi suggested that the girls take the station wagon and look for the rusty red van. "Maybe we can find her, since that van is so obviously hippie that it looks out of place around here. If we see it, we can call the police." Lynette and Cori agreed.

Alisa didn't think they should try to go after Olivia. "She always turns up," she said, "sooner or later. She shouldn't have gone over there anyway. We all told her not to go."

"I know," said Cori, "but, it's sort of understandable that she should believe her mother, if she thought there was a chance she would come to the wedding and not be mad anymore. Livie's never had a relationship with her mother. Maybe down deep, she thought she could. Maybe she was just hoping...."

"All right, Alisa," said Cindi. "You and Cori stay here with Mom so we can find a phone booth and check in every hour or so to see if there's any news. How's that?"

Cori yelled, "Wait a minute. I'm going, too."

Cindi told her, "Number one, you can't run as fast as we can right now, and number two, one of us needs to be here with Mom, in case there's any news." They exchanged a serious glance, Cori nodded, and Lynette and Cindi headed for the car.

Kate, Alisa, and Cori sat down in the kitchen by the phone fielding phone calls from the guys and the girls, both teams of searchers probing methodically through every friend on both sides of town that might have seen Olivia and every street they thought Olivia might have known. But, Kate realized there might have been other mean streets that Rita and Dink knew better.

Alisa made popcorn to have something to do, and Cori curled up with Cleo and Goldie on the couch to cry. Cleo licked her hand and laid her head on Cori's knee.

Kate sat still, staring at the kitchen wall, watching the clock, and praying that her vision was wrong.

The call came from Detective Fredrick about four in the morning. "Her body was found in Mayberry Park," he said, "less than an hour ago. I'm so sorry, because I know your family cared about her."

Kate was stunned into silence, unable to make a sound.

The detective continued. "We'd searched the park before, and she wasn't there when we combed it the first time, so she must have been dumped there afterward. We've been looking for her all night, ever since you called. I told the coroner I would notify you, myself. I called you right away. Another officer was dispatched to tell her mother and get an identification."

"Thank you," Kate managed to say, though the words tore her throat. She held the receiver with both hands to stop shaking.

"When they found her," the Detective resumed, "she had deep wounds in her neck. If I didn't know better, I'd swear they looked almost like bite marks. There was a syringe sticking out of her arm. I hate to tell you, but I think she overdosed again."

"No," screamed Kate. The girls came running into the kitchen.

"She wouldn't do that! She wouldn't. You're wrong. You're all wrong. She's afraid of needles, and she quit completely with the drugs. It was her sister. Find Rita. She did it! Check the needle. I'm sure it was a hot shot. Rita took Livie against her will. She...."

Kate crumpled to the floor. Cori picked up the phone as Alisa ran for a wet towel to bathe Kate's face.

"Detective, can you tell us what happened," Cori asked.

When the two search parties next called in, Cori told them to come on home, without telling them details. "But I'm sure they could tell the news wasn't good by my voice," Cori told Alisa. Cori's eyes were swollen and red.

The girls arrived first. Then, it was a somber crew that met the guys when they returned, sick at heart.

Phil went straight to Kate and took her in his arms. "I'm so sorry, Katie. We hoped so hard we could find her before Rita hurt her. We tried so hard...." They held each other as his own emotion overtook him.

The rest of the kids sat disconsolately on the floor pillows and couches in the living room as Cori tried to tell Roger and the others what the police had found.

Roger paced the floor with clenched fists. "I'll kill her!" he said. "The police better be the ones to find her, 'cause I'll kill her."

Cindi rose to hug him. "That won't bring her back, Roger," she said softly. "It would only get you in jail, and Livie wouldn't want you to spend a single minute there."

They looked in each other's eyes for a long moment, and then Roger collapsed against her small frame, his arms around her, and his head on her shoulder. Cindi motioned behind his back to Rick, and he and James came over to help Roger sit down. The young man sobbed quietly as Lynette and Cori each took a place beside him, holding his hands.

"There appears little we can do for now," said Kate. "Detective Fredrick will be coming over in another hour or two to get everyone's statement about the confrontation with Rita in the park. It may give them more clues to find her, and he thought they would have more information by then."

Cori said, "He also said we should make arrangements for Livie's funeral after the coroner is through with her body...." Further words stuck in her throat.

"I can't, Cori," said Roger. "I just can't do that." He sobbed into his hands. "That's so final. I don't want this to be true. Couldn't it be a mistake?"

"I wish it were, my dear," said Kate, walking over to pat his head. It's going to be hard for all of us, Roger, but we'll all help you. We're family."

Cindi rose quietly, took Rick by the hand and went toward the kitchen. "We'll make some breakfast," she said. Ever the practical one, she added, "I know no one feels like eating, but you have to keep your strength up for all we'll go through the next few days." Then she turned to Rick, and he took her in his arms while she cried out all her practical ideas, and mourned for Olivia.

James and Rick went to get Mrs. Gonzaga for Olivia's funeral. She was red-eyed, but comparatively calm, considering the police had informed her that one of her daughters had killed another, and that Rita would most likely spend the rest of her life in prison. "She didn't believe it," Rick whispered. No way would I trust that women. You could smell the liquor on her breath."

"This is one time I suppose she's entitled," James said. "If I thought a drink would take away this awful loss, I'd take one myself. Surely she must know that she could have helped Olivia years ago if she had just loved her."

The young men all wore their varied military uniforms, and the girls, at Roger's request, wore their long rainbow dresses. Bridal flowers bedecked the casket and altar.

"She wanted the rainbow," he said, with tears in his eyes, "and this is the best we can do for her."

When Kate and Phil went forward to say goodbye to the little girl they had loved and hadn't been able to save, Kate said, "She looks more peaceful now, in death, than she ever was in life, doesn't she?"

Phil put his arm around her. "She *is* at peace, now, Katie, at least I certainly hope so. No more confusion about where she belongs. She tried, Katie. We all tried."

"This is the way I saw her in my vision, in the dress. How I wish I could have changed the outcome."

"I guess none of us could," he said. "Even Livie couldn't have changed the outcome except by not believing her mom."

As the family walked from the church, Kate saw Gina waiting in the foyer. Gina didn't walk away, but stayed until Kate approached and then held out her arms and hugged her.

"I'm so sorry, Kate. I shouldn't have butted in. I knew so little of what you and Phil were trying to do. It's so sad for you. The papers said Olivia overdosed on drugs. I know how hard you two tried to keep her away from drugs. It's so sad that after all your family went through, she went back to the drugs after...."

Kate stopped abruptly and said, "Gina, the police will find that Olivia's so-called 'overdose' was given to her by her sister because Livie refused to sell drugs for her. It was a murder, pure and simple, not an overdose. Livie's been off drugs for a long time. It was never about what we went through—it was about what she went through. She, herself, chose not to be part of the drug culture anymore. She was ours, Gina, and we loved her. We all struggled to understand her, and she struggled to understand herself."

When Kate realized that Gina had stepped back in disbelief, she said to all the bystanders. "Olivia made a difference in all our lives." She was sobbing now, as Phil held his arms around her. "Nobody understood her, but she wasn't just one more druggie found dead in an alley. She changed us all. Her life mattered for something! It mattered."

Kate turned away from her old friend, crying. After a time she looked back into the church. There stood Roger by his bride, touching her hand. Livie was dressed in her tiny white wedding dress, just as she had said she would be.

Kate wiped away her tears and said to Phil, "I'll be all right, dear." She motioned back inside.

Phil nodded and walked back into the church to put his arm around the young airman in Air Force blue.

"We buried a part of ourselves, today, and we'll never forget her. Come on, son," Kate heard him say, "Let's go home."

Afterward

Phil and Kate grieved for Olivia, the child no one could save. They had tried to give her the only life *they* knew, yet it hadn't seemed to fit well with the only life *she* knew. Was the clash of cultures too great to be bridged? Though she always called the two teachers her "bridges over troubled waters," trouble seemed to follow her anyway.

"After all the love and heartache and pain and fun she brought into our lives, were we wrong to even try?" asked Phil. "But," he added, "we couldn't have turned her away."

Kate found no answers, either. The family tried to give Olivia choices that would give her more control over her own life, yet she had learned some of it and had walked away from the rest.

Their sadness and concerns were no different from other parents or substitute parents who love their children, yet who wonder if they've done the parenting job right or wrong. Their parenting style was based on the theory that everything that one did should be examined from the teacher's view of "What message am I sending, if I choose to do this, or that?" But it seemed that sometimes, messages were not received—a short circuit of sorts. Was there just too much damage already in Olivia's head, the memories and night terrors she could never erase, for her to live a life of *consistent* responsibility? They had all loved her. Yet, as most parents know all too well, sometimes love is not enough.

It's always tragic that a young person is lost when she seems on the brink of putting trouble behind her with marriage to Roger, and their leaving Southern California and its temptations behind. Perhaps the old street smart One-Ways would have eventually called them back, but one *wants* to believe they could have made a happy, constructive life together.

Roger needed his chosen family's support to overcome his grief and complete his Air Force assignment. He moped over photos of his dear Olivia. But he eventually met a nice young woman, married, and had a son that he vowed to raise with love and good citizenship...and he did.

Cindi and Alisa became teachers, Cori went into the business field, and Lynette into banking. Lynette was the only one from the Gonzaga family not in jail or dead. This was probably because after Olivia was gone, she never went back

Rick, was killed while on active duty as a firefighter. He and Cindi had always been in contact as friends, but they never were able to be together before his death. Ned graduated into the New York business scene. James made a career of the military. Princess Cleopatra died of bone cancer, and Goldie Buttercup wouldn't eat without his partner. He died three days later. They were buried together in the back yard golf course, the holes of which had filled in with time.

After three more children by Bettina's "old man," he beat her up and ran off to live with another girl of the streets. Neither Bettina nor Belle Starr nor Alice Blue Gown ever broke out of the drug and gang and welfare cycle.

Mrs. Gonzaga never gave up alcohol or her abusive ways. In fact, her next abuse 'victim' was her older daughter's little girl while Betsy was in prison for a few years. Concussions and broken bones—another generation abused. Rita, of course, went to prison for Olivia's death, and for the drugs found on her, but the murder was ruled unpremeditated by the judge, since Livie, also, was considered *officially* as "just another drug death."

Cori overcame most residual effects of her accident by sheer determination, though she was never again pain free. But true to her "mind over matter" theory, she never allowed the pain or disability to get in the way of her chosen activities.

In discussions over the years, the kids had different takes on Olivia. Some saw her as a success story cut off too soon. Others felt she had too many scars to have ever made it to respectable status, anyway. Some felt that she could have solved some of her problems with more "gumption." Though all felt Olivia's weaknesses caused pain and a certain resentment to those who loved her, no one believed that one should abandon even a hopeless fight.

Lynette felt Livie didn't have enough innate good sense to take advantage of her opportunities, and often wasted them.

Just as families change and grow up and move away, places do as well. All three schools of the Johnson kids, elementary, junior high, and high school, were closed due to budget shortfalls not long after the kids graduated. Cori's long distance softball throw in competition still held the record for both boys and girls at high school. When Phil died young, and Kate, devastated, moved away, it seemed the whole neighborhood of "picket fences and PTA" eventually evolved into another One-Ways, as did many Los Angeles suburbs.

Of course, today, we would ask if we had gained or lost ground in the drug culture from those early naïve days. With new drugs like meth, new gang threats in big cities, and new drug cartels smuggling volumes of poison across our porous borders, it's hard to tell. Were we fighting a losing battle then? Are we still?

But the joint task force of teachers at Sunnyside had inadvertently started something. The day Olivia stumbled into Kate's naïve arms asking for help with a drug problem brought the teachers together to ask districts and legislatures for more knowledge and for changes in the identification and treatment of juvenile drug users. Perhaps Livie's loss was not in vain, after all. Concern of teachers for her, helped bring change for other kids.

Not long after Olivia's death, the state passed laws to investigate charges of child abuse more actively, placing children in danger from their parents into protective care. The idea of an alternative school for troubled young people grew and flourished, with many such schools across the country now making available extra academic help, extra counseling, and extra rehabilitation. Drug rehab facilities for children began to appear, and in-service training for teachers in spotting and remediating children caught up in the drug culture became available across the country. Eventually, they were standardized and required.

Would any of these opportunities have helped save a girl like Olivia, had they been available sooner? One would wonder for a lifetime.

Acknowledgements

It is always hard to say just how a story comes into being. One takes known events that affected one at a certain time of her life and transforms them into a conglomeration of fact and fiction, adding natural emotions that arise from those events. These ideas come from many sources.

Having taught in the Los Angeles area during the time of the sixties, before any of us knew drug and gang problems even existed, much less what to do about them, I must thank my teaching colleagues for supplying many anecdotal comments and events as we all struggled to meet the needs of our students with special problems.

I must thank my husband and family for their enthusiastic support. It would be impossible to continue writing if they hadn't kept up the encouragement. The same goes for former students who continually ask for "one more" story, and the CMNC, Curves –Manitou, and DoDDS friends who helped choose titles..

Critique partners are indispensable to the creative process, with the constant necessary reminders to "show, not tell," and the constant necessary assurance that the story is on track. These include, Sue and Sue (both of you), Dave, Wendy, and MB. I cannot thank them enough, especially those willing to do "just one more read through." Pikes Peak Writers

Finally, I must thank the principals and superintendents of school districts, both in California and in Europe under the Department of Defense Dependent Schools (DoDDS) who have allowed teachers the academic freedom to teach to a child's needs, not merely to some high-stakes test. These people who have confidence in their teachers' instincts and dedication are priceless, and I've been lucky enough to have them in my corner during thirty years of teaching before retirement. Out of this teaching experience many ideas and incidents for this novel have been gleaned.

About the Author

Author M. J. Brett (a.k.a. Margaret Brettschneider) spent most of her life teaching, over thirty years of it, though dancing, public speaking, child-rearing, PTA, softball mom, adult education, military wife, skiing, and journalism also contributed to what she calls an active and mostly satisfying life.

Raised in wartime Los Angeles, graduating from Bell Gardens High School, University of California at Fullerton, and various post-graduate institutions, marriage in a Downey church, and teaching in Whittier for nine years, the author's roots are in Los Angeles and Orange Counties of California

Yet Europe called in the form of an opportunity to continue her teaching career for the Department of Defense Dependent Schools (DoDDS) and live in Germany for twenty-one more years.

Though her first three books were set in this European experience, for this novel, *Street Smart on a Dead End,* Ms. Brett goes back to her Los Angeles roots. The early days of emerging problems in teaching a growing number of troubled and drug-addicted children seemed a story that needed to be written, and offered a fertile field for imagination.

Modern young people may find this novel truly "historical fiction." Even the author's own grandchildren were surprised that life even *existed* before cell phones, text messaging. and computer games. For them, we'll call this novel "educational."

Currently enjoying the backyard wildlife in her Colorado home, Ms. Brett says she will continue writing as long as her readers keep demanding more novels.

Other Novels by M. J. Brett

Mutti's War
ISBN 0-9748869-0-4

    Based on the true story of a young mother who smuggled her three children out of East Prussia and walked halfway across Europe during World War II to find her missing and mysterious husband.

    Midwest Bood Review calls this novel, "A vivid, unforgettable story of courage and determination (in WWII) told with fluid dialogue and heart-rending detail."

Shadows on an Iron Curtain –
ISBN 978-0-9748869-1-6

    A tale of recovery from loss on the Cold War Border where intrigue leads the teachers and warriors of Bamberg-Hof area to rely on their camaraderie and the "family" they create for themselves in the face of the Soviet threat.

    Comment from one CAV aviator who flew the East-West Border during this era, "Thank you for being the one to finally get the Cold War right." This one needed military security clearance.

Between Duty and Devotion,
ISBN 978-0-9748869-2-3

    The story of a fast-track military officer who can command a unit, but not his private life. His longings and betrayal lead to the most difficult choice of his life.

    Comment from a reader, "I loved this unorthodox love story where the characters step right out of the story."

    website at www.mjbrett.com